# Row Away from the Rocks

*"Trust in God, but row away from the rocks."*

— *old Indian proverb*

# ROW AWAY FROM THE ROCKS

### LISBETH J. THOM

*Lisbeth J. Thom*

COURT STREET PRESS
Montgomery

## Acknowledgments

Thanks to my husband, Doug, who allows my fictional characters to walk along our path, to my loyal friends and family, to my many writing mentors, especially Rosemary Daniell, and the members of the Zona Rosa writing group, and to Randall Williams, my hardworking editor, for his expertise.

Court Street Press
P.O. Box 1588
Montgomery, AL 36102

Copyright © 2004 by Lisbeth J. Thom
This book is a work of fiction. Names, characters, places and incidents are either products of the author's imagination or are used fictiously. Any resemblence to actual events or locales or persons, living or dead, is entirely coincidental. All rights reserved under International and Pan-American Copyright Conventions. Published in the United States by Court Street Press, a division of NewSouth, Inc., Montgomery, Alabama.

Library of Congress Cataloging-in-Publication Data

ISBN 158838-154-4

Printed in the United States of America

For Doug, Cathy, Mark, and Kristen

and in memory of
Eleanor Daugherty

# Chapter One

Wailing sirens made Carrie Barnes nervous as she hopscotched between puddles in the hospital parking lot. Dark angry clouds in the midwestern sky matched her mood and her head pounded. Carrie felt like she was slipping into a deep crevice. She opened the hospital door and walked past the flower shop to the elevator. Waiting, she tapped her foot nervously on the speckled tile floor. Her thoughts swung like a pendulum—she wanted to be there and she didn't want to be there.

"Calm down," Carrie told Gram on the phone the night before. Gram sounded anxious and out of breath. Without even saying hello, Gram released the bomb, jet-propelling words about a mass in her chest. At first, Carrie assumed her melodramatic grandmother was trying to get her back to Wisconsin. However, when Gram's voice rose shrilly with fear, Carrie began to pay attention. Gram was in trouble. She knew she had no choice but to go back home. It didn't matter that when she married Michael a year ago, she had cut the cord.

The smell of antisceptic, urine, and cafeteria food made her stomach gyrate as she stepped off the elevator on the fourth floor. She walked past the nurses' station and headed down a long hallway. At Room 416, she tapped the door three times, then entered. Gram sat in bed writing in a small green notebook with the flowered pink and gold ink pen Carrie had given her for her birthday.

"Caroline, you're late."

"Not really. Here, I got you *People, Woman's Day,* and *McCall's.*"

"Thanks, Caroline." Everyone called her Carrie, except Gram. Reaching down to kiss Gram on the cheek, Carrie smelled her lavender perfume. Gram pulled away. She didn't like people touching her. Never had. Putting her notebook aside, Gram made herself comfortable in the bed, arranging the pillow behind her back, pulling up the white thermal blanket, smoothing it out. Gram's slight, five-foot frame made her look like a small child in an oversized bed. Her glassy eyes wore a veil of fear. Carrie stared at Gram's swollen, Cabbage-Patch-doll face, feeling uneasy. She couldn't help but wonder where she and Gram were headed. She envisioned the crack in front of her widening to a point of no return.

"You worry me when you're late."

"I didn't give you an exact time. How can I be late?" Carrie had no patience with Gram's obsession with punctuality. Gram was always the first to arrive anywhere. Carrie considered Gram's habit of arriving early annoying and rude.

"You shouldn't wear blue jeans when you travel," Gram said, frowning at Carrie's light tan jeans and periwinkle sweater. Gram, who had always dressed to the hilt, would never change. Even now, in spite of her swollen face, she looked good. At seventy-four, she had short, thick, stylish white hair and a trim figure with only the slightest bulge at her middle. She wore a red velour robe over her hospital gown, makeup—including her trademark fire-engine red lipstick—and gold dangling earrings. Carrie was sure Gram's tombstone would one day read, "Madeline Louise Whitfield. She always looked her best."

"How's Sophie-dog?"

"Fine," Carrie said. Gram loved Carrie's miniature schnauzer and always lavished on her the kind of attention she'd never given people.

Carrie wanted to tell Gram about Atlanta but knew there was no point. After a year, Gram was still angry with her, and especially with Michael, for moving her down south. Gram, who had always lived in Sheboygan, Wisconsin, wore blinders to the world outside her domain.

"Has the doctor been in to see you?"

"He's coming this afternoon," Gram said, twisting the corner edge of her blanket between her thumb and forefinger. Carrie stared at her bright red nails.

"Can I get you anything?"

"Get me a cigarette." Gram coughed.

"Are you sure it's okay?"

"Who cares? I need a cigarette, Caroline. Get my purse out. It's over there." Gram pointed to the closet beside the entry door.

"I'd better check with the nurse."

Gram scowled, then started coughing. She hacked and sputtered. Putting her thumb and left forefinger to her throat, she took quick, short breaths. Her eyes watered. Spasms shook her body as she rocked back and forth on the bed, trying to eject the phlegm inside her lungs.

"Should I call for help?" Carrie tried patting her on the back. Gram shook her head, no, motioning with her right arm for Carrie to back away. Just as Carrie started to run for help, Gram gagged up a glob of mucus then fell over onto the pillow, closed her eyes, and began to snore. Carrie loved her grandmother, especially when she was sleeping.

Carrie was a baby when Gram took on the job of raising her. Gram was fifty-one when Carrie's parents, Richard and Mary Caroline Whitfield, died in a car accident. Richard was Gram's youngest child. His older sister, Nella, was five when Richard was born. Aunt Nella always claimed Richard was Gram's favorite child.

Carrie feared bad news about Gram's condition. Feeling restless after sitting most of the day, she left the room and paced the corridor. Carrie hated sitting around. She liked to move. There had been no time for her morning walk. Back in the room, she settled down in the bedside chair.

"Here, want some water?" Carrie said when noise in the hallway awakened Gram. Gram reached for plastic container.

"I'm so thirsty, always so thirsty." Gram drank the water, a few sips at a time, until it was gone.

"Did you take the shuttle from Milwaukee?" Gram said.

"Yes," Carrie said. She told Gram how she'd stood in the cold, waiting for thirty minutes. "Guess who was driving the van?"

"I have no idea, and I don't feel like guessing."

"Herman Grothe." Herman used to own a neighborhood grocery store around the corner from their old house on Sixth Street. His wife had been dead for years. Each evening, he'd stroll past and wave to Carrie and Gram as they sat on the front porch swing. "He was concerned when I told him you were sick."

"Herman's a good friend," Gram said.

"I had him drop me off at your place. He took me to your car. I found the key under the mat on the driver's side—just where you said it would be."

"I think my car needs some gas," Gram said.

"I'll stop at the gas station when I leave." Gram's old Buick had 90,000 miles on it. Driving her mammoth car always made Carrie feel like she was driving the living room around. "By the way, Gram, do you still think Herman's good looking?"

"Hell no. Not anymore. Did I tell you he lives in my building? He asked me to go to lunch with him at the Big Boy a few weeks ago." Gram explained they both had the fried chicken plate and apple pie for dessert. Right after he took his last bite of pie, Herman had fallen over at the table, lifeless. "One minute he was telling me a boring story about a flood in his basement, the next minute he was slumped down. I thought he was dead."

"Gram, that's terrible," Carrie said.

"It was. But, just a few minutes or so later, Herman popped up as if nothing happened. The waitress called 911. Herman went off to the hospital in an ambulance, and I had to drive his Chevy home. His doctor thinks he may have had a small stroke."

"He seemed okay today. Have you gone out with him again?"

"No, and I'm not going to. He's involved with Iona Cochran from Ootsburg. They deserve each other. Iona's falling apart too."

"Gram, it's Oostburg." Gram had a funny habit of turning words around. Once she decided how to pronounce a word, she forever said it the same way. "I think Herman's got a thing for you."

"Forget it. I'm over seventy, Caroline. I don't need any guy's shoes under my bed." Gram threw her arms into the air, making Carrie laugh.

"Whatever happened to people talking to one another?" Gram said when Carrie mentioned that she hadn't been able to reach Aunt Nella.

"I left several messages on her machine." Gram wrinkled her forehead, scrunching up her face. She hated answering machines and had vowed never to have one. She wrote letters by hand and acted insulted when Carrie sent her typed letters. Gram was not computer literate and proud of it.

"Nella's a vagabond daughter. She never tells me where's she going." Gram held her palms up and shrugged her shoulders. Gram and Nella got along about as well as snakes and baby chickens.

"Maybe she's visiting Jennifer in Minneapolis," Carrie said, though in truth, she suspected that Aunt Nella had hopped a plane to Las Vegas. Like Gram, who loved playing poker with her friends, Aunt Nella loved to gamble. Ever since Uncle Jim had died, Aunt Nella was a free spirit. She rarely spent time with Gram.

"I'm telling you, the food's terrible here," Gram said.

"Hospital food sucks, doesn't it?"

"Caroline, don't talk like that. You know I hate that word." Carrie shook her head. She wished Gram would get off her case and stop telling her what to say. Growing up, Carrie hated Gram's tirades about her behavior. She'd have screaming fits, yelling at Carrie. If Carrie dared to talk back, Gram would berate her, giving her a speech about containing her anger. She wanted Carrie to be a *nice* girl.

Using the remote control, Gram turned on the television. Carrie walked over to the window and looked outside. It was raining harder. The wind was blowing. Autumn leaves swirled past the window doing a frenzied dance. Carrie felt like a gerbil on an exercise wheel, going nowhere. She longed to be at home with Michael, out from under Gram's scrutiny. Pacing the floor, wondering when the doctor would show up, she looked at her watch. Three-thirty. She hoped she wouldn't have to stay cooped up with Gram too long.

"Gram, what did the doctor say about the mass in your chest?" Carrie asked. "As The World Turns" blared from the television set. Gram coughed.

"Did you know that Bob and Kim are getting back together?" Gram said, changing the subject.

"No." When Gram didn't want to talk about something, she clammed up like she had a mouthful of Elmer's glue.

"Carrie. It's been a long time," Dr. Edgar said, striding into the room, his eyes twinkling. He was tall and slightly stooped with a nearly bald head and a white, neatly trimmed beard. Carrie stood up, reaching for his outstretched hand. His large, long-fingered hand felt warm.

"Had any stitches lately?" he asked. Gram chuckled, turning the television off.

"Madeline, this girl still holds the record in my office. Never did see a child who had more accidents. I used to say that we needed a chute between my office and your house next door, so you could scoot Miss Carrie over for repairs."

"You did indeed," Gram said.

"Madeline, I'm going to be frank," Dr. Edgar said. "I have bad news. You have a tumor the size of a mango in your lung." He placed his tanned hand on Gram's. She yanked her hand away, looking up at him with dark brown beady eyes. He explained how they had compared an X-ray Gram had in January to the present one. "In January, your lungs looked clear which means the mass is growing fast. Makes us certain that it's malignant. I'm suggesting you start radiation treatments."

"Forget it." Gram said. I will not have my hair falling out." She sat up straight, turning her gaze away from him. Carrie felt beads of sweat pop out on her forehead.

"Come on, Madeline. You're a strong lady. You can manage a few weeks of radiation. It would shrink the tumor and make you more comfortable."

"I said no." She scowled. "Now, when can I go home?" Gram edged over to the side of the bed and scooted off. Standing on her tip toes, she shook her fist at Dr. Edgar. "My mind's made up. It's my body and *my* decision." Gram pointed to her chest.

"Okay, okay," he said, backing away from her. "Just give it some thought."

"I want a cigarette. Now."

"Go ahead and smoke, Madeline. I'll see you in the morning."

"Might as well send me home right now. I hate this place. It smells bad."

"You can leave in the morning." Not wanting to argue with Gram, Dr. Edgar turned around and went out the door. As Carrie followed him, she swallowed hard. Her throat felt dry.

"I can't believe you're letting her smoke?" Carrie said when they reached the end of the corridor.

"It can't hurt anything. Not now. Carrie, try and convince Gram to have the radiation."

Carrie explained that Gram's friend, Margaret Davis, had lung cancer, endured both radiation and chemotherapy, and died anyhow.

"I know Gram doesn't want to suffer like Margaret did."

"What she doesn't realize is that she'll suffer, even without radiation."

"How long does she have?"

"Probably less than six months. With treatment, maybe a year." He kept his professional manner, but his eyes looked sad. Carrie stared at the floor. She felt like a balloon without any air. Dr. Edgar gave her a hug. "Young lady, you bear a striking resemblance to your mother," he said, releasing her. "When your dad brought Mary Caroline here from Vancouver, she caused quite a sensation. She was tall like you, a beautiful woman with the same huge blue eyes and striking brandy-colored hair. And, she looked good in blue, too." Carrie smiled.

After he walked away, Carrie felt ambivalent. She didn't want to lose Gram or her freedom. Gram had called the shots, her whole life. And now that Gram had received her death sentence, Carrie felt more bound to her than ever. She wanted to flip the page back to the day before when she'd felt in control of her life, but she knew that wasn't possible.

Back in the hospital room, she got the Salems out of Gram's black purse. Gram sat in bed, clutching her Bic lighter, her hands shaking. Carrie held out the pack of cigarettes. Gram snatched it from her.

"I'm going to take a walk while you smoke," Carrie said. She hurried out the door and down to the end of the hallway. Carrie watched as children piled off the school bus at the corner and scurried down the sidewalk. Mothers waited with umbrellas. She remembered how Gram would come to the corner to meet her when she was little. Those days seemed like a hundred years ago. A lot of muddy water had rushed in to cover up that carefree part of her past.

"Carrie, welcome home," a familiar voice said. She turned around and smiled as Helen Newby, jovial and pear-shaped, came over and hugged her. Helen was a nurse at the hospital. The Newbys had been across-the-street neighbors and their house had been like a second home to Carrie. Helen's daughter, Liz, was Carrie's closest childhood friend. "I just spoke with Dr. Edgar at the nurses' station," Helen said. "I'm so sorry to hear about Madeline's cancer. You doin' okay?"

"Not really. Gram's dying of lung cancer, and she's nixed the idea of having radiation."

"I know, honey. Dr. Edgar told me she refused treatment. Can't you get her to change her mind?"

"Probably not. You know Gram—no one tells her what to do." Carrie questioned Helen about Gram's swollen face.

"Most likely, it's swollen because the tumor is blocking the blood from getting to and from her brain. The tumor will grow bigger, and before long, it will close off her throat. Then, she'll choke to death. It could happen anytime. It's a horrible way to die, honey. Believe me, I know. I've seen it happen."

Just then a jagged bolt of lightning flashed in the sky followed by a loud clap of thunder. Carrie's stomach heaved as the ham and cheese sandwich she'd eaten on the plane tried to climb her throat. The back of her neck stiffened. She massaged it with her fingers.

"Honey, I'd better get back to work." Helen started to leave, then turned around and asked Carrie if she wanted to sleep at her house, in Liz's room. "My back door's unlocked. You just go on in whenever you want." Carrie accepted the offer. She didn't want to sleep in Gram's smoke-filled apartment.

As she headed back to Gram's room, she wondered how Liz was doing in college. She hadn't talked to her for several months.

"Get it straight, Caroline. I've already made it clear. No treatments, not now, not ever," Gram shouted when Carrie tried to change her mind. "If I'm going to die, I'll do it my way." She inhaled her cigarette, then blew a stream of smoke toward Carrie. It swirled in the air like a tumbleweed. Minutes later, Gram dropped the cigarette butt into her water glass, something Carrie had never seen her do before.

"I've got a list of things for you to do." Gram said. "The laundry. Grocery shopping. How long can you stay?"

"I'm not sure."

"You know, I'm not sick, Caroline. Not really. I just have a mass in my chest," Gram said, lighting another cigarette.

"I'll be back in a few minutes," Carrie said, anxious to escape the room. She waved to Helen when she passed the nurses' station. In a phone booth near the elevator, she dialed Aunt Nella's number. No one answered. Carrie left another message. Next, she tried calling Aunt Nella's daughter, Jennifer.

"Thank God you're there." Carrie told her about Gram. "Where's your Mom? I've been trying to reach her."

"On a trip. She's supposed to call me tonight."

"When she calls, tell her I'm desperate. I can't handle Gram alone, not this time."

"Mom is not available," Jennifer said.

"I don't believe this. For God's sake, Jennifer, she needs to know that her mother is dying." Carrie hated Jennifer's smug tone. Her cousin didn't get it. As Jennifer went into a monologue about how Gram and her mom didn't get along, Carrie watched a very pregnant young girl, a goofily happy expression on her face, walk past in navy pants and a white maternity T-shirt, announcing *It's A Boy* in red letters. Carrie envied the girl's carefree attitude.

"It's all Gram's fault that she and Mom don't get along," Jennifer said.

"Geez, Jennifer. You're not making any sense."

"Believe me, you don't know the half of it. There are things Gram never told you. Ask her about them sometime." After offering to come see Gram the following weekend, Jennifer said she had to go. "Give Gram my love. Please talk her into having radiation. You can do it, Carrie."

Carrie slammed the phone onto the receiver, irritated that Jennifer was dumping everything on her shoulders. She didn't feel like dealing with family secrets? All she wanted was some help, and Aunt Nella was her last hope.

"You can go now, Caroline, I'm fine," Gram said when Carrie entered. "My dinner arrived. I've got fish and some mysterious dark green vegetable." Gram poked her fork into the pile of collard greens. "At least the Boston Creme Pie looks good."

"I'll see you in the morning," Carrie said, picking her denim purse up from the floor. "Call me when you're ready. I'll be at your apartment doing some cleaning for you." She told Gram that Helen Newby invited her to stay at her house. "Stay out of trouble, okay?" Carrie teased on her way out the door.

"Like I have a choice," Gram said.

When Carrie walked out of the hospital, raindrops pelted her face, but she couldn't feel a thing. After climbing into Gram's rusty green Buick Regal, she pounded her fists on the steering wheel. Carrie wondered why everyone was so sure she could convince Gram to have the radiation treatments. Didn't they realize that changing her grandmother's mind was close to impossible?

Carrie took deep breaths. She'd recently read a newspaper article on how you should take deep breaths, then let the air our slowly to relieve stress. She breathed deeply and exhaled. She half-listened to REM's new song, "Orange," on the car radio. Carrie thought about the people in the cars she passed. She wondered if they were also dealing with a crisis.

She pulled into the parking lot at Randall's restaurant. Inside she ordered bratwurst on a hard roll, fries, and a Diet Coke to go. At Gram's place, she took one whiff of the stale smoke and rushed to open a window, then turned the heat down.

After eating, she called Michael. He didn't answer, so she left a message. "Hi. It's me. Hope you accepted Kay's invitation to go out to dinner. Gram's in bad shape. It's *not* a false alarm. I feel like a sack of wet sand is strapped to my back. Don't call back. I'll call in the morning. Love you. Bye."

Carrie wished she and Michael hadn't argued on the way to the airport that morning. He had insisted that Gram was playing games. Carrie disagreed, shouting at him. Now, she realized that Michael had every reason to think Gram was crying wolf. She'd done it many times before. Carrie longed to be home. She had looked forward to going out to dinner with Kay and Dave.

She looked around Gram's messy apartment. The tables were littered with books, magazines, and junk mail. The sink was piled high with dishes. Dust balls were congregating on the living room carpet. Clothes lay on the floor like permanent sculpture. She found it difficult to believe her usually tidy grandmother was living in such a mess. Carrie remembered how, as a child, she had to help clean the house every Saturday morning, polishing the tables to a shine, using a toothbrush on the tile floor in the bathroom. Gram shouted orders like an army sargeant until their home passed inspection. Carrie felt claustrophobic and too tired to deal with it. She decided to tackle the clean up chores the next morning. After closing the door, she made sure it was locked, then headed to the car.

Carrie started to cry when she reached Helen Newby's driveway. Gram was the only parent she'd ever had. She didn't want Gram to die.

Carrie entered the back door grateful that Helen wasn't home. After unpacking her things, she dropped down onto Liz's bed, happy to be alone. She stewed about the secrets Jennifer had mentioned. She worried about how she was she going to juggle her job, her responsibilities at home, and also help care for Gram.

Wanting to clear her mind before she tried to sleep, she got out the blue journal she wrote in at the end of the day and began to write.

## Chapter Two

Journal, Saturday, September 5, 1987

Today has been a day from hell. I'm so tired I can hardly think. My brain feels out of whack, like its been through a meat grinder. Shooting pains stab my gut, like there's a crazed rooster inside, trying to claw its way out. Gram's slipping away from me, and I'm a genuine basket case. I knew Gram's stupid cigarettes would win. She's been chain smoking them for as long as I can remember. All I can do is pray that Gram won't suffer too long and that I'll have the strength I need to get through this nightmare.

The thought of losing Gram scares me silly. I keep thinking of how she blurted out the facts on the phone last night, shouting like a newspaper boy on the street corner. Gram is often self-centered and flamboyant. The woman thrives on drama and has always blabbed bad news by flinging it right at the fan and to hell with preparing anyone. After she unloaded her grim news, she shut up and waited for my response. Knowing what she expected of me, I told her I would be on a plane the next day.

When I told Michael my plan, as usual, he didn't say anything. He likes to think things over. This morning he questioned my decision to rush off to Wisconsin. He didn't want me to leave, and Gram wanted me to come. I felt like a ragdoll, yanked from both ends. Michael said I was indulging her. I insisted that this time, she really needed me.

I hate it when Michael acts authoritative, like he knows everything.

He doesn't understand that I can't turn my back on my grandmother. She took care of me for years, and now it's my turn. After we turned off Highway 400 and got onto I-285, we rode in silence. Michael had on some radio talk show. I tuned it out. I kept thinking about Gram and wondered if it was as serious as it sounded. By the time we turned onto Camp Creek Parkway, I fought to keep from crying. When Michael told me good-bye at the Delta curbside check-in, he hugged me and kissed me on the cheek. I hugged him back, then walked over to stand in line. I waved as he drove off. I miss him already and wish that we hadn't gotten into an argument. Oh well, I can't worry about him right now. I've got enough weighing on my mind.

This afternoon, with a desperate look on her face, Gram pleaded not to let her die alone. That's when I told her not to worry and agreed to be there for her. Now, I'm wondering how I can keep my promise.

I'm trying my best to figure things out, so I won't have to handle this caretaking job by myself. I'd like to do my share to help out with Gram and arrange for someone else to help the rest of the time. Aunt Nella remains my only hope.

I never have been able to figure out Aunt Nella. She drives me crazy, but I like her anyhow, because she knows how to laugh and have a good time. I often think about the fun I had at her house. Aunt Nella used to stay up half the night playing cards with Jennifer and me. The next day I'd feel blitzed from a lack of sleep, but not Aunt Nella, who only requires a few hours of sleep. I envy that trait. With Aunt Nella's outgoing, funloving personality, she attracts people like a magnet. What puzzles me is why she and Gram don't get along. It doesn't make sense. I'd leap at the chance to spend time with *my* mother.

I have a strange feeling regarding Aunt Nella's whereabouts. She's famous for disappearing when the pressure is high. Knowing the slim chance I have of convincing her to help out with Gram is tying me up in knots. I've got to figure out a way to play on Aunt Nella's emotions, so she'll offer to help take care of her dying mother.

I wish Liz was home. She knows all about the murky water I've waded through with Gram. Lying here on her bed is like taking a journey to the past. I just spent a few minutes looking around her room. It looks the same—the canopy bed, the blue and white flowered bedspread, the mahogany furniture. Faded photos are thumbtacked onto her blue felt bulletin board. I got up to look at them. In one photo, I'm standing next to our homecoming float, and Liz is sitting on a white halfmoon, in front of a light blue background, as a homecoming queen candidate. I remember all of the hours we spent stuffing chicken wire with crepe paper, spelling out the letters, *She's Heavenly*, on the side of the float. Those high school days seem so long ago.

Out the window I can see the Wilcox house next door. I remember one summer night when we were eleven. That night, Liz and I sat on this same bed, in the dark, watching out the window as Darla Wilcox and her tall, skinny boyfriend, on leave from the Navy, necked on the porch swing. We went into giggle fits at the performance they were putting on for us.

Liz and I have always had lots of laughs together. We relate to one another. Like me, she grew up an only child. Her parents, Helen and Ben, always had this notion that I was a good influence on her. That wasn't always the case. We did some pretty crazy things, like the time we took Helen's white Cadillac out to the community pool in the middle of the night. We climbed up over the restroom wall, dropping down into the pool area, took off our shortie pajamas, and went skinny dipping. As far as I know, Helen never found out. Nor did Gram, who is a master at hiding things herself.

Gram is especially good at concealing her constant financial disasters. Tomorrow, I'm going to search her metal strongbox where she keeps her records. I hate to be nosy, but it's necessary. Gram and money are like an unhappy marriage. Michael and I have tried to help her with her finances, but it's a lost cause. She spends money whether she has it or not. According to Aunt Nella, there used to be family money. Gram runs her credit cards to the limit and gets loans from everyone, which she has no intention of repaying. Before, Michael and I got married, she even borrowed money from his parents. I still shudder thinking about that humiliation.

Michael's good money sense attracted me. I have no intention of following in Gram's financial footsteps. I'm determined to live within my means. I'm certain I also fell for Michael's stable background. His family members don't come close to mirroring the soap opera characters in my Whitfield clan. Michael and the rest of the Barnes family are loyal, hard-working people with nothing to shove under the rug. What you see is what you get. Unlike my family, they hug a lot. I like that. When we leave their house, after a visit, we have to go around the room twice, hugging. It takes forever, but it's great.

Speaking of family, I'm quite curious about the secrets Jennifer mentioned. Could it be that she's just playing around with my mind? In the past, I've known her to overdo the mysterious bit. Time will tell. Jennifer's always been an itch under my skin, not exactly my favorite person. For now, I intend to put my worries about her so-called secrets on hold. My brain is on overload.

I keep thinking about how Gram taught me to take one day at a time. Today is today, and I have done with it what I can. I already know that I will honor my commitment to her, with or without help. A promise is a promise. Besides, who but Gram painted Indian faces with iodine on my scabbed knees? Who curled my hair before the spelling bee? Who carried me across the snow on blizzardy evenings? Who made dozens of Christmas sugar cookies, cut in different shapes—stars, bells, wreaths, candy canes, and Christmas trees—with me every Christmas? Gram did it all. Now, it's my turn. Somehow I will steer myself through the choppy waters ahead.

Right now, my heavy eyelids keep trying to shut. I'm more than ready to crash. Who knows what tomorrow will bring? All I know for certain is I don't wish my dreams on anyone.

## Chapter Three

*A*dark-haired woman wearing a lavender chiffon gown darted after Carrie. Her name was Serena. She had milky white skin and round violet eyes. Her thin lips, painted with mauve lipstick, curved down into a permanent frown. Carrie kept trying to get away from her, but no matter how many turns she took, Serena stayed by her side. Carrie's condo was filling with water as she tried over and over to reach the front door. Serena, who moved easily, blocked Carrie's attempts to escape. An odd assortment of people from Carrie's past stood around the room—Willie, the grade school janitor, who cleaned up the coat room the day Carrie barfed inside everyone's galoshes; her high school Latin teacher, Mrs. Clementine Burosky, who always smelled like dried rose petals; Emma Otto, a client at the travel bureau who recently planned a honeymoon trip to St. Lucia with her balding, overweight boyfriend; and, the personable checkout clerk, Zeta, who always wore a white, sleeveless blouse and greeted her with "Hey," at the Kroger store. The water kept rising. No one except Carrie seemed to notice.

Carrie awoke from her dream curled in a fetal position. She pulled the covers up, tucking the flowered bedspread under her chin. When she realized where she was, she threw the covers back and climbed out of bed. Hearing Helen clanking dishes in the kitchen made Carrie feel comfortable. After a shower, she dressed in her light blue faded jeans, a pink and blue madras T-shirt, and her old Reeboks.

Even though it was Sunday, she nixed the idea of going to mass. There was no use taking the chance some local might see her there and tell Gram, who came from generations of Lutherans. Gram, who didn't know she had started going to the Catholic church with Michael, would throw a fit when she found out.

"You sleep okay, honey?" Helen asked when Carrie walked into the kitchen. Helen stood at the sink in her pink terrycloth bathrobe; her permed gray-brown hair was as fuzzy as a Brillo pad.

"Fine," Carrie said. It was easier to lie than to explain how she'd tossed and turned most of the night.

"Want some coffee?"

"No, I still drink tea. But, that coffee smells so good. Does it have vanilla in it?"

"Could be. It's some kind of fancy breakfast blend I bought at Sendik's in Milwaukee." Helen picked up her mug and took a swallow. "Umm, honey, it's delicious." Helen turned the back burner of the stove on and set the tea kettle on it.

"I keep saying that I'm going to start drinking coffee someday—when I grow up—and who knows when that will be?"

Helen chuckled loudly, then got a loaf of zucchini bread from the refrigerator. "Ben said to say hello. He went down to Terry's. You know—that little breakfast place on the south side—to meet some buddies early this morning. They're going fishing out on the lake." Helen placed a few slices of bread on a pewter tray, then sat at the kitchen table across from Carrie. "Honey it sure was great of you to come here and help Madeline out—you're such a nice girl." Carrie clenched her teeth; she hated the *nice-girl* label. One of these days, her allotment of nice was going to run out. "Madeline did a mighty fine job raising you. It wasn't easy for her, you know."

"I'm sure it wasn't." Carrie had heard that line many times before. She got up when the kettle whistled, and poured hot water into the yellow ceramic mug Helen had set out.

"Here, have some." Helen said, passing the bread platter to Carrie.

"Thanks," Carrie said. "I haven't talked to Liz since we moved to Atlanta. Is she doing okay?"

"Fine, she'll finish graduate school in May. Seems like she just started. Where does the time go?"

Carrie savored each bite of the moist, sweet bread that won Helen blue ribbons at the State Fair. When Carrie was growing up, Helen used to invite Carrie across the street to sample her baked goods. Carrie's all-time favorite was Helen's Why-Go-By banana cream pie. Helen loved telling the story of how she got the pie recipe from a restaurant in southern Indiana called, Why-Go-By?

"I stopped in to see Madeline last night right before my shift ended. She was in good spirits. She had me laughing."

"Sounds like Gram. She's good at shelving her concerns."

"I mentioned the tumor, and . . ."

"I know what you're going to say," Carrie interrupted. "She calls it a mass. She can't bring herself to say tumor."

"Give her some time. She's having trouble accepting the bad news," Helen said, staring out the window. "It's windy out there today, but nice and sunny. Those leaves are getting mighty high in the backyard. I hope Ben doesn't wear himself out fishing. I think I'll prop the rake up by the back door, just in case." Carrie laughed, then cleared her dishes.

"I'd better get going. If I know Gram, she's packed up, and ready to go home."

"They won't release her 'til later in the morning. I know the routine," Helen said in an authoritative manner.

"That's fine with me. I've got plenty to do at her apartment." Helen handed Carrie several slices of zucchini bread wrapped in foil. Carrie thanked her then went out the door. Walking to Gram's car, she listened to the gentle clinking of the wind chimes in Helen's backyard.

Driving down the tree-lined street, Carrie thought back to fall mornings when she and Liz walked up the hill to Lincoln School together. After school, they would run home and change clothes, then head outside to play as bright yellow, orange, and red leaves from the oak, birch, and sycamore trees drifted to the ground. Carrie remembered the burning-leaf smell in the air and how she and Liz would pile up leaves, then have giggle fits as they crash landed in the pile. They also played hopscotch on the sidewalk, often singing out, "Step on a crack. Break your mother's back." Carrie smiled at the memory.

Liz and Carrie, born just two days apart, walked up the hill together on their first day of school. During summer vacations, they were inseparable. They often pretended they were sisters. The week they turned nine, they went out behind Newby's garage and pricked their fingers with a needle to become "blood sisters."

They formed a club, sold lemonade at a stand in Carrie's front yard, joined Girl Scouts, 4-H, and organized a neighborhood circus several summers in a row. In junior high school, they wrote, produced, and directed a play about Columbus landing in America. When they went off to high school, they joined the same clubs and double dated.

After high school graduation, Liz went off to college. Not Carrie. Ignoring Carrie's pleas, Gram said there was no money for college. She told Carrie to find herself a job. Gram, who had always hated school, refused to discuss the matter further.

Now that she was on her own, Carrie hoped to start on her degree in Atlanta in the spring or summer, even if she could only take a class or two at a time. Michael was supportive of her decision.

As soon as Carrie walked into Gram's apartment, she threw her coat and purse down, and started cleaning up the mess. First, she dumped loaded ashtrays into the garbage sack in the kitchen, adding trash from the overflowing wastebaskets. She filled a second bag with junk mail and a stack of old catalogs. She tossed two long-dead house plants in the sack, then hauled the bulging bags to the bin at the end of the hallway, around the corner from the elevator. Returning to the apartment, she opened wide the living room window.

What is this gunk, she wondered as she dusted the end tables, coffee table, the windows, the television screen, and the ceramic figurines on the curio shelf? Carrie guessed the thin coat of a gluey, brown goop somehow related to the hundreds of cigarettes Gram had smoked in the apartment. Carrie didn't want to think about what the inside of Gram's lungs must look like.

Opening the refrigerator door, Carrie took one whiff, then shut it quickly. A few seconds later, holding her breath, she opened the door again—this time tossing out rotting vegetables and containers filled with long-forgotten leftovers. Holding her nose, she threw the plastic containers into the garbage sack. Carrie took a welcome break after she finished scouring the kitchen.

Sitting on Gram's green paisley sofa with a glass of ice water, Carrie thought about Helen's warning about how Gram might choke to death if she didn't have the radiation treatments. Carrie envisioned Gram gasping for air, her eyes bugging out. Swallowing hard, she set her glass down on a metal coaster on the coffee table, then shifted her weight on the sofa and stared out the window. She wondered what she could say that would convince Gram to have the radiation treatments. She knew she didn't have the nerve to tell her that she might choke to death.

Carrie made a list of things to do after she retrieved Gram. She wrote down the items: *Make a grocery list. Grocery shop. Cook—make extra to freeze. Offer to help Gram with her bills. Discuss radiation issue with Gram.* The phone rang, just as she finished. It was Michael. Carrie told him about Gram's lung cancer. "Helen Newby offered to let me sleep at her house." She gave Michael the Newbys' phone number and told him she'd be leaving soon to pick Gram up from the hospital. Michael wanted to know how long she would be gone.

"I have no idea," Carrie said. "Gram's not doing well at all. I can't reach Aunt Nella. She's off somewhere. God only knows where."

"You'd better work at finding her."

"I'm trying, Michael." Michael loved telling her what to do.

Michael told Carrie about his dinner out with her friend, Kay, and her husband, Dave. "We went downtown to Rio Bravo. Things were jumping there. I had a chicken enchilada, beef burrito, beans, rice, and a couple of Coronas, and came home stuffed. Today, the three of us are going hiking at Amicolola Falls. Kay said she'd handle things at work for you." Carrie smiled. The only good thing about working at the travel bureau in Dunwoody was making friends with Kay.

"Tell her I said thanks. I'd love to be going hiking with you guys." Carrie told Michael she loved him, then hung up before she had a chance to start complaining.

"This stupid sofa smells like a cat litter box," Carrie said, getting up.

She already hated being stuck in Gram's apartment. When she tore the dirty sheets off of Gram's bed, she found holes with jagged brown edges in the dirty sheets and also in the clean ones. Carrie knew they were cigarette burns. Gram had obviously been smoking in bed. What had the woman been thinking?

Carrie took a load of clothes to the laundry room. On the way back, she passed Cordelia Turner, Gram's tiny, birdlike neighbor from across the hall. Cordelia had white frizzy hair, a crane-like neck, pink circles of rouge on her cheekbones, a wide smile, and an irritating, high-pitched voice.

"Hello, dear," Cordelia said. "Are you visiting Madeline? I hear she had to go to the hospital."

"She hasn't been feeling well," Carrie said.

"I wondered." Cordelia waited, anxious to get fuel for the apartment hotline.

"She's coming home today. Nice to see you." Carrie hurried into Gram's apartment, knowing if she had started talking to the lonely Cordelia, there would have been no getting away.

Carrie found Gram's strongbox in the back of the linen closet, behind a pile of towels. Leafing through the bills, she piled them, then went through them. Gram had only paid the minimum due each month on her charge accounts at Sears, Penneys, and Pranges. Carrie felt a knot in the pit of her stomach, knowing she and Michael would have to use their funds to help pay off her debts. The interest charges on her accounts were more than her payments.

At the bottom of the strongbox, she found an unfamiliar red payment book, listing payments on a five-thousand dollar loan. Gram had borrowed the money in 1986, from the Lutheran church credit union, where she had worked as a receptionist. Carrie wondered why Gram hadn't mentioned the loan back in May when she and Michael came up for the weekend to go over her bills and help her out of her latest financial mess. Just as Carrie returned the loan card to the box, the phone rang.

"Caroline. I'm ready to come home," Gram said. "Dr. Edgar said I could leave. Come get me, right now." Carrie told Gram she would leave soon. "Hurry, Caroline. I can't tolerate this place for another minute."

After hanging up the phone, Carrie returned the strongbox to the closet. She freshened up, grabbed her coat and purse, and hurried out.

"Gram, you look great," Carrie said. Gram sat on the side of the hospital bed dressed in a red blazer, white blouse, and black and white plaid slacks, wearing plenty of makeup. Her dangly earrings matched the gold owl pin on her lapel.

"The nurse said I have to go downstairs in a wheelchair. I hate their stupid rules."

"I'm sure we have to sign some papers."

"I did that already." Gram scooted off the bed.

When the nurse arrived in the room, Carrie offered to get the car and meet Gram at the admissions entrance. "Take that vase of roses down to the car with you," Gram said, pointing toward the window sill.

"Who are the roses from?" Carrie asked.

"Herman."

"Gram, I told you," Carrie said, "he's sweet on you."

"Nonsense. He's just showing off because you're around. I've told you—we're just friends. You don't understand." Gram scowled at her. "Get going, will you. I cannot stand this place for another minute. I'm never going to another hospital, not ever." Carrie hurried out the door, carrying the vase of roses. Gram's mood gave her a warning about what lay ahead.

"I saw your neighbor, Cordelia, this morning," Carrie said on the drive home.

"I hope you didn't mention the mass in my chest to that busybody. News like that travels around our building like a dirty joke." Carrie assured Gram that she hadn't passed out any information. Gram let out a sigh of relief.

Carrie held Gram's arm and helped her to the sofa in her apartment. She got a pillow from Gram's bed and put it beside her.

"I'm about to die of thirst," Gram said. "Bring me some iced tea."

Carrie brought the iced tea and a couple of slices of Helen's bread to Gram, then sat down across the room and reworked her grocery list, adding a few things that Gram wanted. "I guess I'm ready to go to the store in a few minutes. You'll be okay, won't you?"

"Lordy, Caroline. Don't go treating me like an invalid. I'll be fine." Gram flipped on the television with the remote control. "You've got the list, don't you?"

"Yes, Gram," Carrie said, anxious to leave. "I'll fix lunch as soon as I get back. Try some of that bread. It's wonderful." Carrie leaned down, kissed her on the cheek. Gram smelled like she had just licked an ashtray. She had a Salem in her hand, ready to light up, when Carrie walked out the door.

Carrie drove the few blocks to the Piggly Wiggly on Eighth Street. Walking across the parking lot, she smelled bratwurst cooking and knew lots of people in town would follow local Labor Day weekend tradition. They would parboil Johnsonville bratwurst in beer and onions, grill them outdoors, then serve the brats on Sheboygan hard rolls. In Atlanta, when Carrie mentioned she was from Sheboygan, Wisconsin, people would say, "Isn't that where they make the famous bratwurst?"

She bought a firm head of lettuce, bananas, still a little green, a bunch of seedless red grapes—the size of marbles, two cans of tuna packed in water, Grape Nuts, wheat bread, ham and turkey from the deli—sliced thin, chicken breasts, a chuck roast, eggs, milk, and fresh bread from the bakery. Then, she got the items Gram had added to her list: Hershey bars with almonds, two cartons of cigarettes, and a Bic lighter.

At the checkout lane, Mavis Harmon, Gram's childhood friend, stood in line in front of Carrie, smelling of honeysuckle. Mavis wore church clothes—a navy dress trimmed in white and navy heels. She wore a white carnation corsage and carried a navy purse. Mavis still looked the same. Her hair had been permed into tight curls and her face had a healthy glow. Mavis appeared years younger than Gram.

"Carrie, honey, it's good to see you. What are you doing in town?"

"Gram's sick." She shared Gram's diagnosis with Mavis.

"Gracious me," Mavis said. "I wondered why she wasn't at Sunday School this morning." Mavis looked alarmed. She asked Carrie how she liked Atlanta.

"I love it," Carrie said, smiling at Mavis who had always encouraged Carrie to follow her dreams. "It's a wonderful place filled with grand old trees and flowering plants. You should come visit in the springtime when the woods are filled with the lacy dogwood blossoms and the azalea bushes explode all over the city. It's breathtaking, a virtual panorama of color."

"Sounds lovely, dear," Mavis said as she picked up her sack of groceries from the counter. "Did Madeline tell you about our reunion? It's coming up next week." Carrie nodded, wondering if Gram would be able to join her high school friends. "I'd better get on home." Before saying good-bye, Mavis said she'd give Gram a call.

On the drive back to the apartment, Carrie thought about Gram's friends. She'd always had trouble keeping their names straight. Mavis Conrad, Mary Lou Fischer, Marie Schmidt, and, of course, Gram was Madeline. Before Marian Trilling died, there had been five of them. They had loved calling themselves the M and M's. They'd been getting together, once a year, for the past ten years. Gram and Mavis were the only ones left in Sheboygan. Mary Lou lived in the Chicago area, and Marie lived in North Carolina where her husband was mayor of a small town, a fact that impressed Gram. According to Gram, all of her friends had done better than she had. By that, she meant they had more money.

When Carrie got back to the apartment, she put the grocery bags down on the floor, then searched her purse for Gram's door key. She could hear Gram coughing. The hallway smelled like a mixture of burned bacon, cooked cabbage, and Pine-Sol.

She took the groceries to the kitchen, then went in to see Gram. A large vase of amber chrysanthemums with a huge yellow bow sat on the round table near the side window next to the closed light green draperies.

"More flowers? This place is starting to look like a . . ." Carrie paused. She had almost said it looked like a funeral home.

"Nella and Jennifer had them delivered," Gram said. "They came from that new flower shop near the bank. It opened up a year ago, right after you moved away. I called Jennifer to say thanks. Turns out Nella had called her. She's coming home soon."

"Glory, halleujah—where's she been?" Carrie said.

"Jennifer didn't say."

"Surely Jennifer knows where her mother is."

"If she knows, she didn't say. Jennifer's coming here, next weekend. That girl is just the sweetest thing. So thoughtful." Gram beamed. Carrie cringed. Gram had always doted on Jennifer and had treated her like a first-prize granddaughter. Carrie had been more like a daughter than a grandaughter. Carrie crossed her fingers, hoping Aunt Nella would come with Jennifer.

When Carrie opened the pantry to put the carton of cigarettes away, she found two more full cartons. Obviously, Gram did not plan on running out any time soon. After the rest of the groceries were shelved, Carrie made a ham and cheese sandwich and cut it in quarters for Gram. She peeled a banana and got out a carton of raspberry yogurt for herself.

"I don't know how you can eat that yeegurt stuff," Gram said, sitting down at the table.

"It's yogurt, Gram. Want some?"

"Lawsy sakes, no. I hate yeegurt." Gram scrunched up her face as she picked up her sandwich.

"I saw Mavis at the store. She mentioned your reunion next week. I hope you're going to feel like having your friends around."

"I wouldn't miss it. We're going to have fun, fun, fun. We're going out to eat every night, and we've got tickets to a play, *Our Town*, at the Arts Center."

Carrie admired Gram's positive attitude. She wondered if it would be the last time Gram got together with her old friends. Probably so, if the doctor's diagnosis was correct. When Carrie was growing up, Gram's friends gave her lots of attention. She felt the closest to Mavis, who had come along on trips to the park, to the zoo in St. Louis, and on shopping excursions.

Gram only ate a few bites of her sandwich, then covered it up with her paper napkin. They decided to play cards, something they'd done many times over the years. "The cards are over there." Gram pointed to the familiar wicker basket beside the sofa. Carrie smiled at the memory of how Gram had taught her to play blackjack, using buttons for money.

"Are the stakes the same as always?" Carrie asked when they began to play gin rummy. Gram nodded. They played a quarter for a gin, a dime for a lay-down. Carrie shuffled the cards, then dealt out ten to each of them. Gram skunked Carrie, winning seventy-five cents. Except for the fact that she kept checking to see if she held the right number of cards in her hand, Gram did fine. Finally she announced, tiredly, "I'm ready to call it quits," and headed back to the sofa.

Carrie put the cards back into the basket that had held them for as long as she could remember. Gram had always said that someday the round wicker basket would be hers. It had been in Gram's family since her ancestors moved to Sheboygan from Hanover, Germany. When Carrie's great-grandparents first arrived in Sheboygan, they opened a small mercantile store. Gram's husband, Henry Whitfield, worked in the family business where he and Gram met. Henry died in 1960, five years before Carrie's birth. When he died, he left Gram the little house on North Sixth Street where Gram had raised Carrie. However, right before Carrie married, the bank took over the little house. Gram had refinanced it several times and could no longer make the house payments. That's when she moved into her apartment.

Gram had turned on a soap opera, and then had fallen asleep. Carrie turned off the television just as John Dixon screamed at some young nurse at Memorial Hospital. Carrie used to watch "As The World Turns" with Gram, who never tired of telling her how in 1963 she'd been watching the soap when Walter Cronkite interrupted with news that President Kennedy had been shot. A cigarette burned in the ashtray on the table beside the sofa. Carrie snuffed it out, then covered Gram with her rose-colored afghan.

She tiptoed to the hall closet, taking out the metal file box for another look, then went around the corner, out of sight, into the bedroom. Knowing she had replaced it earlier, Carrie was puzzled when she found the loan card missing from the strongbox. Had Gram removed it while she was at the grocery store?

Carrie decided to go for a walk since Gram was snoring, She left a note saying, *I'm taking a walk. Be back soon. Love, Carrie.* She erased *Love, Carrie,* and wrote, *Love, Caroline* and placed it on the TV tray right beside Gram.

Once outside Gram's building, she hurried to the corner and across the street to the cemetery. She walked the winding path past the tall, proud oak trees whose brilliant hand-shaped leaves danced in the gentle breeze as shadows wavered from grave to grave just like Carrie's feelings about caring for Gram. A wreath of wilted red carnations covered a mound of dirt on a freshly dug grave.

She stopped to read the names on the gravestones of people she didn't know, wondering if, one day, would people stop and read the name, Madeline Louise Whitfield, on a gravestone and wonder about her. She read the names—Arliss Reese. Wilbur Nottling. Edith Schroeder. Ulrich Gardner. Who were they? What secrets did they take to the grave with them? Did anyone remember them? Kicking a rock along the cracked sidewalk, she took deep breaths, trying to calm her shaky insides.

As she walked through the cemetery, her head was filled with questions. Carrie couldn't help but wonder how long Gram would last. For the remaining months of Gram's life, she knew, like it or not, that they were in the boat together. Carrie dreaded the thought of watching Gram deteriorate, but she couldn't let her sink by herself. She would figure out a way to stay on in Sheboygan, at least for awhile.

When she returned, Gram was still sleeping. Sitting in a chair across the room, Carrie stared at her pitiful grandmother, whose swollen cheeks drooped like the hanging fern in the corner window. Every now and then she let out a cough, spraying a mist into the room. Her weary figure was a result of her addiction and her rejection of sunlight, fresh air, new places, children's faces, conversation with meaning—the very things she had considered important during the years when Carrie was growing up.

Carrie wished at that very moment that she could have a real heart-to-heart talk with Gram about her problems. She couldn't, not this time. This time Gram *was* her problem. There was no stopping the slide.

# Chapter Four

Journal, Friday, September 11, 1987

Gram's habit of keeping the apartment blinds shut makes me feel claustrophobic, like I'm stuck deep inside a cavern. I'm relieved to be out of there and back at the Newbys' place. Helen and Ben went out for batter-fried pike at the Elk's club, so I've got the place to myself. Gram ate at five, way too early for me. After I left her apartment, I got Randall's takeout—a hamburger with the works and cole slaw. Even though it's cool, I ate outside, in the Newbys' backyard sucking in the fresh air, watching the squirrels scurry after acorns. I could hear the two little boys next door chasing each other, squealing with laughter. It was music for my muddled brain.

Gram's freezer is now full of ready-to-thaw dinners, enough small meals to last her a couple of weeks. In the past few days, I've cooked most of the things she said sounded good to her—chicken soup, meatloaf, barbecued pork, chocolate chip cookies, and homemade bread. I'm sick of working in the kitchen, and I'm also sick of Gram's Grizelda-the-witch personality. She's angry at the world.

I try to be patient, but she's hammered on me for a week now, and I'm feeling bruised. At times I admire her courage, but most of the time, I feel like shaking some sense into her. Her constant criticism probes inside me, digging up unplesant memories. Knowing how sick she is, I try to be understanding, but my wick is getting short. I realize that what she wants is to feel like her normal self. Even so, it's not easy. Gram remains captain of her own ship; she told me to muffle my mouth when I pleaded with her to try the radiation.

Liz called Tuesday night and let me bitch for awhile. It felt good. Liz was glad that I'm staying here with her parents. She suggested that I read Elisabeth Kubler-Ross's book, *On Death and Dying*. Liz studied it in one of her classes, and she thinks it will help me to understand the stages Gram must go through. I checked it out at the library, using Gram's card. I've tried reading it at bedtime, but it's slow going. I usually fall asleep after a page or two.

At the library, I looked through a book on cancer and jotted down a list of lung cancer symptoms. I found out that cancer patients often lose their sense of feel, and that hit home. One day this week at lunch Gram sat at the kitchen table with this huge glob of peanut butter stuck on her cheek. When I asked her to wipe it off with her napkin, she insisted there was nothing on her face. I guess she couldn't feel it there. She gave me a stern look when I reached over and wiped it off. The book also described how cancer cells attack vital organs. Now, I keep picturing these little-monster cancer cells feasting on Gram like Wisconsinites at a smorgasbord.

On Wednesday, before we went to the Lean Bean restaurant in Kohler for lunch, we drove past Lake Michigan. Gram stared out the window at the lake. "Some days, the lake is a Carolina blue just like your eyes. Today, it looks muddy brown, like your father's bath water used to look," she said, making me laugh.

At the restaurant parking lot, Gram inched along unsteadily, stopping often to catch her breath. I suggested getting her a walker. She looked at me like I had stepped out of a spaceship.

Gram told our waiter, a young boy, skinny as a broomstick, that she wanted a tuna sandwich, iced tea, and chocolate mousse. I ordered an Oriental chicken salad. Waiting for our food, Gram told me a joke about this old geezer who was buying a nightgown for his wife. She forgot the punch line. It didn't matter. I laughed anyhow. Gram always waves her arms in the air like an Italian diva when she tells a story. Through the glass wall, we could see the indoor pool from our table.

We rated the guys coming out of the pool, just like we used to do. Melvyn Bean, my potbellied former high school science teacher, got a two. Muscular Dean Kaufman, who took me to the junior prom and now sells Oldsmobiles, got a seven. Gram gave Roger Simpson, her eye doctor, who could double for Robert Redford, a ten. I agreed with Gram—he's a hunk. He's almost as good-looking as Michael. For a while there, it seemed like I had my grandmother back.

But when lunch arrived, Gram looked at it like someone else had done the ordering. She tore her tuna sandwich into bits and made a mess of it on her plate. I looked around to see if anyone was watching. She never put more than three or four bites into her mouth. When she told me her sandwich tasted like chalk and pushed her plate aside, I canceled her dessert order. The waiter cleared our table. She glared at him as if it was his fault she couldn't taste the food.

On the way out, we saw Larry Siegel with his wife, Cheryl, and their little boy, an ugly kid with protruding ears and a very large mouth. Larry actually said hello. Amazing. Gladys Siegel, Larry's mom, used to play in Gram's pinocle group. Gladys and Gram always wanted Larry and me to become an item. What a joke that was. I used to wish he would ask me out—though I was pretty sure it was beneath him—just so I could turn him down. After Larry got Cheryl Wilcox pregnant our junior year, Gram never discussed Larry Siegel again.

Laughing, as we left the parking lot, I asked Gram if she remembered Larry. A silent Gram stared out the window, ignoring my told-you-so insinuation.

Back at the apartment, while Gram napped, I got my little blue notebook and looked over the list of cancer symptoms. Gram has most of them—poor appetite, hoarseness, shortness of breath, drooping eyelids, thick fingernails. I stared at her hard, brittle nails when we were playing cards. She definitely has trouble swallowing. I have to crush her pills in ice cream, same as she used to do for me when I was small. Our roles have flipflopped. Now, I am the mother, and she is the child.

I bumped into Herman Grothe in the laundry room today. He asked questions about Gram, sounding concerned. I don't care what Gram says; I think there's something going on between them. It wouldn't surprise me. Gram's had her share of boyfriends over the years.

I remember one boyfriend, George Fletcher, quite well. How could I forget? I barged in on George one time when he was peeing in our bathroom. Talk about being embarrassed. George was a short, bearded man with bad breath. The right side of his mouth turned upward at an odd angle, because he crashed his bicycle into the back of a truck when he was a teenager. George traveled the Midwest selling a line of women's clothing. All of his samples came in size eight, perfect for Gram. She almost married him, just for the clothes. Typically, when he stopped coming around, she never explained why.

More rain is forecast for tomorrow. I can hear the raindrops now, dancing on the awning outside the kitchen window. I'd love to go home and sleep in my own bed tonight. But, I can't go. Not yet. I've got several things to do before I can leave. I still need to confront Gram about her finances and about the cigarettes burns in her sheets. Then there's the unavoidable visit to the funeral home—just in case it's necessary before I come back. I dread that. Today, when I mentioned leaving, Gram, looking like the last wallflower at the dance, told me to go ahead and leave her all alone.

Some days I think I'd better get out of here before Gram gets so bad that I can't leave. When I do go back home, I've arranged for Mavis and Helen to check up on Gram. Jennifer arrives tomorrow, and possibly Aunt Nella. I know Gram will act like a different person in front of Jennifer. I've often wanted to trade places with my cousin. She's always seen a different side of Gram. Right now, I don't want to trade places with anyone. I just want to get on a plane and head home.

How long will Gram last? I know she's dying, but I can't imagine her dead. Not Gram. I try to envision what it would be like knowing that death is waiting around the corner. These last few days, I've been obsessed with death. Scary thoughts inhabit my head. I question my sanity. Tonight, I looked into the mirror and thought, we are all going to die. Somehow. Some way. Some day. It's just a matter of time.

## Chapter Five

Carrie sat in a rowboat. Gram bobbed in the water nearby holding onto the side of the boat with one hand, trying to reach out for Carrie with the other. Their fingers touched, but Carrie couldn't get her over the side and into the boat. Gram tried to speak, but no words came out. Panic filled her glazed eyes as she thrashed in the choppy water wearing the pale green Eileen West nightgown her friend Mavis had given to her, the one Gram said she'd never wear.

Awakening, Carrie blinked her eyes, trying to erase the image of Gram struggling in the water in the green nightgown. "What a terrible gift to give a sick person," Gram had said the day she had received it. Knowing the gift had insulted Gram, Carrie had folded the nightgown and put it in Gram's dresser, way in the back.

Carrie opened the blinds. She could hear the Newbys' next-door neighbor, Fred Stengl, outside on a ladder, hammering the window frame on the side of the house. His brown and white springer spaniel, Shakespeare, chased a butterfly. The bright sunshine lifted Carrie's spirits.

Carrie could heard Helen and Ben in the kitchen, clinking their forks. The smell of bacon drifted down the hallway. Helen made Ben bacon and eggs almost every morning. Carrie thought that Helen, as a nurse, should know that diet wasn't good for either of them.

Carrie dressed in her light blue running sweats, then headed to the kitchen. Helen was standing in front of the maple cabinet, pouring herself a cup of coffee. She offered to fry some eggs for Carrie.

"No thanks. I'm going out for a run."

"Honey, I don't know why you do all that running. You're plenty slim and trim."

"I won't stay that way for long, not around this house. I'll have some cereal when I get back." She got a glass of water, then sat down in the breakfast nook beside Ben. He asked about Gram.

"She's having a tough time, but I know she'll perk up today. My cousin Jennifer's coming to visit."

"And you, dear, how're you holding up?" Helen asked as she wiped her plate clean with her last scrap of toast.

"I'm doing okay, I guess." Ben lay down the *Milwaukee Sentinel* sports section. Carrie picked it up and glanced at an article about the winter Olympics in Calgary, Canada.

"Is your aunt coming with Jennifer? I haven't seen Nella for ages." Helen put a second piece of homemade bread into the toaster. She had the butter on her knife, ready to lather her toast.

"I hope so." Carrie put her hands in a praying position. She told Helen and Ben good-bye, then turned and hurried out the back door.

Outside, she did some leg stretches, then ran to the corner, jogging in place until the traffic went past. She watched a thirtyish man in a gray business suit come down the front steps of her childhood home. Irene Beckman, who used to give Carrie piano lessons, tooted the horn and waved as she drove past. Carrie waved back, then jogged across the street toward their old house.

Glancing at the front steps as she went past, she remembered how, at age five, she had tried to ride her tricycle down those concrete steps. That brainfart idea had earned ten stitches in her forehead at Dr. Edgar's office next door.

Carrie passed by the large willow between their old house and Lorraine Spencer's house. Picking up her pace, she ran down to the corner and up the hill. Thinking about Lorraine reminded her of the prize-flower incident. One spring day when she was six, Carrie had gone into Lorraine's back yard and picked the bright red-orange flower that had commanded so much attention from the neighborhood ladies.

Carrying it inside, she'd presented it to Gram, who was smoking in the living room.

"My God, girl, that's Lorraine's prize flower," Gram had screamed.

She had wished she could stick it back on the stem. "I'm sorry. I just wanted to surprise you with something pretty."

"Don't tell me you're sorry. You go over to Lorraine's house and tell *her* you're sorry, and don't ever do anything so dastardly again."

Dastardly was a foreign word to Carrie, but the look on Gram's face told her it reeked of evil. She had trembled on the long walk out the back door, over to Lorraine's yard, and up her back steps. With the prize flower in hand, she had tapped on the porch door hoping no one would hear her. No such luck. Lorraine had appeared at the door wearing a broad smile.

"Oh, my sweet little honey. Don't those pigtails look darlin' on you."

"Here." Carrie had said, holding out the flower. "I picked your flower. I don't know why I did it. I didn't mean to, and I'm really sorry. I'll never pick a flower in your yard again."

She dropped the prize flower into a stunned Lorraine's hand, and ran off without another word. Thunder crashed in her head as she scurried up their back steps. In the kitchen, she grabbed two oatmeal raisin cookies, ate them as fast as she could, then ran into her room. Plopping down on her bed, she covered her face with the pillow.

Now, as she ran north on Sixth Street, Carrie smiled at the memory. After that day, she'd never felt confortable around Lorraine, but she'd never taken another flower from anyone's yard again, not even a dandelion.

Just beyond North Avenue, Carrie went past the big stone house where Aunt Nella used to live. The house reminded her of the summer when she was ten. That was the summer she'd gone to Girl Scout camp for a week in June, then she had moved in with Aunt Nella and Uncle Jim for six weeks, sharing a room with Jennifer, who was twelve going on sixteen. That was the summer Gram was drying out.

One morning, as Carrie stood at the kitchen counter waiting for her pop tart to toast, Aunt Nella had told her how she had discovered that

Gram had a drinking problem when Carrie had been away at camp. One day, Aunt Nella had gone over to Gram's to help can peaches. Reverend Grey, the Lutheran minister, had stopped by. "That cold beer looks mighty good," Reverend Grey had said. So, Aunt Nella had offered him a beer. She asked Gram if she wanted something to drink, offering to get her blackberry brandy from the basement.

"Absolutely not," Gram had said, giving Aunt Nella a stern look. Trying to redeem herself, Aunt Nella explained to Reverend Grey how each Christmas her husband, Jim, had given Gram some blackberry brandy.

When the minister left, an outraged Gram scolded Aunt Nella, who stopped canning peaches right then and there. But before she left, she took some jars to the basement storage shelf. That's when she discovered that the blackberry brandy was all gone.

No wonder Gram had said no. There had been at least four bottles on the shelf the last time she'd looked. Aunt Nella confronted Gram, who made a teary-eyed confession. According to Gram, she had been drinking brandy at bedtime to help her sleep. Then she had started dipping into the brandy several times a day, buying her own supply. According to Aunt Nella, Gram had been more than ready to get help for her alcoholic addiction.

Carrie remembered going to the AA club. She had liked sitting up at the bar with Gram, drinking Cokes. "Why dosen't anyone ever ask for beer or wine or something like that?" Carrie had asked Gram one time.

"We can't," Gram had said, with no further explanation.

Carrie later learned more about alcoholism from reading literature. Gram had a relapse and had signed herself back into the hospital. After that, she'd stayed sober. Carrie was proud of Gram's thirteen years of sobriety.

Carrie checked her watch, then turned around and headed back toward the Newbys' house, remembering how Gram helped others in town get involved in AA. Many times, she had gone out on a 12-step call in the middle of the night, leaving a note in the kitchen for Carrie.

"Do you ever feel like having a drink?" Carrie had asked once.

"Sure," Gram had said. "All the time. Trouble is, if I got started, you'd have to fill up the bathtub and give me a straw." Over the years, Carrie had tried not to upset Gram, fearing it might make her start drinking again. In many ways, alcoholism had given Gram the control she loved.

Carrie showered and changed quickly, then headed to Gram's apartment.

---

"Hi Gram," Carrie said. "It's gorgeous outside, the kind of day that makes people around here forget it'll be blustery cold before long."

"You don't have to worry about the cold anymore, do you?"

"We get some cold weather in Atlanta, but it never lasts long."

"Sounds nice. I'd like that."

Carrie gave her a questioning look.

"Jennifer called to say she'd be here a little before noon. And, guess what? She's got a surprise for me." Gram smiled. Carrie was pretty sure she knew what the surprise would be—Aunt Nella's pretty face surfaced in her mind.

"Mind if I open these drapes? Jennifer won't want it gloomy looking."

"Leave them alone," Gram said.

"Fine." Carrie shrugged her shoulders. She wasn't going to let Gram ruin her mood. Jogging always made her feel good. Carrie turned on the radio in the kitchen. Cleaning up the breakfast dishes, she sang "Lady" along with Kenny Rogers. Then she made Gram's bed and straightened up the living room. She could hear Gram in the bathroom, gagging. Peeking around the corner, Carrie saw her leaning over the sink, her finger stuck way into her mouth.

"Gram, let me help you," Carrie said, running to her side. Gram grasped onto Carrie's arm, moaning as she leaned into her like a dead weight. They inched across the room to the sofa, and soon Gram was fast asleep. Covering her with the rose afghan, Carrie sighed. She knew Gram would be passed out for awhile.

In the kitchen, Carrie swallowed two Tylenol tablets with a glass of water. She'd never felt anyone else's pain before. It hurt more than any pain of her own.

At the kitchen table, Carrie tried working the crossword in *The Sheboygan Press*. Unable to concentrate, she drew geometric designs on her notepad. As she doodled, her mind wandered to a conversation she'd had with Gram the day before.

"Your father was a wonder, such a special child," Gram had said. "Even at a young age, he was sensitive to others. And, he shared his feelings. Most males can't, you know." Carrie nodded her head in agreement. Gram had lit a cigarette, inhaled, then let the smoke curl out of her mouth, before she added. "He and his sister, Nella, were absolute opposites. Yet, they were very close." She laughed.

"What's funny, Gram?"

"Oh, just Richard. He was born the middle of November, a Scorpio—so confident and so much his own person. He always loved being right. I'm surprised he didn't become a lawyer." Gram told Carrie how her dad failed a college economics class twice because he disagreed with his professor and wouldn't budge on his stand. He passed on his third try, just barely."

Carrie laughed. She knew that sometimes she was stubborn, just like her dad. "What about my mom?"

"I don't know that much about her. She just showed up one day," Gram said, adding that it was painful when her son brought home a bride she'd never laid eyes on. Carrie had asked more questions about her mother, but Gram wouldn't say more.

While Gram slept, Carrie took a photo album from the bookcase and flipped through it for photographs of her parents. She found the familiar one of them standing beside their bicycles. On the bottom edge of the photo, *The day we met*, was written in black pen. Her mother's short hair was blowing in the wind. She stood, hands on her hips, a mischievious grin on her face. Her dad appeared cocky, like he had just hooked a keeper. They looked like kids at a carnival.

She remembered Aunt Nella saying that her dad had worked in the food industry, selling meat to restaurants. One year he had taken a business trip to Vancouver, and that's where he met Mary Caroline Campbell, a young girl with auburn hair and blue eyes, while bike riding in Stanley Park.

Three weeks later, they had married in a small ceremony in Vancouver with only Mary Caroline's parents and a few friends in attendance. "Your grandmother almost died of shock when your dad called with the news of his marriage. A few months later, when he brought her to Sheboygan to live, things got pretty tense," Aunt Nella had said, "especially when your Gram found out that Richard's new bride was a Catholic."

Carrie found a picture of her mother in a one-piece, navy blue maternity dress with a sailor collar. She stood beside the large oak tree in front of the house on Sixth Street, looking very pregnant. Carrie touched the faded photograph, tracing her finger around the outline of her mother's face.

As she had so many times, Carrie wondered about the car accident that killed her parents. Gram said her parents' car had hit a slick spot on County Trunk J on their way to Aunt Nella's cottage at Elkhart Lake. Their car skidded across the road and into the oncoming lane. A large truck, coming the opposite direction, smashed into their car. The truck driver told the police that he'd braked hard but couldn't avoid the collision.

Her dad died instantly. Her mother, who suffered internal injuries, had been in surgery for several hours and afterward developed pneumonia from having too much fluid in her lungs. Carrie was born a few days later. Giving birth weakened Mary Caroline. Three days later, she died.

Aunt Nella told her how her grandparents, Thomas and Elizabeth Campbell, came from Vancouver to be at their daughter's bedside. Before they arrived, Gram arranged to have Reverend Grey, from the Lutheran Church, come to the hospital and baptize both Mary Caroline and baby, Carrie. "I couldn't let her die a Catholic and go to hell," Aunt Nella quoted Gram as saying.

Thinking about the baptism made Carrie angry. Her mother had probably been too weak to protest. Carrie always felt a strange tension in the air when Aunt Nella or Gram spoke about her parents' accident. She had always known there must be more to the story than they were willing to share.

Carrie often wondered why she'd never heard from her mother's parents. Gram told her one day that her Campbell grandparents wanted to take her back to Vancouver with them. Gram had refused. "If we can't take the baby with us," Thomas Campbell said, "then we will never have any contact with her." Evidently, they had kept their word.

Carrie rubbed her stiff neck, then put the album away. She lay on the carpet, in front of Gram, and did stretching exercises, lifting her legs, one at at time. Holding onto her hamstrings, she felt the pull. She was doing tummy tucks when the doorbell rang. Gram awoke, startled.

Opening the door, Jennifer charged into the room, with her usual air of confidence, looking like a fashion model in her long watchplaid skirt, green sweater, and granny boots. She went over to the sofa and gave Gram a hug.

"Close your eyes," Jennifer said. "Don't peek." Gram held her eyes closed. Jennifer held out her left hand. "Okay, you can look now."

"What's this? Oh my. Look at that big diamond."

"I'm engaged. I got my ring last Sunday night." Carrie went over to look at Jennifer's diamond. Obviously, this was the big surprise. So much for expecting Aunt Nella.

"Tell us all about it, dear. Oh, I'm so excited. I'll need a new dress for the wedding," Gram said. "What color should it be? Blue? Purple?"

"Slow down, Gram. We'll talk about that later. Let me get something to drink. Do you have any soda?" Jennifer headed to the refrigerator and came back with a Diet Coke. Carrie asked Jennifer for details.

"Well, my fiance's name is Kevin Millwood." Jennifer told them Kevin graduated from the University of Minnesota in June, that he'd taken a job at Arthur Andersen in Minneapolis, near where Jennifer worked. "We met at a Twins baseball game. I was there with my roommate, Dawn. Kevin was in front of me, and we started talking. He was impressed when I started spitting out statistics about the players. We've been dating ever since. We're getting married the middle of March."

"I'll be there with bells on," Gram said. Carrie had her doubts.

"Why don't I order a pizza for lunch? We'll have a party to celebrate. Is that okay with you two?" Carrie said.

"Sounds great. I'm starved," Jennifer said.

"A party. Yes, I'd like that." Gram, sure she wasn't dressed up enough for a party, asked Jennifer to help her change clothes.

Looking down at her own sweatshirt and jeans, Carrie watched them go into Gram's room. Gram would think she was a slob, but that was just too bad. She had no other clothes with her. She dialed Papa John's and ordered a large pepperoni, black olive, and mushroom pizza. She could hear squeals of laughter coming from the bedroom.

She was anxious to learn more about Kevin. If Jennifer had picked him out, he had to be perfect. For years, Carrie had tried to hate her popular cousin, but she couldn't. Jennifer frustrated her, but her natural confidence and sense of humor made her fun to be around. She was a lot like her mother.

When the doorbell rang, Carrie smelled the pizza in the hallway. She paid the pudgy delivery boy who had marinara sauce splatttered on his white shirt, then hollered for Gram and Jennifer. Gram came into the room on Jennifer's arm, wearing gray pants and a hot pink sweater. Her dangly silver earrings jingled as she walked across the floor. "Do you like my new shoes?" she said, pointing to her black suede heels. "I ordered them from Marshall Field's." Carrie shook her head. Sick as she was, Gram still managed to spend money she didn't have.

"Doesn't she look great?" Jennifer said. "Don't try to tell me that this lady is sick." Gram beamed. Much to Carrie's surprise, Gram wobbled across the room on her high heels, without assistance.

"Come on over here." Carrie pointed to the kitchen table set with green and white checked placemats, matching napkins in wooden holders, and Gram's best silverware. Carrie put a slice of pizza on each white plate. While the two girls ate, Gram played with her pizza, turning it into an unappetizing doughy sculpture.

"You'd better eat, Gram," Jennifer said. Gram ate a few pieces of the crust, then said she was full.

"That mountain of stuff on your plate looks gross, Gram," Jennifer said.

"Well, I don't like that paparonni stuff."

"Pepperoni, Gram," Carrie said. She and her cousin laughed as they devoured the rest of the pizza. True to form, Gram covered her plate with her napkin. Kicking her heels off first, she headed back to the sofa and lit a cigarette.

"Great party," she said several minutes later, stubbing out her cigarette. Gram lay down, turned on the television, and started watching one of her favorite old movies, Humphrey Bogart and Katharine Hepburn in *The African Queen*.

"Does it have to be so loud?" Jennifer said, rolling her eyes.

"Get used to it," Carrie said.

"It's way too dark in here."

"Tell me about it. Don't even try to open the blinds. Gram will go ballistic." Carrie gave Jennifer a hug. "I'm happy for you, and I'm anxious to meet Kevin. Do you have a picture of him?" Jennifer ran off to get her purse and showed Carrie a photo of Kevin.

"He's very nice looking," Carrie said. Kevin had dark wavy hair, big green eyes, and a dimple in his chin, below a charming smile. "Your Mom must be excited. Is she coming here today? I sort of expected her to come with you."

"She couldn't make it." Jennifer looked away from Carrie.

"Jennifer, I'm confused. Where is your mom, anyhow? Gram's been asking for her." Jennifer didn't answer. Instead, she ran off to the bathroom, slamming the door behind her. Carrie shook her head, wishing for an explanation. Carrie peeked around the corner. Gram still slept on the sofa. Waiting for Jennifer to return, Carrie did the dishes.

"What's wrong? Are you okay?" Carrie said when Jennifer came back with puffy eyes.

Jennifer shook her head no.

"Let's go in here." Carrie said, pointing to Gram's bedroom. Carrie sat down on the edge of Gram's bed. Jennifer sat on the vanity stool across from her. "Tell me what's going on, please," Carrie said. "I didn't mean to upset you, but I really need your mom's help. I need to go home. I can't handle Gram alone."

"She can't help you, not right now." Jennifer said.

"Why not, Jennifer? I don't get it. Gram *is* her mother." Carrie glared at Jennifer.

"It's too soon. She just got out."

"Out? Whatever are you talking about? Where's she been? In jail?" Carrie stood directly in front of Jennifer.

"Get off of my case, Carrie. Of course, she hasn't been in jail. She's been in a detox center."

"Oh great." Carrie sat back down, leaned over, and put her head into her palms. Jennifer started to cry. "I give up," Carrie said, raising her head. "This family is major league dysfunctional." Carrie left the room.

"I'm sorry about your mom. Really, I am," Carrie said, when Jennifer followed her into the kitchen. "I didn't mean to lose it. It's just that I'm tired. And, I'm worried about Gram. I hate having everything on my shoulders. How's Aunt Nella doing?"

"I don't know. It's hard to tell. They only let her make a phone call once a week. I had to tell her about my engagement on the phone." Jennifer explained that her mom's drinking problem had been going on for awhile. She told Carrie about the time she'd come home from college and had gotten up in the middle of the night and had found her mother sprawled out on the bathroom floor, crying out, 'Momma. Momma, help me.' I couldn't lift her up, so I had to leave her lying there until the next morning."

"Sounds awful," Carrie said.

"She doesn't want Gram to know that she's been in detox, so don't say anything."

"Fine. My lips are glued shut."

"I blame Gram for Mom's drinking."

"Oh please, Jennifer. Your Mom probably inherited the tendency toward alcoholism. I can't believe that you think it's Gram's fault?"

"Carrie, I told you there are secrets in this family. When Mom was high on booze, she revealed some pretty unbelievable things."

"Like what?"

"I can't say. Mom swore me to secrecy. Besides, I hear Gram coughing. She's waking up."

"Don't leave me hanging."

"Trust me. I know what I'm talking about." Jennifer went in to visit Gram. Carrie felt drums pounding her temples. She couldn't think a clear thought.

"I'm going out for a walk," Carrie said. She slammed the door when she left. Outside, she hurried across the street, walking on North Avenue toward Lake Michigan. In the distance, a siren wailed. Carrie kicked a pile of wet leaves gathered on the sidewalk. They barely moved. She held her arms across her chest to ward off the wind and the light, drizzly rain. After half an hour, she turned around. She would figure things out. She had no choice. Throwing her shoulders back, she stood up tall, took a deep breath through her nose, then let it out slowly. Swinging her arms at her sides, she thought about her conversation with Jennifer. Someday she would unravel the family secrets.

For now, Gram took center stage. Nothing else mattered. Carrie made a promise to Gram, one she intended to keep.

# Chapter Six

Journal, Saturday, September 19, 1987

I'm finally on my way home. The plane is crowded, and I'm stuck between two businessmen who are using both armrests—like it's their God-given right—leaving me with no place to rest my elbows. I'm too blitzed to deal with their rudeness.

After two weeks with Gram, I'm a first-class zombie, and I can't wait to get home. I miss Michael and feel crummy that our last few phone calls have ended in argument. Michael, who just doesn't get it, is upset with me for not coming home sooner. He has no idea how I've busted my buns arranging things so I could come home. He doesn't realize that supervising Gram's care has landed in my lap. Perhaps his attitude will improve once I get home. Right now, I can't worry about Michael. It's Gram who causes me the most concern. She's hit an ironclad denial stage.

According to her, the tests are all wrong, and the doctor is senile. If I dare to mention the word cancer, she sidesteps the subject. Gram is a master at shelving reality.

For now, she's transferred her problems from her shoulders to mine. So, what else is new? We've been down this stream, many times. However, this time, I can't steer her in another direction. The facts are in big, bold letters. She has a malignancy that will eventually kill her. All I can do is help her stay on course.

Jennifer arrived at Gram's right before Herman showed up, ready to drive me to the airport. He brought white baby roses for Gram. I inhaled their fragrance, then put the long-stemmed beauties in a crystal vase and set them on the top of the television set. Gram can look across the room at them from her nest on the sofa.

As he lifted my suitcase off the sidewalk and up into the van, Herman told me not to worry, that he would keep an eye on Gram. He offered to get her mail and run errands, and I accepted his kind offer even though I may catch hell from Gram. Well, tough tootie to her. I'll take whatever help I can get. Besides, these days, I'm the chief, and she's the Indian.

Herman knows the schedule. He'll offer his services when Gram's M & M friends leave after their four-day visit. On the ride to Milwaukee, he said he knew all about the reunion. In fact, he's picking Mary Lou and Marie up at the airport. I feel like I have the bases covered. Jennifer will stay with Gram until her friends arrive on Sunday.

I feel pretty good about conning Gram into using a walker. Jennifer helped me out. She told Gram last weekend when she visited that the walker was all her idea, even though I was the one who called Dr. Edgar and arranged to pick it up. Jennifer and I rode downtown in her red Chevy Beretta to get it. Riding with her made me think of high school days, when I walked the nine blocks to school. Jennifer would drive past me almost every morning, never once stopping to offer me a ride.

"I hate this damn thing," Gram said, holding onto the walker,

"It will keep you from falling and breaking something," I said.

I'm amazed Jennifer agreed to visit Gram again this weekend. Perhaps Kevin's a good influence on her. With her perfect family falling apart, my guess is she needs the rest of us. I didn't dare ask when and if Aunt Nella planned to come visit Gram. I do know that last night Jennifer picked her mom up from the detox center.

Gram spent the past week raving to her friends about her precious Jennifer's upcoming visit. And, she moaned to her friends about me. According to Gram, my list of flaws is endless. I don't know how to fold clothes; I put them away in the wrong drawers. I lose important papers when I pay the bills, and I cook her food too bland, or too spicy. I make up stories about her, and I lose things. She told her friends how I had tossed out her perfectly good houseplants, in a voice loud enough for me to hear.

Gram insisted in a huff that she had not been smoking in bed when I mentioned the holes in her sheets. She said it was a mystery to her how the sheets came out of the dryer that way. Truth is a foreign commodity in our family. Lily-white lies. That's what Gram calls them. She says that sometimes it's necessary to switch sails midstream, in order to protect people. Makes me think of Aunt Nella. Now, there's someone who can switch sails. Why can't she be honest with Gram? It seems to me that Gram is the one person who could help Aunt Nella deal with her alcoholism.

I begged Jennifer to let me tell Gram about her mother. Jennifer simply gave me a stern, raised-eyebrow stare and told me to can the idea. Sometimes, my cousin grates on me. Jennifer is spoiled. Aunt Nella and Uncle Jim always made sure she had whatever she wanted. She lives a fairy tale life with few restrictions. Princess Jennifer and I come from the same shore, but we ride on different boats.

After spoiling Aunt Nella and my dad, Gram told me she was determined not to make the same mistake with me. God knows, she rarely bought me new clothes. I was forced to wear Jennifer's hand-me-downs or the home-sewn frocks Gram made. I could only go out on Friday and Saturday nights. My curfew was eleven—my dates teased me about that little rule. Gram preferred that I go to a church-sponsored event. She served me liver four nights a week, saying it was good for my blood. When Jennifer came to our house for dinner, she'd bring her own sandwich just in case it was a liver night. Who could blame her? I could barf thinking about it. I vowed I'll never let liver touch my lips again.

I'd like to hate Jennifer, but I don't. In spite of the fact that she drives me crazy at times, she has her good points. We had a fun dinner Saturday night. We went to the Hoffbrau for medium-rare tenderloin sandwiches, fries, salad with french Roquefort dressing and a beer. We had lots of laughs and a good visit. Jennifer's worried about her mother. Aunt Nella sounds fragile. Jennifer and I are both concerned about Gram. That's one area where my cousin and I stand on common ground.

I about toppled out of my chair when Jennifer asked me to be the maid of honor in her wedding. I have no idea why she asked me, unless, to please Gram. Not knowing what else to say, I told her that I'd be honored. She filled me in on her wedding plans. When Jennifer mentioned that Gram couldn't decide whether to wear a suit or a long dress, I clenched my jaw to keep from saying anything. Who knows if Gram will still be alive in March?

Jennifer called last night and praised me for taking good care of Gram. I smelled a rodent. She said she just knew I wouldn't be able to stay away long. She painted a picture, a vivid family scene of Gram on a journey. I felt she as if she were putting a rope around me and hanging me on a hook. That girl has nerve. I wanted to tell her to cut the b.s. Instead, I slammed the receiver down, then felt sharp knives between my shoulder blades for the rest of the evening.

Jennifer's a whiz at work, where she sells computer business forms, designing them herself. She told me between working and planning a wedding, she has no time to deal with Gram's problems. With her recovery in progress, neither does my elusive Aunt Nella. Jennifer's call made it crystal clear. Like it or not, I've won the caretaking role.

I have no choice but to put my life on hold. Michael thinks I'm the ultimate pushover and insists that we can find someone to care for Gram. He likes to be right, but this time he's wrong. Dead wrong.

## Chapter Seven

Carrie stepped off the train at the baggage exit and hurried toward the steep escalator. She didn't see the malted milk balls the boy in front of her had spilled. One minute she was on her feet, the next she lay flat on her back.

"Are you okay?" a man behind her asked.

"I'm fine," she said, trying to get up.

"Here, let me help you." He grabbed her hand and pulled her to a standing position. "You took quite a spill." Carrie wobbled, hanging onto his arm.

"My right ankle hurts." She let go of his arm, then reached for it again, when she lost her balance. Looking up at his face, she realized he was the man who had sat next to her on the airplane, the one whose elbow she had knocked off the armrest while he was sleeping, so she could have more room. He helped her move toward the wall near the escalator.

"I'm Tom Egan. I believe we were seatmates on the plane. I slept almost the whole way," he said.

"I know," Carrie said, letting go of his arm. She leaned against the wall. "I fell asleep right before we landed, and I'm still kind of groggy. I guess that's why I didn't see that little kid drop his candy."

"Is this yours?" Tom asked, reaching down for her blue journal lying on the floor near the escalator.

"Yes." She reached out for it, quickly tucking it into the side pocket of her blue tote bag.

"You ready to try walking?" With Tom's help, Carrie limped toward the escalator. They rode up to the baggage area, then walked slowly to the luggage carousel. The suitcases hadn't arrived yet.

"I didn't catch your name," he said.

"I didn't give it to you," she said, reaching out to shake his hand. "I'm Carrie Barnes." Tom shook her hand, then reached inside his coat pocket, pulled out a business card, and handed it to her. "I see you live in Atlanta," Carrie said, glancing at the card.

"Do you live here, too?" he asked.

"Yes. And, believe me. I'm glad to be here. I've been in Wisconsin taking care of my dying grandmother. I'm blitzed."

"Sounds like a rough assignment," Tom said. "My Mom died not too long ago. I helped out with her sometimes. I know how difficult caretaking can be."

Carrie nodded her head in agreement. She glanced down at his business card. He was a Buckhead lawyer. It figured. He had a confident attitude and a Sean Connery smile. A smooth talker, she figured he could pull whatever information he needed out of anyone. No wonder he wanted to know if she'd hurt herself. Carrie looked over when the luggage carousel started.

"Let me know when your stuff arrives. I'll get it for you."

"Thanks," Carrie said, looking for Michael, who had a habit of running late. She didn't see him, but she did recognize her suitcase.

"Just point to it. I'll get it for you." Tom said.

"There it is, right there. The green one right beside that huge black duffel." Tom pulled it off the carousel and set it down beside her.

"Here you go." She thanked him. Tom hurrried over to grab his own suitcase.

She liked his rugged good looks. "Good luck with that ankle," he said, touching his hand to her shoulder. He told her good-bye.

"Bye. I appreciate your help." She waved as he started to walk away, certain she'd never see him again.

"I could give you a ride home. I'm going to the northside," he said turning around.

"Thanks, but that's not necessary. Michael, my husband—he'll be here any minute."

"Okay, but I hate leaving you alone."

"Trust me. I'll be fine."

"Be sure to call. Let me know how you're doing. You know, you could be injured and not know it."

"Okay, fine. I'll call," she said, anxious for him to leave.

Just minutes after Tom left, Carrie saw Michael coming. "That feels good," she said, when he gave her a vise-grip hug. He smelled like rain and leather. She kissed him in the crook of his neck, then let go.

Michael carried her suitcase as Carrie limped beside him. "What happened to you? You can hardly walk." Carrie told Michael about her fall.

"You know how clumsy I can be. Believe me, I felt like a doinkus lying on the floor. This guy from my plane—he had sat right beside me—helped me up. He got my suitcase for me too."

"Sounds like a nice guy," Michael said. "Sorry I was late. It's drizzling out, and that always makes the traffic worse." Carrie held onto Michael's free arm as they headed to the parking lot across from the baggage pickup area. A blur of people hurried past.

"Slow down, honey. I can't go too fast."

At their car, while Michael put her luggage into the trunk, Carrie watched a large olive-skinned woman in a bright red dress hug a barrel-shaped man, in a white sweatshirt and black jeans. The balding guy with a gray handlebar mustache was three inches shorter than the woman. Carrie remembered seeing the woman standing next to the luggage carousel. She liked to watch reunions and make up her own stories about other people's lives.

"You'd better get off of that foot," Michael said, slamming the trunk. Carrie got into the car. "What were you staring at?"

"That big woman over there was on my plane, two rows in front of me. I was just curious about that woman. I saw her earlier and wondered who was meeting her." Michael laughed.

"You are such a wierdo." He smiled at her. "I missed you."

"I missed you too. And, I missed Miss Sophie-dog. How's she doing?"

"She's fine. When I got her home from the kennel, she ran all over the house looking for you. I thought we'd go to the River House for dinner?"

"Sounds great," Carrie said. She didn't care where they ate as long as she didn't have to fix dinner.

As they drove north on I-85, Carrie loved seeing the familiar scenery. Even the freeway exit signs looked good. She was home. Right after they passed Fulton County Stadium, she lay her head back onto the seat and closed her eyes. The next thing she knew, they were in the parking lot at the River House, just down the road from their condo. She yawned and stretched.

"I've been resting," she said.

"Yeah, right. Could have fooled me," he laughed. They followed a tall waitress to a booth by the window.

"I'm sorry I look so gross," Carrie said. She brushed her hair behind her ears.

"You look fine."

"Look again. Check these bags under my eyes." The waitress walked up just in time to hear her comment. She stared at Carrie, who stared back, thinking, what's it to you sweetie, go ahead and look.

"What'll it be?" she asked. "We've got specials. Red snapper, broiled or blackened. A 12-ounce strip steak. And, ribs, barbecued ribs."

They skipped the specials and ordered their usual—grouper sandwiches, home fries, and salad with honey mustard dressing. Michael ordered a draft beer, and Carrie had the house chardonnay. When the drinks arrived, they clinked their glasses. "To us," he said, winking at her. As always, Michael looked good. They had gone to see *Wall Street* on their first date, and she had told him afterwards that he reminded her of Michael Douglas, except for his curly hair. She loved the way he dressed. Tonight, he wore a short-sleeve, light blue and white striped shirt, a navy sweater vest, khaki pants, starched and ironed, and his brown loafers.

"Are things going okay at work?" she asked. She wanted to tell him all about her ordeal with Gram, but she decided to let him talk first.

"Things are good, and getting better. I've told you how the paper business is cyclical. We're in a rather neutral stage right now. But I can see an upward swing on the horizon," he said. He told her about the list of new customers he'd secured for the company. Michael, an energetic and methodical guy, had a good business head. He related well to people and loved his job selling corrugated boxes for the Georgia-Pacific plant in Doraville, a suburb of Atlanta.

"I wish our food would come. I'm starved. Look at those," Carrie said when their waitress walked past with a plate piled high with french fried onion rings. "They smell so good I can almost taste them."

"We can order some," Michael said. She turned him down, saying they had ordered plenty. "How's Gram doing? Any better."

"Michael, she's not *going* to get better," Carrie said. "That's something I'm trying to face."

"How's her attitude?"

"Well, it's trying. I'll admit she doesn't complain about being sick—I admire her for that—but, believe me, she bitches about everything else. She's one hardheaded, controlling woman. I was more than ready for a break. I couldn't wait to get out of there. First, she didn't want me to leave, then she acted like she couldn't wait to get rid of me. Her attitude flipflops."

"Sounds like your grandmother is about the same as always," Michael said. He signaled for the waitress to bring another beer.

"I think she wanted me out of there so she could chain smoke without getting another lecture from me. I don't know why I worry about her smoking now. Quitting at this point isn't going to do any good. It's just that she hardly has enough air in her to breathe, let alone smoke. Michael, she's pitiful to watch."

Carrie finished her wine and Michael ordered her another glass. "This looks great," she said, taking a bite of her grouper sandwich. Juice from the grouper dripped down her hand. She set it down and wiped her hands with her napkin. They both inhaled the food. Carrie grimaced when the woman in the booth next to them lit a cigarette. She waved her hand in front of her face. "My gut gets tangled when I think about what lies ahead. I'm stuck taking care of her, Michael. It's all up to me."

"Now, wait a minute. Who says you have to be Florence Nightingale? What about your aunt or your cousin. Can't they help out too?"

"Some. They will help some, but I know they expect me to take charge."

Michael shook his head, then got up, telling her he wanted to go check on the baseball score in the next room. "I think it's going to be the Twins and the Cardinals in the series this year," he said. She listened to his ankles crack as he walked away.

It felt good to be out with Michael, who had a way of calming her down. She vowed to put Gram on a shelf for the rest of the evening and concentrate on Michael. Waiting for him to return, she remembered the summer evening she and Michael met, right after he moved to Sheboygan for his first job out of college. They had both gone to the lakefront for the Fourth of July fireworks, she with Liz and other friends, Michael with some guys from work. They ended up sitting on the same hillside and started talking. Michael had asked for her phone number, then called the next day and asked her to a movie.

She turned him down for the next couple of nights, then agreed to go the next Saturday night. After the movie, they went to the Horse and Plow restaurant in Kohler for a sandwich and a beer. That night, Michael told her not to get serious about him, that he had a longtime girlfriend in Milwaukee who had gone to Europe for the summer.

"I have no intention of getting serious with anyone," Carrie had said. They had a fun evening, laughing and talking. She loved his dry wit. "You smell like beer," she told him after he had kissed her goodnight.

"What did you expect, Old Spice?" he had said, making Carrie giggle.

After that evening, she never dated anyone else. Neither did he. A year later they married. She still teased him, saying she would keep her promise not to get serious about him.

"Let's go home, okay?" Carrie said when he returned to their table. They walked out the door holding hands.

At home, Sophie-dog went berserk, running in circles and leaping like a circus animal when they let her out of the laundry room. When Michael took Sophie-dog outside, Carrie poked through the mail.

"Why don't you save that for tomorrow," Michael said. "I'm heading upstairs." Carrie smiled.

"Be right along." She read an encouraging note from Liz and looked at a few bills. Upstairs, she half emptied her suitcase, took a hot shower, and then put on her navy nightshirt. When she went around the corner to the bedroom, Michael lay in bed, reading *Trinity*. She took off her nightshirt, hung it on the bedpost, and slid between the sheets. Michael closed his book, turned off the light, and reached for her.

The next morning at mass, Carrie stood next to Michael singing. She tried to harmonize her soprano voice with his deep alto. After communion, she knelt and prayed for Gram, that she would not suffer long. And she prayed for the strength she would need in the months ahead.

On the way home from church, Carrie remembered how Gram had opposed her marriage to Michael, especially after she'd found out he was Catholic. She knew that one day Gram would find out she was converting and vowed to stand up to her. Carrie wanted to go to the same church as Michael. Going to mass with him made her feel at home. At first, she'd been concerned about changing her religion. That is, until she had spoken with the youth minister at the Lutheran church in Atlanta. "You have nothing to worry about," he had said, "there's only one God." The minister's comment gave her a sense of peace about her decision.

After church, Michael fixed his Sunday morning specialty—eggs over easy, Canadian bacon, and fresh fruit. "Looks great," Carrie said, when he set the plate in front of her. She put two slices of wheat bread into the toaster. Growing up, she had always turned down eggs, because Gram's fried eggs had always looked like bad sculpture—the whites singed, and the yolk hard. Michael's eggs looked like works of art in comparison, not hard, not runny, and always perfectly arranged on the plate. Even Gram liked Michael's eggs.

"Want more tea?" Michael asked when he came back to the table with a fresh cup of coffee.

"No, thanks." Carrie threw Sophie-dog's sock across the kitchen floor. The dog scurried after it.

"Just yesterday I found out that I'm going to be taking a few trips to the New England area on business. Actually, I have a surprise. Since I have to be up that way in two weeks, I made a reservation for us at a bed and breakfast in Bar Harbour, Maine, for the weekend."

"I can't go," Carrie said. "I simply can't go. I can't even stay home long. I know that I'm going to have to go back to Wisconsin."

"Get someone else to take over, Carrie. You would love New England in October." Michael picked up the front page of the *Atlanta Journal-Constitution* and stared at it.

"I can't. I'm sorry. It just won't work out. I'd be bad company anyhow."

"I thought you'd want to come along," Michael said.

"Michael, I do want to come," she said, raising her voice. "Don't put pressure on me. I've got enough to deal with right now. I appreciate the invitation. Really, I do. But, I've made a commitment to Gram. We'll have to go another time." Michael didn't say a word. He got up from the table, taking the paper with him.

His lack of understanding irritated her. The whole world didn't revolve around him. For the first time in their short marriage, they had hit a for-worse category. And he wasn't handling it very well.

Carrie knew the routine. He would go off by himself, ignoring her while he sorted out his feelings. She didn't care. He could stew if that's what he chose to do. She wanted some time alone anyhow.

Carrie got up. She picked up Sophie-dog's sockie from under the chair and threw it across the room. Sophie-dog skidded across the floor racing for it. Carrie cleared the table and put the dishes into the dishwasher. Then she tossed the sock again. It hit a crystal bud vase—a wedding present – that had been on the kitchen table, knocking it onto the floor.

"Geez. What was that," Michael hollered from the great room. He came running to the kitchen.

"Don't worry about it. I'll clean it up," Carrie said, stepping carefully through the shattered glass. "Go on back in and read your paper. I'll take care of this." She lifted Sophie-dog and carried her out to the screened porch, then began picking up the tiny slivers of glass. Michael put the paper down and began helping her.

"You throw a pretty mean curve," he said.

"You didn't seem to mind my curves last night." Carrie tossed the shattered pieces and the glass-covered sock into the garbage can.

"No, ma'am, I didn't mind them at all." Michael laughed, patting her on the butt. He helped her clean up the mess. They had just finished when the phone rang.

"I see you made it home okay," Gram said.

"It was too late to call when I got home last night. You doing okay?"

"I'm fine. You could have called. I was up late. Jennifer rented *Kramer vs. Kramer*. We stayed up until almost eleven. That Dusty Hoffman is a good actor."

"Dustin, Gram. It's Dustin Hoffman. Is Jennifer still there?" Gram told her that Jennifer was on her way back to Minneapolis.

"Did Nella come see you?"

"No, she has a cold." Carried doubted that. "Mavis, the other girls, and I are going out to dinner at the Executive Inn tonight," Gram said.

"Are you sure you're up to that?"

"That's no concern of yours, Caroline. I'll talk to you later."

Carrie hung up, glad that Gram sounded so upbeat. She put a load of wash into the washing machine. Michael's dirty clothes were piled high on the laundry room counter. The room smelled like sweaty jock straps. "Didn't you do any wash while I was gone?" she asked Michael when she walked into the great room.

"Some. I did some sheets and towels and changed the bed, too."

"Good," Carrie said. "I'm taking Sophie-dog for a walk. I need to get some fresh air." Carrie took two Tylenol tablets before she left the house, hoping it would keep her ankle from hurting. She and Sophie-dog headed out the door and down to the corner where they turned into a neighboring subdivision. Carrie felt the wind in her face. She felt more like herself than she had in days.

"Hello there," a familiar voice said. Her friend, Kay had slowed down her red Toyota Corolla, stopping to say hello. "Welcome home. Michael mentioned that you'd be home soon. Can you stop by for a visit?"

"Sounds great. Let's sit outside, okay. I'm kind of sweaty."

Kay drove on down the street a block to her house. Carrie met the tall, dark-haired Kay at the travel bureau where she worked, then discovered that they lived in the same neighborhood. Carrie loved Kay's sense of humor and artsy ways. They enjoyed reading and often discussed books. They both joined a neighborhood book club. Carrie liked to write and Kay painted huge landscapes, mostly of trees.

They headed out back to the patio. Sophie-dog crashed in the shade under the dogwood tree in the corner. Carrie sat on the chaise lounge. It felt good to prop her foot up.

"How are things in Wisconsin?"

"Grim. Much worse than I expected." Carrie gave Kay the rundown on Gram. Then she described her fall at the airport. "This guy, who just happened to be movie-star handsome, helped me up." She explained how he had sat next to her on the plane, then told Kay how she had shoved his elbow off the armrest.

"Way to go, girlfriend." Kay laughed.

"He gave me his business card. I think he's looking for clients."

"He was probably trying to pick you up."

"Oh, please. You should have seen me. I looked like Dracula's aged Aunt Lavidia." Kay laughed. "I know I'll be heading back up there. Things are handled for now, but they won't be for long."

"What about work?" Kay asked.

"I'll explain things tomorrow and hope for the best. I really need to keep my job. We're going to have to help with Gram's finances."

"Mr. Raymond's been a grouchy boss the last week or so. Very moody."

"What else is new?" They both laughed. Kay told her how much she and Dave enjoyed Michael's company. "I'm not on his hit parade at the moment." She explained how she'd turned down a trip with him. "He's acting insulted."

"He'll get over it. Give him some time. So, when's your cousin getting married?"

"Next March. She asked me to be her matron of honor. It doesn't make sense to me. We aren't that close." Carrie crunched on an ice cube. "You look uncomfortable. Are you okay?"

"No, my back's killing me. I went to see this neurosurgeon my internist recommended. He says I have spondylolisthesis—the same thing my Dad has—which means my back disks are out of alignment and sitting on nerves. I'm having a fusion in January."

"Sounds awful."

"I know. But, I'd do about anything to make the pain go away. The recuperation takes a couple of months. I'll go crazy staying home that long. I have no patience, you know."

"Right." Carrie had trouble imagining Kay, an active person, always on the go, stuck at home. She never missed a gallery opening and saw every movie the minute it came out. Carrie stood up to leave, then sat back down.

"I forgot. I wanted to tell you about my trip to the funeral home."

"Gee, I can hardly wait."

"I forced my cousin, Jennifer, to come along. A social butterfly, she usually talks to anyone and everyone—she's a real jabberbox—but, not at this place. She just sat frozen in place, like a cadaver herself, and made me do all of the talking. I filled out forms and answered the questions. Then, I got this creepy tour of the casket room. I forced Jennifer to come along. At least, now we're prepared, just in case."

"Do you think your grandmother's going to die that soon?"

"Who knows?" Carrie stood up, called out to the sleeping Sophie-dog who opened one eye and then closed it fast. "Come on lazybones." Sophie sauntered over to her side.

"Call me—anytime," Kay said.

Carrie left by the side gate. As she walked home, she thought about losing Gram. It all seemed so unreal. Her grandmother was supposed to be around to play with the children she and Michael would have. She wondered what she would tell the kids she would someday have about their great-grandmother. She'd probably tell them how her Gram had been in her fifties when she started raising her, an age when most people had finished with child rearing; how Gram had always said that Carrie kept her young; and, how Gram had always claimed to have a perfect memory, when the truth was that she cleverly twisted facts to make her stories more interesting. She would make up a story for her children about how Gram loved shoes and had a pair in every color.

Carrie laughed remembering how Gram used to have a window full of African violets. She had a name for each one. There was the one called Simply Violet that was periwinkle blue with a tiny off-white center. It always got the center spot. Some of the others were: Olga, the dark pink droopy one; Regina, the royal purple one; Edwina, the lilac one who thrived the longest; and, Pearl, the bright white one with the fluffy petals. Yes, she would tell her children about the violets and many other stories.

As she turned the corner to her condo, Carrie made a mental grocery list. She'd ask Michael to grill chicken for dinner, and she would make pasta and tossed salad. Walking in the door, she called out, but got no answer. Reaching down to unleash Sophie-dog, she saw his note on the desk. *I went to Ace Hardware. Be back soon. Your boss called. He said to call back as soon as possible. He's at the office now. Call him there.*

Carrie wondered why Mr. Raymond would call her on Sunday. She dialed his number. "Hello, Mr. Raymond, it's Carrie. Michael said you called."

"Yes, I did. Good to hear from you Carrie. I'm sorry that your grandmother isn't doing well. Carrie, I hate doing this on the phone. I know it's rude, but I have to go off on a trip to Miami tomorrow. I have a meeting there, and I didn't want someone else to tell you. I regret having to inform you that we have eliminated your position. You do not need to come in tomorrow. We will send you your last check." He paused. Carrie swallowed hard. "We'll be happy to give you a good reference when you need it. Good luck to you." Mr. Raymond said goodbye and hung up.

Carrie slammed down the reciever. That big creep. He had his nerve. She opened the refrigerator and took out a bunch of red grapes. She stared out the window as she started popping them into her mouth. The "seedless" grapes had seeds in them. It figured.

She'd have plenty of free time the next day and the day after that. She decided it was time to go out and buy a black dress. Just in case.

## Chapter Eight

Journal, Monday, October 8, 1987

I dreamed that I searched all over for my beat-up black shoulder-strap purse and finally spied it under Gram's arm. She sat on the bed in her black velour robe clutching onto my purse like it held bars of gold. On her neck, she wore a rhinestone-studded dog collar. "It's too tight," she kept saying as she tugged at the collar. I tried to loosen it but only managed to get it tighter. I never did ask her why she had my purse. It was a weird dream, but at least I didn't have her on a leash.

I woke up at 5:30 a.m. glad to discover I'd been dreaming. I rarely sleep in these days; sleeping is no longer one of my great talents. Most nights, when I go to bed, I lie awake for hours stewing about Gram. I don't need a psychology degree to figure out why I keep having bizarre dreams.

I'd like to look for a new job, but I can't, not with more trips to Wisconsin on the horizon. I certainly don't miss my job at the travel bureau. Michael's the one who had seen the travel agency ad and suggested I check it out. Like a robot, I went in for an interview, and it happened fast. Bingo. Bango. Bongo. I landed on the boat. Michael thought I'd get great perks, but that didn't turn out to be the case.

A few weeks after I started working for Diamond Travel, they sent me on a weekend cruise to Nassau with Rosie, also a neophyte travel agent. We found out about the familiarization trip on a Thursday afternoon and left the next morning. Rosie, a recent high school graduate, had never traveled outside of Georgia, and her batteries were charged. We flew from Atlanta to Miami, then got on a Carnival Cruise Line ship.

Rosie shook with excitement as we boarded, so hyped I practically had to tie her down. "Honey, I'm going to have myself some fun, fun, fun," Rosie said in her best Southern accent after we got our bags unpacked. She remained true to her word. I watched as she rolled her big brown eyes and wiggled her little rear end as she paraded past the crew members who lavished her with attention. I about threw up my crab and spinach quiche at breakfast the next morning when she described the evening she'd spent with the Indonesian waiter with a long, skinny face and Howdy Doody ears. Sparing no details, she told me about positions I'd never imagined. When I got home, I asked Michael if these were the perks he had in mind.

I've been setting some goals for myself. College looms on the horizon. I'm determined to get started on my degree as soon as this ordeal with Gram is over. I'm trying to save money for college, but it's a tough assignment. Right now, we need to help pay off Gram's debts.

I tried talking to Gram about her careless spending, telling her that we need to get her charge accounts paid off. She reminded me that she was very careful about making the minimum payments each month. Any talk about high interest goes right past her. Her attitude makes me want to whack some sense into her.

When I gave Michael the rundown on Gram's finances, he shrugged his shoulders and went on reading his *Sports Illustrated*. He's used to dealing with large amounts of money and thinks Gram's financial problems are just a ripple in the stream. "It's really not a lot of money. When she dies, we can take care of it," Michael stopped reading long enough to say. I knew he didn't want to hear any more about my concerns.

Sometimes, Michael frustrates me. There's a lot I love about him, but I hate the way he states his opinion like an edict, then clams up. We are opposites. I feel better if I can analyze things, a trait that he says is a pure waste of time. Sometimes I wonder if I married Michael just to get away from Gram and if he's the father figure I always longed for. Probably not. He's only five years older. Here I go, analyzing again.

According to Michael, I'm obsessed about Gram. He could be right. I'll admit that I leap off the high dive too often these days. I'm smart enough to know that I've got to calm down, that my problems with Gram aren't going to dissipate into the fog. Reality says that I'm in for a long haul, so for now, I'd better keep myself afloat.

Michael's off on a business trip, and I'm home alone. I'm savoring every moment, because I know I'll be heading north again soon. When Michael kissed me good-bye this morning, he sugggested I think about moving Gram to Atlanta. He wants me to find a nearby nursing home. I don't feel at all comfortable with his idea. Lord knows, Gram would spit a cat if she knew we were even thinking about a nursing home.

I've been getting a lot of phone calls. Aunt Nella called from Milwaukee today, and we had an okay visit. She's immersed in helping Jennifer plan her wedding, a good diversion if you ask me. Aunt Nella thinks Kevin, her son-in-law to be, is the proverbial knight on the unicorn. Jennifer wants the girls in the wedding to wear hot pink. I hope she changes her mind, because I look like crap in that shade. Jennifer and I are north and south in the clothing arena. I'm conservative, and she's loud and flashy. Some people say we look alike, that we have similar mannerisms. But I don't see it. It could be, I don't want to see it.

Aunt Nella reported that she had visited Gram this week. It's about time. I felt like insisting that she spend more time with her mother, but I didn't. She sounded too fragile, and I had this sense of déjà vu. I was afraid she'd get upset and start drinking again. Hanging up, I knew that Aunt Nella wasn't going to be worth a wet noodle in the caretaking department.

Mavis called with her version of the reunion she had with Gram and their other two friends, one that differed from Gram's. According to Mavis, Gram was all dolled up the night they went out to the American Club in Kohler for dinner. She had on a fancy purple suit and purple suede high heels—new duds she had ordered from Marshall Field's in Chicago. Of course, she never told me about her new outfit. I dread seeing her Marshall Field's bill. According to Mavis, Gram looked terrific. Jennifer took her to Raylene's on the southside of Sheboygan for a permanent. I conjured up this mental picture of Gram, Mavis, Mary Lou, and Marie sitting at the American Club, sucking on their Winstons. They all started smoking in the '40's when movie stars like Lauren Bacall and Bette Davis had cigarettes hanging out of their sultry mouths. Gram and her friends still paint their mouths bigger than they really are with bright red lipstick, like those old movie stars, not seeming to notice that the habit has been out of style for decades.

Gram adores bright colors. On my eleventh birthday she let me invite three friends over for hamburgers, french fries, corn on the cob, and chocolate eclairs from Prange's bakery. I wanted to push a button and disappear when Gram arrived wearing black pedal pushers and a bright red tube top with no bra. Her boobs jiggled when she walked. She wore flaming red lipstick to match. No one said anything that night, but the next day at school, my friend Karen asked me why Gram painted red lipstick all over her face. I was mortified. Gram often tells me to make my own lips fuller. God forbid. I don't even like to wear lipstick.

I guess Gram scared her friends silly on the drive home. She missed the exit on Highway 23, so she slowed down and backed up. "We were shaking, clutching onto the edge of our seats, and praying hard," Mavis said. After they got home, Mavis took the car keys away, and she still has them. Now, Gram won't speak to her. Sounds like Gram. I can remember times when she would go days without talking to me. Then a few days later, she'd act like everything was fine again.

Herman's phone call was the real zinger. He called to tell me about the fire in Gram's apartment. She'd been smoking in bed again, and the sheets caught on fire. Cordelia, her across-the-hall neighbor, saw the smoke coming from under her door. She called Herman, who rushed in, and found Gram, batting a dishtowel at the blaze.

Hearing about the fire set off an alarm in my head. I know I can't leave Gram alone much longer.

The whole idea of moving her to Atlanta frightens me. It's so final, like I'm signing up for a long tour of duty. I hate to admit it, but there are times when I wish she would go ahead and die. That way, she wouldn't have to suffer, and I wouldn't have to worry about her. I break out in hives when I have these thoughts.

 I know it's time to make a decision. I can't keep leaving home. Each time, I have to stay in Wisconsin longer. The promise I made to stay by Gram until the end keeps replaying in my head. Reality stares me in the face.

## Chapter Nine

"It's nasty out," Carrie said, walking into Gram's apartment. "Listen to that wind howling. There's lightening and thunder—it's as black as soot outside. You'd never know it was one in the afternoon. If you didn't have these drapes closed, you could see for yourself."

"Caroline, you look like a soused cat and you're dripping on my carpet. Take off your wet raincoat and hang it in the bathroom," Gram said, ignoring Carrie's comment.

"Yes, ma'am." Carrie saluted Gram, then headed to the bathroom. She hung her black raincoat coat over the tub. When she returned, she gave her grandmother a kiss on the cheek. She wrinkled her nose at Gram's cigarette smell.

"Driving from Milwaukee, Herman could hardly see the road," Carrie said sitting down across the room. She stared at Gram's ugly wallpaper with the fan-shaped oyster-white flowers that looked like strutting turkeys on the sandy brown background.

A loud clap of thunder made them both jump. "It always rains a lot in October. Has for years," Gram said. "I probably won't see the fall rain next year."

"You might."

"I won't. A person knows."

Carrie swallowed hard. Gram, perched in her familiar spot at the end of the sofa, looked frail. Her face was more swollen, making Carrie wonder if the tumor stood ready to close off the blood supply to her brain. Gram wore black polyester pants and a red turtleneck sweater. Her dangly gold earrings swayed as she reached for a cigarette. She lit up, then closed her eyes and sucked in on her cigarette like she was trying to vacuum out the insides. Gram and her cigarettes were lovers.

Carrie made Gram's bed then reached for a box of Tide from a shelf in the bathroom closet and set it in Gram's dirty clothes basket. "I'll be back in a minute," she said, picking up the basket. She went out the door and hurried down the long hallway anxious to set the basket down. Gram's clothes smelled like an outhouse. In the laundry room, she sorted the clothes, making piles on the floor, and stuffed a load of light-colored laundry into the machine and fed it two quarters.

"I'm not hungry. I had a big breakfast," Gram said when Carrie asked if she wanted some lunch. Carrie decided it was a good thing Gram's nose didn't grow when she lied. "I think this is a rerun," Gram said after turning on the television set with her remote control. "I've seen that lady before." Gram pointed to the game show. "Her name is Wenonah, or something strange like that. I remember that screechy voice. Doesn't it sound terrible?"

"Right," Carrie said, not particularly interested. She left the room to make her own lunch.

"Nella came to see me twice last week," Gram said when Carrie returned with a plate on which she had put a scoop of tuna salad, a few Ritz crackers, and an apple she'd cut up in slices. Carrie asked Gram how Aunt Nella was doing.

"That girl's hiding something. I can tell. Have you spoken to her?"

"Yes, but we talked mostly about wedding stuff." Carrie wished her aunt would tell Gram the truth. As a recovering alcoholic, Gram should be more understanding than most people.

"Nella slapped me when she was here the other day," Gram said.

"She slapped you? Good heavens. What for?"

"I don't know. I mentioned the mass in my chest. And, that's when Nella got all upset. She yelled out that no one in our family had ever had cancer. Then, she marched across the room and slapped me on the face. Right here." Gram pointed to her right cheek.

"I can't believe she'd do a thing like that." Obviously, Aunt Nella wasn't handling sobriety very well. "I'm sorry Gram. I'll get after her about it."

"Oh, just leave it alone. I don't know what's wrong with Nella. She's acting pretty uptight."

"Well, she'd better not lay a hand on you again, or she'll have me to deal with." Carrie put the last forkful of tuna on a cracker and stuck it into her mouth.

Gram started hacking, gasping for breath, as she attempted to cough up the junk in her chest. Carrie watched Gram's chest rise, then fall. Holding onto the walker, Gram struggled to pull herself up, then shuffled across the room in her furry red slippers. Carrie knew better than to offer help. After Gram reached the bathroom, Carrie listened to gagging noises as she struggled to force up the thick, green mucus.

Taking her plate to the kitchen, Carrie glanced down at a large pile of bills piled up on the dinette table. Picking it up, she examined the bill on top of the pile. It was a billing statement from AARP for medical insurance. Carrie's stomach nosedived. She wondered why Gram would have a bill from AARP when she had Blue Cross insurance. Carrie scanned the bill for a date. Gram emerged from the bathroom and huffed her way back to the sofa. Her tired face was chalky gray.

"I noticed this bill from your AARP account lying here. I don't understand it."

"What's your problem? It's my insurance bill." Gram scowled.

"I thought you had Blue Cross."

"Well, I used to, but I changed it," Gram said, taking slow quick breaths.

"Gram, for God's sake, you can't change insurance companies. Not now."

"Well, I sure as hell can. It's a done deal." Gram let out a deep, husky cough. Her eyes watered.

Carrie flipped through the insurance papers. If Gram had switched insurance companies after her cancer was discovered, the new company wouldn't pay for a previously diagnosed condition. Carrie forced herself to breathe in and breathe out, to maintain control.

"Gram, why in the world did you change companies?" she said, her voice controlled.

"I did it to save some money. The monthly premium is less, and I needed more cash. It's as simple as that."

"I can't believe it," Carrie said, raising her voice. "Do you have any idea what you've done? This could be a disaster. It's just plain stupid. Sometimes you do the dumbest things." Carrie threw the bills back down, then paced the floor. Gram would never change. In order to save a few bucks a month, she had probably created a financial mess.

"When did you make this change?" she asked.

"I'm not quite sure. Here, take these. Go through them if you wish, not that it's any of your business. I don't want to talk about it anymore." She looked up at Carrie like a child caught stealing candy. Gram turned up the volume and stared at a commercial for Comet cleanser. Carrie put the pile of bills beside her purse on the kitchen table. She would study them later, at Helen Newby's house. She dreaded confirmation of her suspicions.

"Michael's playing in a golf tournament this weekend at Lake Lanier. It's some kind of business outing. He'll be gone all next week, too, so it was a good time for me to come back." Carrie turned down the volume on the television.

"I'm glad you came back," Gram said in a quiet voice. "How's puppy dog?" Carrie explained that her neighbor Kay had offered to keep Sophie-dog until she got back.

"I remember your friend, Kay. We went to her place on Christmas Eve, didn't we? I'm certain I had on my fancy silver pants outfit. Kay and her husband gave me a tour of their house. I remember those big paintings on the walls."

"Kay paints oil landscapes, Gram. She has her paintings in a gallery in downtown Atlanta. She's my only close friend in Atlanta. Did I tell you that she's having back surgery before long, some kind of fusion?" Gram shook her head no.

"We all need close friends," Gram said. "They make a person feel human. People need that." Gram fired up another cigarette, then turned the volume up again. The noise, and the smoke, gave Carrie a headache. She opened the drapes and cracked the window open. The sun was out.

"Here," Carrie said, minutes later, handing Gram a plate of food—a few Ritz crackers, several cubes of cheddar cheese, and a small bunch of red grapes before she left to grocery shop.

She returned with milk, bread, fresh fruit, lunch meat, tuna from the deli, milk, and enough stuff to make vegetable soup. Each time Carrie made soup, she experimented with different ingredients.

"Get me some iced tea," Gram said. Carrie checked her lunch plate. Only the crackers were gone. Gram was watching "As the World Turns." Carrie made three trips from the car, carrying groceries. Before her soap opera ended, Gram fell asleep. She slept while Carrie cooked.

After she finished making the soup, Carrie tiptoed out of the apartment and went to the Newbys' house, taking Gram's insurance bills with her. Helen and Ben had gone on a trip to London, so Carrie had the house to herself. After unpacking her clothes and cosmetics, she sat down at the table beside the bay window in Helen's kitchen with a cup of Earl Grey. She sipped her tea and sorted through Gram's bills. The room smelled like lindenberry potpourri.

She dialed the AARP customer service number on Gram's statement, asking when the account originated. The clerk told her, last July. Carrie started breathing easier. Gram's cancer had been diagnosed in September, so Gram was fully covered.

Carrie felt guilty. She never should have hollered at Gram. What had she been thinking? Trying to wash away the guilt, she showered before she went back to Gram's. The stream of hot water pounded the tight muscles in her back. Stepping out of the shower, she wrapped herself in a thick pink towel, then wound a smaller white towel around her wet hair. Just as she finished drying her hair, the phone rang. It was Liz Newby calling to say she was coming home the next evening for an overnight. They made plans to go out for dinner.

"I'm hanging in there," Carrie said, when Liz asked how things were going. "I'll give you the details tomorrow."

After hanging up, Carrie left in a hurry. She stopped at Hoffman's flower shop on Michigan Avenue to buy pink roses for Gram. "How's your grandmother doing?" asked the girl who waited on her. Everyone in town seemed to know about Gram's illness. The Sheboygan grapevine was efficient.

"Not that well." She explained how Gram had refused to have treatments.

"Don't make her have them. My Dad had lung cancer. He went through radiation treatments, and it didn't do a bit of good. He died after a few months anyhow. He was just a shell of a person those last days. He hurt so bad. We couldn't even touch him, not with one finger."

Carrie paid for the roses and hurried out the door. Why were people so anxious to share their own horror stories? As she drove, she cried, thinking about what lie ahead for Gram, who seldom complained about her illness. She was trying hard to be the same person she'd always been. Gram had courage. Carrie liked that about her. As she drove along North Avenue, she had a mental image of Gram lying dead on the sofa. She stepped down on the gas pedal.

"Here," she said, happy to see Gram sitting up, even if she was smoking. "Sniff them. They smell like the roses on the bushes we used to have." Gram sniffed the pale pink roses.

"I can't smell much these days." She sniffed them again as if her sense of smell would return. "Why did you bring me these?"

"I just felt like it."

"Thanks, Caroline."

Carrie arranged the flowers in a crystal vase and put them on the table beside the recliner. "Gram, I've cleared up that insurance thing. I called and found out that you took out the AARP policy in July. So, everything's okay. What still confuses me is that when I asked you on the phone last week if you'd paid your Blue Cross premium, you told me yes."

"I lied."

"Why?"

"I didn't like the tone of your voice." Carrie realized that Gram had a point. Concerned about Gram's bills, she remembered how impatient she had been on the phone that day.

"I was a grouch that day. I'm sorry. I'm also sorry that I got on your case about changing your insurance. I've had a lot on my mind."

"Mostly me and my problems, I suppose."

"Well, I have been thinking about you." Carrie swallowed hard. "Gram, how would you like to come to Atlanta and live with Michael and me?" The words fell out of her mouth before she had time to catch them. She pictured a little person standing inside of her head screaming out, *now you've done it.*

"Oh, I'd like that, Caroline. I'd like that a lot." Gram's humped figure straightened. Her brown eyes sparkled.

Carrie told Gram that they had a lot to do. They needed to get an appointment with Dr. Edgar, call a lawyer and arrange for a power of attorney, decide what things to take to Atlanta and what things to give away, and arrange for movers. Carrie's wheels were spinning. She started a to-do list.

Gram grabbed a pencil and a piece of paper and started diagraming where her things would go in Carrie's extra bedroom, the one on the first floor that she and Michael had been using for an office. Gram would have to stay in that room, because she could no longer climb stairs. After climbing the three steps to get into her apartment building, she had little breath left. "Breathing has become something I have to think about. It's not natural anymore," Gram, said earlier in the day.

While Gram did her planning, Carrie set the table with fancy lace placemats and pink cloth napkins. She lit a votive candle at each place setting. They ate the vegetable soup Carrie had made and a salad with mandarin orange slices on top of cottage cheese. She added a dollop of mayonnaise on top of the oranges and then sprinkled grated cheddar cheese on the top.

"Take a few more bites, Gram. I made brownies for dessert," Carrie said, coaxing her like a mother would a child. Gram took a few bites of salad and a sip or two of soup.

Carrie heated the brownies in the microwave, then placed them on pink dessert plates, adding a scoop of vanilla ice cream. Gram ate almost all of her dessert. After Carrie cleaned up the dinner dishes, she helped

Gram get ready for bed. Before she left, she told Gram she had a joke for her.

"Gram, what's invisible and smells like worms?"

"Oh, Lordy, Caroline. I don't know."

"Bird farts," Carrie said. They both laughed.

"Caroline, you know I don't like that word. But it is pretty funny. I'll have to tell that one to Mavis."

When Carrie left, Gram was on the phone repeating the joke to Mavis. Carrie knew she would also tell her about her moving plans. Gram was more upbeat than she had been in weeks.

That night in bed, Carrie wondered how long her grandmother would last. What had she signed herself up for? And, how would she get Gram, who was probably too sick to fly, to Atlanta? Gram didn't have enough air in her to blow out a candle.

Carrie pictured Gram at her house, camping out in her room, chain smoking. It wasn't a pretty scene. Carrie was afraid Gram would take charge of her life. However, in spite of her reservations, she knew she'd made the right decision.

The next day, after getting boxes at the Piggly Wiggly, Carrie started filling them. Gram supervised. Carrie sat on the floor in the midst of a pile of Gram's belongings: some extra clothes, linens, knicknacks, kitchen utensils, dishes, and wall hangings. Gram was courageous in her effort to get rid of her possessions. "Toss it, toss it," she said when Carrie held up a Christmas tree ornament, an angel for the treetop.

Gram got on the phone. First, she called Jennifer to see what she wanted. Then, she called the caretaker at the Lutheran church rectory, offering him her sofa, her kitchen table and chairs, and her leftover Christmas decorations. She told him to come over and select what he wanted. "You can have the things as soon as I have definite moving date," she told him. Gram was going full speed ahead on a get-me-to-Atlanta mission, and she wasn't going to let a few possessions get in her way. Carrrie's throat tightened when she realized that, once Gram came to live with her, there would be no turning back.

Carrie held up a tiny figurine—with a smiling pumpkin for a head, wearing an orange and black checked skirt, an orange blouse, a black vest, and black tights she found in the back of Gram's dresser drawer.

M A D E L I N E was printed on the base of the figurine in black ink. "What's this?"

"A dance favor. I got it in high school school when I went to a dance with Joe Franklin. Oh, he was quite the popular one. He got a full basketball scholarship to the University of Illinois." Gram smiled at the memory.

"I'll put it in the box of things to keep," Carrie said. Gram rested while Carrie spent the rest of the day sorting through her things. When Gram awakened, she gave her a few rules to be followed once she moved to Atlanta. "You can smoke in your room, not anywhere else. Smoke gives me a headache. We'll have to put an air filter in your room." Gram made no comment. Instead she studied her latest floor plan. She erased one square and moved it to the other side of the rectangle she'd drawn.

"I'll need that antique desk of yours for my important papers, and a space heater, too. You keep your house too cold."

Carrie turned away and scowled. She packed three more boxes for storage, then threw a pile of questionable stuff into a green garbage bag for the homeless shelter. "That's it, Gram," I've had it for today." She couldn't wait to leave.

After fixing Gram a ham sandwich in case she got hungry, she kissed her good-bye. "Don't forget to take your medicine." Dr. Edgar had prescribed an anti-depressant for Gram which helped her sleep at night. Gram told her to have a fun visit with Liz. Carrie drove away trying to put her fears about moving Gram on a shelf for the evening. Liz greeted her when she opened the front door. They hugged.

"Let's go eat. I'm dying to have some fun," Carrie said.

"Let's try the Lone Star Bar. They have great Mexican food." Liz drove down Eighth street toward Pennsylvania Avenue. "Carrie, I love your outfit. You look great in green." Carrie thanked her.

"I don't feel like I look great in anything right now. I'm blitzed."

Inside the Lone Star Bar, they found a table in the corner. A muscular blond waiter brought warm tortilla chips and salsa. Carrie ordered two margaritas with salt. Carrie told Liz about her plans to move Gram to Atlanta.

"What does Michael think about Gram coming to live with you?" Liz said as she dipped a chip into the salsa.

"I'm not telling him until I get home. He's been wanting me to move Gram to Atlanta, but he wants me to put her into a nursing home. I can't do that."

"Are you sure you can handle her?" Liz asked.

"No. I'm not sure of anything. All I know is that I owe it to her, after all the years she took care of me."

"You're a saint."

"Oh, please. You, of all people, know that's not true. I'm just doing what has to be done. I have no choice."

The waiter put the margaritas down onto the table. He got out a tablet and a pencil. "I want a chicken tostada with guacamole," Liz said. "Skip the sour cream."

"Same here," Carrie said. They clinked their glasses together.

"Carrie, you amaze me. You've always been loyal to your grandmother, in spite of her dreaded rules. I can remember times when we all went out for the evening, and Gram made you stay home."

"Oh, I know. She was a real pain sometimes. She still is," Carrie said as she sipped her margarita.

"She had her good side too," Liz said. "Overnights at your house were a blast. Remember the night we went sneaking out after she fell asleep. We went to that new restaurant called The Night Owl. Then, the next morning, she asked if we'd been up late. She even called us night owls."

"And we about died," Carrie said. They both howled.

"I'm hoping to cross the waters to the past after Gram comes to Atlanta."

"That sounds mysterious," Liz said. Carrie told her how Jennifer had mentioned family secrets, telling her to ask Gram for details. "Did you ask?" Carrie explained that so far, the timing had not been right. Liz wanted to know if she would eventually put Gram into a nursing home.

"It depends," Carrie said. "Gram says no one's sticking her in an old folk's home." She told Liz how Aunt Nella had taken Gram to Morningside Nursing Home to see Gram's older sister, Aunt Rae, who has Alzheimer's disease and how Gram asked if they could leave. "Gram got so upset she barfed all over the inside of Aunt Nella's Cadillac."

They both laughed.

Carrie mentioned Aunt Rae's roommate, who had half of her face, including her mouth, eaten away from cancer, and explained how Aunt Nella and Gram had taken a bouquet of flowers to Aunt Rae. "Gram took two of the flowers and gave them to the roommate, who had been thrilled. She had tears rolling down her cheeks as she smiled with her eyes."

"That sounds like something your grandmother would do." Carrie nodded. The waiter was singing a Mexican melody when he set the tostadas down in front of them. Liz ordered two more margaritas. They attacked the pile of beans, chicken, lettuce, cheese, tomato and guacamole. Between bites, Carrie asked Liz about her love life.

"My friends in Madison keep fixing me up with blind dates. We go out a few times, and then it fizzles. There's no one lighting my fire right now."

The wind whistled outside the door. The Saturday night crowd at the bar was lively. Carrie did a double take when a tall, good-looking man passed. "You know him?" Liz asked.

"No . . . he reminds me of this guy I met at the airport the last time I flew home." Carrie started laughing. She told Liz how she'd fallen at the airport, and how Tom Egan had helped her. "He's been calling me ever since."

"Hmm. What for?"

"At first it was to see if I'd hurt myself. Now, he calls to see how Gram's doing. His concern seems genuine. His mom died of cancer, so he understands what I'm going through. For a guy, he sure knows how to share his feelings."

"Watch out," Liz said, giving Carrie a goofy grin. "This guy sounds interested in you."

"It's nothing like that. We're just friends. There's nothing wrong with having a male friend." Liz agreed. They split the bill, leaving their money on the table.

When they got back to the house, Carrie stretched out on the couch. Liz lay on the floor moaning. They stayed up late laughing and talking about childhood fun. The next morning, Carrie slept in until eight.

"I called Mayflower," Gram said, when Carrie came in the door. "They're going to come give me an estimate." Gram was commandeering her move to Atlanta. After hanging up, she told Carrie she had good news. "Nella called and offered to drive me to your house in Atlanta. She says we're going to have a mother-daughter trip. Isn't that nice?"

"So when is this going to take place?" Carrie said, looking surprised.

"Some time in November. I ordered a new suitcase for my trip from the Sears catalog."

"You did what?" Carrie would never understand Gram. Whatever did she need a new suitcase for? She had luggage in her closet. Only Gram would order a new suitcase for the last trip of her life. Who knew what else she had ordered?

For the next week, Carrie packed and moved as much as possible to storage, leaving Gram with just enough to get by for a few weeks. Eventually, the belongings in storage would be tossed out. Gram didn't know that, or maybe she did. Carrie told her they would store things until later and then send for them. Gram decided what things she wanted to take to Atlanta.

Aunt Nella had been strangely nice. She had offered to spend time with Gram as often as possible, until their November trip. When Carrie questioned her about slapping Gram, Aunt Nella said Gram was driving her crazy that day, and she just lost it. She promised never to do it again. Carrie hated the look of glee on Aunt Nella's face. She was obviously relieved that Carrie would soon be in full charge of Gram. Aunt Nella would do her part for a few weeks, then drop Gram in Carrie's lap. Carrie wished they could trade places.

Carrie wondered if, after Gram arrived in Atlanta, she would ever have any time alone. At least she'd be able to go upstairs and hide out once in awhile. That thought consoled her. She missed Sophie-dog, she missed Michael, and she missed the life she had put on hold.

Carrie told Michael on the phone that she'd decided to move Gram south. "Sounds good," Michael said, sounding pleased. "I told you it was time for you to stop going back and forth." He didn't ask, and she didn't tell him, even though she wanted to get it off her chest, that Gram was not going to a nursing home.

# Chapter Ten

Journal, Saturday, November 28, 1987

I'm at the kitchen table trying to calm down. I can't stop shaking. I know it's because any minute now Aunt Nella and Jennifer will drive up my steep driveway and deposit Gram on the doorstep. If Aunt Nella has her way—and she usually does—they will stay overnight, and then they'll beat it out of here tomorrow, anxious to leave Gram in my care. I've been trying not to dwell on what my life will be like with Gram here. I have a foreboding that I'm better off not knowing.

Michael went out to run a few errands and I've been trying to drink in this last little bit of serenity. Giving up time by myself is something I dread. I've been pampering myself this morning. I did my nails and took a long walk around the neighborhood. I listened as the birds sang and the wind rustled through the tall pines. I've vowed to continue walking, even with Gram here. It's good for my psyche. I relish the rush of endorphins I get when I walk fast. Right before I got back home, just as I started to slow down, I spied a crushed cigarette butt lying in the street near the curb. It made me cringe. I picked it up and hurled it into the woods.

I'm glad Jennifer agreed to ride along with Aunt Nella and Gram. Her concern for anyone besides herself seems to have popped up out of nowhere. Who knows where her change of heart came from? Perhaps Kevin's a good influence on her. Jennifer phoned and told me she was worried that the long drive from Sheboygan to Atlanta might be too much for her mother. I can understand her concern. Aunt Nella's still recovering from her bout at the detox center. She's treading water and doing some strange things. I'm still angry with her for slapping Gram.

Two days ago, on Thanksgiving Day, Aunt Nella called to say the three of them would leave her house in Mequon and start their drive to Atlanta the next morning. Jennifer and Kevin helped move Gram out of her apartment. According to Aunt Nella, Mavis cried when they had stopped by her place so Gram could say good-bye. But not Gram. She never shed a tear. "Well, I guess this is it. I've got to get off on my trip now," Gram said to Mavis as she turned away. A stoic Gram never looked back.

Gram has always been able to change gears and move on. She knows how to shelve the past and charge full speed ahead in a new direction. Right now, getting to Atlanta is her top priority. Gram announced on the phone the other day that living at my house was her idea of living in style. Since the day I invited her to come live here, most of her sentences begin with, "When I get to Atlanta . . ."

Gram ordered me to get my computer out of our downstairs room and to put our antique desk on the front wall across from her daybed. "I'll sit there and write letters to all of my friends and daydream as I look out that big window," Gram said. She thinks that moving to Atlanta will turn things around.

The last three weeks flew by like a raging stream. I remember coming home all tied up in knots. Standing at the luggage carousel, I let out a sigh of relief when I saw Michael. I heard his ankles crack as he walked over to meet me. On the way home, we stopped at the Rio Bravo restaurant for dinner. I ordered a glass of wine and a taco salad. Michael asked for a Corona and an enchilada platter. After a few sips of wine, I told Michael I'd invited Gram to come live with us. Knowing I wouldn't feel right until I was assertive, I presented my case like a trial lawyer, expounding on my overwhelming sense of duty to Gram. I talked fast. I was bold, and I was strong. Michael tried to interrupt, but I kept going. He stopped trying and listened.

"You win," Michael said, as our short, round waiter set our food in front of us. After a second beer, Michael managed to throw in a few digs about Gram's complex personality, saying her illness might make her more controlling than ever. He could be right. I promised to look into nursing homes for future reference—it seemed like a fair compromise.

These past few months have taken a toll on both of us. Gram continues to be a financial burden. Michael said that at least now we won't have to pay her apartment rent anymore. He suggested that we dig deeper into our savings. We'd like to move out of our rented condo and buy a house. I don't see how we can. Gram's social security check is barely enough to cover her expenses. Michael seems to think we can still move before long. Does that mean he thinks Gram will die soon? Maybe she will.

One evening, Michael answered the phone when Tom Egan called. "Did I hear you say you are meeting this guy you met at the airport?" he said after I hung up. I told him yes, explaining that Tom wanted to talk to me about doing some work for his law firm, that I could do the work at home and also care for Gram. Michael shrugged his shoulders. I wanted to tell him how supportive Tom had been but left it alone.

The next day I met Tom at Altobeli's in Roswell after my visit to Dr. Kirkland's office. I made the appointment for myself so I could arrange for help caring for Gram. "How did the doctor's appointment go?" Tom asked when I joined him at a table. I told him the doctor wanted me to bring Gram in for an evaluation so he could arrange for hospice care. I felt relieved, because the doctor had made it sound simple.

I ordered manicotti for lunch. Tom wanted the chicken tortellini special. While we ate, I talked too much, but Tom didn't seem to mind. I told him how I'd gone to the lawyer's office in Sheboygan and arranged for power of attorney. He could relate. He was his mom's power of attorney.

When he mentioned that I'd soon be buying adult diapers, I told him about the day I took Gram out for a ride. We'd driven past Lake Michigan on that windy, cold day, and Gram insisted I stop so she could get out and look at the water. At the time, it had seemed like a strange request. After I had pulled into the parking lot, across from the YMCA, she ordered me to stay in the car. She got out and walked a few feet away from the car in her tan polyester pants, a brown sweater and her short wool camel coat. I described to Tom how she stood right there and peed, then acted like nothing unusual had happened when she got back in the car. But I had seen her tan pants turn dark. I had seen the puddle form at her feet. On the way home she smelled strong. Gram stared out the window, squinting in the bright sun. I had no idea what to say, so I drove home quick as I could, knowing she was probably freezing in her wet clothes. She changed into a black sweats outfit as soon as we got inside her apartment. When I finished my tale, I felt strange, sharing such a private moment with Tom.

"I know how you felt," Tom said. Then, he told me how embarrassed he had been when his mother had an accident at a fancy restaurant in Milwaukee. When he finished his story, we laughed together. "You'll need that sense of humor," he said, making me feel comfortable.

I agreed to work for Tom's firm making travel arrangements and doing some typing and proofreading. It's perfect for right now. I drove home feeling good after our lunch. It's nice to have a friend who's traveled a similar path.

The downstairs room is ready and waiting with a new daybed, the antique desk, a bedside table, a cozy tan chair with a matching hassock, a small television set, an air filter, and a smoke alarm. Michael moved the furniture for me, changing the arrangement until it seemed just right for Gram.

Last weekend, Michael and I rented a cabin near Brevard, North Carolina. We hiked in the mountains, played gin rummy, ate fun dinners out, laughed a lot, loved a lot, and slept in late. I tried to ward off thoughts of what lie ahead. Of course, Gram slipped into our conversation now and then. I told Michael about the black dress I'd recently bought. "A sexy one?" he wanted to know.

"No," I told him, "a plain black dress, long sleeves, knee length, not too low in the front. Something appropriate for a funeral."

I mentioned the letter I found while packing up Gram's things. Before I was born, it arrived from Vancouver, British Columbia, from a friend of my mother's family. This friend had written to Gram in order to introduce my mother. Gram refused to let me read it, until after she moved to Atlanta.

Michael and I discussed the mysterious family secrets. He thinks Jennifer is just trying to be dramatic. I'm not so sure about that. I intend to find out what she's talking about. All in all, Michael and I had a great weekend. I wanted to freeze the clock.

Of course, I couldn't. And now, reality is moments away. I know I have to accept what's happening and deal with it. If I couldn't put my thoughts down on paper, I think I'd drown. I'm grateful for people like Kay. I don't know what I'd do without her support. She's had her back surgery, and I've called her every day since she got home from the hospital. Just yesterday, I joked about how I wanted to run away. "At least you *can* run," Kay said laughing.

Oh, no, I can't. It's definitely too late for that. I hear a car coming up the driveway.

## Chapter Eleven

Opening the door, Carrie's stomach churned when she saw a frail Gram standing on the doorstep hanging onto to Aunt Nella's arm. "Come on in," Carrie said. "You look so nice." Gram wore navy pants, a white blouse, and a blue and white striped cardigan sweater.

"Here, you hold onto Gram," Aunt Nella said to Carrie. "I need some Tylenol. My head's about to split open. It feels as big as the state of Utah." Aunt Nella let go of Gram and rushed past Carrie to the the sink.

"The glasses are in the cabinet on the right," Carrie said as she helped Gram inside the door. Aunt Nella downed her pills, then headed back outside to help Jennifer with the luggage. Gram stood, holding onto the edge of the table, her chest heaving. "Sit down, please, catch your breath," Carrie said as she scooted a chair out for Gram.

Sophie-dog jumped off of her pillow in the corner and ran in excited circles on the hardwood floor. "Come here, puppy dog," Gram said. Sophie-dog put her front paws on Gram's bony leg. Gram patted her on the head. "I've missed you, puppy dog. I've come here to live. What do you think about that?" She scratched Sophie-dog behind the ears. Carrie felt the back of her neck stiffen.

"How'd the trip go?" Carrie asked when Aunt Nella came back in carrying a suitcase. She looked disheveled from her many hours on the road.

"Well, I can assure you, it was no party under the apple boughs," Aunt Nella said. "Suffice it to say, it was a *long* ride. She set the suitcase down, her eyes scanning the kitchen. "You've got a nice place. I like that pineapple border up there." She pointed toward the ceiling. "Did you do that stenciling?"

"Yes, with a lot of help from my artistic friend, Kay. You can take your suitcase upstairs. You and Jennifer will be sharing the first room on the right. It has a connecting bathroom."

"Sounds good. Jennifer's outside, unloading stuff. I've got to go lie down until this screaming headache calms down." Aunt Nella hurried out of the room, relaying a message loud and clear. She was no longer in charge. She had handed Gram over to Carrie.

Carrie went outside. Seeing the mountain of boxes and suitcases in the garage, she shook her head. "Looks like you've been busy. I can give you a hand. Sounds like you guys had a tough trip?"

"Thank God it's over. I can assure you Mom and Gram drove me batty. Those two are poisonous snakes out for the kill. They're always at each other's throats."

"Let's get this stuff inside," Jennifer said. She and Carrie hauled Gram's things to her room. Gram stood on the screened porch, just outside the kitchen, smoking.

"I can't believe she has enough air left in her to smoke," Carrie said, after they finished carting the boxes and luggage inside.

"We wouldn't let her smoke in the car. By the time we got here, she was having a major nicotine fit. She lit up in the driveway, the minute she got out of the car," Jennifer said.

"Maybe I should get her to come back inside."

"Let her smoke. She needs her nicotine, or we'll all pay."

Jennifer told Carrie about their overnight stay at a Holiday Inn in Murfreesboro, Tennessee, where they had two rooms, one for Jennifer and her mother, and a connecting room for Gram. "After we arrived at the motel, Gram chainsmoked for over an hour, then fell asleep and coughed all night long. Mom and I hardly got any sleep."

"Sounds grim," Carrie said, handing Jennifer a Diet Coke from the refrigerator. "Gram's so thin. Her arms look like pipestems."

"She doesn't eat much of anything. Believe me, she may be sick, but she's still a real case. You're going to have your hands full." Carrie swallowed hard. She knew it was going to be tough and didn't need a reminder.

Carrie glanced out on the porch at Gram, who stood staring out at the swaying pine trees, blowing out a trail of smoke. Sophie-dog stood right beside Gram, her paws on the window ledge.

"You ready to take a look at your room, Gram?" Carrie said, opening the sliding door to the porch.

"In a minute, Caroline, in a minute." Gram took a last drag on her cigarette, then lit another one. Carrie pulled the door shut and sat down at the kitchen table. Gram sat down on a porch chair. Jennifer headed upstairs with her bag.

Waiting for Gram to finish her cigarette, Carrie remembered how Gram used to sit at her dressing table on Saturday nights getting ready to go out. Carrie would watch as she put on pancake makeup, rouge, eyeliner, eye shadow, and her bright red lipstick on her pretty face. Ruthie Olson, a high school girl who lived around the corner on Jefferson street, would come over to baby sit for Carrie while Gram went out dancing at the American Legion. Gram was a only a shell of her former self.

Carrie felt like she had a belly full of wax. Why had she invited Gram to come to Atlanta? What had she been thinking? She knew there was no backing out now.

Gram banged on the door with her cane. Carrie hurried over to push the door open. "Let's go take a look at your room," Carrie said helping her inside. "I know you're going to like it. Michael helped me get your room ready for you."

"Where is he, anyhow?"

"Running errands. He'll be home before long."

In Gram's room, Carrie helped her sit down in the chair in front of the window. She pointed out the daybed, the desk, the television set sitting on the dresser, the empty dresser drawers, the door leading to the bathroom, and the night stand. "I've never been so tired," Gram said, yawning. "Traveling wears me out."

Carrie offered to fix Gram something to eat. "All I want right now is some sleep."

Carrie reminded Gram to go to the bathroom before her nap. Gram gave her an odd look, but did what she said. Carrie realized, from this point on, she would be mothering Gram, whether she liked it or not.

"Michael and I have some rules for you, but we'll go over those later." Gram lay on her bed, her eyes closed. "We'll get your things unpacked after you wake up," Carrie said, kissing Gram on the cheek. Gram smelled yeasty, like she needed a bath. Carrie picked up Gram's familiar rose afghan from the top of a pile of boxes and lay it over her. It was a new beginning for both of them, she thought as she shut the door.

"Mom's sound asleep," Jennifer said. "I know she has to be blitzed from all that driving. I drove for a little while, but you know Mom. She gets bored if she can't drive. Besides, she likes to be in charge."

"Did you notice the box of Attends?" Jennifer asked. "We had to stop and get them yesterday. We couldn't stand another day of riding in a car smelling like a cat litter box. Gram wet her pants and got Mom's back seat cover all smelly. It'll have to be replaced. Make her wear them all of the time or she'll ruin your furniture." Carrie wrinkled up her nose and sighed, not wanting to hear any more sordid details.

Jennifer left to call Kevin, and Carrie worked on the dinner she had planned. She peeled and deveined the shrimp for her artichoke-shrimp-mushroom casserole. She put the cleaned shrimp into a 9 x 13 glass dish, then added a layer of quartered, marinated artichoke hearts and a layer of sauteed mushrooms. She mixed together cream of celery soup, pale dry sherry, Worchestershire sauce, and seasoned salt, then spread it on top, sprinkling it with grated cheddar cheese. She hoped her relatives appreciated her efforts.

"How's it going?" Michael said, when he arrived home.

"Oh, fine," Carrie said with little enthusiasm. "Gram and Aunt Nella are crashed, and Jennifer's on the phone."

"Does Gram like her room?"

"I think so. She was too exhausted to say much about it." Carrie wanted to tell Michael how apprehensive she felt but knew it wasn't a good idea. After all, she was the one who had begged to let Gram come stay with them.

After Gram awakened, Michael went into her room to say hello. He turned the television set on for her and offered to come get her when dinner was ready.

"Thank you. I'd like that," Gram said.

At dinner, Carrie served fruit salad and French bread with her cassserole. Gram pushed her food in circles on her plate. While the rest of them ate, Aunt Nella was at her social best, raving about her dinner, entertaining everyone with stories about her AA meetings and the interesting people she'd met. Carrie was surprised to hear her speaking candidly about her drinking problem. Obviously, she'd told Gram. Carrie had decided to forego wine for dinner. There was no need in creating an uncomfortable situation for Aunt Nella.

Jennifer went on and on, talking about her efforts to find the perfect wedding dress. Carrie gave Michael a grin, knowing he was getting bored. He winked at her, and cleared the table. Carrie could hear him in the kitchen, putting the dishes into the dishwasher.

"You've got your husband well trained," Aunt Nella said.

"Thanks," Carrie said, smiling. She could hear the coffee grinder going in the background. Michael always made his own coffee. After he brought coffee in for Aunt Nella, Gram and for himself, Carrie served cutout Christmas cookies for dessert. Gram took a frosted bell and licked the icing off the top.

"Michael and I picked out a Christmas tree last night. I think it would be special if we could all trim it together." What Carrie didn't say was that she wanted Gram to share a last tree trimming with them.

"Sounds good to me," Jennifer said.

"Is it December yet?" Gram asked.

"It will be in two days," Carrie said.

"We need to get going before noon. If we decorate the tree, it will have to be early," Aunt Nella said, getting up from the table.

"I'm going back to my room," Gram said. Carrie helped her down the hallway. As Gram held onto her arm, leaning into her, Carrie wondered why Gram wasn't using her walker. As they neared the doorway, Gram almost toppled over. Carrie caught her just in time.

"Gram, you need to use your walker," Carrie said. Gram ignored her. "Good night. Have a good sleep," Carrie said, after Gram got ready for bed.

"Goodnight, Caroline," Gram said in a tiny voice. Carrie turned out the light. She left the room with mixed emotions. In many ways, she was glad Gram had arrived, but, still, she felt uneasy.

Knowing Aunt Nella wouldn't turn down a game, Carrie suggested they play hearts at the game table in the great room. "Sounds good to me," said Aunt Nella who proceeded to skunk everyone. "You make up some strange rules," Michael accused Aunt Nella when she took all of the tricks, shooting the moon.

"Same rules as always," Nella laughed. "You just hate losing."

"Nella, did anyone ever tell you, you're a fruitcake?"

"Watch out. No name calling," Aunt Nella said, laughing.

"I'll clean your clock the next time," Michael said, getting up from the table.

"I'm headed to bed. I can't believe I'm going to bed before midnight," Aunt Nella said, "but tomorrow will be another long driving day." Carrie told her Aunt Nella goodnight, then sat down with Michael. After she gave up trying to read, she kissed Michael goodnight and went upstairs. It had been a draining day. Carrie fell asleep as soon as her head hit the pillow.

The next morning, Carrie and Michael went to early mass. When they returned, Jennifer was the only one up. "I dread saying good-bye to Gram, knowing I may never see her again," Jennifer said, as she stood in the kitchen sipping on her coffee.

"It doesn't have to be the last time. You could fly back down some weekend."

"I doubt if I'll have time for that. I've got tons to do at work and lots of wedding planning to do."

"Right," Carrie said. "I'd appreciate it if you would think about it. I may need some moral support."

"I love all of the trees in your back yard," Jennifer said, changing the subject. "I can't believe how many bird feeders you have. Look at that big black bird flapping his wings in the bird bath."

"Michael loves birds. Me too. He made most of those birdfeeders. He buys enough birdseed to feed half the birds in this area." They continued making small talk until Jennifer decided to take a shower. "Jennifer, I need to know about the family secrets you mentioned," Carrie said, before she got up to leave. "I tried to get some information from Gram, but she played dumb."

"Forget I ever said anything. I should have kept my mouth shut."

"Don't leave me hanging," Carrie said.

"All I can say is that the secrets relate to your parents' car accident. Ask Mom about it sometime. I'm not supposed to say anything."

"Okay, fine. I will. How's your mom doing anyhow? She seems okay."

"I worry about her, but she's making progress."

"I'm glad she's opened up to Gram about her drinking problem," Carrie said.

"Me, too. Gram took it well."

"I knew she would," Carrie said.

"These past few weeks have been hard on Mom. Taking care of Gram has been difficult," Jennifer said, walking away.

Carrie wanted to scream. What was three weeks? She had gotten her aunt all kinds of help. Mavis stopped in to see Gram almost every day, Herman went grocery shopping, and Helen brought food over. The visiting nurses Dr. Edgar ordered were there twice a week. Carrie could hardly feel sympathetic.

When Michael came back downstairs, he offered to cook breakfast. Carrie accepted his offer. Hearing noises from down the hallway, she hurried to Gram's room and helped her dress for breakfast. After twelve hours of sleep, Gram had more pep. "We stopped in Chattanooga yesterday, at a gift shop, and I got you a present," she said, handing a small box to Carrie.

"Thanks," Carrie said, opening the box. She pulled out a blue and yellow ceramic tea bag holder in the shape of a teapot. "That's perfect, Gram." Gram looked pleased.

At breakfast, Gram ate one of her eggs and a few bites of coffee cake. Then she covered her plate with her napkin. "I know. I didn't finish," she said when she saw Carrie staring at her. "I try to eat. I just can't. Every night I think I'll be hungry the next day. But I'm not. I know one thing for sure. When I get to heaven, I'm going to have me a big steak and a hot fudge sundae." They all laughed.

After breakfast, Michael put a tree stand on the frazier fir, and brought it inside. Carrie hauled the ornaments down from the upstairs storage closet. "You guys start decorating. I'll go get Gram."

Returning from Gram's room, Carrie looked disappointed. "She said she's too tired and doesn't want to help." Carrie put a Neil Diamond Christmas CD on. Aunt Nella and Jennifer hung ornaments while Carrie set a wooden sleigh with a fat, floppy Santa on the coffee table. Then, she decorated the fireplace mantel with fake greenery and brass candlesticks holding red and green candles.

"I wish Gram had joined us," Carrie said. "She isn't herself anymore. Christmas doesn't seem to matter to her this year."

"She's probably just too tired. That long ride blitzed her. She coughed the whole way which had to exhaust her. Maybe we should just leave. We decided to hang around for her benefit."

"Mom, that's rude," Jennifer said, handing Aunt Nella a Santa Claus ornament to hang on the tree.

"Okay, fine. But, we need to leave in an hour," Aunt Nella said, looking at her watch.

"You have lots of angels," Jennifer said. She held up a pink angel with a glittery halo. "I have an ornament just like this one."

"Gram gave us the same ornament each year. I thought you knew that."

Carrie took a picture of Aunt Nella and Jennifer hanging ornaments on the tree. She would show it to Gram later on. "You need the flash on, Carrie," Michael said. "You always get red-eye in your pictures."

"Give it a rest, Michael. It's my picture. Let me take it however I want." She turned the flash on, shaking her head at Michael. He loved to manage people. She asked him to take some of the boxes they had unloaded back up to the storage closet. "While you're there, see if you can find the wreath for the front door."

"Yes, ma'am," Michael said, putting down his newspaper.

"Aunt Nella, before you leave, could you tell me about my parents' car accident?" Carrie asked when Jennifer went upstairs to finish packing.

"Oh, Carrie. That was so long ago." Aunt Nella hung a silver star near the top of the tree, then looked over at Carrie. "I don't know that much about it." Aunt Nella's tight face told a story. Carrie was sure she knew plenty.

"I'd appreciate it if you would tell me what you know," Carrie said.

"Some things are best left buried. Gram's dying now. So why bring up the past, the muddy past." She checked her watch again. "I'm going up to see what's taking Jennifer so long."

"Let's go say good-bye," Aunt Nella said, when they were ready to leave. Carrie went with them to Gram's room.

"Good-bye, Gram. Be a good egg for Carrie."

"I will, dear." Gram handed Jennifer a photograph album. "I want you to have this, dear."

"Thanks, Gram." Jennifer said, reaching out for the familiar album, filled with childhood photos. Gram spent years making it. Jennifer hugged her, knowing it was Gram's way of saying good-bye.

"You two be careful," Gram said. "Drive safely." Gram was putting her puzzle pieces in place.

"We'd better get going," Aunt Nella said, holding onto her mother's hand. "I hope you and Carrie have fun together," she said. Gram looked spaced out, like she had traveled into another world. "Bye, Mom," Aunt Nella said, touching her on the arm.

"See ya, Gram," Jennifer said, trying not to cry.

Carrie and Michael waved good-bye as they drove off. Carrie wished she could trade places with them. She stood in the driveway until after they were out of sight. "I'm going to spray these junipers," Michael said.

"Some kind of bug is attacking them."

Carrie couldn't have described how she felt to anyone. She felt uneasy, like she had climbed inside of someone else. Wondering if Gram felt strange too, she went to her room. Gram sat in her chair, looking out the window. "They're gone now," Carrie said. Gram didn't say anything.

"I love looking at these trees," Gram said. "I remember how the dogwoods were blooming when I visited you last spring. I like it here." Looking away from Gram, Carrie rolled her eyes. For someone who had never liked Atlanta, Gram had certainly changed her tune. Carrie figured it was time for her to hum some new bars too.

Carrie pointed to a tree on the right side of the yard. "See that oak tree over there with a pine tree lying across it. The pine fell into the oak, and, over the years, the tree trunks have grown together. Now, they are bonded forever."

"Isn't that nice," Gram said, after studying the two trees. Carrie offered to turn on the television for Gram. "See if you can find me a movie to watch." Carrie flipped through the channels, finally finding a Fred Astaire musical that interested Gram.

"I'm going for a walk," Carrie said.

"You won't be gone long, will you?" Gram said. Carrie felt a noose tighten around her neck.

"No. I won't be gone too long. I need some fresh air. Don't worry. Michael's outside working in the yard. I'll ask him to come in and check on you in a little while." Before she left, Carrie let Sophie-dog into Gram's room. The dog curled up on the floor beside Gram who reached down and patted Sophie-dog on the head. Usually, Sophie-dog went crazy when Carrie mentioned going for a walk. Not today. She seemed content to stay with Gram.

"I'm going to walk over to Kay's house," Carrie said to Michael. He agreed to check on Gram. Carrie walked fast in the cool air. The faster she walked, the less she thought about anything.

At Kay's house, she tapped on the front door. Dave opened it for her. "Carrie, hi. How are you doing? Did your grandmother arrive?"

"Oh, yes. She's here."

"Kay's having a bad day. Maybe you can cheer her up."

"I'll try."

She walked into the family room where Kay lay in the recliner in her clamshell back brace. "Hey there, hello," Carrie said. "What's new?"

"Not much. How's it going?"

"Okay, I guess, but I already feel like my house is no longer mine."

"You've taken on quite a job."

"I know. She just arrived, and I am already whining. Gram's much weaker and very withdrawn. She seems to have disappeared inside herself. I honestly don't know if I can handle this."

"You need to get some help."

"That's my first priority. I'm taking Gram to see Dr. Kirkland tomorrow, so I can arrange for hospice care." Carrie took her jeans jacket off and put it on the arm of the sofa.

A crossword puzzle book scooted off Kay's lap. Carrie picked it up and handed it back. "Are you feeling any better?" Carrie asked.

"I'm still taking pain pills," Kay said. "You know me, I'm not the patient type. I'm going bonkers just lying here. Reading is out. I can't concentrate. Even these easy-to-do crossword puzzles are a challenge. I peek in the back for the answers."

"Taking those pills can mottle your mind." Carrie told Kay to call her anytime she felt bored. She reminded Kay that, with Gram at her house, she was going to be stuck at home.

"I promise to call and bug you. Everyone I know is off at work in the daytime. By the way, have you heard from that guy you met at the airport?"

"You mean Tom Egan?" Kay nodded yes. "Well, he's coming by the house tomorrow. He wants me to do some work for his law office, and the good news is I can do it from home. At least I can make some money. Besides, I'll need a diversion from Gram to save my sanity."

"Your grandmother sounds like a real case," Kay laughed.

"You've got that right. I dread giving her the house rules. She smokes way too much. It gags me. Tomorrow, I'm taking her cigarettes away."

"You can't do that. She'll go crazy."

"I'm going to let her smoke, but I plan to dole her Salems out to her. If I let her have them, she'll chain smoke. She falls asleep a lot, and I'm afraid she'll burn the house down. We put a smoke alarm in her room, and that makes me feel some better."

"I'd hate to be in your shoes."

"Yeah, me too." Carrie stood up. "I'd better get going. Thanks for letting me vent. You hang in there. Each day you're making progress. I think you look great."

"Stop lying. We're friends, remember."

"Okay, you look like crap."

"I do not," Kay said, laughing. "Don't make me laugh. It hurts."

Carrie headed home with a smile on her face.

"Gram's been asking for you," Michael said when she got home.

"I'll let her know I'm back." Carrie hurried inside.

"Gram, it smells like a wet ashtray in here," she said walking into Gram's room. She checked to see if the air filter was on.

"I spilled some tea in the ashtray. It's no big deal. You're still Miss Supernose, aren't you? By the way, Michael was very nice to me when he came in to check on me."

"Good. What did he do that was so nice?"

"Oh, he told me about the birds outside, and he fixed the TV. The picture's clear now."

"Good," Carrie said. She helped Gram up and out into the great room. "Doesn't the tree look great?"

"Umm, hmm," Gram said, sitting down on the sofa. Carrie vowed to make Christmas special for Gram.

When it was time to eat dinner, Carrie got Gram's walker out of her room and insisted she use it. "I'm not sure I need this," Gram said.

"You need it, Gram. I'm afraid you'll fall."

"Have it your way," Gram said, glaring at Carrie.

Gram was quiet at dinner. After only a few bites, she went into a coughing fit. When the coughing died down, she asked Carrie to help her get to bed. Carrie followed behind Gram and her walker. Watching Gram struggle to breathe, as they headed down the hallway made

Carrie's own chest felt tight. She had to remind herself to breathe.

"I like your grandmother better when she's sick," Michael said when she returned to the table. "We had a good visit this afternoon."

"That's what she told me. She seems to think you are quite okay now."

"Well, I am okay."

"I know it, silly goose." Carrie thanked Michael for agreeing to let Gram live with them and promised that she wouldn't let Gram take over their lives. After dinner, she and Michael read the Sunday paper, then went to bed.

Carrie tried to fall asleep. Michael turned over, his breathing deep and steady. Carrie hugged her pillow, holding her eyes shut, anxious to get to the doctor the next morning. She knew arranging for help would benefit Gram and make her feel more at ease. She got up once, went downstairs and checked on Gram who was sound asleep. Back upstairs in bed, she snuggled up against Michael's back remembering some of the things Gram had pounded into her head when she was growing up—be a good girl, don't act uppity, always do what is right, hold your tongue. As she drifted off to sleep, she felt like she was floating on a dark cloud.

# Chapter Twelve

### Journal, Tuesday, December 10, 1987

Thank God Gram's asleep. Today has not been a good day. There's no longer any such thing as a good day around here. The last two weeks have been a struggle. I don't know what made me think I could do this job. It turns out I'm a lousy caretaker.

Tomorrow, I'm taking Gram to see Dr. Kirkwood. She refused to go to the first appointment two weeks ago, claiming she was too exhausted. I kept the appointment and went by myself. I told the doctor how sick Gram was and begged for hospice help. He said he couldn't help me until I brought Gram in to see him.

"Why bother," Gram said, when I told her I was taking her to the doctor. "I'm dying, and there's nothing he can do about it."

Gram insists we are doing fine, that she does not need anyone besides me to care for her. We disagree on that score. I don't know diddly-squat about caring for a dying person. She may not need any help, but God knows I do.

Gram hates my rules. When I spelled them out for her, I became the enemy. She blew a gasket when I explained how I would dole out her cigarettes, five at at time, for safety's sake. She has to ask for more when she runs out. I keep her carton of Salems in the kitchen cabinet and keep track of how many she has with her. She tries to outsmart me by hiding cigarettes like a squirrel storing nuts. I've found cigarettes hidden in her bed, in the dresser drawers, and in her pockets. She calls me a wicked witch. So be it.

Gram's always thirsty. Michael gave her a cowbell, the one he got in Germany on a business trip, to ring when she needs something. She clangs it all day and sometimes at night. Usually, she wants more iced tea. I remember reading about this symptom in the cancer book. I think it has something to do with the cancer cells attacking healthy cells.

"Thanks, it's nice," Gram said, when I brought home the plastic thermal pitcher she keeps in her room. She told me not to worry, that I'd be able to use it later, after she's gone. I hate it when she talks that way. Does she think I'm just waiting for her to die? I don't want her to die. Or do I?

Gram likes Eva, a lady about her age, who sings alto in our church choir. Eva brings communion every Tuesday. Gram doesn't ask, so I don't tell her that her communion wafer comes from a Catholic church. Eva, who always stays an extra thirty minutes or so to visit, knows about our Lutheran-Catholic conflict and says it doesn't matter to God which denomination the wafer comes from. She has a good point. Eva has become Gram's only link to the world outside.

Michael is gone traveling almost every week. I sometimes wonder if it's his way of dealing with having Gram here. When he's home, he visits with Gram each morning and stops in again after work. He always gets her laughing. I continue to be amazed at their new relationship. Gram has forgotten that she didn't like Michael. Now, the two of them have a new rapport, one that excludes me.

Gram and Sophie-dog are big pals. The other day, Gram dropped pieces of cutup hot dog to the floor, and Sophie-dog gobbled them up. I had to warn her that table food does something strange to Sophie-dog's pancreas, making her insides bleed. Looking alarmed, Gram promised not to feed Sophie-dog from the table again.

Gram now eats even less than she did when she first arrived. She does everything possible to make me think she's cleaned her plate. At dinner tonight, she slid her chicken breast into the pocket of her robe. Last weekend, I caught her flushing her sandwich down the toilet.

Tom Egan met Gram last week when he delivered some work to me. He brought her a box of Fannie Mae chocolates and asked how she was doing. "I'm dying, but otherwise I'm fine," Gram said. Tom chuckled at her candid response. After he left, Gram wanted to know why he'd brought her candy and acted miffed that he knew so much about her. She raised her eyebrows when I told her I was doing some work for him.

"He's sweet on Caroline. They spend a lot of time together." Gram told Michael when he arrived home last Friday evening. I felt like screaming. I think she was getting back at me for taking her cigarettes away. Tom Egan doesn't mean anything to me. I like visiting with him, because he understands my concerns about Gram. He's coming by again tomorrow, and I'm looking forward to seeing him. I promised to tell him about our visit to the doctor. Tom has become a good friend, and I must admit I like listening to his deep, penetrating voice.

Phone calls have become a lifeline for me. Jennifer calls often with news about her wedding plans. She wants me to come to her shower in February. I'd leap at the chance to get out of here for a couple of days. Maybe I can hire a nurse to stay with Gram. After Jennifer and I talk, I hand the phone to Gram. The other day I heard her finking on me. She told Jennifer that I am no longer a nice person. And, of course, she's right. Sometimes, I can't afford to be nice.

On rare occasions, Aunt Nella calls. Gram insists that Aunt Nella has a worse drinking problem than her own ever was. I can't be a judge of that. Besides, what difference does it make? At least, these two finally have some common ground. Gram encourages Aunt Nella to keep going to her AA meetings.

Kay and I phone each other every day. I'm not sure how I'd survive without her. She tells me stories and keeps me laughing. Kay is an A personality, someone always in a hurry. Yesterday, she told me about the time she backed into her garage door. She had climbed into her Toyota in a hurry to get to a meeting, had started the engine, and had stepped on the gas pedal. That's when she heard the crashing noise and realized she hadn't opened the garage door. Another time, in a hurry to deliver some oil paintings to a gallery, she backed the car out, forgetting that her father-in-law's Buick Regal was in their driveway. She slammed into it, scrunching the front end. Hearing her story, I laughed until I cried. Kay's calls keep me sane, and, lying at home recuperating, she's a captive audience.

Today, I told her how Gram still hacks all of the time. Her coughing fits are indescribable. She sounds like she's trying to cough up stuff from her feet. When I hear her gagging, I run into her room. Most of the time, she motions for me to go away. I live in fear that the gunk in her chest will get stuck in her throat, and she'll choke to death right in front of me.

She's sleeping now. I just tiptoed into her room and covered her. Her head is propped high on a pile of pillows so she can breathe. When she's asleep, I wonder how I can get so angry at such a fragile soul. Each night, I vow to try and be more patient the next day. But by noon my patience heads downhill.

The life I used to know is gone. When Michael's home, I'm on edge. I want to talk to him about Gram, and I do. But, I hold a lot back, knowing he only wants to hear so much. I pretend my jaw is wired shut, letting him tell me about his sales calls, about sports and current events. I know he's trying to keep my mind off of Gram. But, the trouble is, I need to vent. The feelings I'm keeping locked inside are creating a wall between us.

When Michael comes on to me, I try to respond, but most of the time I'm too tired. When we do make love, I can't stop thinking about Gram, wondering if she's calling out for me. Some nights I sneak downstairs in the middle of the night and sleep on the sofa in the great room, where only a wall separates me from her daybed.

Right now, it's time to get to bed. Tomorrow is an important day. I know Gram will come up with several reasons why she can't get to the doctor tomorrow. She doesn't see the point. We've talked about hospice care, but Gram isn't ready to face the fact that soon she will need the kind of care I can't provide. All I know is that want to get some help before my brain backfires.

## Chapter Thirteen

Carrie sat in a small room sewing a bright green dress. Six other women, sitting near her, stitched similar navy sheath dresses. "My grandmother's very sick. I'm going to have to watch her die," Carrie told the women beside her. "No one wants to help me." When she completed attaching the last tier of satin ruffles on the dress, Carrie got up and told an exceptionally tall man in a black suit standing in the doorway that she had finished her sewing project. He gave her permission to leave. She went to her grandmother's apartment and stood at her bedside, wearing the frilly green dress. "Should I have made a navy sheath like the other women?" she asked.

"Oh, no," her grandmother said, clapping her hands together. Looking bright-eyed, as if Carrie had just fulfilled a prophecy, she raved about the green, ruffled dress. "I'll never have to go see another doctor," she said. "Not ever again."

Carrie sat up in bed, rubbing her eyes. The strange dreams she kept having disturbed her. They didn't make much sense, or did they? Carrie heard a car engine start up outside. Peeking out the window, she saw her neighbor, Frank, back his silver Audi out of his garage and go down the driveway. Carrie stared out the window, seeing only a few clouds. It looked like it would be a sunny day. She brushed her teeth, pulled her gray nightshirt over her head and dropped it onto the brown tile floor. After a quick shower, she slipped on her underwear, khaki pants, a red cable-knit sweater, white socks, and her Nikes.

Downstairs, she peeked in on Gram and found her with her head propped up on her pillow, her elbow under the pillow, leaning toward the wall in a fetal position. Carrie tiptoed out of the room. She would have a quiet breakfast and then awaken Gram in plenty of time to get ready for her doctor's appointment at noon. She could hear Sophie-dog squealing in the laundry room. "Okay, okay," she said, opening the door. Sophie-dog raced to the back door. Carrie took the dog with her when she went outside to get the morning paper. Sophie-dog ran ahead, stopping to piddle in the grass. As Carrie walked to the end of the driveway, brown leaves spiraled to the ground. Soon, they would turn to dust.

Back inside, Carrie poured boiling water into her Green Bay Packers mug, then added an Earl Grey tea bag. She sat down at the kitchen table with her tea and ate a bowl of Grape-Nuts and a banana. When the phone rang, she jumped. It was Michael calling from out of town.

"Jim Tunney, the former NFL referee, is the featured speaker at our meeting this morning. He gives motivational talks, and I hear he's terrific."

"Sounds interesting," Carrie said. "I miss you."

"I'll be home Friday afternoon, not tomorrow. I had to add an extra day." He asked if she wanted to go out to dinner Friday night and suggested inviting Kay and Dave to come along."

"Sounds good to me, but they can't come," she said, adding that Kay was scheduled to have a second back surgery to remove some scar tissue."

"Too bad. No wonder she's been in such pain. How are you and Gram getting along?" he asked.

"Okay, I guess." She related some of Gram's antics from the day before and voiced her concern about getting her to the doctor. Michael didn't comment. She knew his silence meant that she had carved her own path, and he didn't want to hear about her problems with Gram. Michael chose to remain neutral.

"I'd better hang up. I'll call tomorrow."

"Okay. Bye." Carrie hung up. She couldn't believe Michael's nonchalance about her trials with Gram. Was she just supposed to assume he cared about what was going on in her life?"

"What am I suppposed to say?" Michael asked one day when she questioned him about his lack of concern.

"Can't you be sympathetic once in awhile?"

"I just don't know how to do that."

She shrugged. Michael was Michael. He wasn't going to change. Saying nice things that she wanted to hear wasn't part of his repertoire.

Carrie grimmaced when she heard the cowbell. Reaching up to the top shelf in the kitchen cabinet, she got five cigarettes from the carton of Salems and hurried down the hallway. Sophie-dog followed her. Opening the door, she saw Gram sitting in the bedside chair in her tired-looking white chenille bathrobe. Gram was holding her small brown prayer book.

"I want a cigarette," Gram said.

"Did you have a good sleep?"

"I guess." Gram put the prayer book down in her lap, then grabbed the cigarettes from Carrie's outstretched hand. She set four of them down on the TV tray beside her chair, then slipped the other cigarette into her mouth and snapped her Bic lighter. Carrie made Gram's bed, then left the room carrying the empty iced tea pitcher. She knew Gram wanted to be alone so she could chain smoke all five cigarettes. Carrie didn't dare remind Gram of her doctor's appointment until she'd had her nicotine fix.

Carrie reached down under the desk for Gram's metal file box then sat down at the desk to pay some bills. Each month, she'd been sending as much as she could to each of Gram's accounts—Chase Manhattan Visa, Sears, Marshall Fields, and J. C. Penney's. Carrie handled all of her finances, because Gram could no longer add or subtract. Sometimes, she couldn't even sign her own name.

"Whatever are you talking about, girl?" Gram said when Carrie mentioned the missing loan card. There had been no word from the credit union, even though the balance was several hundred dollars. The missing card remained a mystery.

Carrie wrote out several checks, then put the stamped and sealed bills beside her black purse. Opening the freezer compartment on top of the refrigerator, she took out two pounds of ground beef. She had decided to make a meatloaf, English muffins, and applesauce for dinner. Gram used to love meatloaf. Perhaps, she could get her to eat some. Michael would be delighted to have a meatloaf sandwich for lunch on the weekend.

Carrie heard footsteps in the hallway. Peeking around the corner, she saw Gram struggling behind her walker on her way to the kitchen.

"Want me to fix a bowl of cereal for you?" Carrie asked.

"I can do it." Gram poured herself a bowl of Rice Crispies. She spooned sugar on top, spilling half of it onto the counter. With the palm of her hand, Gram shoved the sugar off of the counter onto the floor. Carrie narrowed her eyes at Gram, not knowing what to say. She couldn't believe Gram, the neatness freak, would brush the sugar onto the floor. Carrie decided not to say anything. She would clean it up later. Over the years, Carrie had spent hours helping Gram shine their house as if the President himself was coming to visit. There was no point in scolding Gram.

"No, you don't," Carrie said when Sophie-dog came running over to lick the sugar off the tile. She grabbed the little dog and put her outside on the screened porch. "Can you bring my breakfast to the table?" Gram said.

"Sure." Carrie took the bowl of cereal and a glass of orange juice to the table and sat down across from Gram. She knew better than to offer her coffee. Gram used to drink several cups every morning, but now it made her cough. Carrie noticed that the swelling in Gram's face had gone down.

"I need some new bras. These are too small," Gram said later when Carrie helped her get dressed. As Carrie pulled her pink flowered nightgown over her head, she watched Gram's hanging breasts sway. Her right breast was twice the size of the left one.

"Let me help you," Carrie said, trying to fasten Gram's bra. "It's really tight, Gram. I can't get it fastened. We'll get you some bigger ones soon. I think you'd better go without your bra today."

"My stars, Caroline. I'm not going to that doctor's office without my brassiere."

"Fine, Gram." Carrie stretched the elastic on Gram's bra, struggled with the clasp and finally got it fastened. It cut into Gram's skin. Carrie wondered if the tumor had switched position. She guessed that perhaps the fluid buildup had moved to her chest, making one boob bigger than the other.

Gram took two more hours, with a stop for a short nap, to get ready to leave the house. By the time Carrie threw a biscuit on the floor and put Sophie-dog securely in the laundry room, Gram stood leaning on her walker by the back door dressed in her gray striped pants, a pink silk blouse, and her black suede heels. She wore silver hoop earrings and a silver pin in her lapel. Every white hair in her bouffant bob was fixed in position. She had sprayed herself with enough White Shoulders perfume to gag an army of ants.

Carrie had fought with her about the heels. Gram wouldn't budge. She had slipped one on, then the other, ignoring Carrie's protests. Gram almost toppled over just going down the hallway. Carrie figured she'd have to get a wheelchair to transport her from the car to the doctor's office. Before she went out the door, Carrie called the doctor's office and made sure they had a wheelchair for Gram to use.

"Why didn't you wear your flat shoes, Gram?" Carrie asked as she drove down the driveway. "You can barely walk in those high heels."

"I only brought one pair of flat shoes. You've seen them. I had them on the day I arrived. They're navy blue, and they wouldn't go with this outfit."

"I remember them, Gram. The only thing you've worn on your feet since then are your bedroom slippers. I can't believe you put on high heels." Gram stared out the window, ignoring Carrie.

They sat at a red light at Northridge and Roswell Road. The car next to them blared loud rock music. A young man with milky white skin, greasy hair, and a gold ring in his nose, tapped his hand on the steering wheel, swaying his body back and forth in time to the music. Gram eyeballed him, shaking her head.

"For God's sake, Gram, why didn't you bring your other flat shoes with you?" Carrie said as they turned onto Northridge Road. The ring-nosed guy went straight on Roswell Road.

"I thought when I moved here, I'd feel better," Gram said as if it made perfect sense. She tilted her chin up and pursed her lips. Carrie swallowed hard. She put a George Winston tape into the player. Gram liked piano music. She couldn't blame Gram for wanting to get well. She reminded herself of the rough seas in Gram's path and vowed to be more patient.

"Wait here," Carrie said after she parked. "I'll be right back." She hurried inside the medical building to get the wheelchair. Returning to the car, Carrie paid no attention to Gram who refused to use the wheelchair. She scooted Gram out of the car and sat her down in it, knowing there was no way Gram could walk across the parking lot in her three-inch heels.

She took Gram up to the second floor in the elevator. Inside the doctor's office, the receptionist handed Carrie two sheets of paper on a clipboard. Gram leafed through a *Vogue* magazine while Carrie filled out the forms.

"Gram, I need some information from you. How did your parents die?"

"My father died of pneumonia, and my mother had a stroke. She died in 1959, the same year as my father." Gram continued thumbing through the magazine while Carrie finished the forms. A young girl with straight brown shoulder-length hair in jeans and a purple cotton turtleneck sat in a loveseat across the room peeling an orange. Carrie looked up at the girl who had dark circles under her eyes and a hoarse cough.

"I'm going to get me some of those one of these days," Gram said, pointing to the young girl's tight demin jeans.

"Oh, sure," Carrie said. Gram had never owned a pair of jeans. The young girl stuck an orange wedge in her mouth, slurping as she chewed. Carrie handed the forms to the receptionist.

"Caroline, could we have fried chicken for dinner tonight?" Gram said.

"Well, I had planned on fixing a meatloaf, but I guess chicken would be okay. I'll have to stop at the store on the way home." If Gram wanted chicken, they would have chicken. The ground beef would keep one more day.

"I want some of those maldarin oranges too," Gram said.

"Mandarin oranges? I think you mean mandarin oranges, Gram."

"Whatever. I like those."

Gram had hardly eaten for days. Carrie was willing to prepare anything she wanted just to get some food into her. Fried chicken always made Carrie think of Sundays when she was growing up. Lorraine, from next door, used to go out early every Sunday morning, get a chicken out of the hen house, and chop its head off. Carrie would watch out her bedroom window as the headless chicken twirled around doing the tango, until it fell over dead.

"When you stop at the store, get me some Ex-lax." Gram said. The young girl looked up, staring at Gram and Carrie. Carrie told her okay in a quiet voice. Gram had been constipated since she arrived.

"Gram, I saw you had a note from Mavis yesterday," Carrie said. "What did she have to say?"

"She told me that Mary Lou's husband made a killing on some kind of mechanical invention. Something to do with cars. Don't ask me for details. All I know is now they're rolling in dough."

"Good for them."

"My high school friends have all done better than me."

"Gram. Don't say that. You've done just fine."

"No, Caroline. I haven't. I've always had to struggle to pay my bills. And I've made some grave mistakes."

"Gram, I paid the bills this morning," Carrie said. "I still can't find that loan card from the church credit union."

"You didn't get that dressed up, Caroline," Gram said avoiding any mention of the loan.

"Gram, what did you want me to wear? These are my good pants, and my red sweater fits with the Christmas spirit, don't you think?" Carrie looked at her watch, wondering what was taking so long.

"You told me that Michael got a promotion to sales manager. That means you should dress better," Gram said. Carrie winced. Gram got hung up on titles. She wanted to tell her that Michael was the sales manager, not her.

"Come on in now, Mrs. Whitfield. You too," the nurse motioned to Carrie. Carrie pushed the wheelchair down a long hallway. They stopped halfway, at a scale where the nurse weighed and measured Gram—106 pounds, ten pounds less than in September. In the small examination room, the nurse checked Gram's blood pressure and temperature. "The doctor will be along soon," the nurse said, going out the door.

"Mrs. Whitfield, I'm pleased to meet you," Dr. Kirkland said, striding into the room a few minutes later. "My, my. I'm quite surprised," he said. "I didn't expect to see someone as lovely as you." Gram glanced up at him, smiling. "I have looked over your chart, and your granddaughter has told me all about you. I was prepared to see a very sick woman." He reached his hand for hers.

"Thank you," Gram said, reaching out to shake hands.

Gram put on a stellar performance for the doctor. He asked questions. She told lies. She told him, no, she didn't cough much. She had no trouble swallowing, and, yes, she could eat just about everything. Yes, she had complete bladder control. No, she wasn't constipated, wasn't hoarse, and didn't feel tired.

"I just love everything about Atlanta," Gram said as if she had been on one excursion around town after another.

"She's been constipated since she arrived," Carrie said. Gram shot her a look of disapproval. Dr. Kirkland wrote down the name of a stool softener and handed it to Carrie.

"We need some nursing help, and I'd like to arrange for hospice care," Carrie said. Gram gave Carrie a disapproving look. The doctor asked Gram why she needed a nurse. "Well, a nurse could help us when we go to the mall."

"Gram, please," Carrie said, "tell the truth. We do not go to the mall, and you know it. We don't go anywhere."

"I would prefer that you let your grandmother do the talking," the doctor said. Carrie wanted to scream, but she buttoned her lip and listened as he questioned Gram. After studying his notes, he recommended that Gram have radiation treatments to shrink her tumor.

"I've decided against any kind of treatments," Gram said.

Dr. Kirkland asked her to reconsider her decision and recommended that she see an oncologist. He gave Carrie a card with a Dr. Baker's phone number on it. "You are way too vibrant to just give up," he said, patting Gram on the arm. "Perhaps, down the road, when it becomes necessary, we could look into getting you some nursing help."

At Carrie's request, he wrote a prescription for a rental wheelchair, then shook hands with both of them. He told Carrie to make sure Gram got a balanced diet before he went out the door.

Carrie felt like a squashed bug. She was way too angry at Gram to say anything. She would call Dr. Kirkland and try to explain that, because of Gram's pride, she had lied to him. As she wheeled Gram to the elevator, she couldn't decide who she disliked the most, the doctor or her grandmother. Gram deserved an Oscar for her performance.

On the way home, Carrie stopped at a medical supply store to rent a wheelchair. Gram, who was sure she didn't need one, waited in the car. After getting the wheelchair into the trunk of the car, Carrie got onto the freeway and headed toward home.

"I won't be long," she said, getting out of the car at the neighborhood Kroger store. She left a window open, knowing Gram would light a cigarette the minute she got out of sight.

"I need some Salems," Gram called after her.

Carrie shopped for all of the things she needed for the blasted chicken dinner she didn't feel like cooking. Then she added the Colace stool softener, Ex-lax, Attends, two Fleet enemas, All-bran cereal, and prunes. As she stood in line at the checkout, she felt conspicuous and hoped no one she knew was in the store. She wanted the young male clerk to hurry. She wondered what he was thinking. He'd probably looked at her face and decided that she was the one who was constipated.

After they arrived home, Gram lay on her bed, exhausted, and soon fell asleep.

"Oh my God, it was horrible," Carrie said when she called Kay. "I try to be nice to her, Kay. Really, I do. Then she pulls a stunt like this. I wanted to drop her off at the nearest corner and let her fend for herself. The woman is driving me batty."

Kay laughed when she described the trip to Kroger. Carrie asked if she had gotten the word about the surgery?

"I'm all set for next Monday. I can't stand this pain any longer. Come over and visit if you can get away."

"I'll come over this weekend, when Michael's home," Carrie said. "I'd better peel the potatoes. Gram wants mashed potatoes with her dumb chicken dinner. I hate fried chicken." Carrie hung up feeling better.

At the dinner table, a sullen and silent Gram played with her food, refusing to make eye contact. "Gram, I thought you wanted fried chicken. You've hardly touched anything on your plate."

"It doesn't taste right," Gram said. Not wanting to scold Gram while she was eating, Carrie excused herself from the table for a few minutes. When she returned, she found Gram dropping bites of chicken on the floor for Sophie-dog, who now always sat at Gram's feet when she ate. Carrie grabbed the chicken out of Sophie-dog's mouth.

"I'm sorry," Gram said. "I forgot." Carrie shook her head, knowing it wouldn't do any good to say anything. After clearing Gram's dinner plate, she gave her a brownie she'd bought at Kroger bakery. Gram took a bite of the brownie.

"Gram, why did you lie to the doctor?" Carrie said.

"Oh, I just knew you were going to bring that up."

"Well, why? Just tell me why. You acted like you didn't have a thing wrong with you. We both know better."

"This tastes good," Gram said, taking a big bite of her brownie. She started gagging. Putting her hands to her throat, she made choking noises. Then, there was no sound at all. Jumping out of her chair, Carrie patted Gram's back. Gram gasped, thrusting her head forward. Phlegm and food shot out of her mouth and onto the table. Gram held onto the table, taking quick breaths. Her chest heaved up and down.

Carrie hurried down the hallway and came back with the wheelchair. Gram felt heavy when Carrie helped lift her into her chair. She got her into her room and into bed. Within minutes, Gram was passed out.

Back in the kitchen, Carrie cleaned up the mess. There was no point in making big meals for Gram anymore. From now on, she would only serve her small portions of soft food. Carrie fixed a chicken salad for herself and took it into the great room. She still felt shaky knowing Gram had almost choked to death. The house was quiet. All she could hear were ice cubes dropping into the icemaker. Carrie stared at the ceiling, looking at a brown, lopsided ring in the oyster white paint, wondering if the roof had a leak.

When the doorbell rang, she was startled. Then she remembered that Tom Egan had said he would stop by. Passing the entry mirror, she noticed purple bags under her eyes. She ran her fingers through her uncombed hair, then looked out the peephole.

"I almost forgot you were coming," she said, opening the door.

"You look beat."

"After the day I've had, I'm not surprised."

"That bad, huh?" He walked inside. "I brought you more work to do. You're doing a great job."

Thanks," she said. "The work keeps me sane." She led him into the great room. "I'll be back in a minute," she said. She ran upstairs, washed her face, brushed her hair, and put on lipstick. Back downstairs, she opened a bottle of Pinot Grigio and poured two glasses.

Sitting in the recliner, across from where Tom sat on the sofa, she told him about taking Gram to the doctor. "She took forever to get ready. Actually, she looked pretty good." Carrie described Gram's performance.

"Did he arrange for hospice help?"

"Are you kidding? I couldn't even get a visiting nurse, not after Gram said we only needed a nurse for our trips to the mall." Tom raised his eyebrows.

"Don't give me that strange look. We never leave this house." Carrie took a sip of her wine. "What really frosts me is that Dr. Kirkwood made me feel guilty. He acted like I wanted Gram to die."

"He sounds like a jerk. Do you want me to call and talk to him?" Carrie scooted to the edge of her chair.

"Heavens, no. I can handle it. I'll call him tomorrow." She told Tom about Gram's choking fit.

"Sounds like a bummer of a day. Maybe this is too much for you to do by yourself."

"God, you sound like Michael. Maybe it is. I don't know. All I know is that I expected to leave that office today with hospice care. The doctor refused to talk about it. He doesn't thinks she's sick enough."

Carrie got up and listened outside Gram's bedroom door when she heard her coughing and moving around. "Iced tea," Gram said when she opened the door. Carrie poured some tea from Gram's thermal pitcher, then helped her take a few sips.

"Is Michael home?" Gram asked.

"No—he doesn't come home for two days, not until Friday."

"I heard some man talking. Do you have company?"

"Just Tom Egan. He stopped by to bring me some more work."

"Kind of late for that, isn't it?"

"Gram, it's only nine. Tom will be leaving soon. Do you want anything else?"

"No." Gram lay back down. "You can turn the light out."

"Goodnight. I'll see you in the morning," Carrie said, leaning down to kiss her on the forehead.

"Maybe," Gram said.

Carrie closed the door. When she got back into the great room, Tom and Sophie-dog were playing tug-of-war with the sockie.

"Tom, I want to be nice to Gram, but she makes it difficult. I feel like she's at war with me."

"She is. You're the caretaker. You make the rules and that makes you the enemy. She resents you. You've taken away her independence. My Mom acted that way too. It was a bad scene. I had no choice, and neither do you."

"Thanks, I needed that."

Tom stood up to leave. Carrie walked him to the door. He patted her on the back, "Just remember, in the middle of all of this, that your grandmother still loves you in her own way."

After Carrie shut the door, she thought about what Tom had said. She wanted to believe, that in spite of everything, Gram still loved her.

# Chapter Fourteen

### Journal, Sunday, December 29, 1987

It's early evening, and I'm hiding out in the extra room upstairs, trying to shuffle through the madness inside my head. Gram's asleep, and Michael's watching a football game. The Christmas tree came down today, and we shelved the rest of the decorations. It was none too soon. The new year is around the corner, and it's time to move on. I'm certain that I'll always remember this holiday season.

We made it festive for Gram, knowing it would probably be her last Christmas. Michael went to midnight mass on Christmas Eve, and I went to 7:30 a.m. mass the next morning. It felt strange going alone. Michael stayed with Gram, who has never asked where we attend church. Perhaps, I'll tell her one of these days that we go to a Catholic Church.

After I came home from mass, I helped Gram get dressed in her new red crocheted sweater, black velour pants, and her Christmas tree earrings. Gram joined us at the dining room table, set with crystal and linens, for a traditional Christmas brunch. Michael put on a Mannheim Steamroller CD. I lit red and green candles floating in a white ceramic sleigh centerpiece as we listened to "We Three Kings." For brunch, we had eggs over-easy, ham, fresh fruit, and cinnamon rolls, like the ones Gram used to make each Christmas. She smiled and her eyes brightened when she saw the cinnamon rolls on the Spode platter that used to be hers.

Gram ate a few bites of everything on her plate and raved about Michael's eggs. She wouldn't touch the fried eggs I made her for dinner last week and gave me a lecture on how disgusting they tasted. Michael thought it was pretty funny. Sometimes, I think he and Gram consider me their mutual enemy.

After breakfast, we went into the great room to open packages. Gram sat on the sofa beside the tree playing with her thin fingers, twisting them like a child acting out "The Itsy Bitsy Spider." Watching her while we waited for Michael to get out of the bathroom, I thought about other Christmases and how Gram had flitted around the room like a windup toy, so excited she couldn't contain herself. When she opened a gift, she would ooooh and ahhhh, whoop and holler. Not this year. Instead, she showed little enthusiasm.

Nella sent her some fancy body lotion, and a bright blue cardigan sweater with matching pants. Gram smiled at the large white teddy bear, wearing a red bow, that Jennifer had mailed, along with a large basket of fresh fruit. Mavis sent her a gold cross. She fingered the cross and wanted to put it on, so I fastened it around her neck. Herman sent a box of white chocolate fudge from a small candy shop in Milwaukee. Gram nibbled on the fudge.

Michael and I gave her several little packages—bath powder, earrings, pink furry slippers with rubber soles, red Clinique lipstick, shortbread cookies in a fancy gold tin, and a dried dogwood blossom pressed between two pieces of glass to hang in her window. She held onto the dogwood blossom. "This reminds me of springtime," she said. Gram keeps asking when the stick trees will get leaves on them. She seems to be waiting for the renewal of spring.

Gram gave me the green Eileen West nightgown she'd never worn, the one her friends in Wisconsin gave her. I thanked her, not knowing what else to say. I doubt that I'll wear it either. It holds too many memories I'd just as soon forget. Gram gave Michael some golf socks and a brown leather wallet, items she had ordered from Sears. She smiled when Michael gave me a gold necklace with matching earrings.

After all of the gifts under the tree were opened, Gram handed me a manilla envelope. Inside was the letter from a friend of my mother's family, the one Gram had promised I could read after she got to Atlanta. "I received this letter on December 31, 1962. I'd like you to read it on New Year's Eve this year," Gram said. I'm very anxious to read this mysterious link to my past.

Gram's been living with us for over a month now. She has good days and bad days. Her moods shift from passive and remote to feisty and controlling. I'm trying to deal with the ups and downs of caring for her; however, it isn't as if I have a choice. She shifts from being quite alert to being very confused. Last week, she got out her address book and thumbed through it over and over.

"What's Nella's last name?" she asked. I looked at her, surprised. I couldn't believe she didn't know her own daughter's name. I dialed the number for her. "Who's this?" Gram said when Aunt Nella answered. I reminded her that she was speaking to her daughter.

A deck of cards with a white rubberband around them sits on Gram's bedside table. On the front of the cards, a dreamy-looking barefoot girl sits at the foot of a huge tree. She is wearing a red dress with a low-cut bodice, and a bonnet. The scene reminded me of the covers of the historical romances Gram always loved to read. She can no longer read or play gin rummy, or any other card game. Perhaps the cards remind her of the person she used to be.

Today was gray and cloudy. There seems to be a permanent cloud over this house. I try to be cheerful for Gram and for Michael, but I often wonder what happened to the carefree newlyweds who used to live here. I try taking one day at a time, but that is easier said than done. Like Gram, I hang onto threads of hope. Each night, I pray the next day will be better than the day before; I wonder how long I can keep this up.

I called Dr. Kirkland after Gram's performance at his office a few weeks ago, trying to explain her behavior. Making no comment, he simply repeated his suggestion to take Gram to Dr. Baker, the oncologist. At least, when I called and asked for Dr. Baker, he spoke with me and asked questions. He wants to see Gram, but first he wants her to have a lung biopsy. He said it needs to be done to verify that her tumor is malignant. Once that is done, Dr. Baker has promised to arrange hospice care. All I can say is yeah, hurray, bring out the balloons. Help is on the way.

"If you don't have the biopsy we're putting you in a nursing home," Michael said to Gram, looking directly into her dark brown eyes, when she refused to go to the hospital for the test. Michael's abruptness surprised me. Gram dropped her head, and I swallowed the football that climbed my throat.

Gram stared down at the tan carpet as if what she wanted to say would appear on it. "Okay, fine," she finally said, getting up. I offered to help get her back to her room, but she refused.

"Leave her alone," Michael said. At the time, I thought he was being cruel. Now, I realize that she needed to be in control of something, even if it was only getting back to her room on her own. I listened to the thump of the walker as she slowly went around the corner.

Gram ate dinner alone in her room, watching television. She was quiet when I went in to tell her good night and looked like a puppy waiting for a reprimand. When Michael went in to say good night, I stood outside the door expecting to hear her lashing out at him. She didn't. Instead, she said, "Michael, watch out—Caroline is having men over for the evening when you're gone."

At first, I couldn't believe what I'd heard. Michael is the one who ordered her to have the biopsy, but she stood up for him. I wondered if Gram was striking out at me, because I'm the one who's determined to get hospice care.

"It's no big deal," Michael said when I explained how Tom had come over one evening to bring work. I told him that Gram had read it all wrong. He said not to worry, that he believed me. I hope he does. He refused to discuss it any further. When he's through talking about something, not even the Pope could pry words out of his mouth.

I'll never figure Gram out. At times I wonder if she's trying to put a wedge between Michael and me. I refuse to let that happen. I had a life, a good life, with Michael before she came to live with us.

I love Gram, but I often despise her actions. Sometimes, she makes me so angry I could spit fire. Other times, I see this frail, vulnerable person who simply wants to go on living, and I want to rock her in my arms. I'm so confused. Some days I pray that she'll fall asleep and not awaken. Other times, I wonder how the only parent I've ever known can dare to walk out of my life? Gram flipflops too. She can be loving one minute, and the next, she's angry and bitter. I'm guessing it may be because I'll go on living after she dies.

The only thing I am certain of right now is that I'm too tired to analyze her feelings or my own any longer. For now, all I want is to get to sleep, get up in the morning, and get the biopsy over with, so I can get some help.

## Chapter Fifteen

Carrie ripped a page off the *Far Side* calendar on the kitchen desk. The nurse called with a report on Gram's biopsy. Carrie was ready to punch her fist into the wall. The biopsy failed because the doctor didn't take enough tissue from Gram's lung. Carrie felt as frazzled as the cartoon character on the New Year's Eve calendar page. Couldn't anything go right?

Trying to keep her cool, Carrie decided to make a loaf of banana bread, hoping that Gram would want some for lunch. She preheated the oven, then got out the ingredients. After buttering a loaf pan, she cracked the eggs on the edge of the countertop and dropped them into the blender, then added the dry ingredients to the eggs and turned it on. The mixture whipped around in circles, then shot out of the blender onto the cabinets, the counter, the floor, the ceiling, and all over Carrie.

"God bless it all," Carrie screamed, wiping batter from her face. "I forgot to put the lid on the stupid blender."

It took her almost an hour to clean up the mess. She had to stick Sophie-dog out on the screened porch, so she wouldn't lick the batter off of the floor. Carrie didn't need a sick dog in the middle of the mess. She had to get a small step ladder to climb onto the kitchen counter to wipe a few blobs of batter off the ceiling.

Finally, she sat at the kitchen table and tried to read the morning paper. But she could think only about the day before when she and Gram had spent hours in the outpatient zoo at St. Joseph's hospital. Lying in the hospital bed, in an oversized blue and white checked gown, an IV tube connected to her bony arm, Gram looked so frightened. Carrie was relieved when a nurse gave her a sedative.

While Gram slept, Carrie sat across the small room on an uncomfortable metal chair, doodling on her notepad. She drew blobs, looking like jellyfish with long tentacles, then penciled in polka dots on the jellyfish. Then two nurses came in and wheeled Gram out and directed Carrie to a waiting room.

She shook her head to bring her mind back to the present. What a waste of time, Carrie thought as she got up from the table. Standing at the kitchen sink in her black jeans, last summer's Peachtree Road Race T-shirt, her feet comfortable in her old moccasins, she felt guilty for making Gram go through with the biopsy. Rain pelted the window like it wanted to nudge her into action. She cut a Granny Smith into wedges and ate them. Then she dialed Dr. Kirkland's office.

"He's with a patient. I can put you on hold," the receptionist said. Carrie paced the kitchen floor listening to elevator music. Dr. Kirkland's image popped into view—his bald head, dark-framed glasses, long, skinny face, sagging cheeks, topping his small-framed body. At five feet seven, Carrie was at least two inches taller than the doctor. When he answered, his abrupt voice startled her. Carrie explained that Gram saw Dr. Baker, the oncologist, whom he had recommended.

"I took her in for the biopsy yesterday, but it didn't work."

"What do you mean, it didn't work?"

Carrie talked fast. "He didn't take enough tissue, so we still don't have proof that her tumor is malignant."

"Slow down, please. I can hardly understand you. Are you saying that the biopsy failed to confirm a diagnosis?" She told him yes. She felt like telling him to chill out.

"My grandmother is getting worse every day, and I'm having a rough time trying to care for her. Believe me, Dr. Kirkland, I am desperate for help," Carrie said in a slow, deliberate voice.

"She needs radiation," the doctor said.

"I understand that, and I've tried my best to talk her into it, but she refuses to have any kind of treatment. I can't force her to do it." Carrie felt hammers pounding her temples.

"When I saw her in my office, Mrs. Whitfield looked quite good."

"Looks can be deceiving," Carrie said, ready to explode. "I'm with her day and night, and I can assure you she is on a downward spiral. Gram can barely walk, even with her walker, and she can't write her own name anymore. She can no longer read. She's often confused; sometimes, she doesn't even know who I am. She has difficulty swallowing and coughs, this deep, raspy cough all of the time." Carrie pushed her bangs away from her sweaty forehead.

"Perhaps the biopsy should be redone."

"No. I can't make her go through that again. I just can't." Carrie told him how Gram had slept for fifteen hours, without waking, after they had returned home from the hospital.

Dr. Kirkland let out a loud sigh. "Okay, fine. I'll try to arrange for a visiting nurse to come to your home. Someone will call you." Carrie thanked him. He hung up without saying good-bye.

Carrie slammed the receiver down. What *was* his problem? Did his lack of interest have anything to do with the fact that dying patients don't bring in the bucks? Carrie decided that, yes, it probably did. She went down the hallway.

"Lunch is ready. Let's go out to the kitchen," Carrie said, opening the door to Gram's room. There was no point in telling her about the useless biopsy.

"I'm not hungry, but I am quite thirsty. My iced tea pitcher is empty." Gram pointed to the pitcher.

"Here, you hold this," Carrie said after she got Gram into her wheelchair. She handed Gram the pitcher. Gram didn't put up a fuss like she ususally did when Carrie insisted on using the wheelchair. The day before, trying to walk down the hallway behind her walker, Gram lost her balance and fell to the floor. Carrie wrenched her back trying to get her up on her feet. Gram, who now weighed ninety pounds, felt like dead weight to Carrie.

"It's cold in here, Caroline," Gram said, when Carrie scooted her up to the table. Carrie turned up the thermostat. Gram crossed her arms and held them close to her chest.

Sophie-dog ran in front of Carrie over to get her sockie and then dropped the worn-out gray sock at Gram's feet. Reaching down to get the sockie and throw it was impossible for Gram; it would make her too short of breath.

"It should warm up in here soon. Kay says it's always cold and damp around here on New Year's Eve," Carrie said. Gram asked how Kay was doing. "She had more back surgery, and now she's home recuperating."

"Too much surgery is a bad idea," Gram said. "I hope they don't ruin her back. These doctors just want to make money. That's what I think."

"I agree with you. Though, I suppose there are still *some* decent doctors out there." Carrie set a glass of iced tea down in front of Gram.

"Where's Michael?"

"Working, as usual. I hope he gets home early. I get tired of his long hours." Carrie set a plate with a scoop of chicken salad, mandarin oranges, and a slice of Pepperidge Farm white bread in front of Gram. She didn't bother to tell Gram about her banana bread fiasco.

"Don't be so hard on Michael. He's got an important job," Gram said.

"I know." Carrie shook her head. Obviously, Michael had climbed up another notch. While Gram ate, Carrie emptied the dishwasher.

"Michael reminds me of your father," Gram said.

"He does?"

"Yes, Richard was kind, just like Michael."

No wonder Gram had changed her mind about Michael. Carrie remembered Aunt Nella saying that her brother, Richard, had been Gram's prize child. She had detected jealousy in Aunt Nella's voice.

"I can't eat anymore. I can't taste anything, and besides, I hurt too much."

"Where's the pain, Gram."

"Up here—down there." Gram pointed up, then down. "I don't know. It jumps around, everywhere." Gram jiggled the ice cubes in her glass.

"Just eat what you can," Carrie said, pouring her more iced tea. At least Gram ate her chicken salad.

The sun coming in the window had turned the kitchen yellow. For Gram, the warm rays had a hypnotic power. Her head bobbed down to her chest. When the phone rang, Carrie snatched it off of the hook. Gram's head popped back up.

"Oh, you're home," Liz said.

"Yes, I'm still here. Where else would I be?" Carrie said, laughing. She told Liz that the doctor might arrange for a nurse to help out. "I'll walk over to see you after while," Carrie said, after they had chatted for a few minutes. Gram was awake now, and Carrie didn't want her eavesdropping.

"Did you say something about a nurse coming here?" Gram asked.

"Yes, I did. I talked to Dr. Kirkwood this morning, and he said he may send a nurse here to help out." Gram pursed her lips, staring at Carrie.

Across the room, Carrie could see the letter Gram gave her at Christmas sitting in the front of the letter box on the desk. Now was as good a time as any to ask if she could read it. Besides, Carrie wanted to change the subject.

"May I read the letter you gave me? It's New Year's Eve. You said I could read it today."

"Sure. Go ahead."

"Tell me more about the person it came from," Carrie said.

"It came from Rebecca Stone, a friend of your mother's family. She sent it to me after Richard and Mary Caroline got married. It arrived a week or so before Richard brought your mother home to meet me." Carrie was amazed at how clear-headed Gram sounded. There were brief moments, especially when they discussed the past, when Gram's mind was lucid.

"It's a strange letter." Gram said.

Carrie pulled the thin pages from the envelope and carefully unfolded the letter. It was writttten in elegant longhand. She started to read:

*My dear Mrs. Whitfield. You will doubtless be surprised to see the penmanship of a perfect stranger. I am a friend of the family of Mary Caroline Campbell. It has occurred to me, that since your son married suddenly, you might appreciate the unprejudiced appraisal of the new member of the family. I will venture to make a few comments on her behalf.*

*Your son, Richard, met Mary Caroline while on a business trip to Vancouver. Richard and a few of his friends went to a carnival in the city and met Mary Caroline and her friends there. Your son and Mary Caroline experienced one of those love-at-first-sight things. Though their courtship was brief, it was so intense that the short period of time seemed insignificant.*

*As far as Mary Caroline is concerned, she is a refined young lady who possesses high ideals and good principles. You will never have to offer any apologies for this bright, young Catholic girl. She loves to read and, according to her mother, she keeps a daily journal. Some of her poetry has been published. I believe this tall, small-boned girl with big blue eyes and striking auburn hair will be an asset to your family.*

*I have no doubt that the marriage will be a long and happy one. Richard and Mary Caroline make a trim-looking young couple and appear to be thoroughly oblivious to the world at large.*

*I trust, Mrs. Whitfield, that I have helped you in expressing myself. I did want you to know what a lovely bride your son has selected. Yours very sincerely, Rebecca L. Stone.*

Carrie clutched the letter to her chest. Why in the world hadn't Gram shown her the letter before now?

"Gram, I didn't know that my mother was a Catholic."

"She was baptized a Lutheran right before she died. You and your mother were both baptized in the hospital room." Carrie gave Gram a puzzled look. "Check that envelope. I think there's a an old newspaper clipping inside there."

Carrie peeked inside the envelope. Folded up at the bottom of the envelope, she found a yellowed obituary from *The Sheboygan Press*. The caption read

*Death of Mrs. Richard Whitfield*

*Mrs. Richard Whitfield, age 22, died early this morning from injuries she received in an automobile accident which occurred two weeks ago on County*

*Trunk J. The deceased, formerly Miss Mary Caroline Campbell, was married in May of 1964 to Richard Whitfield at her home in Vancouver, B.C. Mr. Whitfield, who preceded her in death, immediately following the car accident, brought his new wife to Sheboygan to live last fall. They had one daughter, Caroline Louise Whitfield, born September 20, 1965. Both Mrs. Whitfield and her daughter were baptized as Lutherans at the hospital, just two days before Mrs. Whitfield died. Mrs. Whitfield was the daughter of Thomas and Elizabeth Campbell of Vancouver, B.C. She had one brother, Harry, also of Vancouver. Funeral arrangements are pending.*

"Gram, thank you for the letter and the article."

"I'd like to go back to my room now," Gram said, paying little attention to Carrie's excitement. She had climbed back inside herself. Carrie knew better than to try to open the door. She had a feeling that Gram hadn't wanted to share the old letter and the obituary with her. Perhaps for Gram, it had been a form of bargaining for more time.

"I need a cigarette. Right now," Gram said when she got back into her room.

"I'll bring you some. But first, could you answer a question?"

"Okay," Gram said. Carrie asked Gram if she had any of her mother's written work.

"There might be some in my old trunk." Gram told her she hadn't seen the trunk for years, that it might be in Nella's attic. "Now, can I have my cigarettes?" Carrie left, then returned with the Salems. Gram grabbed them out of her hand and lit one up. Carrie told Gram she planned to walk over to see Kay.

"I won't be gone long." Carrie put Kay's phone number beside the phone on Gram's bedside table. Carrie decided to wait to leave until Gram finished smoking. Sophie-dog ran in circles around the room. "Sophie-dog, you stay here and keep Gram company." The dog curled up at Gram's feet.

"Michael should be home any time now. I'll leave him a note."

Before leaving, Carrie made sure the answering machine was on in case the doctor's office called about the visiting nurse. She grabbed her windbreaker from the hall closet and went out the door.

"Come on in," Dave said, opening the door. "Kay's waiting for you."

"Hello there. I hope your New Year's Eve is going better than mine," Carrie said. Kay lay stretched out on the recliner in a burgundy sweat shirt and black stretch pants. "You look pretty chipper today."

"I feel much better than I did after the first surgery. I think they got it right this time. How are you doing?"

"Not that great." Carrie told Kay about the failed biopsy and about her conversation with the doctor. "What makes me furious is that Dr. Kirkland makes me feel guilty. He makes it seem like I *want* Gram to die."

"At least you'll be getting nursing help," Kay said. "What about hospice? Did he sign you up?"

"No, because he doesn't think she's terminal. The biopsy was supposed to prove that her tumor is malignant. Without that proof, he says he can't sign the papers."

"What a mess," Kay said. She wanted to know how the doctors in Wisconsin had known that Gram's tumor was malignant. Carrie repeated Dr. Edgar's words, telling Kay that the tumor hadn't shown up on an X-ray they had done a year ago. However, when they had X-rayed her in September, only eight months later, the tumor had grown quite large in a short time. "Did you tell Dr. Kirkland that?"

"Of course, I did. I even offered to ask Dr. Edgar to send his report and the X-rays from Wisconsin. He ignored me." Carrie stood and stretched. "I feel like such a blob. I never get any exercise anymore. Sorry I'm such poor company. I look like crap too." Carrie told Kay about the banana bread explosion all over the kitchen.

Kay laughed. "Hang in there. Things have to get better."

"I'm not so sure about that," Carrie said, sitting back down. "When I agreed to care for Gram, I had no idea what I'd signed up for." Dave came into the room and brought a plate of oatmeal raisin cookies.

"Did you make these?" Carrie asked. "These are my favorite cookies."

"Actually—no," Dave said, laughing. "Bernice Frazier, from down the street, brought them over after she heard Kay had surgery again." Dave left the room, saying he would be working in the backyard.

"I do have some good news. I almost forgot," Carrie said, after she wolfed down four cookies. She told Kay about the letter.

"Did you know your mother was Catholic?"

"Aunt Nella mentioned it once."

"How ironic that you plan to become a Catholic. Must have been fate."

Carrie told Kay about the old trunk and how she planned to look for it when she went to Jennifer's wedding shower in Wisconsin. "I hope I can get away. If this nurse thing works out, maybe I can hire one of them to stay with Gram." Carrie got up. She was reluctant to leave, but she knew she'd better get home.

"Here's to good things in the New Year," Carrie said. "Visiting with you is saving my sanity."

"Mine too," Kay said.

※

Walking into the house, she saw Michael on his hands and knees srubbing the hallway carpet with a brush. A plastic bottle of carpet cleaner sat on the floor beside him. "What happened?"

"Sophie-dog barfed on the carpet. I got home about twenty minutes ago and found the dog upchucking and Gram having a nervous fit. The dog's in the laundry room with the door shut. Gram's happier now. I gave her some cigarettes."

Carrie checked on Sophie-dog. The laundry room smelled like a portapotty. Newpapers lay on the floor. The dog stood in a mess of barf and runny poop, having the dry heaves. "Yuck," Carrie said, shutting the door. She hurried to the kitchen and called the vet. The receptionist told her to bring Sophie-dog right in. Since it was New Year's Eve, they planned to close early.

Carrie told Michael where she was going. "Could you please clean up the laundry room?" she asked him, giving him a crazy grin. He rolled his eyes and made a face at her. "Welcome to my world," Carrie said. "Fun, isn't it? I'll tell Gram where I'm going."

"What's wrong with puppy dog?" Gram asked after Carrie explained.

"We don't know. She's very sick."

"Aren't you going to change your clothes?" Gram asked. "You look as ratty as Eudelle Biggs." Carrie glanced at her soiled jeans and T-shirt, covered with stains from the banana bread caper.

"I'll put my jacket over this shirt. I don't have time to do anything else." Carrie said. A picture of Eudelle Biggs popped into her head. Eudelle, who used to come to their house in Sheyboygan to hang wallpaper, always wore faded jeans and white men's shirts with food stains all over them. "Gram, remember Eudelle's husband? He always came along with her and held the ladder for her. He would sing 'What A Friend I Have in Jesus' over and over while she hung the wallpaper."

"Oh, I remember that old coot. His fly was always open." Carrie left Gram's room laughing.

Not wanting the dog to mess up the car, she hurried out the door with Sophie-dog in a box. On the drive, Roswell Road was jammed with New Year's Eve traffic.

Carrie thought about how pitiful Gram looked. Reading the Elizabeth Kubler-Ross book had clarified for Carrie the stages of death. Gram had passed from the denial stage to the angry stage. She was complaining more, making more demands. "Don't leave me out. I'm not dead yet," Gram had said several times in the past week. Carrie knew Gram hated giving up control of life. Who could blame her? Her comment was understandable. No wonder she was angry.

"We're here, finally," she said to Sophie-dog.

"Go right on in. He'll be with you in a few minutes," the receptionist said. A nervous Sophie-dog began to whimper.

"I think it's another pancreas attack," the vet said. "We'll have to keep her a couple of days. She's probably eaten some table food. Do you have little children in the house?"

"No," Carrie said. "No, we don't."

Lionel Richie's "You Are the World" played on the car radio as she drove home. In the middle of the song, it dawned on Carrie—they *did* have a child in the house. No wonder Gram's chicken salad disappeared at lunch. Gram must have dropped it onto the floor for Sophie-dog. Carrie ran her fingers through her hair, brushing it behind her ears. She was anxious to get home. Somehow, she would manage a New Year's Eve celebration with Michael.

By seven, Carrie had showered and dressed in her peach cashmere sweater and gray pants. Gram was down for the night. The potatoes were baking in the oven. While Michael grilled steaks, she tossed salad with Romaine lettuce, tomatoes, feta cheese, Chinese noodles, and balsamic vinegar dressing.

"To good things in 1988," Michael said, clinking wine glasses, after they sat in the dining room. As they ate, they told each other funny stories. Michael told her how, as a little boy, he had taken his wooden hammer and knocked holes in every watermelon in his grandfather's garden.

"Geez, you must have gotten into big trouble."

"More with my mom than Grandpa." Carrie laughed. Michael was handsome in his burgundy turtle neck and khaki pants. Burgundy was a good color on him. He smelled good too. She stood and kissed him on the back of the neck and touched him lightly on the cheek.

"Thanks," he said. "You sit down."

He poured her another glass of red wine. "I'll put this stuff in the dishwasher." Carrie accepted his offer.

It wasn't until after he came back to the table that Michael dropped the bomb. While sipping his coffee, he told Carrie about the call from the doctor's office.

"Did they call to say when the nurses would start coming?"

"No, there's a bit of a complication."

"I'm not so sure I want to hear this," Carrie said. She put her thumbs under her chin and held her forehead on her fingertips.

"According to the girl who called, someone from the Visiting Nurses Association called here this afternoon, when we were both gone. Gram answered the phone. When the nurse tried to set up an appointment,

Gram told her that next week would not be a good time for a nurse to come."

"Oh, great?" Carrie said. "What did she do that for?"

"Brace yourself," Michael said. "Gram told the lady that she had to work at the hospital every day next week, doing her volunteer job in the nursery."

"What!" Carrie screamed. "That woman is trying to drive me crazy. She volunteered in the hospital nursery several years ago. I can't believe she said that." Carrie's dinner nosedived in her stomach.

"The girl I spoke with said, if Gram was able to do volunteer work, that she wasn't eligible to have a nurse come."

"I tried, but didn't get anywhere. You need to call on Monday and clear things up."

"I never should have brought her here. You were right. Gram should be in a nursing home."

"I don't mind having Gram here," he said, reaching for her hand.

"Well, I do," Carrie said pulling her hand away. Carrie ran out of the room and up the stairs. "Stop it. Stop it. Don't let her ruin your life," she screamed at her own image in her vanity mirror.

Carrie went to the bathroom, then washed her face and put on fresh lipstick. She went back downstairs wearing a skimpy black nightgown under her red velour robe.

"Want to play gin rummy?" Michael asked when she walked into the great room.

"Sure." Carrie got the cards out of a small drawer in the antique chest sitting next to the game table then sat down across from Michael. "You won last time. It's your turn to deal." Carrie won the first game, and he won the next two. They finished a few minutes before midnight. Michael turned on the television set, so they could watch the big apple fall in Times Square.

At the stroke of midnight, Carrie fell into Michael's arms for a kiss. "Let's go to bed," Carrie said, pressing her body into Michael's.

"Yes, ma'am," Michael said.

"Go on up. I'll be right there, after I check on Gram."

Carrie opened Gram's door and tiptoed into the room.

"Happy New Year, Gram," she whispered, then left the room, careful not to make any noise closing the door.

Upstairs, she threw off her robe. Climbing into bed, she reached for Michael, vowing to drown out any clangs of the cowbell.

## Chapter Sixteen

JOURNAL, MONDAY, JANUARY 25, 1988

We're making some progress around here—at least Gram likes Annie and Rhonda, the nurses. She thinks they bathe her better than I do, and I say glory, hallelujah, they can have the job. "Oh how I loved to dance," Gram said to Annie today. "I'd wear one of my fancy dresses, my spike heels, and stay out until the dance hall closed. And," she said, raising her eyebrows, "I never missed a dance." While they bathe her and check her blood presure and temperature, Gram keeps the nurses entertained. They only come twice a week, thirty minutes each time. It's just a pebble in the pond, but I'm grateful.

I still can't believe Gram almost sabatoged my efforts to get this smidgen of help. When I phoned the visiting nurses' place, I talked fast, presenting my case, and, finally, the lady said she would send the nurses here. Who knows why Gram made up the story about how she had to go to work? She probably doesn't know why herself. Sometimes, Gram puts herself in the past as a means of coping with the present.

One thing is certain. I was naïve to assume that the nurses know how to deal with a dying patient. Annie, Gram's tall, skinny black nurse, ran into the kitchen hollering for me today. "Miz Carrie, Miz Carrie, your grandmother is coughing so hard, she's choking. Come quick. I'm 'fraid she's gonna gag herself to death," she said. I rolled my eyes, then hurried down the hallway to Gram's room. After Gram calmed down, Annie bolted out of here, and my shoulders tightened. I am still alone at the helm.

Rhonda, the older, roly-poly nurse, has agreed to stay with Gram next Friday, so I can go to the wedding shower. She'll stay here until Michael comes home from work. He offered to take care of Gram on Saturday and Sunday, and I accepted his offer with reluctance, knowing that he'll have his hands full. I plan to take along an empty suitcase, then return it with some of Gram's things we left at the storage place. Jennifer said that she found Gram's old trunk in her mother's attic, and I'm anxious to see if my mother's journals are in the trunk. I can't wait to get out of here; God knows, I need a break.

Dr. Kirkland, who remains a major pain, called today complaining that Gram's nurses are phoning him way too often. This guy gets under my skin like poison ivy. His attitude is discombobulating my insides. I swallowed the negative comments that dared to come out, because I wanted some information, like why was Gram getting so shaky?

"It's probably because she needs food. You must get her to eat," he said.

"That would be as easy as getting her to walk on stilts," I said, then told him how Gram could hardly swallow and only ate stuff like jello, pudding, and baby food. He suggested a liquid diet supplement, then hung up. I pounded my fist on the kitchen counter.

This morning it was bright and sunny, so I took Gram for a ride in the car. She insisted on dressing up in her navy blue and red flowered silk blouse, navy polyester pants, and dangly gold earrings. I vetoed high heels. She protested, but I forced her to put on her blue flats, then struggled to get her out to the car. "I hate seatbelts," she said, as we drove away. I stopped the car at the bottom of the driveway and waited.

"You have to buckle up, Gram. It's the law."

"Phooey. Why bother? These things are a nuisance." Gram glared at me, giving me her pursed-lip look. I started to tell her that wearing a seat belt had saved a lot of lives, but didn't, knowing the comment seemed a bit absurd.

We took 285 and headed to Stone Mountain Park. Driving around the park, we went past the sightseeing train, the riverboat, and the antebellum plantation house. "Remember the carving, Gram?" I said, stopping near the immense Confederate stone carving on the side of the mountain. "It's as big as a whole football field. We saw it last spring." She didn't say anything. I couldn't tell if she remembered or not. Sunlight danced on the trees. The blue granite on the sides of the road glistened. It made me want to get out and hike to the top of the mountain, Michael and I used to hike often.

"How long before we get there?" Gram asked on the way home. She fell asleep before we got back onto the freeway. On the floor beside my seat sat a bag of Attends, baby wipes, and a thermos of iced tea. I wonder if caring for Gram was practice for the children I want to have some day. I don't know if Gram enjoyed getting out of our prison, but just going for a drive made me feel like a kid at the circus.

Sophie-dog, who is doing okay now, did flips when we arrived home. I gave Gram a stern lecture about *never* feeding her table food again. She seems to have gotten the message; but, of course, the soft food she eats now isn't as easy to drop onto the floor. After Sophie-dog came home from the vet Gram wanted to know if the dog had cancer. I told her no, that she'd had some kind of pancreatic attack.

"I thought she might have cancer. It runs in our family, you know," Gram said. "You'll get it, too, Caroline."

I clenched my jaw, wanting to scream at her to shut up. The way Gram sometimes says whatever she's thinking irritates me. I'm the opposite. Trying not to lose control, I often shelve my thoughts, and, at this point, my shelf is getting full. I'm like an unvented dish in the microwave oven.

Most of the time, I indulge Gram, caretake her feelings, even though she shows no regard for mine. Earlier this week, I dropped my guard.

"My God, Gram, if you aren't careful, you're going to burn the house down," I said, when I found a cigarette burn in the carpet beside her chair. She acted unconcerned until I mentioned that Michael would be upset. Then, she agreed to be more careful.

Michael's gone way too much. In the past three weeks, since New

Year's weekend, we've spent little time together. At least I got out of here last Saturday to go shopping. Once I left, I wanted to keep on going—to the mountains, or wherever. Instead, I went to Perimeter Mall and bought an expensive silk dress. I figured—life is short—so why not? I bought Gram a new pink and white striped cotton bathrobe. That evening she smiled when Michael told her she looked nice in her new robe. She wants to wear it everyday. It's interesting. Now, I'm the one who talks about putting Gram into a nursing home, and Michael, who has become Gram's buddy, insists it isn't a good idea, that she belongs with her family.

Yesterday, I ran down the hallway when Gram clanged the cowbell. (I swear, when this is all over, I'm going to bury that blasted thing.) When I got to her room, Gram was in bed watching a "Roadrunner" cartoon and didn't remember ringing the cowbell. I sat down in the chair next to her bed, baffled that the cartoon kept her entertained.

"I don't think of Jesus in fancy robes," she said, when the cartoon show ended. "I just think of Him as a good friend, and—he looks just like Michael."

"Right," I said with sarcasm. Obviously, Michael remains perched on a pedestal. When I told Michael the Jesus story on the phone, he thought it was pretty funny. Gram asked over and over when Michael would be home from his meeting in "Prebble Beach." I told her that her savior would be home soon. The sooner the better—I'm about to dig a hole to China.

Gram talks about Jennifer's wedding and describes her new dress and her grandmother's corsage. Attending the wedding is an absolute impossibility for her. I think she knows that but can't give up hope.

Aunt Nella needs to get her buns down here and visit her mother. Just yesterday, I asked her to come for a visit, and the excuses flew out of her mouth faster than a stunt clown out of the cannon. She's tied up with wedding plans and trips to Las Vegas—another addiction, I suppose. "Force her to come," Tom Egan said, insisting that she'll feel guilty if she doesn't get see Gram again before she dies. He has a good point.

Tom's been a good friend. Desperate for company, I invited him over after Gram fell asleep tonight. We had a glass of wine, and I went over some travel arrangements he and his partners want me to make. Tom listens while I do a running monologue, voicing my concerns. Tonight, when he left, he gave me a big, tight hug. I needed that. I can still smell his musky aftershave.

Right now, my hand is limp, just like the rest of me. I'm ready to crash.

## Chapter Seventeen

"Step right this way, young lady. I'll get your suitcase for you."

"Herman! Hello." Carrie hurried over toward his van. "Geez, it's cold out here," she said, "the hairs in my nose are starting to freeze."

He chuckled. "Aw, you've been in Georgia too long. Your blood's all thinned out."

"Maybe so."

"I saw your name on the list of pickups today and arranged it with Bert so I could come get you." He placed her suitcase in the back of the van, then opened the front passenger door. Carrie climbed in. She put her gloves in her pocket, then unbuttoned her red wool coat.

"How's Madeline doing?"

"Terrible. She's in bad shape."

"Sorry to hear that. Do you think she'll ever get back this way?"

"Oh, no. That's out of the question. She's wants to come to Jennifer's wedding, but she knows she can't."

"Too bad. I suppose that gets her down."

"Oh, yes. She and Jennifer have always been very close. Gram told me about a dream she had last week. In the dream, she was dancing at Jennifer's wedding reception, wearing a fancy lilac flowered dress and a big orchid corsage."

"I miss Madeline. I miss her a lot."

"She's really enjoyed the cards you've sent."

"My wife, Iona, helped pick them out. Did I tell you that I got

"You did? Well, congratulations." Carrie gave him a puzzled look.

"Yep, right before Christmas."

"You know," Herman said, as he passed a rusty red pickup truck. "Madeline and I were close friends. I don't mind telling you that we were in AA together. She got up in the middle of the night one rainy October evening and went on what we call a 12-step call. I was fresh out of detox, and I craved booze that night like the dickens. Madeline stayed up half the night talking to me. She told me one funny story after another."

"Did she? That sounds like Gram."

"Without her, I'd still be nursing the bottle. She kept me going to AA meetings, and I called her many times for moral support. I've been sober for over ten years now, and, believe you me, Madeline deserves the credit for that."

"I'm sure some of the credit belongs to you." Carrie was surprised that Gram had never mentioned seeing Herman at her AA meetings at the 1907 Club.

"You seem surprised," Herman said. "You know—what we shared at meetings—well, that stuff is confidential."

Carrie decided that made sense.

"When we had parties at the club, Madeline was quite popular. We used to stand in line for a chance to dance with her. She could outlast us all."

Herman hummed a few bars of "New York, New York," bouncing his head up and down in time to the music. Carrie pictured Gram all dressed up, twirling around the dance floor, her high heels clicking.

Herman said, "I read a quote from this poet the other day, and darn if it didn't remind me of Madeline."

Carrie glanced over. Herman didn't seem like the poetry type. She watched out the window, studying the farms alongside Highway 43, just north of Port Washington. The landscape looked like a Norman Rockwell painting—picturesque barns and silos, white snow piled up on the ground like fluffy frosting. The scene made her think of cold snowy days as a child, sitting near the fireplace playing gin rummy or double solitaire with Gram.

"I've got it in my head now," Herman said, interrupting her thoughts. "I remember the quote. The poem went something like this, 'Life is a party and death is having to go home, all the while knowing, that the party will go on without you.' I bet that's how Madeline must be feeling about now."

"You know Gram pretty well."

"Yes, dear, I do." Herman appeared lost in thought.

Staring out the window, Carrie thought about Gram and wondered how she and Rhonda were getting along. Gram had seemed nervous when Carrie kissed her good-bye, leaving her with the nurse. She checked her watch. Michael would be home by late afternoon.

"You're looking kinda sad," Herman said as they passed the turn off to Cedar Grove.

"Well, I am. I've been thinking about Gram and how she wants to die. She insists that it won't be long. At bedtime, she tells me good-bye, not good night. It's tough. I keep telling her she's not the one in charge." Carrie laughed. "I'm sure I don't have to tell you. Gram likes to call the shots."

"Oh, yes, indeed." Herman smiled, shaking his head. He turned on the radio.

"It will be clear and cold this evening," the announcer said. "The low temperature will be two degrees. Tomorrow it will be sunny and cold with a high of twelve degrees and a wind chill of four below zero." Carrie folded her arms, holding onto her elbows, and shuddered.

"Hope you brought along your warm clothes," he said, then asked when she was returning home.

"Sunday."

"Sounds like a quick trip."

"I can't be gone long. My husband's staying with Gram, and I can assure you, he's in for a difficult weekend."

"Don't you worry. It'll all work out," Herman said as he pulled into the Newbys' driveway. "Iona and I will keep Madeline in our prayers."

"Thanks, I'll be sure and tell Gram you said hello."

"You're a special young lady," Herman said, carrying her suitcase to the front door, "so good to your grandmother. Madeline did a right fine job raising you. She's always been mighty proud of you. Even if she doesn't show it now, I know she appreciates what you're doing for her." Carrie hugged him good-bye.

The door opened and there was Helen in a flour-covered red apron, and the air inside the house had the aroma of fresh baking. "Honey, it's so good to see you," Helen said, "Just take your things on down to your room, and then come into the kitchen. I have a surprise for you."

In the kitchen, Carrie found a fresh slice of banana cream pie and a cup of hot tea waiting on the round oak table near the bay window.

"Have a seat, honey. We've got some catching up to do." Helen took off her apron off and sat across from Carrie.

The pie was creamy sweet. "Helen, this is to die for. I can feel my waistline expanding." Carrie patted her stomach.

"More?"

"Heavens, no. I can't eat another bite."

"Honey, looks like you've lost weight."

"I don't feel much like eating these days."

"It's getting bad, isn't it?"

"Uh huh." Carrie propped her elbow on the table and rested her head on the fingertips of her right hand. "Helen, you're a nurse. How do you deal with dying patients?"

"It's never easy, Carrie. What you're doing takes superhuman effort." Helen touched her hand.

"I'm losing it, Helen. I've had to give up everything—my time with Michael, my job, going out with my friends, exercising, my time alone—and I'm not dealing with it very well. Besides, I'm a lousy caretaker."

"You've taken on quite a load. I'm sure you're doing just fine."

"I feel guilty when I complain. After all, Gram's dying."

"Well, you can't keep everything all jammed up inside."

Carrie explained her failed attempt to get hospice help and how she hated the doctor.

"Mercy, girl. Seems to me Madeline's a perfect candidate for hospice."

"She is. I'm disillusioned with the whole medical world," Carrie said.

"Some doctors can be a major pain in the rear. That's for sure."

Carrie laughed and excused herself. She called home. Michael sounded frustrated. He told her how Gram had stayed awake all afternoon playing hostess to Rhonda.

"Good heavens, why? I hired Rhonda to take care of her."

"Who knows why Gram does anything?" Michael said. He held the phone away from his ear and asked Gram if she wanted to say hello to Carrie.

"She doesn't want to talk to you."

"Why not? Is she angry with me for leaving?"

"That's not it."

"What have I done wrong now?"

Michael explained how he'd gone outside to blow leaves off the driveway. And, while he was outside, the phone had rung. Gram answered it. It had been Father O'Brien from the church.

"Father O'Brien? Oh geez, why would he call?"

"Eva, the lady who brings Gram communion, told Father O'Brien about Gram, and he called to see if she wanted to receive the Sacrament of the Sick."

"Oh, good Lord."

"So I had to tell Gram that you're planning to convert. I'm sorry. I didn't know what to say, so I told her the truth."

"Oh well. She had to find out sometime."

Michael described the scene—Gram, beady-eyed, shaking her finger at him, telling him that Carrie was doomed. "I told her you were becoming a Catholic for me."

"Well, that's not the truth. I'm doing it for myself."

"Whatever," he sighed. "I've got to go. She's clanging the cowbell."

Carrie stifled a laugh. She could relate.

She took a long, hot shower, then dressed in her matching tan pants and cable knit sweater. She put a gold chain around her neck and stepped into her leopard print loafers.

"Carrie, are you ready?" a familiar voice called out.

"Jennifer, come on in." Carrie gave her a tight hug. "You look like you've spent the last three weeks in Florida."

"I've been going to the tanning salon," Jennifer said. Next to her cousin, Carrie knew she looked pasty white. Carrie held her red woolen coat tight around her as they walked to the car. It was black outside. She had forgotten how early it got dark in Wisconsin in December.

Driving to the shower, Jennifer rattled on and on about wedding details. Carrie half listened as she thought back to her own wedding day, remembering the happy look on Michael's face when she walked down the aisle on Uncle Jim's arm. Before the wedding, Carrie had worried that the world would end before she could marry the man she loved and spend happy days with him. Who would have guessed that in just over a year their lives would change so much?

"Did you like being an only child?" Jennifer asked.

"Not really—though I never thought much about it. I didn't have much choice," Carrie said. "How about you?"

"I always wanted a brother or sister, but Mom always told me it wasn't possible, that she couldn't have another baby. Kevin and I want a bunch of kids."

"Michael says he wants four. I want two. We'll just have to see what happens. I'm not in any hurry. Besides, I can't think about it right now."

"How's Gram?" Jennifer asked. "She looked pretty bad when we brought her down to Atlanta."

"She's much worse. Her face isn't as puffy now, but it looks distorted—her eyelids droop, her bones protrude, and her skin has this eerie yellowish cast."

Carrie paused, then said, "You'd better get down to see her before it's too late."

"I'd like to, Carrie, really I would. But I don't know. I have a really big project to complete at work and last-minute wedding details to handle."

"Don't wait too long," Carrie said.

Jennifer stopped at the curb in front of her friend Amy's house, then glanced at Carrie, not saying anything. Carrie stared into Jennifer's bright blue eyes, big and round like her own. At least she had given her cousin food for thought, she decided as they got out of the car.

The wedding shower seemed long to Carrie. She enjoyed seeing familiar faces, but the light-hearted chit-chat and silly games did nothing to squelch the apprenhension knawing her insides. There was no escaping the problems at home.

On the ride back to Helen's, Carrie thought about Gram and the religion issue. She would explain to Gram how at first she'd simply wanted to go to church with Michael. However, kneeling beside him at mass, she had felt a sense of belonging, a sense of peace that had triggered her decision. She hoped Gram would understand. This is between me and God, she thought, not between me and Gram.

Dropping Carrie back at Helen's house, Jennifer said she would pick her up at nine the next morning for breakfast at the pancake house with Aunt Nella. Then, they would go to the storage place and go through Gram's things.

"Will your mom be coming to the storage place with us?"

"No, she's going to visit Aunt Rae at the nursing home."

"Okay, see you tomorrow." Carrie ran up the steps and hurried inside. She hung her coat in the front hall closet, then peeked into the den. Helen sat in the blue leather recliner, two pillows behind her back, with her feet outstretched, working on a cross-stitch project. Ben had already gone to bed.

"How was the shower?"

"Oh, fine," Carrie said. "What are you making?"

"A sampler for Liz, for her graduation in May. She called tonight. I just hung up the phone. She said to tell you hello. She asked if I would tell you what I know about your parents' car accident."

"Tell me, please. What do you know?" Carrie said, slipping off her shoes. She sat on the sofa next to Helen's chair, propping a flowered pillow behind her back, waiting for Helen to tell her the story.

"Well, honey, I remember the time Madeline told me that she wished she could turn back the clock to the day of the accident. That day she had called your dad, and whatever it was she said to him—I don't know what it was or I'd tell you—anyhow, whatever she told him made him hurry out to Nella and Jim's cottage at Elkhart Lake. Of course, the accident occurred on the way out there." Helen shifted in her chair. "I do know that Madeline felt responsible."

"That doesn't make sense," Carrie said. "I thought a truck skidded out of control and crashed into them."

"Yes, dear, it did. But your grandmother felt guilty, knowing she had sent them out to Elkhart Lake that rainy evening."

"That sounds like Gram. She shelves things that upset her. I can't get her to talk about my parents."

"I can tell you this much, Carrie. At the time of the accident, your parents were planning on moving away from here, and the thought of that devastated Madeline. You might ask your Aunt Nella what she knows."

"I tried. She claims she doesn't know anything."

"That's strange." Helen threaded her needle with three dark gold strands. "Perhaps it's best left alone. Knowing won't erase your parents' tragic death."

"I'm off to bed," Carrie said, getting up.

"Wait a minute," Helen said. "One more thing. Liz said to tell you she'd be happy to come down to Atlanta the weekend of the wedding and stay with Gram."

"That's a nice offer, but I can't let her do that. It would be too much for Liz, really it would."

"Well, think about it," Helen said.

Later, Carrie lay in bed rehashing her conversation with Helen. What had Gram told her dad on the phone? Why wouldn't Aunt Nella talk about the accident? She knew she couldn't ask Liz to come stay with Gram. She tossed and turned.

*

*It was a warm spring day. The grass was green, the azaleas and dogwood trees were in bloom. Carrie stood up at the softball game during the seventh-inning stretch. Across the grassy park, beyond the ballfield, she saw Aunt Rae sitting on a red and black plaid blanket. Hurrying down the bleacher steps,* she ran over to say hello. "Who is that?" she asked pointing to a shriveled-up doll on the blanket beside Aunt Rae.

"It's your grandmother," she said, smiling sweetly.

Reaching down, Carrie picked up the doll that looked like ET with frizzy white hair, and held it in front of her. The strange figure dressed in black with arms and legs that hung loosely like a puppet, stared at Carrie with a fixed grin and broken teeth. "The game is about to start," Aunt Rae said, acting like everything was normal. Carrie propped the puppet-figure next to Aunt Rae and bolted out of the ball park, down the street, and into the parking lot. Where was her car? She zigzagged across the aisles, searching. "I've got to find my car," she said. "Where did it go?" She wanted to jump into her car and drive far away, where no one would ever find her.

Carrie awoke with a start and squinted at the digital clock. It was 4:46 a.m. She got up and walked down the hallway to the bathroom, stepping carefully as if the shriveled up puppet-figure might be lying on the hallway floor. She tried to go back to sleep when she climbed back into bed, but couldn't for fear her dream would continue.

※

That morning she packed up her things and waited for Jennifer to arrive. Helen and Ben had left for a shopping trip to Milwaukee. Carrie wrote a note thanking Helen for the overnight stay.

"That wind is nasty," Carrie said when she climbed into Jennifer's car. They drove down Eighth Street, turning on Kohler Memorial Drive and on to the IHOP where they met Aunt Nella.

"Give us a booth," Aunt Nella said to the young boy who seated them. "Don't you give us any trouble, okay." The young waiter smiled at Aunt Nella. Carrie laughed. After they ordered, Carrie mentioned the time Aunt Nella came to Atlanta to visit. "I acted pretty crazy at that Mexican place, didn't I?" Jennifer gave her mom a puzzled look.

"Your mom and I both ordered these scrumptious California quesadillas," Carrie explained to Jennifer. "While waiting, we munched on warm chips and salsa. Your mom spilled a glob of salsa on the pink placemat. She tried to wipe it off, but the salsa left a stain on the placemat, so she simply turned it over. After we finished eating, your mom handed the waiter her plate, then turned over the place mat, showing him the stain. 'Do I get a prize for telling you I made this mess?' your mom said."

"What did the waiter do?" asked Jennifer.

"Well, when he returned with our check, he handed your mom a shot glass with La Paz written on it. He gave me one too. Your mom asked him why I got a prize, too."

"She gets a prize just for putting up with you," he said. They all laughed.

"Aunt Nella, how about coming down to stay with Gram next weekend, so Michael and I can go away overnight?" Carrie said, seizing the opportunity to catch her aunt in a carefree mood.

"I could probably do that," Aunt Nella said. Just then, the waiter brought waffles with strawberries for Jennifer and Carrie, and a mushroom omelet for Aunt Nella. After they finished eating, Aunt Nella hurried off to see Aunt Rae. While Jennifer read the *Milwaukee Sentinel*, Carrie went to the phone booth to call home.

"It's not going well," Michael said. "I can't get Gram to leave her room today. She's withdrawn and refuses to eat."

"Don't worry, Michael. Just make sure she keeps drinking her iced tea. Do you think she'd talk to me now?"

"No, I just checked on her. She's asleep."

"Jennifer got a gift from Gram at the shower, this sexy, expensive-looking, pale blue nightgown and matching robe. I guess she called and charged it and had it delivered."

"Oh well," Michael said. Carrie knew they were going to get stuck with the bill. Perhaps she should move the phone out of Gram's room, better yet, she should cut up Gram's credit cards. When she told Michael that Aunt Nella might come to Atlanta next weekend and stay with Gram, so they could get away, he sounded pleased. Carrie suggested going to Callaway Gardens. Michael said he would call right away and make a reservation.

"This is taking forever," Carrie said while she and Jennifer rummaged through Gram's stuff. They sifted through clothes, knickknacks, photo albums, and miscellany, then made piles, unboxing and reboxing items they wanted to give away, and setting aside things Gram had asked Carrie to bring back. Gram didn't need to know what they gave away. Afterwards, they delivered the giveaway boxes to the Bethesda Thrift Shop downtown, then left for Aunt Nella's place in Mequon.

"Darn these farmers," Jennifer said, zipping past a truckload of baled hay. "They don't know much about driving the freeways."

"Want me to drive?" Carrie asked.

"No. I'm like my mom. I get bored just sitting."

Carrie glanced over at Jennifer. She didn't look anything like her mother, though she did act a lot like her. Aunt Nella had dark brown hair, a round face, white skin, and tiny feet like Gram. Jennifer's face was long like Carrie's, and they both wore the same size shoe—nine narrow.

When they arrived in Mequon, Aunt Nella ordered a pizza for an early dinner, saying she would have to leave for an AA meeting.

"We got rid of everything, except for the few things she wanted," Carrie told Aunt Nella after they finished eating. "Gram asked me to bring home that weird abalone ashtray of hers for Michael, the one she got in San Francisco on the trip she took years ago."

"That ugly thing," Aunt Nella said. "I'm sure he'll be thrilled."

"Do you remember her little Oriental man figurine?" Carrie asked.

"Sure. It sat on her dresser for as long as I can remember," Nella said. "I have no idea where it came from."

When Jennifer got a phone call from Kevin, Carrie excused herself, pretending to go to the bathroom. She headed to the attic, knowing Aunt Nella was leaving soon. After searching for the old trunk, she found it in an alcove under the stairway. Pulling it out and placing the trunk under the single lightbulb on the wall, she sat down on the floor and opened it. Gram's wedding gown, wrinkled and yellowed, lay on top. Someday, she wanted to hear more about Gram's wedding to Grandfather Henry.

Beneath the wedding gown, she found an old scrapbook. In it were several pictures of Gram as a child, some newspaper articles relating to school events and church activities, and pencil drawings of two girls labeled Madeline and Rae, drawn by Rae Whitfield. Carrie smiled. Aunt

Rae had been quite an artist. Perhaps Aunt Nella should take the pictures to Aunt Rae and put them on the wall at the nursing home.

She kept digging. At the bottom of the trunk, she found a partially collapsed gray box. Opening it, she found her mother's journal and a white envelope. Inside the envelope were photographs of a young couple. From the few photos Gram had given her, she knew she was looking at her parents.

There were photos of her parents at an amusement park smiling like they had won first prize. Another picture showed them holding hands near a cascading waterfall at a beach, squinting at the camera on a hot, sunny day; dressed in tailored clothing, stepping onto a train; and standing together, her father's arm around her mother, on the sidewalk in front of the house in Sheboygan where Carrie grew up.

Carrie found one final photograph in the envelope, smaller than the others, of her father, standing beside the large oak tree in front of their old home. She turned the picture over and read: "Richard and his baby girl, 1963." Carrie didn't recognize the handwriting. Whoever had written on the back of the photograph had the wrong date. She was born in 1965, not 1963.

Setting the photograph down, she opened the journal. MY NEW LIFE IN SHEBOYGAN, by Mary Caroline Whitfield, was printed in black ink on the very first page. Carrie started reading.

> May, 1964: We have just arrived on a cool, damp day in Sheboygan, Wisconsin, where Richard spent his childhood. I am weary from the long day of traveling. Mrs. Whitfield met us with a warm welcome. It is quite obvious that Richard is her golden boy. His mother hugged him on the steps of their home, as if she never wanted to let go. Richard's older sister, Nella, husband, Jim, and their little girl, Jennifer, joined us for the evening meal of pot roast, potatoes, gravy, carrots, and a cherry streudel for dessert. The baby has a mop of dark hair and is so good-natured, a little beauty. Richard adores her. Holding her made me want to have a little one of my own. I know I will miss my family and my home in Vancouver; however, I do feel at home here with Richard—

even though his mother does act a bit cold toward me. Time will surely change that.

Carrie slid the envelope of photographs inside the journal and had put it down when she heard the attic door open.

"Are you up here, Carrie?"

"Yes."

"I'm going to the drugstore. Do you want to come along?"

Carrie said no. She wanted time alone to get to know her mother.

## Chapter Eighteen

Journal, Wednesday, February 10, 1988

On Sunday evening, when I arrived home, I took one look at Michael's rumpled clothing and dejected face and knew caring for Gram had taken its toll. "I don't know how you do this," he said, shaking his head.

"Me either." I gave him a tight hug, knowing that now he had an inkling of what I'd been going through.

On Monday morning, when Michael walked into the kitchen in his brown suit—he looks great in brown—his cream-colored shirt, and paisley tie in shades of green and gold, he looked anxious to scoot out the door. When he gave me a quick kiss good-bye, I longed to trade places with him. He's been in San Francisco going to meetings and eating at classy places like Alioto's at Fisherman's Wharf, and Bardelli's. Since he left on Monday, I've only escaped this prison once for a quick trip to Kroger's. Whoopee!

Every time I leave the house, Gram panics. I return to find her shaking all over. She stays in her room full time now, refusing to come out even for meals. Wanting to be alone, she often orders me to go away. She wants me here, and she wants me gone. Gram's a puzzle I cannot solve.

On Sunday evening, I dished out the details about Jennifer's wedding shower—who was there, what they had on, what games we played. I described the gifts Jennifer opened and told her how good the seafood salad and chocolate crunch torte tasted. Gram showed no interest. She's been giving me the frigid shoulder, and I know it's the church issue. She's insulted that I plan to become Catholic. I told her that I wanted to go to the same church as Michael.

"You lied," she said, her eyes accusing me of a grave sin.

I explained that I had not lied, but had simply avoided the subject, knowing she would get angry. I reminded her that I still believed in the Christian principles she had taught me.

"Besides, there's only one God," I said.

Gram blew smoke in my face. I got up and left the room before I said anything I would regret. I'm no psychoanalyst, but I'd bet the bungalow that she's depressed. In her shoes, who wouldn't be?

Yesterday I sifted through the things I brought her from Wisconsin, showing Gram each piece of clothing and every knickknack. Holding up the little Oriental man, I expected to see her face light up. I positioned him on her dresser, next to Jennifer's college graduation picture, so she could see it from across the room. "Do me a favor?" Gram said. "Get rid of that dumb thing. I hate it." She threw her hands into the air, scowling.

"Why did you hang onto it all these years?" I said.

"I got it from . . ." Gram couldn't finish. She started a nasty coughing episode. Her face turned red as she put her hands to her throat. I rushed over. She shooed me away. Beads of sweat dotted her forehead as she ejected a string of yellow-green phlegm. I grabbed several tissues and wiped off her face and the front of her robe. Then, after helping her lie down in bed, I propped three pillows around her. Her head fell over to one side, her eyes closed, and I knew she'd be passed out for awhile.

"Good-bye," I said to the little Oriental man before I dumped him into the kitchen trash can. Outside, I heard a siren wail. Peeking out the window over the sink, I saw a shiny red firetruck zoom up the hill. The kitchen still smelled like the garlic bread I made for dinner last night. I turned on the fan and cracked open the window, then, needing an escape, I went outside and plopped down on the chaise lounge to read a few chapters of *The Accidental Tourist*. I'm about half done with it. Anne Tyler pens words that leap off of the page. When I read, I often get transported to wherever the pages want to take me. It helps me stay sane in this house of madness.

Gram slept more than two hours. I came in from the backyard and heard her coughing again. I gave her a few minutes to wake up, then went into her room, where she sat looking out the window.

"I'm talking to the trees," she said. "They live a lot longer than people, you know." I reminded Gram that the buds on the trees would soon open. "I won't be around to see them," she said. I wonder if a person knows when they are about to die.

Gram says I don't treat her like a person. She could be right. I have to admit that sometimes I question the nurse right in front of her, as if she isn't there. I have to stop doing that. Last night, lying in bed, I prayed that I would remember to treat her with more respect.

This morning, I snipped enough purple and yellow pansies from the planter to make a nice bouquet. I arranged the pansies in the blue and white vase Michael's secretary, Charn, gave us for a wedding present. Tiptoeing into Gram's room, I placed the arangement on the TV tray beside her chair, hoping they would make her smile.

Next, I made an apple crisp. I peeled four Granny Smith apples, arranging them in a baking dish, then added sugar, cinnamon, cloves, water, and lemon juice. On top, I sprinkled the flour, sugar, and butter mixture. While it baked, I reread parts of my mother's journal.

She wrote flowing lines in longhand, in black ink, her cursive letters leaning to the right. I chuckled at her comments about the dialect in Sheyboygan. She described how some one-syllable words became two syllables, then wrote examples like: co-at for coat and bo-at for boat. "They call the drinking fountain a bubbler. How funny!" she wrote. Mother said she missed her home and family in Vancouver, but made positive comments about her new home in the Midwest. She especially liked the people, describing them as, "friendly, good-hearted, and down to earth."

An optimistic newlywed, she sounded determined to win over her mother-in-law, who had so far been cold to her. In February 1965, she wrote, "I'm expecting a baby in September. The doctor thinks it's a girl.

I wonder if he's right." The very last entry in mother's journal disturbed me. I read it over and over, stopping when the oven timer went off. I took the apple crisp out of the oven, then, after hearing the cowbell, I went to Gram's room, carrying fresh iced tea.

"Something smells good," Gram said, when I opened the door. I was amazed that Gram could smell the apple crisp. "Maybe later," she said when I offered her some. She noticed the pansies.

"They're from me," I said. I gave Gram a cigarette from my pocket, before she asked for one. She smiled, probably more at the cigarette than the flowers. Her hands shook as she flicked her Bic lighter. While she smoked, I straightened up her room, wearing a face mask. Then I showed Gram the photograph I had found in the old trunk.

"That's you and your Dad," she said, handing it back like it was a hot-wired spud. I showed her the date on the back, reminding her I was born in 1965. The date on the back of the picture said 1963. It didn't look like Gram's handwriting, but I asked if it was anyhow. She said, no, adding that she was well aware of when I was born. Gram insisted that someone had written the wrong date.

Wanting to get a closer look, I walked over to the window and examined the photograph. The baby bundled in a blanket had dark hair. My other baby pictures showed me with blond hair. I feel certain that Gram is hiding the truth. Sitting on the bed, her birdlike legs dangling over the side, Gram stared out the window, her stern face telling me the subject was closed. I left her alone. I know one thing for sure; my insides aren't going to calm down until I figure it out.

Someday, I will unravel this mystery.

## Chapter Nineteen

"We have to go. I'll meet you at the car in ten minutes," Michael whispered. She wondered why they had to leave the wedding before the bride and groom said their vows. She waited five minutes, then left. She walked down a snow-covered hill and hurried past a man and woman wearing coneheads. He wore a black leather jacket and lime-green satin pants with hiking boots, and she wore Nike tennis shoes and a ratty mink coat, pulled tight around her. The couple pointed at Carrie, laughing. She had no idea why they laughed. She couldn't find the lot where Michael had parked the car. Confused, she stopped at an apartment and knocked on the door. A lady with cigarette breath and white hair sticking out in spikes opened the door.

"Come on in, sugar," she said. Stacks of dusty books, newspapers, dirty clothes, magazines, and empty boxes covered the living room floor. A teenage girl wearing a gold ring in her left nostril sat at a corner desk writing on a yellow legal pad.

"Do you have a phone?" Carrie asked.

"We have a portable phone, but we can't find it," the woman answered. "Go ahead and look for it if you want to." Carrie poked through the piles, searching for the phone.

"Don't bother looking," the young girl said. "My sister probably took it with her on her honeymoon."

"What are you writing?" Carrie said.

"A short story."

"Is it difficult? I've never written one."

"No, not really," the girl said, pulling on her earlobe. "I just get me a main character who wants something real bad—then I get her into trouble. After she runs into one obstacle after another, I get her out of trouble." The girl started writing again, moving her pen quickly across the page.

The older woman coughed. Carrie said good-bye, then stepped over the piles and hurried out the door. She retraced her steps, but still couldn't find the car. When she reached the church, she saw the bride and groom waving at the crowd as they paraded out the front door. Purple and white balloons swirled in the air above them. Carrie reached up, grabbing a ribbon attached to one of the purple balloons, and pulled it toward her. A caricature of an emaciated Gram was painted on one side of the balloon. Carrie screamed and released it. The balloon flew away, then after hitting an icicle on a nearby street light, deflated and fell to the ground.

Carrie woke up clenching her fists. Rolling over on her back, she stared at the narrow strip of molding near the ceiling, trying to clear her head. It took her a few minutes to figure out it was Saturday morning. Michael was up already, probably out running, she decided. After a quick shower, she went downstairs, tiptoeing past the extra bedroom where Jennifer slept. She had plenty to do before leaving for her overnight getaway with Michael. Aunt Nella, who had backed out on her offer to come stay with Gram, had sent Jennifer as her replacement.

Carrie yanked her jeans jacket out of the hall closet and put it on as she went out the back door. Walking down the hill to get the newspaper, she felt a calm breeze on her face. Sun rays shone through the pine trees. On the way back up the hill, she glanced at the front page story about the Winter Olympic opening ceremonies in Canada. Back inside, as she drank tea and ate a bagel, she read an article about Alberto Tomba, Italy's macho skier. Sophie-dog lay curled up at her feet.

Carrie made a list of Gram's daily routine for Jennifer. "I'd better tell her your schedule, too," she said to the dog, who raised her head looking up at Carrie. "You'd better be good. I don't want you breaking any rules, okay?" Carrie knew Jennifer would spoil Sophie-dog. She checked her watch.

Wondering why she hadn't heard the cowbell, she went down the hall to Gram's room. Opening the door, she saw rumpled sheets and blankets in a pile at the end of the bed. But she didn't see Gram. "Gram," she called out several times. She called out louder, then swallowed hard. Where was Gram? Did she fall in the bathroom? Part of her breakfast climbed up her throat. Carrie spit it into a tissue. Then, afraid to look in the bathroom, she shut Gram's door. The phone rang. Carrie ran to the kitchen to answer it. It was Kay calling to ask if she was excited about getting away.

"Kay, I can't find her," Carrie said. "She's not in her room. Her bed is empty. I called out for her and got no answer. I don't know where she is."

"Carrie, you're not making sense. She has to be somewhere."

"I'm afraid she got up to go to the bathroom and fell. She might be lying dead on the bathroom floor. I can't make myself go in there. Michael's out running. I wish he'd get home."

"Just go look, Carrie. I'll stay on the phone," Kay said.

Carrie walked down the hallway, holding onto the cordless phone. "Okay, I'm almost there." Carrie peeked into Gram's bathroom. "I looked. She's not there. Where could she be?" Carrie walked through the house, looking all over.

"Maybe she went outside."

"Outside. That doesn't make any sense. She never goes outside. Unless maybe she got confused . . . I hate to even think about it." Carrie heard a noise in the garage. Michael opened the door. She told Kay she'd call back later.

"Good Lord, Carrie, what's the matter? You look spooked," Michael said. His T-shirt was soaking wet. Sweat dripped down his face and chin.

"It's Gram. I can't find her anywhere."

"Get a grip, Carrie. She has to be somewhere." He filled a glass with water, drank it fast, then hurried down the hallway. Carrie stood around the corner, listening. "I found her," he said a couple of minutes later. "Come on in here."

"Where was she?" Carrie said, staring at Gram who lay in bed, her eyes closed, her breathing steady. "Is she okay?"

"I think so, but she's really out. I found her in a ball at the end of the bed, under a pile of sheets and blankets. She could have suffocated. I turned her ragdoll body around and propped her up in bed."

"Do you think she's unconscious?" Carrie lifted Gram's arm slightly, then let go. Her arm dropped back down beside her. Gram didn't change her expression.

"Carrie, let's just wait awhile. Something tells me that she'll probably wake up. I'm going up to shower now."

"Good idea," Carrie said, pinching her nose with her thumb and forefinger as he passed by her.

In the kitchen, she found Jennifer at the table drinking coffee. Carrie told her where the cereal and bagels were, then explained what happened with Gram.

"Isn't that kind of weird?" Jennifer said.

"Lots of strange things happen around here," Carrie said. "Stay tuned."

Carrie called the Visiting Nurses office to see if one could stop by to check on Gram. "A nurse is coming soon. Don't worry," Carrie said, seeing the look of concern on Jennifer's face. "We won't leave if things don't improve."

"Gram looks pretty bad. How long do you think she has?" Jennifer asked.

"Not long, if you ask me. But then, what do I know?" Carrie said. She handed Jennifer the lists she had made. "I made some suggestions for meals. But there's plenty of food around, so just help yourself to whatever you want. I put a list of emergency numbers by the phone."

"How far away is Callaway Gardens?"

"An hour and a half," Carrie said, wondering if they would be leaving.

While Jennifer read over the notes, Carrie studied her face. People often said she and Jennifer resembled one another. Perhaps they shared some physical traits, but their personalities were miles apart. Jennifer, who loved to shop, had a reputation for always looking just right. Carrie hated shopping and dressed on the conservative side.

"Any questions?" Carrie asked when Jennifer put the lists down.

"No. It all looks pretty clear. Do you think Gram's going to be okay?" Carrie shrugged her shoulders, then left to check on Gram.

"Gram, it's time to wake up," she said. There was no response. Carrie stood and watched Gram's chest rise and fall. "She's still out," Carrie said, returning to the kitchen. She heard Michael outside blowing leaves. Carrie went upstairs and phoned Kay to tell her they had found Gram. "I put your name on a list of people my cousin, Jennifer, can call—that is if we get to leave. I'm beginning to have my doubts."

"Do you like living in Atlanta?" Jennifer asked when Carrie came back downstairs.

"Well, I did, before Gram got sick. Now it wouldn't matter where I lived." Carrie thanked Jennifer for coming to Atlanta.

"It's okay. I don't mind. Mom's fragile right now. Besides, I've been worried about not seeing Gram again."

"Jennifer," Carrie said, "do you remember when we were kids how you'd come over for a sleepover? We'd do such crazy things. That one spring, we boiled dozens of Gram's daffodils trying to make perfume."

"Of course, it didn't work," Jennifer said, laughing. "Just the other day, I was thinking about the night, right after I got my license, when we rode around town in our shortie pajamas, honking at guys. Gram never knew we left the house."

"How's your job going?" Carrie asked.

"I love what I do and can't believe my good fortune. I'm the only girl in our office. I tell you one thing—it sure helps to have a college degree." Jennifer held her head up, looking proud.

"Don't act uppity, Jennifer. I wanted to go to college, but Gram said I couldn't, that she didn't have the money to send me." Carrie's face reddened. Jennifer was an expert at making her feel like a second-class citizen.

"Mom told me how Gram spent the money your parents left you for your education."

"My God, girl, what are you talking about?" Carrie glared at Jennifer.

"You didn't know about it?" Jennifer got up from the table. "Oh jeez, forget what I said. Mom could be wrong. I'm going out for a short walk."

There was nothing left to say. Carrie watched her walk out the door. She whipped a dishtowel against the kitchen counter. She couldn't blame Jennifer for telling her the truth, even if it had gouged her in the gut.

Carrie cleaned the kitchen, finished her packing, then put her mother's journal and the old photographs in plain view on the kitchen table. She wanted to show Jennifer the picture of her dad and the baby.

"You look upset," Michael said, coming in the from the yard. "What's happening around here?"

"Jennifer went for a walk, and the last time I checked, Gram was still passed out." Michael said he would check on Gram. Carrie heard the back door open.

"What do you have here?" Jennifer said, looking at the things on the table.

"Stuff I found in that old trunk in your mom's attic."

"Let me see." Jennifer said, leaning over the table, picking up a photograph. "This has to be Uncle Richard and your mother. They look so young," Jennifer said. "I don't remember your dad. Mom told me I was two years old when he died."

Carrie showed her the photograph of her dad holding the baby. "Is that you?" Jennifer asked.

"Gram says it is," Carrie said, "but I'm not so sure. Turn it over. On the back, it says, 'Richard and his baby girl, 1963.' I guess someone could have labeled it wrong."

Jennifer's eyes widened as she studied the photograph. "Wait a minute. I think it's me he's holding. I have this same picture in my album, the one Gram made for me." Carrie grabbed the picture from Jennifer and took another look.

"She's awake now," Michael hollered from down the hall. Carrie put the photograph down.

"Gram, good morning. You sure are a sleepyhead today," Carrie said, walking into the room. Gram's eyelids were only half open. Her white hair was matted to her head. "I want a cigarette," she said, slurring her words. "Who's that with you?"

"It's Jennifer, Gram. She came last night, remember?" Jennifer kissed Gram on the cheek.

"Get me a cigarette. You know I always have a smoke first thing in the morning."

"Not just yet, Gram. You need to wake up first." Carrie helped her into a sitting position. She sent Jennifer to the kitchen for a fresh pitcher of iced tea and a can of Ensure. She washed Gram's face and hands and brushed her hair before she gave her a Salem. Jennifer offered to stay with Gram while she drank her breakfast.

When the nurse, Annie, arrived, Carrie told her how they had found Gram at the end of the bed. "She just woke up. We thought she was unconscious for a while." Annie headed down the hallway.

"She seems fairly alert now," Annie said, returning to the kitchen. "Her blood pressure's high. She may have had a minor stroke. I had to put a catheter in her. I tried standing her up beside her walker, but she's pretty shaky. She couldn't make it to the bathroom." She gave Carrie a phone number and told her to order a portable toilet to put beside Gram's bed.

"Do you think it's all right for us to leave?" Carrie told Annie about the overnight trip they had planned. "My cousin will be here with her."

"Honey, go ahead. You need to get out of here," Annie said. Carrie agreed.

"I think she'll be okay," Annie continued. "Why don't you call the doctor, tell him what happened, and ask him to prescribe something to calm her down."

After Carrie ordered the portable toilet, she called Dr. Kirkwood. First, the doctor gave Carrie a speech, insisting that Gram was shaky because she needed to eat.

"Get her to eat more," he said, before agreeing to call in a prescription for an anti-depressant. "Make sure you don't give her the Elavil too often. We have to be careful. In her weakened state, too much medication could kill her."

"Right," Carrie said, trying to comprehend his logic.

She sent Michael to the drugstore to pick up the prescription, then had Jennifer take Gram another can of Ensure and a straw. "Try to get her to drink some," Carrie said.

Carrie went out to get the mail. At the bottom of the driveway, she waved to Julaine Reed, her neighbor across the street, who was pulling weeds in her front yard. Carrie told her she would be gone overnight.

"Have your cousin call me if she needs anything," Mrs. Reed said.

"You have two cards, probably Valentines," she said, walking into Gram's room. "One from Mavis and one from Herman."

"Herman and Iona got married," Gram said. "Did I tell you that? Mavis told me in her last letter."

"No, you didn't tell me, but Herman did, when I was in Wisconsin last week. You know, Gram, I used to think that he was your boyfriend," Carrie said.

"Oh, Caroline, no. He's just a good friend." Gram laughed, as she ripped open the envelope.

"Would you read this to me?" Gram said, handing Carrie a typed note from Herman.

"Sure." Carrie said, reaching for the note. "Gram, this is entitled 'God Will Not Desert Us.'"

"'Word comes to me that you are making a magnificent stand in adversity—this adversity being the state of your health. It gives me a chance to express my gratitude for your recovery in AA and especially for the demonstration of its principles you are now so inspiringly giving to us all.

"'You will be glad to know that AAs have an almost unfailing record in this respect. This, I think, is because we are so aware that God will not desert us when the chips are down, indeed, He did not when we were drinking. And so it should be with the remainder of life. Certainly, He does not plan to save us from all troubles and adversity. Nor, in the end, does He save us from so-called death—since this is but an opening of a door into a new life, where we shall dwell among His many mansions. Touching these things I know you have a most confident faith.'"

Herman included a handwritten note which Carrie also read: "'Dear Madeline, this is for you. It's a copy of a letter Bill W. wrote to a sick friend in 1966. I am sending it to you because it applies. I read it in the book, *As Bill Sees It*, and thought of you. Love Herman. P.S. Happy Valentine's Day.'" When Carrie finished reading, Gram had tears in her eyes.

"Herman told me that he knew you from AA," Carrie said, handing Gram a tissue.

"That sentimental old fool. He's not supposed to go around telling people we are in AA together." Gram opened the envelope from Mavis, looked at the card, then handed it to Carrie.

"'Roses are red, Violets are blue. This Valentine sends hugs and kisses to you.'"

Gram smiled. Carrie handed the card back. "Gram, it's about time for Michael and me to leave. I hope you and Jennifer have fun together."

"We're going to watch those games in, Calvary, Canada."

"Calgary, not Calvary, Gram."

The doorbell rang. Carrie left the room. "It's the portable toilet," Carrie said, hauling it into Gram's room. "Michael's back from the drug store with the medicine." Carrie gave Gram an Elavil tablet mashed up in chocolate pudding.

"Stop staring at me, Caroline. I swallowed it." Gram took a sip of iced tea. Carrie and Michael told Gram good-bye.

"Be a good egg for Jennifer," Carrie said as they left the room.

"Have fun," Jennifer said, as they got into the car. Carrie and Michael both thanked her for staying with Gram. They waved good-bye. An apprehensive-looking Jennifer waved back as they drove off.

"I hope Jennifer does okay with Gram," Carrie said as they drove through downtown Atlanta. The dome on the capitol building glistened in the sunshine.

"She'll be fine. We won't be gone that long," Michael said.

As they passed Fulton County Stadium, Carrie turned on the radio, then fell asleep. Michael awakened her when they arrived at Callaway Gardens.

That afternoon they rented bikes. They rode the trails, looking at the colorful azaleas. They parked their bikes to tour the manicured gardens, then continued their ride, stopping at a little church where they sat on a bench overlooking the water.

"I feel strange," Carrie said.

"Just try to relax and enjoy the break."

"Michael, I was thinking about Gram." He raised his eyebrows. "Don't worry. It's nothing gloomy, just a fun story." She paused, smiling. "Last spring when Gram visited us, I took her to lunch at Marquitos, and after we had ordered, these two attractive, well-dressed black ladies came in for lunch. When they walked over to a table near ours, Gram said in a whisper, 'I sure didn't know *they* ate Mexican food.'"

"Sounds like Gram," Michael said. "She's a real character, but I like her. God knows I admire the courage that woman has." Carrie thought about what Michael said. Gram did have her good points—they were easier to see with a little distance.

That evening at dinner they ate grilled, blackened salmon, garlic mashed potatoes, and asparagus with hollandaise sauce. For dessert they shared a mocha cheesecake.

"My butt hurts from riding my bike so long. I'll pay tomorrow," Carrie said.

"I made a tee time for early afternoon." Michael poured more wine into their glasses.

"I'm not too familiar with golf. You know that, don't you?"

"I'll give you a few tips."

"Oh, I'm sure you will," Carrie said. "Jennifer's the golfer in our family. She started taking lessons at Pine Hills when she was six. She was on the high school golf team."

"Didn't you take lessons?"

"No. Don't make me laugh. We didn't belong to Pine Hills."

"I've got a golf story for you," Michael said. "Charlie, the manager at our plant in Naperville told me about playing golf with a buddy of his. The guy told Charlie a long, boring story about some IRS problem he had. So, on the twelfth hole, Charlie reached into his pocket and pulled out a quarter. 'Here's a quarter,' Charlie told the guy. 'Go call someone who gives a shit.'"

"That line could come in handy sometime," Carrie said. They left the restaurant laughing.

"Want to play cards?" Michael asked.

"No, I have something better in mind." She started taking off her clothes. Michael turned down the bed.

"Nice birthday suit," Michael said.

"It's been way too long," Carrie said, reaching for him.

※

Carrie didn't awaken until eight in the morning. She lay in bed, wondering how Jennifer was doing. She showered, dressed, and then made her phone call.

"Gram had a terrible night," Carrie said, hanging up. "She got Jennifer up several times. She finally went down and slept on the sofa. I guess Gram moaned all night long. I told her we were having a great time."

"Let's continue to have a great time. Stop worrying about what's happening at home. We'll be back before you know it."

They made plans to tour the butterfly house after brunch, take a walk, then play golf. "I told Jennifer we'd be home by seven."

That afternoon, on the golf course, Carrie hit more bad shots than good ones, but it didn't matter. She and Michael laughed and talked and soaked up the sun. He tried to give her lessons on the course. She told him to hang it up, that she would work it out herself. After golf, they headed home.

When they arrived, Gram was asleep and a tired Jennifer was delighted to see them. "Mavis called," Jennifer said. "She wanted to thank you both for offering to buy plane tickets to Atlanta for her, and for Mary Lou, and Marie. She's sorry, but they can't come."

"Whatever are you talking about? I didn't offer to buy any plane tickets," Carrie said. Michael rolled his eyes, then left the room, carrying their suitcases.

"Mavis said Gram had the nurse help her make a call last week. Gram told Mavis that you wanted the three of them to come stay with Gram the weekend of my wedding. Gram said you would buy their tickets."

"Oh, great." Carrie said. "I told Gram that Rhonda, one of her nurses, was coming here to stay with her that weekend."

"Mavis sounded very uncomfortable with the whole idea," Jennifer said.

"I'm sure she did. I'd never ask them to take over."

"Some guy named Tom called too."

"He did? What did he have to say?"

"First he said Happy Valentine's Day—in a very sexy voice. He thought he was talking to you." Jennifer raised her eyebrows. "I told him you had gone away with Michael. He knew all about the wedding and other stuff about me." Jennifer gave her a questioning look.

Carrie explained how she'd met Tom at the airport. "I've been doing some part-time work for him. Was Gram awake when he called?"

"Yes, but she was in her room. I didn't mention the call to her."

"Good," Carrie said. "She thinks I'm interested in Tom. Of course, there's no truth to that. Tom's just a very good friend. God knows, I need all of the friends I can get right now."

Carrie's head spun in circles. She wasn't ready to face Gram's antics. Sick as she was, Gram was still trying to control things, in her own rudderless fashion.

The next morning, Jennifer and Carrie played five hundred rummy. Michael had stayed home, working on the phone, so he could drive Jennifer to the airport to catch her plane at noon. They took turns checking on Gram, who was drowsy after taking her Elavil.

"Gram asked me to make a loan payment for her while you were gone," Jennifer said. "She gave me her loan payment book and asked me not to tell you about it."

"She's classic. What next?" Carrie said, laying down three tens. She discarded the two of diamonds. "I've been looking for a missing loan payment book I saw one time, when she was still in Wisconsin. Then, it disappeared. I asked Gram about it, but she played dumb."

By picking up the two, Jennifer was able to lay down her whole hand. "Add up your points," Jennifer said with a cocky smile.

"Where was that loan card? I've looked all over for it."

"Stashed in the lining of her black purse. How many points do I get?" Jennifer sat pen in hand, ready to total her score.

"You get ninety points. I can't figure out why she'd want you to make a payment? She's been totally uninvolved with the rest of her finances."

"I know why. Gram told me she'd made this bargain with God. She'd make a payment on the loan if *He* would get her to my wedding," Jennifer said, picking up the cards. "Isn't she something?"

Carrie nodded. "Let's stop playing," Carrie said. "I concede." Carrie held her head in her hands. Gram needed to hang up the idea of being at Jennifer's wedding.

"I need to get my stuff from upstairs. It's almost time for me to leave. And, I want to say good-bye to Gram." Jennifer's tone was upbeat.

"First, let me ask you a question," Carrie said. "Helen Newby told me one day that Gram made a phone call that triggered my parents' car accident. Is that the secret you've been talking about?"

"Part of it. There's more," Jennifer said. "It's time someone told you the rest. Gram did call your dad the day of the accident. She told him that I was terribly sick and that he needed to hurry out to Elkhart Lake to help my mom. But it was a lie."

"Why would Gram do that?" Carrie said.

"Because, she was desperate. She didn't want your parents to move out of town. Uncle Richard left immediately and drove to Elkhart Lake. You know the rest. They never got there. One day, not long after the accident, Gram confessed to my mother what she had done. Mom's still angry at her, after all of these years. She was very close to her brother."

"So, why didn't anyone tell me this story?"

"I don't know, but I don't think it's right. That's why I decided to tell you."

"Jennifer, where was your dad when this happened?" Carrie's heart raced.

"My stepfather was in Canada on a fishing trip."

"What do you mean, your *stepfather*?"

"I'm adopted—that's another secret. Mom told me a few years ago and made me promise not to tell anyone." There was a sad tone in Jennifer's voice.

"Why are you telling me now?" Carrie asked.

"Because, I have this theory. Last night, I sat staring at that photo of your dad and the baby, and it hit me. I think we're sisters, and that your dad—my Uncle Richard—was my father. It *is* a picture of your Dad and his daughter, just like it says on the back. And, the daughter in the photograph is me. That's the reason he rushed out to Elkhart Lake when he thought I was so sick."

"That's absurd," Carrie said.

"It makes sense to me," Jennifer said.

Not wanting to believe Jennifer, Carrie got up from the kitchen table and ran upstairs. She hated the idea of sharing her father with anyone.

# Chapter Twenty

Journal, Thursday, February 18, 1988

I can't stop thinking about Jennifer's theory that we're sisters. The whole idea doesn't make any sense. "Did Uncle Richard have more than one child?" Jennifer boldly asked Gram right before she left here on Monday.

"Richard?" Gram said, looking puzzled. "I don't know anyone named Richard." Gram wasn't playing dumb. At that moment, she was totally confused and didn't even know her own name. Jennifer dropped the subject. The way she clasped Gram's frail hand and kissed her good-bye made me swallow hard.

Before climbing into Michael's car, Jennifer hugged me, saying she was sorry if she had upset me by suggesting that we might be sisters. I thanked her for coming down to stay with Gram. Hoping to unravel the mystery, she plans to ask her mother for a copy of her birth certificate. I'll see her at the wedding in just a few weeks. She promised to call and let me know if she finds out anything, but, so far, I haven't heard a word.

It feels good sitting here on the patio in the mid-February sunshine, listening to the birds. The other day, when I told Gram I'd seen a Carolina wren, she wanted to know if it was brown. When I said yes, she tilted her head up and informed me that I'd seen a winter wren, not a Carolina wren. "Michael told me the Carolina wren has a lighter breast area," she said. Obviously, Michael and Gram had been talking birds again.

I asked Gram to come outside with me, but she refused, preferring to stay in her smoke-filled room. She sits in there waiting to die—just as I bide my time, waiting to step back into my former life.

There are so many things here in Atlanta that I'd like to be doing. I'd like to go downtown to the Georgia-Pacific building and see *Dawn's Forest*, the controversial sculpture by Louise Nevelson. I'd like to see another show at the Fox Theatre. It's such a grand old theatre. Last year, we had season tickets. I'd like to go back to artsy Virginia Highlands and eat dinner at Tito's, the great Italian place where we spent a fun evening with Kay and Dave last summer. All of these things will have to wait.

For now, I'm a robot. I get up each day, shower, and have breakfast. When Michael's home—a rare treat these days—we have a quick visit while he makes instant coffee in his black plastic commuter cup. Then, before I know it, he kisses me good-bye, and is out the door.

I've reached the point where I'm scared Gram will die, and scared she won't. Lifting her off the bed to use the portable toilet makes my back hurt. I don't know how long I can keep doing it. Several times a day, I empty the amber pee from the bag hanging at the end of her catheter tube. Gram hates having the catheter stuck in her; yesterday, I caught her trying to yank it out. Today, there was blood in her catheter tube. Did she injure herself pulling on the tube?

Gram looks like a concentration camp refugee. I don't look much better. Walking past the entryway mirror this morning, I barely recognized the gaunt person staring at me with eyes no longer bright blue, but dusty gray-blue. Dark bags hang under my eyes. My bangs touch my eyebrows. Who knows when I can leave to get a haircut? My drab gray shorts and faded navy T-shirt reflect my mood. I suppose I could dress nicer, for Gram's sake. Who knows if it would make any difference? Nothing I do seems to please her.

She tells me often that I've taken away everything she likes. She's still irritated about having to beg for cigarettes, but I refuse to budge. In truth, I can't wait to toss her cancer sticks out of my life for good.

"A person can't enjoy a cigarette with you around," she said today, when I offered to sit down and visit. I left the room, but kept checking on her until that cigarette was dead in the ashtray.

"I want Caroline to give me my medicine," Gram said this morning, surprising me. How could she not know me? I waited until she was more alert, then made her take her Elavil pill, because it calms her down. Right now, she's engrossed in watching a "Flintstones" cartoon. She could care less that I'm outside.

She needs stronger medication for her pain. When I ask where it hurts, she tells me it hurts all over. Her back hurts bad. My guess is that the cancer is now feasting on her spine. Weeks ago, when we visited Dr. Baker, the oncologist, he told her he would keep her comfortable. It's time for him to follow through on his promise.

Sitting here soaking up the sun, I've been thinking about how Gram's never going to stand outside again, never going to water the flowers, or feel the wind on her face. She's too sick to care. Across the yard, a female cardinal splashes in the birdbath, while I wonder how I'm going to tell Gram that it's time to put her in a nursing home. On the phone last night Michael nixed the idea, saying it would break Gram's heart. Talk about a turnaround!

"Give it a rest," I said. I don't need Michael telling me what to do. He has no idea how close I am to crashing. Sure, he cares about Gram, but he's not with her day in and day out. I care about her too, but the waves may be getting too high. I'll hang in here a little longer. I will care for poor, sick Gram who is now too frail to hold her glass of iced tea. She says it's too heavy.

Michael installed a monitor that connects our bedroom to Gram's, so I no longer have to sleep downstairs. "I'm so sick. Oh, I'm so sick, someone help me," Gram moans over and over each night. Knowing there's nothing I can do keeps me awake, but at least I'm in my own bed. The fact that I don't know what to do to help her is difficult.

I love sitting out here feeling the breeze, inhaling the clean earthy smell of springtime. It makes me want to plant petunias and impatiens. Sophie-dog is hooked up to her exercise rope. Taking her for a walk is no longer an option.

Gram did make me laugh yesterday. "I'm going to get me some of those fancy jeans when I feel better," she said, pointing to my blue jeans. That cracked me up. It must have been the medicine talking. The sad truth is, these days Gram wears her nightgown all the time. The simple motions of getting dressed make her too tired.

"Don't hover over me," she said. "When I die, I don't want you to moan and groan or throw your hands up into the air and wail." She put her hands up over her head. "Don't you grieve. I'll be fine, and you'll be fine without me." I promised to follow her instructions. "I'm ready to die. I feel like any time now, Jesus will walk right through that door and say, 'Come on, old girl, you've suffered long enough.'"

Gram insists that when she dies, her husband, Henry, and son, Richard, will be there to greet her. I asked if she would be there for me when it was my time. "You mean waiting on you, bringing you iced tea, emptying your urine bag?"

"No, no, Gram," I said. "I mean when I die—will you come to meet me?"

"Yes, dear, I certainly will," she said, without hesitation.

Gram gave me specific instructions for her funeral. "I don't want people walking past, saying how good I look. Dead people don't look good," she said, insisting on a closed casket. "You tell me good-bye while I'm still warm, okay? And bury me in black, right here in Georgia, not in that frozen ground up north."

"Good idea," I said. "It won't cost as much to bury you here." I wanted to gather up those words as soon as they fell out.

"Don't get uppity with me about money," she said. "I have my five thousand dollar life insurance policy. Don't you go telling folks I can't bury myself."

"I won't, Gram." Then—I don't know why I chose that moment—I blurted out that I knew Jennifer was adopted.

"Nella told me never to tell," Gram said. "So I didn't. Nella couldn't have children. But she raised Jennifer like she was her very own." I asked if there was anything more I should know about Jennifer. "No," she said, looking away. I wanted to ask about my parents' car accident, but I didn't.

I'm tired of writing. I think I'll just enjoy a few more minutes out here. The birds are busy, snatching up the makings for a nest, and Sophie-dog keeps racing back and forth on her rope, chasing butterflies. And me, I keep thinking about what Gram said to me.

"I don't mind dying," she said. "I just don't want to suffer."

"Me either, Gram, me either."

## Chapter Twenty-one

Gram's dentures were in a half-filled glass of water on the bedside table. "Something's wrong with them," she said. "They don't fit anymore."

After losing so much weight, Gram's mouth was too small for her teeth. It didn't matter if Gram wore them or not—her diet was only soft food now. Carrie gave Gram a few sips of iced tea, then spooned pureed bananas, containing a crushed Elavil tablet, into her mouth.

"I want a cigarette," Gram said, in a deep whisper, after she struggled to swallow. With a frown, Carrie reached into her pocket for a Salem. Gram grabbed it from Carrie's outstretched hand and quickly lit up.

Hanging over the edge of the hospital bed Carrie had ordered, Gram looked sallow and bruised. Her skin and the whites of her eyes had yellowed. Her hands, ears, and feet had a bluish-purple cast to them. Gram clamped the cigarette in her mouth, inhaling—then blew the smoke into the stuffy room. Carrie adjusted her face mask, then lit the vanilla candle on Gram's dresser. She crossed the room and cracked open the window. Morning dew glistened on the oak leaves. "I see a robin in the dogwood, Gram. That's a sure sign of spring, isn't it?"

"If it's spring, why are those winter games on television?" Gram said.

"Gram, the games are in Canada, remember? It's still cold up there, though I read the Chinook winds are making it warmer than usual this year. The snow is melting. They're having problems with some of the events. Fifty-seven nations are represented in the Olympics. Isn't that amazing?"

"Um hmm," Gram said, blowing out more smoke. Gram closed her eyes, inhaling with fervor. Carrie shrugged her shoulders. There was no use talking to Gram while she smoked.

"I'll be glad when I don't have to light another one of these," Gram said, stubbing her cigarette out. "I'm an addict, you know. Always have been. When I latch onto something, my body craves it something bad."

You hit the bull's-eye with that statement, Carrie thought. She was surprised to hear Gram admitting her addiction. Over the years, Gram had craved many things—cigarettes, alcohol, chocolate, and now iced tea. After giving up alcohol, Gram had craved sugar. She'd often bake a large pan of brownies, topping them with thick chocolate icing. Then she'd eat half the pan while they were still warm. How Gram had stayed so slim was a mystery to Carrie.

"I feel dizzy, Caroline. The room's spinning in circles." Gram slumped over onto the bed. Carrie rushed over to catch her, holding onto Gram's bony shoulders. "Make it stop," Gram said. "I can't stand it."

"I would if I could, Gram, but I don't know how." Carrie helped ease her onto the bed. "Just lie still for awhile. That might help." Carrie stared out the window wishing she had some magic that would make Gram feel better.

"If Michael was here, he could make the room stop whirling around. Call him, Caroline."

"I can't reach him right now, Gram. He's at a meeting at the Peachtree City Conference Center and won't be be home until late tonight. You can see him in the morning."

"If I'm still around," Gram said.

Carrie didn't comment. She was getting used to Gram's flippant remarks about dying. Gram lay in bed, her wavy white hair framing her face. Looking at her, Carrie thought back to her childhood days when she would sit on the vanity stool next to Gram, watching her fix her long dark hair into a french roll. Gram would apply moisturizer, eye shadow, eyeliner, pancake makeup, rouge, and red lipstick, while Carrie daydreamed about getting older.

Sitting down in the bedside chair, Carrie picked up Gram's worn-out prayerbook. She wondered if reading it to her would help steady Gram. Thumbing through the dog-eared pages, she found *The Beatitude* prayer. Knowing it was a favorite of Gram's, she started reading:

"Blessed are the poor in spirit, for theirs is the kingdom of heaven."

"Blessed are the meek, for they shall possess the earth."

"Blessed are they who mourn, for they shall be comforted."

"Blessed are they who hunger and thirst for justice, for they shall be satisfied . . ."

Closing the prayerbook, Carrie heard a soft snoring. She slipped out of the room, quietly shutting the door behind her. She went into the kitchen and phoned Kay, who faithfully asked how things were going with Gram.

"First thing this morning, she made no sense at all. She told me the doctors at the hospital were nice and that her Dad had stopped by to see her. She wanted Michael to come home, so she could tell him good-bye."

"Is she that close to dying?"

"*She* seems to think so."

Carrie asked Kay if she could come stay with Gram while she made a dreaded trip to the funeral home. "Gram's nurse, Rhonda, you know, the one from the Visiting Nurses place, said I'd better have some plans made." Kay agreed to relieve Carrie. "I'll call you when I'm ready to go. I'll make sure that Gram is sleeping while you're here." Hanging up, Carrie felt relieved. She looked forward to getting out of the house, then decided she had to be a nut case to be excited about going to a funeral home.

While she cubed a chuck roast for vegetable soup, Carrie remembered Father O'Brien's words after mass on Sunday. "Don't worry," Father O'Brien had said, reassuring her, when she told him Gram was doing terrible. "Your grandmother's going to be just fine."

Carrie could still see his gentle smile. She realized that he had wanted her to understand that dying wasn't so bad. Perhaps, Gram would be better off after she died. Just about anything would be better than the life she was now living.

"I'm not going to drop anything on the floor," Carrie said to Sophie-dog who stood guard at her feet. She had just added a large can of stewed tomatoes to the copper soup pot when she heard tapping at the back door. "Come on in," she said.

"Sure smells good in here," Rhonda said.

"I'm making vegetable soup hoping Gram will eat some. I may have to put it into the blender." Carrie told Rhonda about Gram's dizzy spell. Rhonda left the room to check Gram's vital signs.

Carrie added more ingredients to the soup—barley, liquid garlic, pepper and Worcestershire sauce, then set it on the back burner. After the soup reached a boil, she turned the stove to simmer, then headed to Gram's room.

"I used to be pretty," Gram said.

"You still are, Mrs. Whitfield," Rhonda said. "You remind me of the actress, Angela Lansbury." Gram smiled.

"Are you still dizzy, Gram?" Carrie said.

"Dizzy? What are you talking about, girl? I'm doing fine. I was telling my black nurse here about my red satin holiday dress with matching shoes, the one I loved to wear when I went out partying."

"Your nurse's name is Rhonda, Gram." Carrie felt like crawling under the carpet.

"I know her name," Gram said. "Don't interrupt, Caroline . . . Rhonda said I look *good* in red."

"That's right, Gram, you do. I'll be in the kitchen if you need me," she told Rhonda.

"I'm sorry about Gram's comment," Carrie said to Rhonda when she was ready to leave. "She grew up in a town with all whites, and she's fascinated by African Americans."

"Don't worry. I know she didn't mean anything by it."

"Gram likes you a lot," Carrie said. "Me, too." She gave Rhonda a hug, then asked her if she had any idea why Gram looked so yellow.

"Well, honey, I'm guessing the cancer's moved on to her liver and made it stop working. Now the bile's causing her to turn yellow. She sure looks like she swallowed yellow Easter egg dye, doesn't she?"

Carrie agreed, waving to Rhonda as she went out the door.

"The nurse is nice, but she doesn't know how sick I am. And neither do you," Gram said when Carrie took her a can of chocolate Ensure. Carrie instructed her to drink as much as she could.

Carrie headed upstairs to change into her jean jumper, a yellow T-shirt and her blue flats. Back downstairs, she found the full can of Ensure on the bedside table. Gram was sleeping. She called Kay to come over.

At the funeral home, Carrie filled out forms and explained her situation to a man in a gray suit. "Just call when you need us. We can pick up the body for you, any time of day or night. We'll be happy to be of service." Carrie gulped at the casual way he referred to Gram as a "body." She refused his offer to tour the casket room, saying she would take care of that later. On the way home, she stopped at Kroger to get milk, bread, lettuce, tomatoes, bananas, and Gram's damn cigarettes.

"You see any goobers down there?" a white-haired man with two front teeth missing asked her, pointing down at some shelves near the checkout line. Carrie looked down at the shelves of candy and nuts.

"I don't see any," she said, assuming he meant a bag of peanuts.

"They just don't get enough of them anymore. They're always runnin' out." The man looked irritated. Carrie tried not to laugh as he walked away. The wrinkled old man picked up his pace as he walked out the door. He moved pretty good for someone who looked about ninety. The fact that he was so agile, and a much younger Gram was bedridden, seemed an ironic twist of fate.

"She only woke up once," Kay said, when Carrie got home. She didn't seem upset. I told her you went to the grocery store. She begged me to call Dr. Baker."

"She did? Whatever for?"

"She asked him for some strong pain medicine. The doctor called in a prescription for Tylenol-3. It's at Kroger."

"Oh great, I was just there."

Kay remarked that she was going to pick up groceries after she left and would get the prescription. "She told me you didn't like her doctor," Kay said.

"Dr. Baker's not as bad as her internist, Dr. Kirkwood. He's the doctor I'd like to nominate for asshole of the year." Kay laughed.

"I don't know how you can stay here day after day," Kay said. "You're a saint."

"Kay, please. Don't put me on a pedestal. I don't know how I do it either. What choice do I have? Believe me when I tell you I'm no saint. I'm impatient. I'm cranky. I feel sorry for myself. I'm telling you—sometimes, I think I'm going to cross over the edge."

"Are you getting any exercise?"

"Very little. I can't go out for a walk anymore—Gram gets paranoid if I leave. Sometimes I run in place in the house. I do stretching exercises. I'm addicted to exercise. I have to get my heart rate up, or I feel out of whack. Maybe that's how Gram feels without her cigarettes."

When Kay mentioned she'd be going back to work before long, Carrie exploded.

"Don't tell me that! Having you at home has kept me sane. Who else can I call anytime of day?"

"You can still call. I'll only be gone a few hours," Kay said. Then she started laughing.

"What's so funny?"

"While you were gone, Gram had to use the portable toilet."

"I hope you didn't hurt your back helping her."

"No, I did fine. I've got my clam shell brace on. When I got Gram off of the portable toilet, there was just this one tiny little marble of poop in the pot."

"'Nothing feels better than a good BM,'" Gram said, like she'd dumped a whole load." They both giggled like school girls.

"Is Michael okay about having Gram here? She seems to think he's perfect."

"Oh, I know. They've bonded. He doesn't mind having her here. Of course, he's not here much. He's traveling more and more for work. When he's home, he works long hours, plays golf, works out at the gym, and trains for his next marathon. I watch him come in and out the door. It's his way of dealing with a tough situation."

"Carrie, *you* need to get out of here once in awhile."

"Don't I know it," Carrie said. When Kay got up to leave, she promised to come back soon and visit. Carrie asked her to leave Gram's prescription in the mailbox on her way home from the store.

※

"My cigarette broke," Gram said later in the afternoon. "I need another one."

"How'd it break, Gram?"

"Kay sat on it."

"Oh, sure," Carrie said. Her grandmother would say anything to get another cigarette. "Are you hungry, Gram?" Carrie held out a can of strawberry Ensure.

"I hate that Endure stuff. My appetite's coming back. At dinner, I'm going to have me a big hamburger and some of that soup you're making."

"That's good," Carrie said, knowing Gram was fantasizing. "It's Ensure, Gram, not Endure. Try some and I'll give you another cigarette."

At dinner, Gram refused the soup. She only ate a small dish of vanilla ice cream topped with hot fudge sauce. After she finished, Carrie insisted Gram get out of bed and sit in her chair for awhile. "You'll get bed sores if you don't move," Carrie said. She got out her pink and white robe, the one Gram had started calling her invalid's robe, and put it on her.

"Gram," Carrie said, "I read an article the other day about about how people don't really die, but live on in others." Gram didn't stay anything. Carrie watched a tear roll down Gram's cheek. "It's okay, Gram, you can cry."

"No, I can't. I cried like an injured dog when my mother died, but I'll never do that again. I made a spectacle of myself."

"Tell me about my great-grandmother Ludke," Carrie said.

"Her name was Elizabeth Louise Ludke," Gram said with an alertness that surprised Carrie. "Everyone called her Lizzie. She hated her nickname. Mother always wore a dress, stockings, sensible shoes, and a hat when she left the house. She favored her straw hat, the one with a sprig of lily of the valley tucked into the band. Mother often walked the nine blocks to the center of town for scraps of material at the dry goods store.

She stitched quilts using small hexagons of patterned fabric. One of the quilts is over there in the closet. She made it using pieces of the dresses she had sewn for me. Would you like to have that quilt, Caroline?"

"I'd love to have it, Gram."

Gram stared across the room, like she had set sail in another direction. She was probably thinking about her mother.

Carrie had always wanted a mother. As a child, she had always dreaded May, when the students made Mother's Day cards at school. "You can make a card for your grandmother," Mrs. Porter would tell Carrie each year.

"I'll come back in and get you ready for bed," Carrie said to Gram, not wanting to dwell on her thoughts. She heated a bowl of soup in the microwave, broiled an English muffin, and sliced up an apple, then put it on a tray and headed to the great room. She watched the news, eating in a hurry. The soup tasted great. Too bad Gram didn't try it.

After dinner, she picked up her mother's journal. On the front cover, giant ocean waves crashed on shore, leaving foamy water on a sandy beach. Carrie sniffed the musty pages, holding them close. She ran her hand across one of the pages, wanting to touch what her mother had touched. Thumbing through, she reread several of the pages. The last journal page drew her back to it. In that last entry, her mother had written:

"We have just received a strange phone call from Richard's mother. I will never figure her out. She wants Richard to go to Elkhart Lake immediately. As soon as Helen Newby, from across the street, comes to stay with baby Caroline, we'll leave. He has insisted that I come along, even though I don't want to go. Richard is acting so very distraught. Sounding mysterious, he said he had something important to tell me once we get on the road, something he hoped that I would be able to understand. So, I must go. I don't understand why, but I feel so apprehensive about leaving. More later . . ." Carrie ran her fingers over the page. *What did her mother learn on the ride to Elkhart Lake? Did she have a premonition of the accident? Is that why she wanted to stay home with her baby? Did Richard tell her that Jennifer was his daughter?*

Carrie sat wondering if she would ever know the answers to these questions. From Gram's room, she heard a loud, gagging noise. Jumping up, she dropped her mother's journal onto the floor, and ran around the corner.

"Oh, Gram, what's wrong?" Carrie knelt down on the floor in front of the chair, putting her arms around Gram whose body lurched forward into Carrie's arms.

"Oh, no. Oh, no. The wedding." Gram said in a tiny voice.

Then, her head bobbed down onto Carrie's shoulder. Her body continued to jerk. Carrie held onto Gram tightly, sure she was dying. Seconds later, Gram was limp. Carrie held on tight, afraid to release her grip.

"Caroline, let go—you're choking me," Gram said, after what seemed like several minutes, raising her head off of Carrie's shoulder. Stunned, Carrie released her grip. "I guess I fell asleep," Gram said, oblivious to what had happened.

"I guess so," Carrie said with relief. She helped Gram get up, out of her robe, and into her bed. She folded the robe and lay it over the back of the chair.

"I'm not me anymore," Gram said, after Carrie kissed her goodnight.

"I love you anyhow," Carrie said.

"Why?"

"I just do. I love you this much." Carrie spread her arms wide, just like Gram used to do at bedtime when she was a child.

"Am I in the hospital?" Gram asked.

"No," Carrie said.

"Do you have your lessons done?"

"Yes," Carrie said. "I'll see you in the morning."

"When I wake up in the morning, I'm always glad to see you," Gram said. "Then, I remember how terrible I feel, and I want to die."

"I'm glad to see you each morning, too," Carrie said. She turned out the light, and left the room.

Once in the family room recliner, Carrie sat dazed. She wished Michael was home. She tried reading a magazine, but couldn't concentrate. Her arms and legs itched. Her throat felt like it was constricting. Frightened, she went into the bathroom and looked into the mirror. Round, red blotches with jagged edges covered her face, her neck, her arms. She stuck her tongue out. It was swollen—three times its normal size. Don't panic, she told herself. *Do not panic.*

Grabbing the phone, she dialed Kay. No answer. She called Michael's voice mail and left an urgent message. Then, she tried Tom Egan, who answered on the first ring. "What's wrong? You sound strange," he said.

"Tom, can you come over quick? Gram had this terrible episode tonight. She almost died. That was just a little while ago, and now I'm covered with hives. I can hardly catch my breath." She struggled to get the words out.

"Sit down. Breathe slow. I'll be right there." She told him she would leave the front door unlocked.

When Tom arrived, he found Carrie sitting on the sofa, a pillow clutched to her chest. Sophie-dog lay at her feet. "This is my friend, Diana Chambers," Tom said. The tall blond standing next to him said hello. "Diana will drive you to the hospital, and I'll stay here with Gram." Carrie gave him a questioning look. She tried to tell him about Gram's attack. "Don't worry," he said. "I can handle it." He told her he had called St. Joseph's emergency room to let them know she was coming.

"Thanks," Carrie said, after Tom helped her into the car.

"No problem." Tom told Diana to call him from the hospital.

Tom peeked into Gram's room after they had left. She was sound asleep. He turned on the television to watch the Olympic skiing competition.

※

"Stay calm." The emergency room nurse held up a needle. "This will pinch a little," the nurse said. She stuck a needle into Carrie's arm. Feeling a stabbing pain, Carrie glared at the nurse. Why did they always have to lie?

"What did you have for dinner?" the doctor asked when he arrived.

"Vegetable soup, an English muffin and an apple."

"Anything else?"

"No, that's it."

"Have you been under any stress?"

"Does a bear go in the woods," Carrie said, rolling her eyes.

"Excuse me," the doctor said, wrinkling his forehead.

"I'm sorry. I didn't mean to be flippant." She told him about Gram's seizure and how she'd been caring for her alone, for several months.

"Sounds like your grandmother may have had a stroke or a heart attack," the doctor said. "You should get in touch with her doctor."

"Right," Carrie said. There was no point in trying to explain to the young emergency room doctor how she had no one to call. At least, no one who cared.

"You're looking much better." Diana said, when she came back into the cubicle. "I called Tom and told him you were going to be okay. He said not to worry. Your grandmother's still asleep."

"Good," Carrie said. "So, how long have you two been seeing each other?" Carrie gave Diana the once over. Diana looked like a model in her tight black T-shirt and black jeans.

"Oh," Diana said, laughing. "I'm just a friend of Tom's. We're next door neighbors. I'm married." She held up her hand, pointing to her wedding ring. Tom and my husband, Steve, are tennis partners. Tom comes over to our house often. Steve wasn't home when Tom called, so I offered to help out." Diana sat down in the bedside chair. "You know, I feel like I know you. Tom sings your praises all the time. He likes you, Carrie. I can tell. He likes you a lot."

After the nurse released Carrie, Diana drove her home. Just before Diana pulled into the driveway, the phone rang inside Carrie's condo. "Barnes residence," Tom said.

"And just who is this?" Michael said.

"Tom Egan. I'm a friend of Carrie's."

"This is Michael Barnes. Please put my wife on the phone."

"I can't. She's not here. She had a severe allergic reaction to something. My neighbor, Diana, took her to St. Joseph's emergency room. I'm staying here with Gram."

Michael said good-bye and hung up before Tom had a chance to tell him that Carrie was okay and probably on her way home. Carrie and Diana walked in a few minutes later. "Your husband just called," Tom said. "Gram's fine." He gave Carrie the once-over. "Boy, you look a heck of a lot better."

"The medicine they gave me worked fast. The doctor thought the allergic reaction could have been from stress over Gram's attack." Tom asked her for details.

"Well, Gram had this weird jerking fit," Carrie said, sitting down beside Tom on the sofa. "I was sitting out here when she called for me in this urgent voice. I ran into the room as she lurched out of her chair. I caught her just in time. I held onto her as she jerked toward me several times. It was like she was getting jolts of electricity. Then, she stopped and lay limp on my shoulder. She had stopped breathing. I kept my arms around her, so sure she had died. It was horrible. It seemed like a long time, but was probably only seconds. I dreaded letting go. I was shocked when she lifted her head and told me to stop holding on so tight, that I was choking her."

"Geez. That sounds pretty wild."

"After I got her settled into bed, I came back into the great room. That's when I broke out in hives. I can't thank you and Diana enough for coming over to help me." When Diana asked if she could use the bathroom, Carrie told her it was around the corner.

Tom reached over and put his arms around Carrie, giving her a tight hug. Carrie hugged him back, resting her head on his shoulder. Just then, Michael walked into the room.

"Carrie, are you okay? I went to the hospital, but just missed you."

"I'm doing much better," she said, pulling away from Tom. She stood up and went over beside Michael. "This is Tom Egan. I've told you about Tom. I called him when I couldn't reach you or Kay." Diana walked into the room. "This is Diana Chambers, Tom's neighbor."

"Thank you both for helping," Michael said. "You can both leave. I can take over now."

"You take care," Tom said, getting up. "Call tomorrow and let me know how you're doing." Carrie agreed to call. Michael walked them to the front door, closing it firmly once they were gone.

"I was worried about you," Michael said when he returned. "Can I get you anything?"

"What you can get is some manners, Michael. Why were you so rude to Tom and Diana? I don't appreciate the way you treated them."

"I'm sorry you feel that way," Michael said.

"Look, Michael. I've had a nasty day, a *really nasty* day." She told him about Gram's fit and her hives, then started to get up. She wanted to get to bed.

"You'd better lie back down."

"Michael. Don't tell me what to do. I run this household just fine, day in and day out, without much assistance from you, I might add. Open your eyes, Michael. I'm not the same naive, young girl you married. I don't need a manager, and I don't need you walking in here, like someone I don't know, dumping on my friends. Where were you when I called anyhow?"

"Having dinner with my boss at the Ritz Carlton, downtown. We had some things to go over before tomorrow's meeting. I'm sorry I forgot to give you the phone number. I called home as soon as I checked my messages. For what it's worth, Carrie, I'm sorry about tonight. When I came home and found you in that guy's arms, I lost it. It made me wonder."

"Michael—don't even go there. Trust me. Nothing's going on, but don't think I haven't thought about it. Tom Egan's a good person, a special friend whose taken the time to care. I'm too tired to deal with this, Michael. I'm going to bed."

"I'll be up soon," he said, giving her a hug. She pulled away from him.

Carrie yawned as she climbed the stairs. Within minutes, she fell into bed, too tired to know how she felt about anything.

# Chapter Twenty-two

Journal, Monday, February 29, 1988

Michael's at the gym and Gram's tucked in for the night. It's been another long day. I glanced at the calender several times today wondering if Gram would die. Wouldn't it be kind of unique to die on the twenty-ninth of February? Gram's death is always on my mind. Since her close encounter last week, Gram seems to be heading to the edge at top speed.

She moaned in pain throughout the night. I finally got up, turned off the monitor, headed downstairs, and gave her a pill which eased her pain for a short while, then it attacked her again. Unable to sleep, she clenched her fists and bit her lip, her eyes pleading. I kept her company while she fought off the suffering.

She wanted to know what I planned to wear to Jennifer and Kevin's rehearsal dinner. When I said I'd wear my new pale pink silk dress, she nodded her approval. I hate talking about the wedding, knowing how unhappy it makes her. We've hired Rhonda to stay here while we're gone for the wedding, but what if Gram dies while we're gone, and I'm not by her side like I promised? I'm not so sure I should leave.

Last night, as I listened to the raspy sounds coming from Gram's chest, I watched the nightlight cast eerie shadows on the wall. The odor in her room made me think of the time a possum crawled under the front porch of our house on Sixth Street and died. It had been dead a couple of days before we noticed the stench. I remember running around the back yard holding my nose while Gram called Otis Cooper, our neighbor from down the street, to come over and dig it out.

Yesterday, Gram asked me if she smelled bad. I couldn't tell her the truth. For years, she's told me stories about how horrible her mother smelled as she lay dying in her hospital bed.

Around four this morning, Gram finally fell asleep. I went upstairs, got my pillow and a comforter from the linen closet, then crashed on the sofa. I wanted to sleep, but couldn't. For some reason, I thought about how I used to come home from high school and find Gram in a starched housedress, her hair looking perfect, makeup on, her nails polished. I hated seeing her like that. I wanted Gram to be like my friends' mothers, who wore jeans and trendy outfits and went to the YMCA to play racquetball. I'd go to my room and not come out until dinner. I fell asleep, wondering why I wasn't nicer to Gram, who put her life on the back burner to raise me.

Morning came. I had my hot tea, and Gram had her iced tea. I apologized for the many times I'd acted like a jerk. Gram told me not to worry, that those things didn't matter. She said that after raising Aunt Nella, taking care of me was like putting butter on toast.

She told me stories about Aunt Nella and her many boyfriends. When Gram said that Jennifer was popluar and pretty, just like her mother, I baited her, saying that Jennifer was like a sister to me. Gram glanced around the room, looking everywhere but at me. I threw out more worms, but she didn't bite. I felt a little guilty for trying to pry information from her, but I forgave myself. After all, I learned my game-playing maneuvers from Gram, the all-time champion.

I'm waiting for Michael to get home. We're making progress in our efforts to hang on to what we have together. I've gotten him to open up a little, but not much. I tend to analyze. I like going over things, settling issues. Michael says it's a girl-thing to rehash things to death. He likes to turn the page. He apologized again for his behavior the night I went to the emergency room. Now, he wants to move on.

I know Michael was jealous that night, even if he won't admit it. I'm pretty sure he'd been sucked in by Gram's insinuations about Tom and me. The whole idea is absurd. I don't have time to be involved with anyone.

Michael thinks I'm trying to be superhuman and insists I can care for Gram and also have fun now and then. I promised to lighten up a bit. That's why I invited Kay and Dave over for dinner last night.

Michael picked up dinner at La Strada—french bread, Caesar salad, and manicotti. It tasted great. After dinner we drank Cabernet Sauvignon and played games. It felt good to laugh. Gram rang the cowbell four times during the evening. First, she wanted the light off, then she wanted iced tea. The other two times, she couldn't remember what she wanted— probably just some attention.

After Kay and Dave left, Michael and I did the dishes together, then sat in the great room, sipping Bailey's Irish Cream, talking about places we'd like to travel. Gram's name didn't come up. When we went upstairs, I brushed my teeth in a hurry. I couldn't wait to climb into bed with Michael. In the caring department, Michael's much better at showing than telling.

I haven't given up my friendship with Tom Egan. He came by last Friday giving me more work and another dose of moral support. When he told me good-bye, he gave me a hug, holding on for a minute or so. I closed my eyes, wishing it didn't feel so good. Michael insists he trusts my judgment where Tom is concerned. Will his trust keep me out of trouble? I hope so.

I've been writing more. Sometimes, I sit in Gram's room and write in my journal. The other day, Gram told me that my fancy words didn't mean a thing. She's certain that I'm writing about her. She's right. The scenes I'm witnessing now are wilder than any fiction I could ever hope to create.

Today Gram did a very strange thing. She sat on the edge of her bed sucking on an unlit cigarette, blowing out air like it was smoke. I'm not sure if she even realized it wasn't lit. Gram has those moves memorized. Simply going through the motions seemed to satisfy her. I stared at her, not knowing what to say. She let out a sigh when she finally put the cigarette down. My guess is she simply doesn't have the air left to inhale.

Father O'Brien stopped by last week to see Gram. I explained our situation, telling him she was a Lutheran and not too pleased that I had decided to become Catholic. He smiled, telling me not to worry. He told Gram that she was a fine Lutheran lady, making her smile. He read the twenty-third Psalm, made the sign of the cross over her, and gave her his blessing, and she seemed pleased. After he left, Gram said he was a nice minister.

I try to talk to Gram about the years we spent together and bring up specific incidents, like the time I sat on the cake she'd baked for the church bazaar. But, she says it's difficult being nostalgic when she can't recall much. Some days she draws a blank on almost everything. On those days, she doesn't recognize me or react to any familiar names. Other days, she's quite alert. I'm not sure what brings her out of her confusion. Perhaps, sometimes there's more oxygen circulating through her brain.

Jennifer calls often, filling me in on wedding details. I don't mind. I enjoy the diversion. I haven't had the nerve to tell her that I'm getting igloo feet, that I might not come to the wedding. I'm wondering if I could get Aunt Nella to fill in for me as Jennifer's matron of honor. Today, I asked Jennifer if she found her birth certificate. She said no, but that she's still working on it. I can't believe that Aunt Nella doesn't know where it is.

Right before I tucked her in bed tonight, Gram was despondent about not going to Wisconsin with us for the wedding. That's when I said, "Gram if you die, perhaps you can be at the wedding." She gave me a strange look, but didn't say anything. After I kissed her goodnight and left the room, I wondered if I had said the wrong thing.

I phoned Kay, telling her what I'd done. Kay said I had given her permission to die, which kind of made sense. I'll never be sure if what I did was the right thing or not. But what's done is done. The truth is I'm not sure about much these days. All I know is I want her suffering to end.

## Chapter Twenty-three

Carrie filled her plate from the buffet—jumbo shrimp, marinated artichokes, gorganzola grits, ziti pasta salad, salami, olives, and stuffed mushrooms, then headed to a round table where her grandmother sat in a sparkly silver dress. When Mavis whirled into the room, in a turquoise chiffon outfit and her hair teased into a bleached-blond pile on top of her head, Gram smiled and waved. "That seat's taken," Gram said, throwing her head back in a full-palate laugh when Carrie pulled out the chair beside her.

Carrie walked across the room and sat at a round table for eight. "I was sorry to hear the terrible news about Michael," said an elderly lady with a hairy mole on the side of her cheek. "I don't know what you are talking about," Carrie said. Michael was okay, wasn't he? She got up from the table, leaving her plate, and headed down a dark, narrow hallway. Several chattering women followed her. One stocky lady, just over five feet tall, pointed to Carrie's pale pink sheath dress. "My goodness dear," she said, "why aren't you dressed in black?"

Carrie awoke drenched in sweat. She climbed out of bed and hurried to her bathroom to splash cold water on her face. She then ran down to the kitchen and dialed Michael's hotel number in New York City. The phone rang four times.

"Are you okay?" she asked when he answered.

"I'm fine," said a groggy Michael. "What's wrong? It's five a.m."

"I had a terrible dream. Several women were chasing me, saying weird things about you. They acted like you had died."

"Rest assured, except for bad breath, I'm fine. I reek of garlic. We ate at a great Italian place last night. How are things at home?"

"The same . . . not so good. Gram's in terrible pain. I got up with her several times during the night."

"You'd better get back to sleep," he said, yawning. "I should too, I've got to be up for a meeting in a couple of hours. I'll call you tonight." Michael hung up. She had wanted to tell him more about her dream, but knew better. Michael, who claimed he never dreamed, lacked enthusiasm about hers.

Carrie peeked into Gram's room and listened to Gram's raspy breathing. Back upstairs, she brushed her teeth, moving the brush in circles around her gums like the hygenist had instructed. She flossed, then swirled cold water in her mouth and spit it out. Lifting her nightshirt over her head, Carrie barely recognized the skinny girl in the mirror. Her rib cage showed. Before stepping into the shower, she weighed herself. She weighed 126 in September. Now she weighed 116.

Downstairs, she ate a cinnamon raisin bagel and sipped her tea, while reading Celestine Sibley's column in the *Atlanta Constitution*. When they first moved to Atlanta, Sibley's columns seemed too folksy, but they had grown on her. When she finished Celestine's tale about her faithful dog, she smiled. Sophie-dog lay at her feet. Carrie knew, if the door had been open, Sophie-dog would by lying in her favorite spot on the floor beside Gram's bed.

When Carrie got up from the table, she turned on the radio. Bobby McFerrin was singing "Don't Worry, Be Happy." Carrie sang along. She took a fresh pitcher of iced tea to Gram's room. Gram lay on the bed, her face gray, her mouth hanging open, looking like a concentration camp figure. Picking up Gram's bony arm, Carrie gently moved it back and forth. Gram didn't respond. Nothing moved, except for the rise and fall of her chest.

"I think Gram's unconscious," Carrie said after she phoned Kay. "She's in the same position she was in hours ago. I hope I didn't give her too much pain medication last night. What if I did? Sorry about my nervous jabbering. I must sound like a real basket case."

"You *are* a basket case. Calm down, Carrie. And stop kicking yourself. You haven't done anything wrong. She'll probably wake up."

"I called Michael at five this morning." She told Kay about her strange dream. "Of course, he didn't say so, but I think he was mad at me for waking him up so early. He never says much when we talk long distance. I'm trying to get him to share his feelings."

"Give it up," Kay said. "Guys don't change."

"Like we *do,* right?" Carrie said. "Michael says I never leave a thought unexpressed." They both laughed.

"Just get busy doing something. You know, like ironing or exercises. I think Gram's going to wake up. Don't ask me why. I just feel it."

"Okay, so you're a psychic, now. I boiled some eggs, so I can make deviled eggs. I actually looked up a recipe. The cookbook said to cover them with cold water, bring them to a rolling boil, set them aside for twenty minutes, then rinse them in cool water. That makes it easy to peel the shell off."

"Tweny minutes! I couldn't wait that long."

"You're so impatient," Carrie said, laughing.

"I know," Kay said. "Go make your deviled eggs. Call me after Gram wakes up."

After hanging up, Carrie checked again. There was no change. She lifted Gram's limp hand, squeezing it tight, but got no reaction. Her skin was lighter than Carrie's, almost white. She lay her grandmother's hand back down on the rose-colored afghan.

"Let's go outside," Carrie said to Sophie-dog, who had followed her into Gram's room. "I think we both could use some fresh air."

Carrie put the monitor on the deck and plugged it in, so she could hear if Gram called her. Then she walked across the yard and around to the front of the house, kicking a pine cone, then another, down the hilly driveway, watching as they rolled into the street. Lacy blossoms on the dogwood trees danced in the spring breeze. Yellow forsythia petals floated to the ground. Puffy clouds paraded through the blue sky. One cloud looked like a spaceship. Carrie wanted to climb aboard.

She chased Sophie-dog around the back yard, their feet leaving a trail in the wet grass. Feeling the warm sun on her back, Carrie ran in place. Sophie-dog circled around her, stopping now and then to chase a butterfly. Out of breath, but feeling better, Carrie unhooked the monitor and went back inside.

"Gram," she yelled, a few inches from her face, "are you in there?" Gram didn't flinch.

Carrie wondered if she should change clothes. If Gram *was* dying, Carrie knew Gram wouldn't approve if she went to the hospital in her scruffy jeans and bleach-spotted sweatshirt. She changed into black pants, a gold turtle neck, and a brown and black embroidered vest. She put on knee highs and her black flats, then brushed her hair and applied lip gloss.

She dug around in her black purse looking for the business card she'd received at the funeral parlor. On the way downstairs, she heard the cowbell clanging. Running to the kitchen, she paperclipped the funeral home card to the blue phone book, then headed down the hallway.

"My goodness, Gram. I thought you were going to sleep all day," Carrie said. She stared into Gram's vacant eyes, wondering if she recognized her. "Here, want a sip?" Carrie asked, offering Gram iced tea. Gram shook her head no. As Carrie set the glass back down on the bedside table, she noticed urine, dark as strong coffee, in Gram's catheter tube. Knowing it was probably not a good sign, she made a mental note to ask Gram's nurse, due soon, about it.

"Cigarette," Gram said.

"Wait a few minutes," Carrie said.

"Must you always tell me what to do? Give me a cigarette. Right now."

Carrie shrugged her shoulders, carefully lifting Gram up. She propped pillows around Gram, whose skinny, birdlike legs dangled over the side of the bed. Carrie washed Gram's hands and face, and brushed her hair before she pulled the pack of cigarettes out of her pocket.

Gram grabbed a cigarette, sticking the wrong end in her mouth. Once again, she acted out the motions—pursing her lips, sucking the unlit cigarette, taking it out of her mouth, then blowing out what air she could muster. Carrie took off her face mask.

"I'm feeling fine today. I'm so hungry. I ate a whole banana. The doctor says I need bananas for potassium." Gram said when Annie, her nurse, arrived.

"That's good, Mrs. Whitfield."

Carrie left the room. Gram hated bananas. And, she hadn't had a bite to eat all day. What was Gram trying to pull? She sure didn't act like someone who was passed out most of the morning. When Annie had finished with Gram, she came into the kitchen.

"I don't know how much longer I can take care of her," Carrie said. "My back's killing me." She told Annie about Gram's restless night and how much pain she was having. "Do you think it's time to get her into a nursing home?"

"I can't make that decision for you," Annie said. "Maybe you should look into hospice care."

"Forget it. I've tried, but neither of her doctors will sign the papers. They claim she's not sick enough for hospice. They have no idea how sick she is; they haven't laid eyes on her for weeks." Annie shook her head. "I know how bad she's getting," Carrie continued. "This morning I thought she'd gone into a coma."

"Hmm—she seemed pretty chipper to me," Annie said.

"Well, she's not. She's putting on a show, for your benefit."

"I'll call the doctor. Her dark urine is not a good sign."

"Like that will do any good. Her doctor told me he hates having you and Rhonda calling him with questions about Gram." Carrie walked outside with Annie.

"Tough tootie to him. I'm calling anyhow, " Annie said, putting one foot into her car. Then she stepped back out and said, "Are you prepared to have your grandmother choke to death?"

"No, of course not. How can anyone prepare for something like that? Thinking about it makes me crazy." Annie touched Carrie on the shoulder, then got into her car and drove off.

Back inside, Carrie grabbed the phone book out of the cupboard. Flipping to the N section in the Yellow Pages, she found the listing for nursing homes. She dialed the number of a nursing home on Ashford-Dunwoody Road. The girl who answered told her everyone was busy. Carrie left a message to have someone call as soon as possible.

"Why do you have that nasty look on your face?" Gram said when Carrie went back to her room.

"I'm angry because you lied to the nurse. You didn't eat a damn banana this morning, and you know it. You hate bananas. I'll bet you haven't eaten one in two years. As for today, you haven't taken one bite of anything. And—you aren't feeling *fine*. You did this very same thing that day at the doctor's office."

"Oh, so that's it," Gram said. "I knew. I just *knew* that would come up some day. That's why you want me out of here. Don't think I don't know. I heard you talking to that nurse about putting me into a nursing home. Why don't you just pick me up and throw me into the garbage?"

"Gram, don't be absurd." Carrie gritted her teeth.

"Go on. Just toss me out. I'm no good to anyone. I've never done anything right in my whole damn life." Gram threw her hands up into the air.

"That's not true, and you know it," Carrie said. She felt the blood rising in her face. Gram stared at Carrie, her eyes like darts. "You listen here, Gram. I'm trying my best to to take care of you, and believe you me—it's not easy. You wouldn't put up with half the stuff I'm tolerating from you." Carrie stood, her hands on her hips, her elbows jutting out in defiance.

"Don't bother. Just let me rot. I'm not worth the trouble anyhow."

"Gram, stop it right this minute. Stop putting yourself down. You've helped lots of people get started in AA. You raised your own family, then took over with me. One time, you told me that the only thing we take with us from this life is the good we've done to others, and Gram—you've done lots of good." Carrie took a deep breath.

"I'm worthless," Gram said, narrowing her eyes at Carrie. "I'm just an emaciated old woman."

"Bullshit, Gram," Carrie screamed.

"Well, bullshit to you, too. Young lady, you don't know what it's like to lie here in pain, so weak I can't even get out of this stupid bed."

"Go ahead, Gram, get angry. It's about time." Carrie paced the floor, clenching her fists. "It doesn't matter. What you can't do anymore doesn't matter. Who you are isn't about what you can do."

"Oh, be quiet. *You* don't know anything except that you're sick of caring for me. After all I've done for you, Caroline, you *could* show me some respect."

"Hold it right there . . . I do respect you, Gram. I've put my whole life on hold for you—my job, my privacy, my social life, my time with Michael, and my physical health. Look at me. I'm a beanpole. I can't sleep or eat. I throw up most of what I do eat. You've taken over my whole life." Carrie took several short quick breaths, trying not to hyperventilate. Her face turned red.

"I always knew that you are a very headstrong girl."

"I have to be headstrong to deal with you, Gram. Could you please tell me why you've sabatoged all of my efforts to get help."

"Oh, so everything is *my* fault." Gram stared at Carrie with beady eyes. "You're just waiting for me to die, and you know it."

"Stop, Gram. Stop right now. I don't have to listen to this." Carrie put her hands over her ears.

"Well, you sure as hell don't like playing nursemaid. You listen here, Caroline." Gram pointed her finger at Carrie. "I gave up a good part of my life raising you." Gram had to stop to catch her breath. "Why are you dressed up so fancy anyhow? Are you going out somewhere? Are you going to leave me here all alone?"

"Of course not." She didn't tell Gram why she had changed. "Don't you try to make me feel guilty," Carrie said. "The truth is—I'm not sure I can take this any longer."

"*You* can't take it any longer. Well, what about me? I hate it when you tell me what to eat, when to go to the bathroom, when to use the telephone, when to take a pain pill. You took away everything I like."

"What do you mean by that?"

"You've taken away my cigarettes and the other."

"What other?"

"You know—alcohol."

"Gram, you aren't making sense. I was a child when you stopped drinking."

"Well, I did it for you." Gram started to cough.

"Are you okay?"

"Hell, no. I'm not okay. I want Nella to come take care of me. She knows how to take care of a sick person."

"Oh, please, Gram. That's nonsense. You and Nella have a war going on. Any fool knows that."

"We do not. You don't know anything." Gram took short quick breaths.

"I know quite a lot," Carrie said, her voice escalating. "I know all about how you called my dad the night of the car accident, sending my parents out on the road to Elkhart Lake. My mother wrote about it in the journal I found in an old trunk in Nella's attic." Once Carrie realized what she had blurted out, she began shaking.

Gram looked like she'd been slapped in the face. She gasped and fell over onto her side. Rushing to her, Carrie caught her just in time.

"Go away," Gram said. "Don't you touch me. I want to be alone."

"Fine." Carrie left the room, exhausted. At the end of her rope, she couldn't wait for Gram to die. She changed back into her grubby clothes, then headed outside with Sophie-dog.

She pulled weeds out of the planter and screamed at a bee to get the hell out of her way. Gram wasn't the only one who could get angry. Perhaps it was time that she released her own pent-up emotions. After all, Gram didn't own *all* of the craziness in the family.

Perish the thought, she said to herself, wondering if she was turning into Gram. She beat at the dirt in the planter, then ripped at the pansies, deadheading them. She dug up one withered, sickly-looking plant nearest the door to the great room, and threw it across the yard. Getting up, she walked over, picked up the limp plant and hurled it into the grove of pine trees in the adjacent lot.

Carrie walked back inside. What did it matter? What did anything matter? She felt limp, lifeless. She wondered how Gram must feel. She opened Gram's door. Gram was crashed. Carrie washed her hands, then lay down on the sofa. She was startled by the phone ringing.

"Did I wake you?" Tom said.

"I'm not sure. I think so." Carrie said, checking her watch. She had been asleep for an hour. She told Tom about her fight with Gram. "I'm not sure what happened. I exploded. I'm turning into some kind of monster. How could I yell at poor Gram?"

"It was probably good for both of you," he said.

"Maybe so. But I feel rotten."

"Is Michael home?"

"No, he's in New York."

"Is it okay if I come over?"

"No, please don't. I'm a mess," Carrie said.

"You shouldn't be alone right now, Carrie."

"Believe me, I'm not alone." She told him good-bye.

Carrie went upstairs to the spare bedroom and wrote a few lines of doom and gloom verse, then scribbled over it with a black marker. Back downstairs, she got a Diet Coke out of the refrigerator and toasted an English muffin. She put a slice of ham and a glob of mustard on her muffin then forced herself to eat. She was startled when she heard the cowbell ring; Gram had been sleeping for more than three hours.

"Gram," she said. "I'm so sorry for yelling at you."

"Me too," Gram said.

"Can I get you anything?" Carrie said.

"No. I just wanted to say thanks."

"For what?"

"For everything," Gram said.

"You're welcome." Carrie fixed Gram fresh tea, then spoon-fed her chocolate pudding. She gave her a cigarette to hold onto.

Carrie picked up a photo album from the top of Gram's wicker basket. "Want to look at this with me?' she asked. Gram nodded yes.

Carrie propped Gram up on her pillows, then stood beside the bed and began turning the pages of the album. "Isn't that Alvina Pickett next to you in this picture?" Gram studied it closely. "I remember the funny stories about Alvina, and how she always claimed the chair by the window in the entryway of your apartment building."

"A person could have sold tickets for that spot when someone was moving in," Gram said. "Alvina was a first-class busybody who never missed anything."

They looked at pictures of Gram smiling, wearing print dresses in the summer, stylish woolen dresses and felt hats in the winter, and sequined outfits for the holidays.

"Gram, I'm proud of you. You have had a lot to deal with, and you've shown so much courage," Carrie said.

"We do what we have to do. We must bear our burdens in this life."

"I know, Gram. I know." She patted Gram on the arm.

"I can't believe you saved this," Carrie said, pointing to a yellowed scrap of lined paper with a child's handwriting. "Mature is being able to accept the fact that you're not always right and being able to listen to other people and control yourself when you need to. Caroline Whitfield, age 6," she read aloud. Gram smiled.

"I guess we both lost it today, didn't we?" Gram said.

"Yes, we did. But it's okay. We both feel better, right?" Gram nodded.

Carrie put the album away and sat down in the bedside chair. The two of them sat in silence facing one another, their silence going beyond words. She's slipping away, like a falling star, Carrie thought, but no matter how far away she falls, she'll always be a part of me.

❦

"Gram," Carrie said. "I've been thinking. If Michael and I have a daughter, I'd like to call her Madeline."

"I'd like that, Caroline. I'd like that a lot." Gram smiled. "Don't call her Maddie, call her Madeline."

"Okay, Gram."

Gram told Carrie she wanted to phone Jennifer. Carrie dialed the number, then handed her the phone. Gram asked Carrie to leave the room. When Carrie returned a short time later, Gram had tears in her eyes. "What's wrong?" Carrie asked.

"I told Jennifer I couldn't make it to her wedding." Gram twisted the corner of her afghan with her hand.

"I've done things in my life that I've regretted," Gram said. "I want you to know that."

"So have I," Carrie said. "So have I." Carrie kissed Gram on the cheek.

"I never meant any harm to come to your parents. So many times I've wished I could turn the clock back and do that night over."

"I know you didn't mean harm, Gram." Carrie wanted so much to know more, but dropped the subject. She had tortured Gram enough for one day.

Carrie heated a Lean Cuisine frozen enchilada in the microwave. While eating, she thought about a comment Gram had made before their fight. "I know that God is with me," Gram had said. "That helps when I'm afraid." Gram's comment had given Carrie food for thought. She knew Gram's anger had come partly from fear. Hers had too.

After dinner, Carrie flipped through the latest *Sports Illustrated* stopping to read an article about Brian Boitano, the U. S. Olympic figure skater. She got up when the doorbell rang. Looking out the peephole, she was surprised to see Tom Egan. "Here," he said handing her a bouquet of daffodils when she opened the door.

"Thanks," Carrie said as he stepped inside the house. She took the flowers to the kitchen and put them in a vase. Tom followed her.

"You don't look so terrible," he said.

"Tom, I look like crap, and I feel like crap." They went into the great room.

"Why did you come over?" she said.

"I was concerned about you."

"I'm doing better. Gram and I made up. She's down for the night now." Carrie sat down beside Tom on the sofa. "The poor woman is dying. I can't believe I got so angry with her."

"I'm sorry you had such a tough day." Tom reached over for her. She leaned into him, resting her head on his shoulder. He put his arm around her.

"No, don't do that," she said, surprised when he lifted her chin and tried to kiss her. He tried again. She started to return his kiss, then pulled away. "Stop, please stop," she said, standing up. She had fantasized about being in Tom's arms, but now, she wanted no part of it. It didn't feel right.

"I can help you relax," Tom said, standing up. He massaged her back with the palms of his hands.

"I can't believe you said that," she said, moving away from him. "My head is already so messed up tonight. I can't deal with this. Besides—I'm not into this free sex bit."

"Oh," he said, laughing, "you *charge*?"

"Tom, I'm not in the mood for flip comments. I don't think it's funny. I have every right to tell you to back off. It's my choice not to get involved with you. Is that clear?" she said holding up her left hand. "I am married. Remember?"

"Fine—I was just feeling bad for you." Tom sat back down. "I concede."

"Look," she said. "I have enough to feel guilty about for today. I can't just change gears and jump into bed with you. I think you'd better leave."

"Okay, I'm sorry. I'm a jerk. I made a dumb mistake. I'll go." He walked to the front door. Carrie followed him.

"Michael must be some guy," Tom said as he walked out the door. Carrie waited a couple of minutes, until his car went down the driveway. Then she slammed the door.

She looked in on Gram, then headed upstairs and got ready for bed. The phone rang right after she turned out the light. It was Michael. He wanted to know how things were going. Carrie told him about her fight with Gram. "I even told her I knew about the phone call she made to my dad the night of the car accident."

"How'd she react?"

"Shocked and hurt."

"Did you ask Gram if Jennifer's your sister?"

"No. I wanted to, but that will have to wait. I felt like I'd done enough damage for one day. I feel guilty, Michael—I really feel guilty."

"Don't beat yourself up, Carrie. You've been dealing with a lot."

"Thanks. I needed to hear that. The good news is that we both apologized and made up. After that, Gram seemed more at peace."

"Good," Michael said. "Maybe she needed to let off some steam. She's probably angry at the world."

"I guess so," Carrie said. "I'm in bed now. My eyelids feel like they are weighted down with concrete. I've got to hang up. I miss you. Hurry home, please."

"Hmm, I wish I was already there. I'll see you tomorrow."

Carrie tossed and turned in bed. Nothing seemed real anymore. She felt like an intruder in someone else's life. She tried to sort things out, to make sense of her day, but her brain was fried. She wanted to stop thinking. Who knew what tomorrow would bring?

# Chapter Twenty-four

### Journal, Wednesday, March 2, 1988

6:00 a.m. I'm a zombie. I'm on the sofa in the great room, shivering. You'd think my jeans and sweater would keep me warm. The wind is howling. I turned the heat up, so it should kick in soon. I'm exhausted. It's a good thing I went to bed early last night. I got up at one this morning when I heard Gram on the monitor crying out – over and over – begging someone to please help her.

I forced myself out of bed. When I got downstairs, Gram wore a look like a wild animal caught in a car's headlights. She writhed in pain. I hurt just watching her. Her fingernails dug into my arm as I lifted her into a sitting position, propping her up with pillows. I gave her a Tylenol-3 tablet crushed in chocolate ice cream.

"Hospital," Gram said several times in a tiny childlike voice.

I wondered if she was serious. Did she really want me to call for an ambulance? Was the pain controlling her thoughts? I couldn't tell. Yesterday, she went ballistic when I mentioned that it might be time to get her to a hospital.

I decided to wait for her to mention the hospital again. I was stalling for time. Sending her to the hospital seemed so final. While I waited for the medication to take effect, I sat in the bedside chair making small talk, chatting about whatever popped into my mind. I talked about the signs of springtime—yellow forsythia blossoms, new green leaves, the buds on the Japanese magnolia trees lining the front walkway, robins and cardinals splashing in the birdbath. Gram lay in bed, her fists in tight balls, her breathing labored.

I knew when the pain medication began to take effect because her breathing slowed. Her face relaxed. She stretched her fingers. She dropped her head back and finally closed her eyes. While she dozed, I looked through the small green prayer book with rag-eared pages that my grandfather Henry gave her many years before. On the front cover, tall trees stood shrouded in fog. Inside was the inscription—*To Madeline, who brought a little bit of heaven into my life. Love, Henry.*

I fingered the tattered bookmark that lay between the pages. I gave that bookmark to Gram for her birthday one year. Scotch tape covered a teddy bear's faded face on the front of the bookmark. Underneath the bear, blue letters spelled out *Don't Forget That I Love You*. On the back, fingerprints and food stained my childish handwriting, *To Gram, Happy Birthday, Love, Caroline, May, 1975.*

Gram had marked a section about suffering in the prayerbook. Over the years, Gram and I had often discussed why some people suffered more than others. I remembered asking Gram why bad things happened to good people. I wanted to know why my friend Susan's brother had died when lightning struck him while he was playing basketball. And why, I wanted to know, had Susan's dad run off, leaving her mother without any money? Gram told me she didn't know, but she did know Susan and her mother would be rewarded for their suffering, that suffering linked people to God.

I wondered if she still believed in that reward system. I read a few more pages of her prayer book, trying to stay awake. Gram would wake up off and on moaning, then fall back asleep. About an hour ago, I gave her more pain pills, mixed in butterscotch pudding. It took a long time for Gram to swallow each tiny portion.

After she got the pills down, she wanted to know if we were going to the hospital. I asked her if she was sure that was what she wanted. She nodded yes, then asked if I would go with her. I said of course I would.

Gram looked relieved. She fell asleep comforted. I jumped into the shower. Now, I sit here hesitating to make the call for an ambulance. I'm afraid to make it. Once she leaves here, she won't come back.

I'd like to call Michael, but I've decided to wait until I know what's going on. At least he's coming home today. My mind is spinning. I'd like to call a doctor for advice. But, I have no doctor who will respond. Here I am, with Gram dying, and no one in the medical world who seems to give a damn. I refuse to call Dr. Kirkland. I'll call the oncologist, Dr. Baker, once I get an ambulance on the way. I plan to tell him what *he* needs to do.

When all of this is behind me, I'm sending Dr. Kirkland a letter and Dr. Baker a copy. I've been composing it in my head the past few weeks. I may as well put it down on paper right now. I need something to keep me from going crazy. Here goes:

*Dear Dr. Kirkland,*

*Last December, I came to your office and explained that my grandmother, Madeline Whitfield, a lung cancer patient, would be coming to live with me. Her doctor in Wisconsin had found a massive tumor in her lung and had given her three to six months to live. You told me to bring Gram in to see you, which I did. You were amazed at how good she looked. I agreed. She did look good, but looks can be deceiving. What you need to know is that Gram spent four hours getting ready for the office visit. (She had to stop for an hour's nap in the process.)*

*You ordered her to have radiation, but she refused. I begged for hospice care. You denied my request, saying it was too soon. You suggested she see Dr. Baker, an oncologist. I took her to Dr. Baker who ordered her to have a biopsy to prove she had a malignancy, a necessary requirement for someone requesting hospice care. My husband and I forced Gram to have the biopsy. The lung specialist did not take enough tissue, so the biopsy failed.*

*After that, I made another appointment with you, begging for help. You once again refused to sign the papers for hospice care. You finally agreed to arrange for nurses to come twice a week for thirty minutes each visit. The nurses who came were not trained in caring for terminal patients. One of the nurses came to me for help one day, when she thought Gram was choking. The nurses often called you with questions. You called me complaining that the constant calls from the nurses were bothering you. You insisted that my grandmother was not all that sick, insinuating that I wanted my grandmother to die. I came to you for help in taking care of my dying grandmother. All you managed to do was make me feel guilty.*

*As a doctor, sworn to the ethics of the Hippocratic oath, I believe you failed in doing your duty. I'm angry and disappointed. When my grandmother dies, I won't be angry because she has died. I'll be angry because you let me down. You only added to my grandmother's suffering and to mine.*

*In the future, I hope that you will show compassion for patients and their caregivers. It is my hope that others will not suffer as I have. I never want another patient of yours to become a prisoner in their own home with no support from you. I trust that I have adequately explained my position.*

I think my letter will get the doctor's attention. He may even figure out that he's been a jerk. My hand is tired. I need another cup of tea—forget the tea. I hear the cowbell ringing.

## Chapter Twenty-five

G ram's urgent eyes spoke volumes. She tried to cough. Her chest made sputtering noises, like a dying motor. When Carrie scooted her up onto her pillows, Gram grimaced, clenching her fists. The March wind rattled the windows. Glancing outside, Carrie noticed a light was on in the house next door.

"Are we going now?"

"Where?" Carrie asked.

"You know . . . to the hospital? You can't wear your jeans to the hospital," Gram said, in a weakened voice.

"I'll go change." Carrie welcomed the opportunity to leave the room. She needed time to think. Was Gram really ready to go to the hospital? Carrie wanted to be sure before she called for an ambulance.

The phone rang when Carrie reached the top of the stairs. It was Jennifer. "For some reason, I can't seem to get Gram off my mind this morning. Is everything okay?"

"No. Far from it," Carrie said. "Gram's in bad shape. She's asking to go to the hospital."

"Are you sure it's time?"

"Gram seems to think so. I'm going to call for an ambulance as soon as I hang up," Carrie said, making her decision. "She can't take the pain anymore. She had a terrible night. I hate seeing her like this."

"Is Michael home?" "No."

"Call me after you get to the hospital. Please."

"I hope they will give her morhpine at the hospital. She won't be coming back here—you know that, don't you?" Carrie said. Jennifer whispered yes. "Please call your Mom for me. Let her know what's going on. I'll call you back after she gets settled at the hospital."

Carrie hung up and changed into an outfit Gram had complimented her on—her black pants and pink and black striped sweater. She put on knee highs, then slipped on her black flats. Before she lost her nerve, she called St. Joseph's Hospital and asked them to send an ambulance. Hanging up, she reminded herself how Gram said months ago to move her somewhere when it got too bad. If their roles were reversed, she felt sure that Gram would send her to the hospital.

She waited ten minutes to call Dr. Baker's office when it opened at eight o'clock. "Dr. Baker's on his way to St. Joseph's to make his rounds," his nurse said. "I'll pass along your message and ask him to look for you either in emergency or up on the sixth floor oncology ward."

"Make sure he gets my message," Carrie said. She felt nauseous when she hung up the phone. She stopped outside the door to Gram's to gain her composure, then walked in. "I called the ambulance," Carrie said, trying to act cheerful. "It will be here soon."

Gram lay propped up on the bed, her brown eyes fixed in position. She refused to look at Carrie. Knowing Gram needed a few minutes alone, Carrie left the room. She took Sophie-dog outside and hooked her onto her rope. Back in the kitchen, she checked her purse to see if she had any cash. She found a twenty, two fives, and several ones in her wallet. Who knew how long she would be at the hospital? She set her journal and *Kate Vaiden,* the Reynolds Price book she'd been reading, in her black and white canvas tote bag and set it beside her purse. Her heart raced. She took several deep breaths, then exhaled.

"Gram, can I get you anything?" she said, walking back into her room. Gram slowly shook her head no. Carrie touched Gram on the hand and said, "I love you, Gram."

She heard three loud knocks and ran to open the front door. Two men stood on the doorstep—a John Belushi look-alike and a tall, skinny blond whose face was dotted with zits.

"Ma'am, I'm Rudy," the Belushi look-alike said, "and this is my helper, Sherwood. You called for an ambulance?"

"Wait here a moment," Carrie said after ushering them inside. "I need to tell my grandmother you're here."

"The ambulance is here," Carrie said. Gram's eyes widened. "Do you still want to go to the hospital?"

Gram nodded yes. Carrie pulled Gram's pink and white striped robe off the closet hook, then motioned for the men to come down the hallway. Their heavy footsteps resounded ominously in the hall. Rudy lifted Gram into a sitting position, his strong hands under her armpits. Carrie put Gram's arms into the sleeves of her robe and pulled it around her, tying the belt in front. She slid Gram's black satin slippers onto her feet.

"You sure have dainty little feet," Rudy said. Gram gave him half of a smile. She'd always been proud of her small feet.

"Hang onto to me," Sherwood said as he hoisted Gram's frail body onto the stretcher, covering her with a mustard-colored blanket. The two men carried her out of the room. Carrie followed.

"Caroline, get my purse," Gram said, once they got to the front door. "And get my glasses, and make sure my wallet and insurance card are in my purse."

"Okay, Gram." Carrie shook her head.

"Where's puppy dog?" Gram asked.

"Outside, on her rope. I'll put her into the laundry room before I leave. Don't worry. She'll be just fine."

"Wasn't my nurse, Rhonda, supposed to come today?"

"Yes, Gram. I'll call and let her know." Carrie was amazed at Gram's ability to orchestrate her exit. Gram was crossing things off her mental list. She had no intention of leaving things undone.

Standing, holding onto the gurney, Rudy and Sherman began to look impatient. "We're off now, ma'am," Rudy said to Gram "It's time to take a ride."

"I'll be right along, Gram."

Gram blinked when the bright sun hit her eyes. Carrie watched them load her into the ambulance. Rudy shut the door with a bang. Carrie felt a corresponding thud in the pit of her stomach. The air was cold and crisp. The leaves on the dogwood trees beside the driveway sparkled in the sunshine.

"Please don't turn on the siren. There's no need for that," Carrie said.

"Okay, ma'am," Rudy said. "We'll keep it quiet."

Carrie took a deep breath as she watched the ambulance wind down the driveway. When it was out of sight, she hurried back inside and called Kay. She left a message on her machine that she would be at the hospital. Then she grabbed Gram's things—hairbrush, glasses, prayer book, driver's license and Social Security card—and put them into Gram's favorite old black purse.

The phone rang as she was going out the back door. "Aunt Nella, I can't talk," Carrie said. She explained that the ambulance had just driven off with Gram.

"But I wanted to talk to mother." Aunt Nella sounded anxious.

"You'll have to wait. I'll call later. Right now, I've got to go." Carrie hung up, not wanting to waste another minute.

Before she left, Carrie opened the kitchen cabinet, reached up to the top shelf, and grabbed Gram's carton of Salems. On the way out the door, she dropped the cigarettes into the garbage.

On the freeway, Carrie checked her watch. It had been ten minutes since the ambulance drove away. Luckily, at the hospital, she got a parking space in the emergency parking lot, near the entrance. Inside, she searched for the emergency room. "Mrs. Whitfield's in the corner room," a nurse said, pointing to a small cubicle.

"Gram, I finally made it here. Aunt Nella called just as I was leaving."

"Is she coming to see me?"

"No, Gram. There's a big snowstorm in Milwaukee. The airport's closed." On the radio, driving to the hospital, Carrie heard about the big Midwestern snowstorm. She had made up the part about Milwaukee. "Aunt Nella wants to talk to you. We'll call as soon as you get settled into a room. Has Dr. Baker been in to see you?"

"No," Gram said. Carrie was relieved. She didn't want to miss him.

"You look nice," Gram said." Carrie thanked her.

Gram's brown eyes appeared too large for her sunken face. An IV dripped into her shriveled arm. "I'm going to check with the nurse," Carrie said. At the nurse's station, she learned that Dr. Baker had called and ordered morphine for Gram. "She should be getting drowsy," the nurse said. "Her room's almost ready."

"Good," Carrie said. When she got back to the cubicle, Gram was sleeping. Standing beside the bed, Carrie stared down. Good for you, Gram, she thought. You have fought a tough battle with courage, never wavering in your determination to die on your own terms. She took Gram's clammy hand and held onto it. Listening to her labored breathing, Carrie knew she had to let go. It had all come down to letting go.

Carrie sat down across the room in a wooden straight-back chair and fell asleep.

"We're moving her now. She's been assigned to Room 626," a nurse said, walking into the room.

"Okay," Carrie said, shaking her head, waking from a dream. In the dream, Gram was dressed in a red satin gown, looking happy and healthy . . . *"This getting into heaven—lawsy sakes, it took some real doing," Gram said, her hands on her hips, as she stood waiting for an elevator. Carrie asked Gram what it was like in heaven. "Oh, they do everything for you here."*

*"They?" Carrie asked, picturing chubby baroque angels. Gram didn't answer. Carrie asked several questions, but Gram, who looked about thirty years old, said nothing. When the door opened, Gram stepped onto the elevator—smiling, her hair short and perky, her eyes bright, her skin smooth.*

"I'm dying. I just know it," Gram said.

"Gram, the nurse is going to take you to your room now." Carrie blinked her eyes, trying to wake up.

"Are you coming, too?"

"Of course."

The wheels of the gurney squeaked as the nurse pushed it onto the elevator. Carrie stood beside Gram, staring up at the numbers as the elevator moved up to the sixth floor. She walked beside Gram as they rolled her down the hallway to her room. Two nurses hoisted her onto the bed. Carrie stared at the number 626 on the door. It figured that dying cancer patients would be sent to the sixth floor, she thought. Carrie hated the number six. She wasn't sure why. Perhaps, because it was a Biblically bad number.

"Your purse with the things you wanted is right here," Carrie said. She opened the deep bottom drawer of the beside chest and put Gram's purse inside. She knew Gram wouldn't use the purse, or her glasses, or her wallet. But she knew a woman surely could not die without knowing the whereabouts of her purse.

"I'm Eileen, Mrs. Whitfield. I'll be your nurse today." Carrie said hello and introduced herself to the tall, thin nurse with curly auburn red hair.

"I'm pleased to meet you both," the nurse said. "Mrs. Whitfield, I want you to speak up when you're hurting."

"You can call me Madeline," Gram said.

"Okay, Madeline," the nurse said.

❦

"How are you doing?" Dr. Baker asked, striding into the room holding onto a clipboard.

"I've been better," Gram said.

"We'll keep you comfortable," he said. He checked Gram's vital signs. "Please come with me," he said to Carrie when he finished with Gram. As they stood near the circular nurses station, nurses darted past. Visitors paced the floor, looking anxious. Three orderlies rolled a gurney past with a completely covered form. A white-haired man, with tears in his eyes, shuffled along behind the gurney. Carrie looked away.

Holding Gram's chart, Dr. Baker pointed to the big black letters on the front. "DNR stands for do not rescusitate. I've put this message on here, because Mrs. Whitfield requested I do so when I saw her in my office. No emergency measures will be performed to keep your grandmother alive."

"Good." Carrie said, knowing that was what Gram wanted.

"I'm not giving her an IV—no food or water in accordance with her wishes. However, I have ordered an oxygen tube hooked up to help her breathe."

"How often can she have the morphine shots?"

"Every four hours," he said, thumbing through her chart. "I see a huge deterioration in Mrs. Whitfield since I saw her six weeks ago."

Carrie wanted to say, *No shit, Sherlock*, but she bit her tongue. "How long do you think she'll last?"

"It's difficult to tell," he said. "I can't say for certain that her death is imminent, because I've no idea how strong her body is. She might not make it until tomorrow morning. Then again, she may last a few weeks."

Carrie's face felt hot. A few weeks? Surely, she couldn't last that long, not in her condition. Or, could she?

"Perhaps we should arrange for hospice care," Dr. Baker said.

Carrie wanted to slap him. "Don't you think it's a little late for that?" she said. The words flew out of her mouth, like bullets. She felt like calling Dr. Baker several choice names but held her tongue.

"I'll be back to check on her later," he said, looking away. He placed Gram's chart on the nurse's desk, then walked toward the elevator.

Back in Gram's room Carrie sat in the armchair in front of the tall, narrow window. She stared at the grayish-mauve walls, the oxygen tube, dangling on the iron bed railing. Gram lay hunched over the mound of pillows. Carrie's intestines felt like spastic snakes. She stared at the scratch marks on the back of the closed door and shuddered. Had someone tried to claw their way out?

"Should I lay her down?" Carrie asked when the nurse returned to the room.

"No. Leave her be. She might start to choke if you lie her down. Sitting up like that is probably the only way she can breathe."

A pink-smocked hospital volunteer walked into the room with a bouquet of flowers—seven red roses surrounded by baby's breath in a milkglass vase. "Please put them down over there, on the food tray," Carrie said. She wanted Gram to see the flowers when she awoke.

"They add a nice touch, don't they?" the nurse said, taking a sniff. Carrie nodded yes as she opened the envelope. The card read:

"Mother, Here are seven roses, one for each decade you have danced through life. Love, Nella."

She propped the card up in front of the flowers.

"You sure you don't want her to have an IV?" Eileen asked. "She's seems pretty dehydrated."

Carrie hesitated, then said, "No. While we waited in the emergency area, she pleaded not to give her anything. I promised I wouldn't do anything to prolong her life. Believe me, she wants to die." Carrie hoped she was doing the right thing.

"Okay," the nurse said, "if that's her wish."

"I'll try giving her a sip of water when she awakens. Could she have some sweetened tea? That's the only thing she likes right now."

"Certainly. I'll have them bring some with her lunch," Eileen said. "The trays should be coming up soon."

"She won't be getting any lunch."

"Sure she will. The doctor ordered a full lunch for her." Eileen left the room.

What had Dr. Baker been thinking? He had just told Carrie that he wouldn't give her any food. Had he forgotten so soon?

Carrie sat down in the gray vinyl chair and closed her eyes. She fought off the urge to call the nurse back into the room and hook up an IV. The room was quiet, except for the raspy noises coming from Gram's chest. Gram looked like a limp doll, arched over the mound of pillows, her mouth hanging open, her eyes shut.

Carrie tried reading, but dozed off after two paragraphs. She awoke to a loud crashing sound in the corridor. Opening the door, she she saw that someone had dropped a tray of instruments in the hallway. The loud noise hadn't disturbed Gram. Carrie left the room. She searched for a phone booth and called Aunt Nella. "The roses arrived. They're gorgeous," Carrie said, when her aunt answered.

"Does she like them?" Aunt Nella said.

"She hasn't seen them yet." Carrie told her how bad things were.

"The timing's bad, with the wedding only ten days away." Aunt Nella said.

"No one chooses when to die," Carrie said, sounding perturbed.

"Gram wanted so much to be at the wedding," Aunt Nella said. "I wish I had come back down to see her." Carrie clenched her jaw to keep from saying anything.

"When Gram awakens, I'll call you from her room. She really wants to talk to you." Carrie said before she hung up.

Next, Carrie called Jennifer at work and gave her an update. She told Jennifer about her confrontation with Gram.

"How did Gram react when you said you knew about her phone call to your Dad?" Jennifer said.

"She clammed up. But, later she told me she'd done things in her life that she regretted. Have you found anything out about your birth father?"

"A tad. Mom said he and my mom gave me up because he felt it was the right thing to do."

"Did she tell you anything more?"

"No, but Gram did, on the phone yesterday."

"She did?"

Just then, Gram's nurse, Eileen, tapped Carrie on the shoulder. "Your grandmother is awake and calling out for you."

"I have to go now. I'll call back later. I want to know what Gram said."

❦

"I'm right here.Gram. I called Aunt Nella and Jennifer. They send their love. Did you see the roses from Aunt Nella?" Carrie carried the bouquet over toward the bed, so Gram could get a closer look. After putting the flowers down, she pulled her chair closer to Gram's bed, then touched Gram gently on the arm.

"No, don't," Gram said, grimacing.

"I'm sorry, Gram." Carrie thought about the day the girl in the flower shop in Sheboygan, whose brother had died of cancer, had mentioned how they couldn't touch him at the end. It hurt too much.

"The pain. It's awful, Caroline. I can't stand it."

"I'm sorry, Gram."

"How long does it take to die?" Gram asked the nurse.

"I can't say, dear. There is no formula. Dying is different for everyone," Eileen said.

"The wedding. The wedding," Gram repeated after Eileen went out the door.

"Yes, Gram, Jennifer's wedding is soon." Carrie paused, then asked, "Gram, is Jennifer my sister?" Gram looked confused. "Remember the photograph, the one of my dad and the little baby. Was he holding Jennifer?"

Someone opened the door before Gram had time to answer. "Lunch time," a short, squatty nurse's aide said. "You'll have to move those flowers and make me some room to put this tray down."

Carrie wrinkled her nose. The meal smelled institutional. "We don't need a lunch tray," Carrie said. "Just leave the iced tea and a spoon." The girl handed over the tea and spoon and left.

"Wa - ter," Gram said, "wa - ter." Carrie dribbbled some iced tea into her mouth. Most of it fell down Gram's chin.

"Here you go, Gram." She tried giving her more tea, with little luck. Gram stared at Carrie, moving her mouth as if she wanted to say something.

"Mo - ney," Gram finally said, in a barely audible voice. She looked over at Carrie like a little girl in trouble.

"It's okay, Gram. Don't worry. You're a good egg, aren't you?" Gram nodded yes. Carrie figured that Gram was worried, because she'd never told Carrie about the mysterious loan. It no longer mattered. Carrie wasn't sure if they would be responsible for Gram's bills or not. Michael had said, probably not.

Carrie was startled when Gram fell forward, her right hand tapping at her throat, like she was trying to clear out her throat. "Oh, no . . . oh, no," Gram said, her body jerking forward, her eyes bugging out. She held onto her throat.

Carrie could see the fear in her eyes and knew that Gram was afraid she was choking to death. So was Carrie. She stood beside Gram, trying to help, but there was nothing she could do. Gram whimpered, then fell forward onto the pillows, her eyes closed.

"Come quick," Carrie said, running out to the nurses' station. She motioned for Eileen to follow her. Back in the room, Carrie was glad to see Gram still breathing.

"I brought you a pain pill, Madeline. Swallow it down," she said, trying to give Gram a sip of water. The pill lay on Gram's tongue. It stayed there. Gram stared at Carrie, her eyes lifeless.

"She can't swallow anymore," Carrie said.

"I'm sorry," Eileen said. "Dr. Baker said to give her the morphine shot, then to give her medication by mouth. I guess I'll have to inject her again."

"He has no idea what she can and can't do," Carrie said.

Eileen left the room and came back with a hypodermic needle. She stabbed Gram's arm. Gram rolled her eyes to the back of her head. Her eye sockets looked too big for her eyes. Carrie looked at the floor, biting her lip. "There. Now, you'll feel better," Eileen said.

Carrie sat back down. Gram closed her eyes, waiting for relief. Carrie wanted the suffering to stop for Gram. She wanted to tell Gram not to worry, that she would get her safely to the shore. "With all you've endured, perhaps you'll go straight to heaven," Carrie said, trying to make Gram feel better.

Gram shot her a beady-eyed look. "Don't talk like that," she said in a tiny voice. Carrie looked away smiling. Gram had no intention of taking any detours.

"You've got it right, Gram. You have a straight shot," Carrie said, trying to correct her faux pas. She admired Gram's spunk. Why had she always tried to turn Gram into someone other than herself? Kay was right. People don't change. We are who we are—take it or leave it.

Carrie heard footsteps coming down the hallway and recognized Michael's cracking ankles. "Well, here you two are," Michael said. "I got home early and found an empty house. I called Kay to find out where you guys had gone."

"Michael," Gram said. "Oh, Michael—please, please." Gram reached her hand toward him. Michael took Gram's hand in his. Gram winced. Michael let go of her hand. He looked over at Carrie.

"We're both hanging in there, aren't we Gram?" She asked Michael to stay with Gram for a few minutes while she went out in the hallway to stretch her legs.

"She's so pitiful looking," Michael said, when she returned. Gram had passed out again. "Have you been here long?"

"Long enough," Carrie said.

Just then Tom Egan walked into the room, carrying a large pink azalea plant. "I called your house, and when I got no answer, I assumed you might be at the hospital, and I guessed it would be St. Joseph's. Don't all Catholics go to St. Joseph's?"

"Tom, lower your voice. I don't want Gram to find out that she's in a Catholic hospital." Carrie laughed.

"Sorry," Tom said.

"Michael, you remember Tom Egan, don't you?"

"Yes, of course."

"Keep your chin up," Tom said. "It's almost over. You've done all you can do for your grandmother. Remember that. I'm not going to hang around. I just wanted to let you know I'm thinking about you." He gave her a quick pat on the back.

"I'll make sure Gram knows you brought her flowers." Carrie thanked him for stopping by.

"Call me if I can do anything," Tom said, walking out the room.

Michael offered to stay. She told him no, to go on back to work, that, with Gram sleeping, she would take a lunch break. Michael said he'd be back in a few hours.

After he left, Carrie wiped the drool off of Gram's chin. Then, she wrote a note saying:

*I went to get some lunch. If my grandmother wakes up, tell her that I'll be back soon. Caroline Barnes.* She left the note on the beside table, then picked up her purse and went out the door. To be double sure someone knew her whereabouts, she stopped at the nurses' station. Gram's nurse was nowhere in sight.

"I'm going to lunch now," Carrie said to a nurse who was thumbing through a pile of charts. "My grandmother is in Room 626. Please tell her nurse, Eileen, that I won't be gone long. I left a note in her room." The nurse nodded.

Wanting a complete change of scenery, Carrie drove less than a mile down the road to Perimeter Mall. She parked near Rich's department store. Once inside the mall, she headed to the Athlete's Foot and bought a pair of Reeboks she had been wanting. Then, she hurried to the food court where she ordered a chicken sandwich, fries, and a Diet Coke at Chick-Fil-A. Walking around the courtyard, she noticed that most of the tables were full. Seeing an attractive gray-haired woman in a denim dress, sitting alone at a table in front of the Yogurt Palace, she walked over to her.

"Do you mind if I sit here with you?" Carrie said.

"Sit right down. I'd love some company."

"Thanks, I'm Caroline Barnes." Carrie sat down, took the wrapper off of her chicken sandwich, and then squirted catsup on the wrapper. She picked up a french fry and swirled it in the catsup.

"Hello, I'm glad to have you join me," the lady said. "My name is Barbara Hanson. Did you find any bargains today?"

"I got some running shoes on sale," Carrie said, wondering how could she buy new tennies with Gram down the road dying? What had she been thinking?

The woman pulled a piece of sheer apricot fabric from her brown leather purse. "I've been shopping for material to make some curtains for our new condo."

"That's a nice color," Carrie said. "Did you just move here?"

"Yes. From the Midwest. We came here a month ago from Chicago. My husband just retired, and he wanted to move south."

"And you, did you want to move?"

"No dear. I didn't want to leave my grown children, my grandchildren, or my friends. I don't really know anyone around here yet."

"You'll make friends. People are quite friendly here. Atlanta is so full of fun places and interesting things to do. My husband and I love it here." Carrie ate her sandwich and fries while the woman told her about her visit to the Cyclorama in Grant Park.

"Michael and I went there one Sunday afternoon. It's impressive. The revolving platform makes it seem real. Have you been to Oakland Cemetery? It has an incredible collection of cast iron, bronze, and Victorian statues. Margaret Mitchell is buried there. The day we visited, a fresh peach rose lay on her grave."

"Sounds like a place I'd like to see." The woman got out her purse and jotted down some notes.

Carrie took a sip of her coke, then found herself telling the woman about Gram. "Now she can barely talk or swallow. It's grim. Her body is arched over a mound of pillows, so she can breathe."

"My dear. I'm so sorry." The woman reached over and patted her on the hand.

"I shouldn't have bothered you with all of this," Carrie said, checking her watch. "I've got to go," she said, getting up. "I can't stay away any longer."

"I've enjoyed our visit. You're about my daughter's age. I feel like I had lunch with her today."

"I know," Carrie said. The woman could have been her mother. She was the right age. She wanted to stay, but instead she picked up the shoe bag and said good-bye.

# Chapter Twenty-six

JOURNAL, WEDNESDAY, MARCH 2, 1988

I'm sitting here in Gram's hospital room where things are quiet, except for the night rain pelting the window. Gram looks like a contortionist in her unusual position, lying over a mound of pillows, her arms outstretched, like she's trying to touch her toes. For now, the morphine has deadened her pain. I keep thinking about the long road that Gram and I have traveled together. We've had rough seas and days of calm. Today, the waves have crashed around us. I watch, wait, and wonder how long it will be until Gram capsizes.

After my lunch at the mall, I returned to find Eileen, Gram's nurse, standing beside the bed adjusting Gram's oxygen tube. Recognizing my voice, Gram looked up, her eyes pleading. According to Eileen, Gram acted agitated when I was gone. I touched Gram lightly on the hand and told her not to worry. Seeing her looking so frightened made me queasy. When some of my lunch shot back up my throat, I ran to the bathroom, closed the door, and upchucked into the toilet. When I returned to Gram's bedside, she had passed out again.

I wondered why Gram wore a strange white contraption that was wrapped around her upper body and hooked to the bed frame. Eileen told me it was a restraint jacket the nurses had to put on her after she tried to climb out of bed. I swallowed hard. Noticing my discomfort, Eileen said not to be alarmed. Gram didn't seem to mind. In fact, Gram told the nurses she thought it was pretty. I smiled. Wanting to look her best, Gram's foggy mind probably transformed the jacket into a fancy garment.

When the morphine wore off, Gram awoke in excruciating pain begging for help. I had no idea what to do for her until it was time for another shot. Not knowing what else to say, I told Gram she was suffering just like Jesus suffered on the cross. Gram rolled her eyes, obviously unimpressed with my analogy. I told Gram I loved her. She responded in a childlike voice that she loved me too. After several long minutes passed, I rang for the nurse who came with a needle and soon Gram was a fallen statue.

A strong odor permeated the room, reminding me of raw chicken gone bad. I opened the door for some fresh air, then stood in the doorway, listening. Phones rang. Nurses shuffled through papers, checking charts. Every now and then, I heard a doctor's name called out over the loud speaker. Visitors with concern imprinted on their faces paced the circular corridor. Doctors rushed past with swaying stethoscopes. I soon grew tired of standing, so I closed the door and sat back down.

I watched Gram, knowing one day soon, her face would be just a memory. I thought about her spunky personality. I laughed to myself, remembering a comment Jennifer recently made. "Gram got her degree from the Slash and Burn School of Public Speaking," Jennifer said. I agreed. Indeed Gram did have a sharp tongue. Not anymore, though. Pain has taken the gusts out of her sails.

I don't remember falling asleep, but I did, because when Eileen came in to check on Gram, I awoke from a dream. In the dream a burly man with a shaved head shoveled dirt in piles all over the front yard of our old house on Sixth Street. The dirt was loaded with nasty red ants. When Gram came out onto the front porch and hollered at the man, I told her not to yell at him, to keep calm, not to lose control. Gram buttoned her lip. When the man got in his rusty white pickup truck to leave, I was the one who exploded, calling the bald guy an asshole.

Did the dream mean, now that Gram was almost silenced, it was my turn to shout out my anger? Who knows?

When Eileen's shift ended at three, she introduced me to Ann, a cute nurse with short dark hair and a bubbly personality. Ann gave Gram her medication. Then, she encouraged me to attend a cancer support group meeting in the hospital. With some reluctance, I agreed to go. I followed Ann down the hallway and around the corner to a meeting room where she introduced me to five people, sitting in a semi-circle on metal chairs. Some were cancer patients, others caretakers like me.

Lois, a nurse, led the discussion. I met Amber, a young, divorced woman with two small children. Amber's dad had died at age forty-six of leukemia. She now had cancer in her lymph nodes. Amber had a positive attitude and was determined to beat her cancer. Next I met Suzanne who had undergone five operations and had endured massive doses of chemotherapy. She had little wisps of white hair. David, an elderly gentleman with thick glasses, joined us. His wife, Tova, was dying of pancreatic cancer. Rachel, a teenage girl who had just found out about her inoperable brain tumor, was also in our group. Barry, a truck driver who had advanced prostrate cancer, was the last member in our circle.

A social worker spoke about Bernie Siegal's book, *Love, Medicine, and Miracles,* emphasizing the positive role faith plays in the healing process. Several people spoke of bargaining with God, including me. I told them that I simply wanted Gram's suffering to end, that I wanted her to climb out of her cocoon and fly off like a butterfly.

We sang a song of hope and prayed. We all asked for the courage to accept God's will, and then we reminisced about good times. I felt comfortable with the group. Surprising myself, I told them how Gram had taught me card games and how she would drop everything to sit down and play. I went back to Gram's room feeling less tension in my neck and shoulders.

Michael returned to the hospital and insisted I go home for a while. At home, Sophie-dog looked excited to get outside. I could relate. I tore the bedding off Gram's bed, then opened the windows wide. I wondered how long the smell of decay would linger. The silenced cowbell sat on the bedside table. I moved it to the dresser, vowing to bury it deep in the ground. I made a ham and cheese sandwich and wolfed it down, then went back to the hospital. Nothing had changed.

Gram was in the same position. Michael stayed with me for over an hour, then left for home. After he left, I read *Rabbit Is Rich*. As I read, I could hear the basketball bounce, see Angstrum shoot the ball toward the makeshift backboard, and feel his pride when he sank it cleanly. After I read several pages, I tried, but couldn't concentrate on Rabbit Angstrum playing basketball with the six young boys. It wasn't John Updike's fault.

I put the book aside, then sat looking around this room where Gram's glasses sat on the nightstand tucked into her rose and black needlepoint case next to the gray container holding her false teeth. I listened to water dripping from the faucet in Gram's bathroom. Just minutes ago, I tried to shut it off, but the rhythmic plop, plop, plop continues. The room smells of roses and sickness.

During Gram's last awake period, I adopted a now or never attitude. I came right out and asked if Jennifer was my sister. Gram didn't hestitate this time. With a blank expression, she told me yes. I asked more questions, but it seemed my words didn't register. I thanked her for telling me the truth. Gram sat wracked with pain, her face contorted. I knew Gram was losing the battle with her naked nerve endings.

Her confirmation about my father and Jennifer has given me a sense of closure and mixed feelings. I'm happy I finally know the truth, but sad for Gram who kept such a deep secret for so long.

At midnight, Sister Julie from the chaplain's office came by and offered to sit with Gram, so I could go home and get some sleep. She told me that Gram could remain in her same condition for some time, so I've accepted her offer. I hesitate to leave, but I am so exhausted. Sister Julie has promised to call me if Gram's spirals downhill.

I keep praying this will soon be over for Gram and for me. Even though I have apprehensions, I know it's time for her to let go.

## Chapter Twenty-seven

The phone's ring startled Carrie. "Your grandmother has gone into a coma." Carrie recognized Sister Julie's voice. "She could go at anytime. I wanted you to know."

"I'll be right there," Carrie said, without hesitation.

"Who was on the phone?" Michael asked. "What time is it?"

"It's 4:15. Gram's gone into a coma. I've got to get to the hospital."

"I'm coming with you."

"You don't have to come."

"I want to," he said, as he climbed out of bed.

Carrie splashed cold water on her face trying to clear her head. She ran a brush through her hair, dressed quickly, then went downstairs and fixed a cup of tea to take in the car. While she waited for Michael, she got her white ski jacket out of the closet.

The neighborhood was dark except for a few street lights. Carrie glanced at the houses they passed, wanting to trade places with the neighbors curled up in their beds. They rode in silence. Carrie felt her heart pounding. Was Gram really in a coma? Even though Sister Julie had said it could take several hours, Carrie worried that they wouldn't make it in time.

"I heard that," Michael said when her stomach growled.

"My insides are doing a native dance," Carrie said. "You know, it just hit me. I'll never get to talk to Gram again."

"You can still talk to her," Michael said, as he turned off the freeway at the Johnson Ferry Road exit.

"What good would that do?"

"She may be able to hear you. People who've been in a coma and recovered have reported that they hovered over their own bodies watching and listening. One man said he could hear his wife talking—and could see her too."

"I've read about that stuff," Carrie said. "Sounds strange. Who knows?"

Michael turned into the deserted hospital parking lot. Carrie stepped out of the car, then tripped, falling to the ground. "I think I twisted my ankle. What's a rock doing in the parking lot anyhow?"

"It probably has something to do with the construction project over there." He pointed across the street. "They're adding a wing to the hospital."

With her left foot, Carrie shoved the rock over to the edge of the parking lot. "Come on," Michael said. Carrie limped over to join him.

The air was cold on Carrie's face. She put her hands in her jacket pockets and pulled it tightly around her as they crossed the street to the hospital. They walked past the visitors waiting area and headed for the elevator. Michael pushed the button for the sixth floor. Carrie's stomach gurgled again.

"That you again?" Michael asked.

"It's me again." She laughed. "I can't believe this is happening," she said as they stepped onto the elevator. "I can't believe Gram is in a coma." When the elevator stopped, they hurried to Gram's room.

Gram lay flat in the bed, motionless except for the rise and fall of her chest. Her head was resting on the pillow, her eyes were closed. Her arms lay on top of the blanket. Gram's face looked peaceful. Carrie scooted a chair over beside the bed and sat down. She picked up Gram's hand, holding it in hers. It felt hot. The skin on her fingers was paper thin. Carrie squeezed her hand. "It's going to be okay, Gram," she said. "Everything's going to be okay."

Michael looked down at Gram from the other side of the bed, shifting his weight from one foot to the other. They both turned around when they heard footsteps.

"I was with her for several hours during the night," Sister Julie said, walking into the room.

"I shouldn't have left," Carrie said.

"Don't worry, dear. I told her you'd be back. Besides, she wasn't in her right mind most of the time. The morphine made her confused."

"I promised to be with her at the end."

"And you are, dear. She knows you're here." Sister Julie smiled. "During the night, I read to her from my prayer book. She liked that. At one point, she sounded very clear. She said she could see her Aunt Margaret, standing in a circle of bright light. Up there." Sister Julie pointed to the right corner of the room, near the doorway.

"Aunt Margaret died before I was born," Carrie said. "She was Gram's mother's sister," Carrie said. "Gram told me lots of stories about her."

"She tried to tell me something about a dress her Aunt Margaret gave to her," Sister Julie said. "She spoke in a whisper. I didn't quite understand her."

"Oh, I know that story. I heard it often. Aunt Margaret bought Gram her first store-bought dress. Gram said the red dress from Aunt Margaret had a thousand and one pleats."

"Perhaps her Aunt Margaret was coming to get her," Sister Julie said.

"Maybe so," Carrie said.

"I'll leave you two alone with her." Gram stopped breathing just as Sister Julie started to leave. Carrie looked alarmed. "Don't worry, dear. She'll start up again. You can expect her to take seven breaths, then pause. A few seconds later, she'll start breathing again. She may continue like that for some time. It's a normal process. Eventually, she won't start back up again." Sister Julie waited to leave until Gram started breathing again.

"I'm glad Gram didn't have to go into a nursing home," Carrie said to Michael. She wiped foam from the edges of Gram's mouth, then washed her face with a washcloth she found in the bathroom, then brushed Gram's wavy, white hair. Even on her deathbed, her hair looked good. Carrie glanced up toward the ceiling and wondered if Gram was watching them.

They counted her quick breaths over and over again. Just like Sister Julie said, Gram took seven breaths, gurgled, then come to a complete stop. Each time, Carrie and Michael stared, waiting. A few seconds later, right on cue, she'd start up again, repeating the process.

"You look puzzled," Michael said.

"I am. I'm kind of foggy. I can't even figure out what day it is."

"It's Thursday, the third of March."

Carrie checked her watch. It had been just over twenty-four hours since she had brought Gram to the hospital. She looked up when she heard a knock at the door to Gram's room.

"Hello, I'm Nadine, the night nurse. Mrs. Whitfield had a rough night," she said, "a very rough night." She checked Gram's pulse. "She begged to go into a coma. I'm glad she finally got her wish."

"Me, too," Carrie said. "She looks so much more comfortable. I hated seeing her contorted in pain, perched up on those pillows. I'll never forget the look in her eyes."

"Last night, she wanted to know when she would pass out for good," Nadine said. "Once, when I gave her a morphine injection, she asked if she was in heaven. I told her no—not yet." Carrie smiled. That sounded like Gram, navigating her life to the very end.

"I'm going to get some coffee. Want anything?" Michael asked after Nadine left.

"Get me a Diet Coke." Carrie watched him leave. "I'm going to miss you, Gram," Carrie said, picking up Gram's hand.

Carrie thought about playing outside as a child, climbing the apple tree in the middle of the back yard. She recalled sitting in the branches singing songs and reciting poetry like Elizabeth Barrett Browing's "How Do I Love Thee?" She often sat in the tree daydreaming about going off on her own. It wouldn't be long now.

Carrie got up and paced the floor, stopping in front of the window to stretch. She looked at her watch. Almost two hours had passed since they arrived at the hospital. "I can hardly think. I feel like I'm in a tunnel. Am I crazy or what?" she said when Michael returned.

"You're exhausted," he said, handing her the Diet Coke,. "We've been through a lot the past few months."

"*We've* been through a lot? You've been gone most of the time. I'm the one whose been with Gram night and day."

"I stand corrected," he said. "I've been really busy at work, you know."

"I know—but, you never traveled this much before. It seems like you've dealt with Gram's illness by avoiding me and keeping yourself away from the chaos."

"Carrie, that's not true."

"Well, you haven't slept with me all that much. How's that supposed to make me feel?" She didn't wait for him to answer. "For your information, it makes me feel pretty crummy."

"I'm not sure how this relates to what we're talking about."

"You just don't get it. I've tried telling you how difficult it's been these past few months, but talking to you is like talking to a rock." Carrie blew her nose and blinked away tears.

"I'm sorry," Michael said, shrugging his shoulders. He walked over to the window and stared out at the darkness. Carrie started counting up to seven again as Gram's chest rose and fell. She didn't feel like herself. Sitting in the sterile hospital room watching Gram die didn't seem real. Did she make a mistake? Should she have let them hook an IV in Gram's arm? No, no, no. That isn't what she wanted. Carrie remembered Gram's appointment with Dr. Baker.

"When the time comes, don't do anything to keep me alive," Gram told Dr. Baker.

"We should talk about what to do after she dies," Michael said, interrupting her thoughts.

"It's all arranged. I told you I went to the funeral home last week."

"I forgot what you said."

"You didn't forget, Michael. You didn't listen."

"Will someone come get her body?"

"Michael, please . . . it's all arranged. I can't deal with these questions right now." She sighed. "Let's try to get along. Gram is probably listening."

"Okay," he said, looking up toward the ceiling. Carrie stood near the dangling oxygen tube.

"My shift's over now," Nadine said, walking into the room shortly after seven in the morning. "Sarah Jane, her new nurse, will be in soon. You'll like her." Nadine wished them luck.

"One, two, three, four, five, six, seven," Carrie counted out after Nadine left. Gram paused, then let out a loud gurgle, like a balloon deflating. They waited a few seconds, expecting her to start up again. Instead of breathing, Gram's mouth opened wide, then stayed locked in place. Holding onto Gram's hand, Carrie felt her give a final jerk. It was twelve minutes past seven, on March 3, 1988.

"She's gone," Carrie said. "It's over." She cradled Gram's lifeless hand in hers, then looked up at Michael, surprised to see tears rolling down his face. Carrie got up and walked over to his side of the bed. He put his arms around her. She lay her head on his shoulder, nestling her face into his dark green sweater vest. It smelled like moth balls. She didn't care.

"So what we are supposed to do now?" Carrie asked.

"I'm not sure," he said.

Carrie walked over and looked out the window at people scurrying about. A line of cars headed toward the parking lot. Michael and Carrie both turned around when they heard a tapping on the door.

"Hello," said a young girl, wearing a white uniform and a pink smock. She pushed a blood pressure machine into the room. Before they had a chance to explain, the girl stuck a thermometer into Gram's mouth and started taking her blood pressure. Carrie glanced at Michael, not knowing what to do or say. He shrugged his shoulders and held his hands out, palms up.

"She's at peace. Her suffering's over," the aide blurted out. Then, putting her hand over her mouth, she ran out of the room, leaving her equipment behind.

"She sure freaked out," Michael said. "She's probably never found a patient dead before. She didn't think we knew." Carrie put her forehead into her hands. She felt like a bit player in a B-movie. This was not the scene she had imagined.

Opening the door, Michael looked out into the hallway. He waved his arm, trying to summon one of the busy nurses. "I'll be there in a minute," a fiftyish nurse said.

"This is ridiculous," Carrie said. Michael opened the door and stood in the doorway.

"Hello, I'm Sarah Jane. I'll be caring for Mrs. Whitfield today." The nurse walked into the room smiling.

"Not for long," Carrie said.

The nurse picked up Gram's arm and began taking her pulse. "She's gone," Sarah Jane said, looking startled.

"Look, we know how this story ends," Michael said. Carrie stifled a nervous laugh.

"I'm so sorry. No one told me," Sarah Jane said.

"A young nurse's aide was in here just a few minutes ago. When she realized my grandmother died, she bolted out the door, leaving her equipment behind." Carrie pointed to the blood pressure machine.

"I apologize. I saw an aide hurry out of this room and go into the restroom. I had no idea that Mrs. Whitfield had died. I'm sorry. Really I am."

"Don't worry," Carrie said. "Just tell us what we're supposed to do, so we can get out of here."

"I'll call pastoral care for you."

Sister Julie arrived minutes later. "First, let's say a prayer." Sister Julie stood on one side of Gram's bed, Carrie and Michael on the other. "Dear God, we pray for Madeline Whitfield and thank you for the time we've shared with her. May we hang on to the things she has given to us and may her love be with us always. I call upon the angels of the Lord to come for Madeline. May she be guided into the light of Your presence." Sister Julie wanted to know if they had made any arrangements. Carrie handed her a business card from the funeral home.

The three of them looked up when a man walked into the room. "Hello, I'm Reverend Quigley, from St. James Lutheran Church," he said, then explained that the hospital chaplain had asked him to visit Mrs. Whitfield.

"I was hoping I could be of assistance," the minister said when he learned that Gram had died. Carrie asked if he would perform a service at the funeral home the next day, explaining that Gram had been a lifelong Lutheran. He said he would be obliged.

"He smelled like a doughnut," Carrie said after he walked out the door.

"It's okay to leave now," Sister Julie said, chuckling at Carrie's observation.

"I'd like a few moments alone with her."

After Sister Julie and Michael left the room, Carrie placed Gram's glasses and false teeth into the wastebasket beside the bed, then gathered her few remaining belongings. "I love you, Gram," she said, kissing her on the forehead. Gram smelled bad. After taking a last glance at Gram, Carrie pulled the sheet up over her grandmother's head and walked out of the room.

In the hallway, she saw Dr. Baker striding down the corridor. "I need to speak with you about transferring your grandmother to the hospice home," he said, stopping beside her. He held Gram's chart in his hand.

"Your timing's off. She's dead," Carrie said. She turned and walked over to join Michael and Sister Julie, who were standing in front of the elevator.

"You're taking this very well. You seem so composed," Sister Julie said, as they stepped onto the elevator.

"Gram told me not to cry. I'm just following her instructions." Carrie felt like her body was novacained. She wanted to get away from everyone. No one had a clue how she really felt.

After thanking Sister Julie, Carrie and Michael headed to the parking lot. Going out the door, Carrie looked at the anxious faces on the people entering the hospital, glad she was leaving.

"Do you want me to go to the funeral home with you?" Michael asked on the drive home.

"No. You can go back to work. I can handle it."

"You sure?"

"I'm not sure of much right now. All I know for certain is that I want to be by myself. After I make some phone calls and get the service arranged, I'm going to get some sleep."

At home, Carrie took Sophie-dog outside and put her on her rope. Then she headed to Gram's room to select burial clothing. She picked out the items Gram had requested—her Liz Claiborne black dress, the one she wore to the banquet at her fiftieth high school reunion; her three-inch suede black heels; her black lingerie; the gold cross necklace her friend, Mavis, gave her for Christmas, and dangly gold earrings.

"Oh God, no!" Aunt Nella said when Carrie phoned her. "I just knew it. I woke up at seven this morning with this unsettling feeling." Aunt Nella started sobbing. Carrie told her that the service would be sometime the next afternoon.

"Jennifer and I will fly down."

"Fine," Carrie said. She suggested that they have a memorial service the following weekend in Wisconsin, the day before Jennifer's wedding. Carrie and Michael had discussed the idea. It made sense to them, especially since so many people would be in town for the wedding.

"Good Lord," Aunt Nella said. "We can't have a service on the day of the rehearsal dinner. You can't do this to Jennifer."

"Aunt Nella, calm down and then think about it. Please call and discuss my plan with Jennifer. I think my sister will agree that it's a good idea."

"Your sister?! Did Mother tell you?"

"Yes. She told me on her deathbed."

"Does Jennifer know?"

"I think so. Why don't you ask her?"

"I'm calling her right now," Aunt Nella said, hanging up.

Carrie hung up the phone and let out a sigh. She filled a glass with cold water and took a long drink. If Aunt Nella and Jennifer didn't like her idea, they could come up with their own plan. She was sick and tired of being the one in charge.

She liked the idea of celebrating Gram's life and then going on with the wedding festivities. She knew Gram would approve. It would work, she knew it would. Besides, she knew there was no chance that Aunt

Nella would take over. Nor would her sister, Jennifer.

Carrie phoned Kay and left a message. Before leaving for the funeral home, she took the cowbell outside and lay it on the grass near the side of the house. With a shovel from the garage, she dug a deep hole. The cowbell made a ringing noise when she dropped it into the hole. Then it was silenced. She filled the hole with loose dirt, then stomped on the ground to smooth it out. "There," she said, slapping her palms together.

She put Sophie-dog back into the laundry room, washed the dirt off her hands, picked up her denim purse, and headed to the funeral home. She rang the doorbell. A short man with wispy, white hair opened the door.

"Come in, Mrs. Barnes," he said, holding the door open for her. "We've been awaiting your arrival. I see you've brought the burial clothing." He ushered her into a room and told her to sit down. Carrie fidgeted, twirling her wedding ring around her finger until a tall man with dyed-black hair walked into the room. He looked like a model funeral director in his dark suit and stiff white shirt, chalky complexion, hands clasped in front of him, like in the movies, his teeth crooked. He smelled like Listerine and dried rose petals.

*I can see it now,* Carrie thought. *He's ready to give me his big sales pitch, to talk me into spending big bucks. Sorry, buster. I don't have a wad of dough.*

He went down the checklist. Carrie told him yes, yes, yes, and then, no, no, no. Absolutely no to the makeup and coiffure. "Closed casket," she reminded him.

"Did I tell you she always wanted to be in the circus?" Carrie said, then wondered why she said it. She came close to telling him to leave the casket open.

The funeral director, a perplexed look on his face, blinked his eyes twice and cleared his throat. "Let me escort you to the casket room," he said in a deadly serious tone. He gave her a tour, stopping near his deluxe models. "These are our most elegant caskets," he said.

"Look, I'm not buying a car. I want something simple."

"Fine," he said, as she hurried past the shiny black, gold, and silver models. She pointed to a pine casket, lined with pink quilted satin.

"That one will be perfect," she said.

She turned down a five-hundred dollar bouquet of roses, then selected a large bouquet of wildflowers in yellow, purple, and white for $350. After agreeing on details for the afternoon service, the director grinned his graveyard grin. "I'll see you tomorrow at one."

Hurrying to the exit door, Carrie almost knocked over the old man who had greeted her. "Excuse me dear," he said. "I was wondering. Is that your grandmother in the cold storage room?" Carrie looked at him like he had two heads. *What kind of question was that?*

"No," she said. "I'd never let my grandmother stay all night in a place like this." Then, she bolted out the door and ran to her car where she pounded her fists on the steering wheel. Why did that idiot have to tell her that Gram was lying in the cold storage room? Envisioning Gram lying naked on a slab, she felt like puking.

She took off down the road. Instead of heading toward home, she turned right on Roswell Road and drove to Interstate 285, heading east. Edging over to the fast lane, she turned up the radio. She drove without any particular destination. "Watch it, creep," she said when a dumptruck flew past, splattering her windshield.

Pulling off the freeway, she turned into the parking lot in front of a Waffle House restaurant. Suddenly, her stomach craved grease. "Good afternoon," the girl behind the counter said, when she walked inside. Carrie sat down in a booth and studied the menu. A waitress with red-orange hair set a glass of water down.

"Thanks," Carrie said. "I'll have a grilled chicken sandwich, hash browns, and a Diet Coke. And some fries. Bring me fries, too." The waitress shouted out the order, then returned with a Diet Coke. Carrie drank it, hoping the caffeine would give her a boost.

When her plate arrived, she smothered the hash browns and fries with ketchup, then bit into the sandwich. Grabbing her napkin, she wiped the grease off her chin. As she ate, she listened to the two men in the booth next to hers. "They say that Dolly Parton had breast reduction surgery," the bald man in a red shirt said.

"Well, if she did, ah sure don't know where," said the younger man who had a mop of blond curls. "She's still got herself a couple of basketballs." Carrie laughed.

"My wife's all tied up with this here weddin' stuff," the bald guy said. "She got this etiquette book to find out how to address the invitations. She explained the proper way to address an invite to homosexuals to me last night. Ah told her, ah didn't know we was invitin' any." He let out a loud belly laugh. My wife said, 'You go by age. If they are the same age, you go alphabetically.' She said it like it was somethin' we needed to know."

"I'll swan," the young man said. They both laughed.

Carrie took the last bite of her sandwich, then started to cry. "You okay?" the waitress said as she put the check on the table. But, Carrie couldn't stop crying. "Honey, I can stay here for a minute. Looks like you need somebody to talk to."

Carrie picked up a clean napkin and blew her nose. "Do you want to talk to the person I think I am, the person others think I am, or the person I'd like to be?" she said, looking up at the waitress who cocked her head and pinched her lips shut.

Carrie wasn't sure where her words had came from. Probably, she'd read them somewhere. No matter, she liked them. The person she would like to be would say something like that. She stared at the waitress, who backed slowly away from the table.

Carrie paid her bill, put a dollar on the table for a tip and left. Outside, she walked to a phone booth in the corner of the parking lot. "Hi, it's me," Carrie said to Kay. "Did you get my message?"

"Yes, I did. I'm so sorry about Gram, but I know it's for the best. You must be relieved that it's over."

"I'm so tired—so tired. I feel strange. I hate everything right now, and everyone. I hate men, women, right-wingers, liberals, healthy people, sick people. I hate dogs, cats, goldfish. I have a case of ugly-itis."

"Carrie, you've had a rough few months. It's difficult to end a lifetime relationship. Please be good to yourself. Where are you anyhow? Michael called here, wondering if I knew where you were."

"I'm calling from a phone booth at a Waffle House, somewhere on

Buford Highway, north of 285, I think. After I left the funeral home, I took off driving and ended up here."

"Carrie, go find out where you are. I'll come get you," Kay said.

"No, that's not necessary. I'm on my way home. Bye." Carrie hung up.

She walked over to her car, got in, and started the ignition, then turned it off. She couldn't drive. Everything looked blurry. She got out of the car, climbed into the back seat, and lay down. All she wanted to do was sleep.

# Chapter Twenty-eight

Journal, Thursday, March 10, 1988

I'm packed and ready to go to Wisconsin for the wedding. It's hard to believe it's been a week since Gram died. Parts of the day she died will be with me forever. I'll never forget watching her take her final breath, kissing her good-bye, taking a last look at her, then pulling the sheet up over her still body. I'm glad it's over. I know Gram's better off now. Taking care of her was tough, but I know someday down the road, I'll be glad I did it. I can't change anything that happened during our last months together. What I can do is accept her death and what I went through while she lay dying and go on.

That doesn't mean that I'll ever erase the events of that day. I'll never forget how Dr. Baker finally offered hospice help right after she died, or how that old man at the funeral home asked me if it was Gram lying in the cold storage room? He must have goose liver for a brain. His question triggered some kind of mental breakdown.

I remember driving away from that funeral parlor and ending up at a Waffle House. After lunch, I fell asleep in the back seat of the car and awakened when I heard a pounding noise. Opening my eyes, I saw a distorted face against the car window.

I was confused. I'd been dreaming about sitting in a church. *Michael sat behind me, and, in the pew right behind him sat a gorgeous young girl with long dark hair, a flawless complexion, and full red lips. The girl rested her hand on Michael's shoulder, acting like she knew him well. The girl asked what was going on and wanted to know who I was. Michael told her I was simply a friend. I felt a stab in my chest. Was I losing Michael to someone else? No . . . no, no. That isn't what I wanted.*

The pounding noise continued. Moving closer to the window, I recognized Tom Egan. He told me he had checked out every Waffle House on Buford Highway north of 285, looking for me. I opened the door, explaining how I'd fallen asleep in my car. He told me I'd picked a strange place to sleep.

Tom drove me home, saying not to worry, that someone would come back for my car. On the way home, I kept thinking about my dream. I was anxious to see Michael. When I walked in the back door, Michael looked worried. I headed to the bathroom, letting Tom explain where he had found me. When I returned to the kitchen, both of them treated me like an egg ready to crack. Michael shook Tom's hand before he left, thanking him for coming to my rescue.

Not much else registers about that day. I recall Michael saying he had to go to the airport to pick up my relatives. He heated the chili Kay had brought over. We ate the chili for dinner before he left to pick up Aunt Nella, Jennifer, and Kevin. I took a long hot shower, then fell into bed and slept for over twelve hours.

Coming down the stairs the next morning, I smelled Aunt Nella's lilac perfume. "Thanks for coming," I said when I saw everyone sitting at the kitchen table drinking Michael's gourmet breakfast blend. I hugged everyone before I sat down with my cup of tea. Over fresh cinnamon raisin bagels, bananas, and cornflakes, we reminisced, telling fun stories about Gram, alternating between laughing and crying.

As we ate, neither Aunt Nella or Jennifer mentioned the sister issue or the memorial service in Wisconsin, so I let it slide, knowing I had to tackle one thing at a time.

Riding to the funeral home that afternoon, Michael looked great in his light gray suit, white shirt, and burgundy necktie, an outfit that had been a favorite of Gram's. I nixed the black dress idea. Instead, I wore my black and white checked blazer, an off-white sweater, and black pants.

Sitting behind Michael and next to Jennifer in the backseat, Aunt Nella filled the car with a monologue of nervous jabber.

Cascading spring wildflowers adorned Gram's simple pine casket. The room smelled fresh and earthy. Our gathering was small-the four of us, Kay and Dave, Tom Egan, Eva, the lady from church who had brought Gram communion, Sister Julie, and a few of the people from Michael's office.

Reverend Daniels spoke kindly of death, emphasizing that Gram had risen to a place where there was no pain. We sang "Amazing Grace" and read the twenty-third Psalm. In her black dress and a wide-brimmed hat with a veil, Aunt Nella dabbed at her eyes with her lacy handkerchief. Jennifer, wearing a navy pants suit, held Kevin's hand. I put my hand in the crook of Michael's left arm. Everyone in the family shed tears except me. I wanted to cry, but I couldn't. Gram's rules held me back.

At Gram's grave site on a hill overlooking a peaceful pond, ducks swam, then waddled on the grass. I watched them shake the water off their feathers as the minister spoke of the separation of the body and spirit. The sun came out during the last prayer. A butterfly flittered above the flowers on top of the casket.

Tom grabbed onto my hand and gave me a quick kiss on the cheek before he left. I knew it was a farewell to what we had shared. I told him to keep in touch, not sure that I would ever see him again. Did I regret that I had not pursued a deeper relationship with him? Yes, for a few moments here and there. But then I thought of Michael whose steady love had not wavered. I knew where I wanted to be.

After the funeral, Michael and Kevin went out for a run while Aunt Nella, Jennifer, and I sorted through Gram's things. I'd already put aside the silver-framed photo of Gram in her wedding gown, a small antique photo album with pictures of Gram's parents and her siblings, her green prayer book, her red and black brocade coin purse, a pearl-handled nail file, and her wicker basket. I told Aunt Nella and Jennifer to take whatever they wanted.

After they made their selections Gram's belongings dwindled down to three plastic garbage bags. I looked at what was left of Gram's life and realized that her things no longer held meaning. It was Gram who would live on.

A lady from the nursing home I phoned the day I felt so desperate returned my call, letting me know that a room was now available. I felt grateful that we no longer needed the room.

After dinner that night, we played cards, drank wine, and finished off the chocolate chip cookies. Sophie-dog, who loved the company, kept a close watch for crumbs under the table. Kevin skunked us all at hearts, with Michael egging him on. He enjoyed every minute of it. Aunt Nella acted miffed at him for beating her. He promised to give her another chance to dethrone him soon. We laughed a lot. It was Gram's kind of evening.

The next morning when Jennifer arrived downstairs, I asked if her mom had mentioned having a memorial service for Gram in Wisconsin. She had, and Jennifer was all for it. The issue was settled. Jennifer said it would be a way of making Gram a part of her wedding weekend. Jennifer had persuaded her Mom and Kevin that my idea was a good one. I thanked her for supporting me.

Aunt Nella had not told Jennifer about her birth parents. Just as I started to mention to Jennifer that I knew we were sisters, Aunt Nella walked into the kitchen. I changed the subject in a hurry. I wanted to speak with Jennifer later, but later never came. In no time at all, Michael herded them out the door so they could catch their morning plane. The good news was—at long last, I had the house to myself.

I accomplished a lot the past week. Though I cleaned and emptied Gram's room, I need time before I can move my things back in. For now, we are keeping the door closed. Sophie-dog is one confused animal. She sits by the door of what used to be Gram's room and whimpers.

While cleaning, I found an envelope containing a note for Jennifer and me tucked between the armrest and the cushion in Gram's chair. When I read it, I cried. It was as if Gram was standing right there talking to me. No mattter how busy the wedding weekend becomes, I'm determined to find a few minutes alone with Jennifer, so I can share the special note with her.

I've written a eulogy for the service tomorrow which Michael has agreed to read. Jennifer will do one Bible reading, Mavis will do one also, and I'll read a prayer. I asked Aunt Nella, but she refused to participate in the service. Jennifer said that her mother is grieving and way too upset to participate. I left her comment alone.

It will take more time, but I'm feeling better about having a sister, even if it is Jennifer. I want things to work out between us. It dawned on me the other day that, by sharing her secret, Gram gave Jennifer and me the gift of family.

Things have a way of falling into place. I keep reminding myself that worrying does no good at all. Everything has turned out for the best. I'm certain Gram will be at the wedding, probably hovering over the altar. Right now, I hear Michael pulling into the garage. It's time to head to the airport. Today, there's no one to leave behind.

## Chapter Twenty-nine

Michael walked to the front of the church. He took out two sheets of paper from the inside pocket of his navy suit, unfolded them, and set them down on the podium. He began:

"We are gathered here to say good-bye to Madeline Whitfield, a special lady who created her own unique biography, one that is now threaded into the tapestry of all of us. In the last months of her life, Madeline displayed an amazing amount of courage and acceptance. Three months ago, before leaving her hometown of Sheboygan, she did not hesitate to give away most of her possessions. Knowing her journey was coming to an end, she wanted everything in its place.

"Madeline loved to play cards, dance, and dress up in fancy clothes. Most of all, she loved being with her family and friends whose lives she often sprinkled with laughter, telling funny stories and pronouncing words in her own distinct way.

"During the last weeks of her life, Madeline talked about her death. She looked forward to meeting her friend, Jesus. One day, not long ago, she told her granddaughter, Caroline, that Jesus would come into her room soon and say: 'Come on old girl, you've suffered long enough.'

"Those of us in her family are proud of Madeline's many years of sobriety. She joined Alcoholics Anonymous fourteen years ago. During that time, she helped many people get started in AA. Because she was brave enough to stand up and tell her story at the local club, others followed in her footsteps.

"Last week we received a sympathy note from a man Madeline knew in AA, who said he felt sure that Madeline was now saying the Serenity Prayer for all of us. She attempted to live by the words in that prayer which goes: 'God grant me the serenity to accept the things I cannot change, the courage to change the things I can, and the wisdom to know the difference.'

"At the end, Madeline struggled to accept her death. However, she died knowing that her fate was not in her own hands. We will miss Madeline, but we are relieved that her suffering is over and take comfort in knowing that she is now in a better place."

Walking back to his pew, Michael gave Carrie an encouraging smile as she walked to the podium in her new black skirt, royal blue jacket, and black patent-leather heels. She took a deep breath and began.

"Thank you for coming here today to celebrate the life of my grandmother. I'd like to share a poem written by an unknown author. It was sent to me by my special friend, Liz Newby." Carrie glanced at Liz, who sat in the second row right behind Jennifer. She recited the prayer, giving each word careful emphasis, pausing between sentences:

"'Do not stand at my grave and weep; I am not there. I do not sleep. I am a thousand winds that blow. I am the diamond glint on snow. I am the sunlight on ripened grain. I am the gentle autumn's rain. When you awaken in the morning's hush, I am the swift uplifting rush of quiet birds in circled flight. I am the soft stars that shine at night. Do not stand at my grave and cry. I am not there. I did not die.'"

Just as she finished, a beam of bright light streamed through a stained glass window near the front of the church. Carrie blinked her eyes as she stepped away from the podium.

"That was beautiful. Good job," Jennifer said, when Michael rose to let Carrie into the pew. Carrie sat down between Michael and Jennifer. On the other side of Jennifer sat Kevin, and next to him, Aunt Nella and her friend, Robert. According to Jennifer, Aunt Nella met Robert at an AA meeting in Milwaukee.

The organist began playing "The Prayer of St. Francis." Carrie sang along, remembering how Gram always told her to open her mouth wide and bring the music out from deep inside. Beside her, Michael sang in his deep baritone voice. She moved closer to him, sharing his song book.

"There is a democracy in death. In death, we all become equal," the minister said in closing, quoting John Donne, the English poet and clergyman. Carrie and Jennifer walked out of the church in front of Michael and Kevin. "I felt Gram's presence," Jennifer said.

"Me too," said Carrie. "Did you see that ray of light come through the window just after I finished reading the prayer?"

"Makes you wonder, doesn't it? Maybe it was Gram."

"I'd like to think so," Carrie said. Then, she asked Jennifer if they could meet for a few minutes before the rehearsal started. At first, Jennifer said no, that she had too much to do. When Carrie explained that she had found a note Gram had written to both of them, Jennifer arranged a meeting at the church twenty minutes before the rehearsal started.

Once they got outside of the church, Aunt Nella and Robert hurried over to join them. "Robert this is my niece, Carrie. Carrie, this is my friend, Robert Grayson." Extending his hand, Robert complimented Carrie on the service.

"Carrie is a wonder. She handles things with such ease," Aunt Nella said. "I don't know how she does it."

"It wasn't *that* easy," Carrie said, a bit sharply. "How was Door County?" she asked, changing the subject. She knew Aunt Nella had gone away with Robert for a few days, leaving Carrie to plan the whole service.

"Wonderful. Robert's cottage at Ellison Bay was the perfect place for me. I needed time to grieve."

"Right," said, Carrie biting her tongue. She didn't dare say what she was thinking.

"I'll see you in a few minutes," Robert said, lighting a cigarette as he walked away. Carrie cringed. She wondered if she was going to turn into one of those freaks who couldn't tolerate smoking.

"Jennifer, we have a problem," Aunt Nella said. "The soloist is missing. No one has a clue as to where he might be. He doesn't know the time of the rehearsal. What if he doesn't show up tomorrow?"

"We'll go ahead and get married," Jennifer said.

Carrie smiled. Jennifer knew how to handle her mother. Walking away from them, Carrie stopped to visit with several of Gram's friends who told her fun stories about adventures with Gram. "Looks like there's trouble brewing," Carrie said to Kevin when she walked up beside him. She pointed to Jennifer and her mother. Aunt Nella was talking loud and fast, her arms flailing.

"Jennifer will handle it," Kevin said.

"So, how are you holding up, Kevin? Getting nervous?"

"Not really. I'm doing fine, thanks to Jennifer. Her attitude is contagious. She keeps saying that everything will fall into place, that we don't need to get uptight over the small stuff. Gram's death has put things into perspective."

"I agree," Carrie said. She smiled and waved across the crowd when she saw Michael talking to Liz Newby. Mavis walked up just as Kevin started to leave. Carrie introduced Mavis to Kevin.

"I hate to run off, but we need to find out if Dad's tuxedo fits."

"He seems like a nice young man," Mavis said.

"He'll make a great addition to our family. Goodness knows, we need more men."

"Speaking of men, who's that man with Nella?"

"Robert Grayson. He's from Milwaukee."

"Hmm . . . so, how long has she known him? My, he's good looking. His mop of wavy hair reminds me of Douglas Fairbanks, Jr." Carrie tried to remember what the old actor looked like, but couldn't.

"According to Jennifer, Aunt Nella met him a few weeks ago," Carrie said. "Mavis, I've got a funny story for you. When Aunt Nella first mentioned Robert to me on the phone, I asked what he looked like. She said he was tall, smart, and *had* hair. It turns out, she'd had several blind dates—bald ones—before she met him." Mavis laughed, then stared down at the concrete entry way to the church.

"Nella and Madeline had a difficult relationship," Mavis said, lifting her head. "They had some unresolved issues." Carrie felt certain that

Mavis knew about Jennifer's adoption and probably knew about her parents' car accident, too.

"She told you, didn't she?" Mavis said, staring directly at Carrie.

"About Jennifer?"

Mavis nodded.

"She told me that Jennifer is my sister the day before she died. That's all she told me."

"Madeline wanted to tell you for such a long time, but she'd promised your dad she would keep it a secret. Besides, Nella didn't want others to know either. Can't blame her."

"There's so much I don't understand," Carrie said. "Jennifer and I are both looking for answers."

Mavis hesitated, then said, "Carrie, why don't you come over in the morning around eleven? Now that Madeline's gone, there's no reason not to tell you some of the things you deserve to know."

"That would be great," Carrie said, surprised. She saw Mavis crying in church. Now she saw tears in Mavis's eyes again. They hugged goodbye. Mavis pulled her coat tight across her chest and walked away.

Carrie saw Herman standing near a tall oak tree on the left side of the church. He turned around and smiled.

"That was me you were talking about in the eulogy when you mentioned Madeline's AA friend, right?"

"Yes," Carrie said.

"I'll miss her. She was a lively one," Herman said. "I can't believe she's gone."

"I feel the same way."

"Honey, you're shivering," Herman said. "This cold wind is coming right off Lake Michigan. You'd better get someplace warm. I'm going home before I catch cold." He turned around and trudged up the hill toward his car. Carrie waved good-bye.

"I'm freezing. I'm sure it's okay to leave now," Carrie said when she found Michael. She put her hand in the crook of Michael's arm as they walked to the car. Even though she felt a twinge of sadness, Carrie was glad the service was over.

"It sure doesn't look like mid-March," Michael said. "The trees don't have any leaves on them yet."

"I know. When I was little, I called winter trees stick trees. Spring comes late here because the cold water in Lake Michigan keeps the temperature down. Some years, it simply goes from winter to summer. There's no spring at all. I can remember shivering at Memorial Day picnics. Sometimes, it was still cool on the Fourth of July."

"Sounds grim," Michael said.

"We survived," Carrie said. "It was a good place to live, still is." Michael gave her a dubious look.

"I met Robert. He teaches psychology at Marquette," Michael said after they got into the car.

"Psychology—hmm. Maybe he can figure Aunt Nella out for us."

"Don't count on it," Michael said, laughing.

"Aunt Nella makes me crazy. She avoided Gram when she was dying, and now she acts devastated over her death."

"She probably feels guilty," Michael said.

"We don't have a whole lot of time. Liz said she wanted to stop by the motel. And, I have to go to the rehearsal a little early," Carrie said, mentioning her meeting with Jennifer and also the one with Mavis the next morning.

"I'm glad you've arranged to see Jennifer. I hope Mavis clears some things up for you."

"Me too." Carrie watched out the window as they drove on Kohler Memorial Drive. "Ebenreiter's is still here," she said pointing to the lumber company. Sheboygan was a town that never changed much. Neither did the people. A lot of them stayed in Sheboygan. Carrie liked being back home to visit. Unlike Atlanta, almost everywhere they went, someone recognized her and said hello. It felt good.

When they got to their motel room, Michael changed into his running clothes. "Don't freeze your buns off," Carrie said when he went out the door.

"Okay." He laughed at her comment. "I won't be long."

She had just put on her purple sweats when she heard a knock. "I went down by Pranges to get some hose," Liz said when Carrie opened the door to their room. She and Carrie laughed at the familiar idiom. The locals always said, "down by Pranges," referring to stopping in at the local department store. Liz pulled out the desk chair and sat down.

"It's unreal, isn't it? Having a memorial service, then a wedding." Carrie propped two pillows against the headboard, then sat down on the bed.

"You doing okay?" Liz asked, turning the chair around.

"I guess so. I haven't had time to think about it." Carrie described Gram's antics in the last few weeks of her life. "She kept telling me how horrible I was, and I believed her. I was this close to giving up." Carrie said holding her right thumb and forefinger just apart.

"But you didn't."

"I know. Thank God for that. I'm just glad it's over with. Those last hours in the hospital were a real nightmare for her, for me too—I still feel guilty."

"Why? After all you did for your grandmother, I can't imagine why."

"Because she got so thirsty—so very thirsty at the end. She couldn't swallow at all. I could have asked the nurse to hook up an IV tube, but I didn't, because she'd begged the doctor not to prolong her life. The doctor decided not to give her anything, and I went along with him."

"Carrie, stop blaming yourself. You didn't do anything wrong."

"Well, it's haunting me. I can't stop thinking about it. I've had this same dream that I'm crawling on the desert searching for water and can't find any."

"You're making me thirsty." Liz stood up. "I'm going to the lobby and get a couple of sodas out of the machine," she said, picking up her purse. When Liz returned, she handed Carrie a Diet Coke.

"By the way," Liz said, "what ever happened between you and the guy you met on the plane?"

"Tom Egan?" Carrie smiled. "He gave me great moral support. I don't know what I would have done without him, especially with Michael gone so much of the time."

"You sound pretty hung up on this guy. Did you sleep with him?"

Carrie laughed at Liz's blunt question. "No, but I came close." She told Liz how Tom had come over the evening after she and Gram had their big blowout. "I told him not to come over, but he came anyway. I looked like crap. After a beer or two, he came on to me. I told him to back off."

"Why?"

"It didn't seem right."

"Are you sorry?"

"Sometimes, yes. But, I feel good about standing up for myself. It's high time I stopped trying to please everyone. I told Tom that I didn't owe him anything, except my friendship. Besides, I didn't want to betray Michael."

"What did Tom think about that?"

"He told me I was old-fashioned. I came right back at him, telling him I was simply standing up for my right to choose, and I chose not to have sex with him."

"Way to go, girl," Liz said.

"I doubt if he'd ever been turned down before."

"Did you see him again?" Carrie nodded yes. She told Liz how he'd rescued her and how they had parted at the cemetery. "We're still friends," she said.

"And everyone lives happily ever after," Liz said. She grabbed her jacket from the bed. "I'd better get out of here. Try to get some rest. I'll see you tomorrow at the wedding." Just as she was leaving a red-faced Michael came into the room. They both told Liz good-bye.

"Do you want to get into the shower first?" Michael asked. He leaned down and kissed Carrie on the cheek.

"Whew," she said, holding her nose. "You better go first. Besides, you need to warm up. Your face is bright red."

❦

"I feel free. I'm not in charge of anything tonight or tomorrow," Carrie said on the way to the church for the rehearsal.

"Not even me," Michael said.

"Pretty funny. When have I ever been in charge of you?" Michael laughed.

When they walked inside the church, Jennifer stood just inside the door, wearing a tea-length blue and white flowered dress. "Let's go in here," Jennifer said, pointing to a small room off of the vestibule.

"You look fantastic," Carrie said.

"You too. I like your pink dress. Is that silk?" Carrie smiled, remembering the day Michael baby-sat Gram so she could go shopping for a dress for the wedding rehearsal. Carrie reached into her purse and pulled out an envelope. She handed Jennifer her copy of Gram's note.

Jennifer opened the envelope and began to read:

Dear Jennifer and Caroline,

I know that someday you will learn the truth—that you are sisters. It has been difficult keeping your father's secret. I wanted you to know that he loved you both very much.

I am very proud of you both. I wish I could have been a better grandmother and done more for you, but I did the best I could. Please love one another. Love, Gram

"Thanks," Jennifer said, putting the note back into the envelope. "It's time for the rehearsal to start." Carrie wanted to give her a hug, but it didn't seem appropriate, not after Jennifer's cold response to the note.

"How'd it go?" Michael said.

"She didn't say much," Carrie said. "I think she's less than pleased to have me for a sister."

At dinner, Carrie and Michael sat at the same table with Jennifer and Kevin, Kevin's parents, Aunt Nella, Robert, and Kevin's grandfather, George. Carrie sat between Michael and George, who was eighty-four and a little hard of hearing. A server placed a green salad in front of Jennifer and Kevin, then served the rest of the table. George ate his salad quickly. His plate was cleared away as soon as he finished his last bite. Within minutes, the server set another salad in front of George. "Excuse me, miss," George said to Carrie. "Didn't I just eat a salad?"

"Yes, you did," Carrie said, trying not to laugh. George started eating the second salad. "You don't have to eat another one. They made a mistake." She chuckled.

"It's okay," George said, continuing to eat the second salad.

"Nella tells me that you live in Atlanta," Robert said, from across the table. "I spent time at a seminar at Emory University last April."

Carrie liked Robert's easygoing manner. Aunt Nella was in rare form, entertaining everyone at the table with stories about Jennifer's childhood. Many of the stories related to both Jennifer and Carrie.

"We took a lot of trips together," Aunt Nella said. "Carrie often came with us, and the two girls got into more trouble. Do you remember the torpedo queens in the bathtub when we took you to Chicago for the weekend?"

"Mother, give it a rest. Do not tell that story," Jennifer said, giving her mother a look.

"Aunt Nella, you wouldn't dare," added Carrie.

"It's time for a toast," Michael said. He held his glass up in the air. "To Jennifer and Kevin, may they have a perfect wedding day tomorrow." Everyone raised a wine glass. Aunt Nella and Robert raised a glass of sparkling water.

"Michael saved us," Jennifer said after dinner. "I thought Mother was going to tell that fart story right in front of Kevin's parents." Carrie howled.

"We had fun on those trips, didn't we?" Carrie said.

Carrie told Jennifer good-bye when Michael pulled the car up to the curb. "Get your beauty sleep. Tomorrow is your big day."

Back at the motel, Carrie brushed her teeth and climbed into bed, without her usual oversized T-shirt on. Michael turned out the light then reached for her.

※

Early the next morning, after breakfast at the IHOP, Carrie and Michael went to the nursing home to visit Aunt Rae, who sat tied into a wheelchair. Carrie put a fuschia azalea plant on the dresser. She and Michael took turns, trying to get a response from Aunt Rae, but only received a blank stare.

"She's hiding inside herself," the nurse said, coming into the room.

"Good-bye," Aunt Rae said, when they got up to leave. That was it for conversation.

"At least Gram didn't have to end up like that," Michael said. "Why can't Aunt Rae just die? She's not really living."

"Gram would say there's a plan. We just don't know what it is," Carrie said. She checked her watch. It was almost eleven.

"Good luck," Michael said, dropping Carrie off at Mavis's house.

"Hello dear," Mavis said, opening the door. Carrie looked around as she walked inside. Every spot on the wall and every table was filled with a lifetime of collecting: oil paintings, watercolors, photos in antique silver frames, figurines of birds, silk flower arrangements, and turtles, a myriad of them in every material imaginable.

"I used to love to play with your turtles. You have quite a collection."

"I know, dear. My place is full of stuff. I've always said that a person simply can't have enough stuff."

They sat down in the living room. Mavis poured Carrie a cup of tea from her china teapot. "Dear, I know you're curious, so I'll begin."

Mavis told Carrie about the day her parents died, explaining how Gram had been upset, knowing Richard was leaving for Indianapolis that very afternoon where he would start a new job "Madeline had a heart of gold, but she did not always use the best judgment," Mavis said. "I can assure you that I often tried to steer her away from the rocky shore."

"Madeline called your father that day and told him that his daughter, Jennifer, was very ill. She knew your dad wouldn't leave town with his little girl sick. Nella had reluctantly agreed to go along with her mother. To this day, I can't figure out what Nella was going to say when he discovered Gram's lie."

"Why did Aunt Nella agree to go along with Gram?"

"Because Gram turned the world upside down to see that Nella got to adopt Jennifer. She's the one who got Darlene Olhmeier to forget about having an abortion. She also convinced your dad to let Nella raise Jennifer as her own."

"So, this Darlene person was Jennifer's mother?"

"Yes, dear. Your dad dated her one long, hot summer. When she became pregnant, he offered to marry her. She refused. And Madeline shouted for joy."

"What happened to Darlene?"

"I'm not certain. She never came back to town. Her parents moved away years ago. They never made any attempt to see Jennifer."

"I can't believe Gram would call my dad and make up a story like that."

"Well, she did—out of desperation. Of course, her plan backfired. Madeline was devastated by the accident, and so was Nella, who resented Gram for taking her brother away from her. Madeline made a grave mistake, and she regretted it for the rest of her life. She did the right thing by telling you girls that you are sisters."

"I'm grateful for that."

"Just remember, dear, you are the one who kept her going. My how she loved you."

Carrie heard a car pull into the driveway. "Michael's here," she said, "I've got to go." Mavis walked her to the door.

"Thanks," Carrie said. "I appreciate what you have shared."

"You take care, dear. You need time to heal. A dying person absorbs all of our energies."

"My head is spinning," Carrie said, getting into the car. She told Michael the highlights of her conversation with Mavis. "I don't see how Gram could have lied to her own son."

"People do strange things when they are desperate," Michael said. "Are you going to tell Jennifer what you know about her mother?"

"I guess so, but not right away," Carrie said. "Perhaps I should have her get the information from Mavis just like I did. That might be best."

❧

On the way to the church for the ceremony, Carrie tried to picture her parents climbing into the car, her father anxious, knowing he would tell her mother about Jennifer. Did they collide with the truck before he told her, or after? Carrie would never know. Michael held her hand as they walked into the church. "Smile when you walk down the aisle," he said when he dropped her off at the door to the room where Jennifer was getting into her bridal gown.

Michael didn't badger her with questions after her visit with Mavis. He would give her time to think it through. Michael's patience was one of the things she loved most about him.

The ceremony began promptly at three. Carrie's face froze in a smile as she walked down the aisle, but her hands shook. Moments later, she stood at the front of the church watching Jennifer come down the aisle on Kevin's arm. As they repeated their vows, Carrie couldn't stop thinking about their dad. Carrie had spent a lifetime wishing that she had known him, and her mother, too.

Lost in thought for a brief few minutes, she had a vision. A man in a dark blue suit appeared in front of her. He wrapped her in his arms. She could feel his arms around her. She hugged him back, and then he was gone. A stunned Carrie knew it had been her father. Jennifer reached her arms out for her bouquet. Handing it over, Carrie smiled. She wanted her sister to be happy.

"I present to you, Mr. and Mrs. Kevin Millwood," the minister said. Everyone clapped. "The Trumpet Voluntary" played as the wedding party walked out of the church.

In the car on the way to the reception, Carrie wiped away the tears that rolled down her face. She could still feel her father's hug. She smiled, knowing the warmth of his hug would stay with her a long time.

# Chapter Thirty

Journal, Sunday, April 17, 1988

It's warm and sunny out today. A spring breeze blows through the trees, enticing the freshly watered purple and white petunias in the planter box to gyrate like dancers in a chorus line. They become back-row performers for the front-row begonias who sit at round tables like diners at a theater club, ladies in pink, men in white, leafed together.

The neighbor's fat black cat is perched on the deck railing. She's watching a Carolina wren hover near her nest in the basket filled with red impatiens that hangs near the back door.

I have my own fantasies like the one about making all A's in my summer classes at Georgia State University. After I graduate, I'd like to teach high school English for a few years, then start a family. Michael wants kids now, but he'll have to wait. I have this dream about writing the story that lives inside my head, the one about a young woman who cares for a cantankerous older lady. I picture myself in a long flowing purple dress, signing copies of my book. I have a pile of notebooks bulging with details recorded during the days, weeks, and months when I cared for Gram, struggling to make it one day at time. I still jot down memories, some good, some bad. It helps me put things into perspective.

Michael and I have paid off most of Gram's bills. Her small life insurance policy covered her funeral expenses. I still can't believe that the loan she kept hidden for months was covered by insurance. Too bad I stewed over that loan for so long. I wonder if I'll I ever learn that worrying doesn't accomplish anything?

Yesterday, a girl from the Sears business office called wanting money from Gram's estate to pay off her several hundred dollar account. I told her to forget it, that the estate balance was zero. I added a dumb cliche about how you can't milk a dry cow. The girl suggested that I pay the bill. I refused, reminding her that her store should have known better than to hand out a credit card to someone with a disastrous credit record. The girl gave up.

I rewrote my letter to Dr. Kirkland and mailed it, with a copy to Dr. Baker. In response to my letter, Dr. Kirkland called saying if he had it to do over again, he would handle Gram's case in a different manner. He admitted making a mistake, saying that he should have looked further into the situation and hoped his phone call had made me feel better. His call gave me a sense of satisfaction, but it didn't erase all of my anger. All I can hope is that he'll think twice if the situation arises again. As for Dr. Baker, he didn't call; however, even though we owe him a healthy sum, he hasn't sent another bill.

As my life falls back into place, I treasure the simple things—taking Sophie-dog on walks, working out at the fitness center at the corner strip mall, reading books like the one I'm on now, *Humboldt's Gift* by Saul Bellow, going out for frozen yogurt with Kay at a moment's notice—without pangs of guilt that I should hurry back home. Three or four days a week I work for a temporary agency, going to different offices. Last week I worked at Tom Egan's law office. It was good to see him again. Our drifting apart feels right. Tom has a new friend, a dark-haired Italian girl named Maria. I met her one afternoon when she stopped by the office, and believe me, I tried my best to avoid staring at her ample chest under her see-through blouse. I rolled my eyes at Tom, and he gave me a cocky little grin. He held his arms out, palms up, cocked his head to the side, lifting his shoulders up, as if to say, *well, you're taken, so I had to move on.*

"So, where did you meet Maria?" I asked when she left to use the john.

"She lives in my apartment building."

"How convenient."

"Yes, indeed," Tom said, with a wink.

Michael laughed when I told him about Maria. We laugh and love a lot these days. I've come home to my husband. Michael's amazed at my turnaround. I am me again—changed a bit, but still me. My newfound confidence feels good. I'm handling my marriage the same way I faced caretaking—one day at a time. The good news is that I'm beginning to see that what I have is what I want.

My writing room, formerly the room where Gram repeatedly clanged the cowbell, is my refuge. Some days, it's hard to forget that it's the same room where Gram labored to breathe, where she came close to choking to death, and where she smoked until she couldn't inhale one more time. We have cleaned the room and painted the walls a pale yellow. The new silver-gray carpet feels squishy on my bare feet. Even though the smell of death is gone, I burn vanilla candles in the room. Gram's presence lingers. I look forward to the day, when, like a mother giving birth to a child, I can forget the pain and think only of the good times I had with my grandmother.

I often think about Gram's final memorial service and the wedding festivities that followed. I'll never forget how Jennifer stood up at the reception and introduced her attendants. "I'd especially like to thank my sister, Carrie Barnes, for being my matron of honor," she said when she got to me, surprising the wedding guests. Aunt Nella gasped, looking stunned. I have to give Jennifer credit for being brave. It was obvious that she no longer feared her mother's reaction.

Since she and Kevin returned from their honeymoon, we've called one another several times. At my suggestion, Jennifer has spoken with Mavis about her birth mother, Darlene Ohlmeier. Aunt Nella has offered to help find Darlene. So far, they've not made much progress, but Jennifer is convinced they will find her. I have to wonder if finding Darlene will be a good thing. Jennifer doesn't want to hurt Aunt Nella; she just wants to meet the person who gave birth to her.

I'm making an effort with Jennifer, and she's acting likewise toward me. I know our father loved us both and would want us to be friends. We are easing into a sisterly relationship. Neither of us knew our father or our mothers. We have that in common. However, it is our bond with Gram that unites us.

I still have unanswered questions, like why Gram hated the little Oriental man. There are times when I want to pick up the phone and ask Gram something. Often, I have the receiver in my hand before I realize she's gone. And, I will always wonder about Gram's phone call that triggered my parents' fatal accident. The priest at our parish told me that the why of things often reveals itself in time and becomes a link between the past and the present, so perhaps some day I'll learn more. What I've come to realize is that what Gram and I had together means more than any resentment I feel toward her. I'm beginning to forgive Gram, and that has helped to ease the pain of losing my parents.

Even though she's gone, I know Gram will always have a say in my life. She stands looking over my shoulder. Just last week, Michael took me along on a business trip to San Diego. Michael and I went outside the hotel to the pool area one evening. While he swam laps in the pool, I relaxed in the hot tub. Sitting there by myself, I saw ripples in the water and felt Gram's presence. I saw her diving in the water like a porpoise, wearing this knowing smile, as if she had all of the answers. Within seconds, *poof*, she disappeared. I looked toward the sky just in time to see a bright light slip out of sight. I wondered if Gram's quick visit was her way of telling me that what we were to one another we still are.

Eerie dreams haunt my sleep, dreams where Gram begs me for water. I awaken thirsty, drenched in sweat. The good news is that pleasant dreams are beginning to surface. I'm slowly beginning to realize that caring for Gram was a gift. It gave me the opportunity to share the last days of her life. Now I can leave the past behind and row away toward my own future.